You Don't Know Me

Mandy Lee

Copyright

The moral right of the author has been asserted.

All rights reserved. Without limiting the rights under copyright reserved above, no part of this publication may be reproduced, stored in or introduced into a retrieval system, or transmitted, in any form or by any means (electronic, mechanical, photocopying, recording or otherwise), without the prior written permission of both the copyright owner and the publisher of the book.

You Don't Know Me

Copyright © 2015 Mandy Lee

First print edition.

Acknowledgements

Huge thanks to Jackie Bates for her wonderful editing skills, and to Sue Hart for her Beta reading.

Thanks also to Julie, my biggest fan!

Last, but by no means least, thanks to my wonderful daughter for putting up with my writing obsession. I love you!

Chapter One

The Northern Line tube is crammed this morning, filled to the brim with humanity: hot sweaty bodies in a hot sweaty space. And even though my best friend is currently sitting right next to me, dishing out half-hearted moral support in between flicking through the pages of *Heat* magazine, so far none of it seems to have made a difference. Anxiety is creeping through my body like a poison.

'Are you okay?' Lucy glances at me.

'Yes, I'm fine,' I lie.

'The first day's always the worst.'

'I know that.'

'Well, if it's any consolation, you look good, Maya.'

She smiles weakly, knowing full well that I totally disagree. I take a look down at my legs and decide that I can see far too much of them.

'This isn't me,' I mutter.

'It's not about being you. You can't wear jeans and a tatty T-shirt for this type of thing. You've got to be professional.'

While she goes back to pretending to read an interview with some C-list celebrity, I busy myself with wondering how I've managed to end up like this.

'How is this professional?' I groan, pulling at my blouse which is actually Lucy's blouse. I borrowed it first thing this morning when I realised that my own wardrobe had coughed out anything remotely suitable years ago. 'People are staring at me.'

She glances back up. Her eyes widen. 'They're staring at you because you look stunning.'

Stunning? How can I possibly look stunning? 'They're staring at me because I look like a tart.'

I shift about in my seat and peer along the tube carriage. Yes, they are staring at me. There's no doubt about it. For a start, there's a teenage boy sitting three seats down who doesn't know what to do with his tongue. And then there's the old man at the opposite side of the carriage who seems to have come over all hot and bothered. And that's not to mention the pervert in the seat to my right who smells of crisps and keeps rubbing his leg against mine. I'm being stared at, good and proper, and I know exactly why. It's because my skirt, if you can call it a skirt, is far too short. It barely covers my legs and finishes off precariously close to my knickers.

'If I bend over in this,' I grumble under my breath, 'someone's going to try and park a bicycle up my backside.'

'Don't be such a prude. You look much better in it than I do. You've got great legs. You should show them off a bit more. And you've got great boobs too, Maya.'

I gaze down at the blouse, a white chiffon number with a plunging neckline. It's a hot June day and I've not bothered with a jacket ... but I should have done. While Lucy's exactly the same size as me from the waist downwards, from the waist upwards, she's at least three cup sizes smaller and my boobs are ready to explode out of the bloody thing.

'I need a bigger blouse.'

'Trust me, you don't. You're oozing sex appeal in that one.'

I suck in a deep breath, silently willing myself not to grab her celebrity magazine and screw it up into a ball.

'Why would I want to ooze sex appeal, Luce?'

'You never know.' She turns a page. 'There might be some sexy beast of a rich businessman on the prowl.'

'I don't need a man in my life.'

'That's what you say now,' she laughs, turning to an article about cystitis. 'But eventually it's going to happen.'

Is it, now? Well, not any time soon. I've only just shaken off the after effects of the last one, and I'm not about to wade into that particular minefield again. It's been an entire year now since Tom smashed my world into pieces, taking off with another woman and leaving me in the debris.

'This isn't a hunting trip,' I groan. 'I'm not out to bag a man. This is a job, to earn money so I can pay my way. I'm doing what I need to do ...'

'When you should be doing what you want to do,' she interrupts.

I let that one go. I'm heartily sick of all the little reminders to get my life back on track, and I certainly don't need them today of all days, when I'm starting a new job and I'm dressed like a hussy and I'm wedged in next to a pervert on the tube. I curse myself for avoiding a shopping trip over the weekend, leaving myself desperate for an outfit first thing this morning.

'Calm down,' she mumbles, flicking over to the horoscopes. 'You'll be there soon.'

I shake my head, but she doesn't notice. She's poring over Pisces.

The old man in the opposite seat has gone now. I can see my reflection in the dark glass, broken up every now and then by the flash of a light. A lock of thick, blonde hair has come loose from its up-do, and oh God, the make-up. I'd forgotten about that. I'm wearing way too much of the bloody stuff. Industrial quantities of it. I've been sponged and brushed to within an inch of my life. My eyes have been smothered with kohl and mascara. Apparently, it's the smoky eyed look, but I'm not too sure. I look like I've gone ten rounds with Mike Tyson. If the house-mate hadn't taken it on herself to give me a make-over first thing this morning, then I wouldn't be looking like a cross between a tangerine and a clown right now. She's good at plenty of things, Lucy, such as managing an art gallery and navigating her way around the London Underground, but she's certainly useless when it comes to make-overs. I'll swing by a shop when I get off the tube and source a packet of wipes.

The train begins to slow, scratching and screeching its way to a halt. Lucy thrusts the magazine into her handbag and I make a move only to find that I'm held back by her hand.

'Not yet.' She shakes her head. 'This is my stop. Tottenham Court Road. You take it on to Waterloo, remember? Jesus, you only went down there last Friday.'

'I can't help it if I'm crap on the tube. Which line was it?'

'Jubilee,' Lucy sighs. 'The grey one. You take it to London Bridge. It's the second stop and you're off. And then,' she grins, pushing herself up from her seat, 'you go and find yourself some top totty.' The train jolts and she glances up. 'I've got a bastard of a day.' She grabs hold of a hand rail and wobbles precariously. 'It's the exhibition soon. Are you still coming?'

I rearrange my hair one more time. 'Of course. See you later.'

She cocks me a grin. 'Come on, Maya. You can do it.'

I nod uncertainly. I've been a bad tempered bitch all morning, and suddenly I'm regretting it. I may look like a hooker, but Lucy's done her best. 'Get some wine on the way home,' I call after her. 'I've got a feeling I'm going to need it.'

3

Chapter Two

I stumble out into the early morning sunlight and stand in a daze at the front of the station, desperately trying to get my bearings. I can just about find my way around North London on a good day, but south of the river might as well be another planet. I manage to get myself across a major road without being flattened, turning for a moment to take in the low-lying blackened bricks of London Bridge station, and behind it the Shard slicing its way up into the sky. And then I head for London Bridge itself. It's not far and before I know it, I'm tottering down a set of steps and veering off to the right along the south embankment. Another couple of minutes and I reach my destination.

The narrow walkway widens out and there it is, towering above my head, the central offices of Fosters Construction. I come to a halt, standing absolutely still, an island of inactivity in a flowing river of bodies, and I look up to count the storeys. Fifteen of them in all, fifteen floors of dark glass, glaring out across the Thames. My body gives a quick shudder. I'm about to start a job with the largest construction company in the country: a money-making machine with no heart and no soul. It goes against everything I've ever believed in, everything I've ever loved. But it's a job, I remind myself. And I need the money.

Ahead of me, a set of revolving doors is busy swallowing up its morning quota of workers, and I know that in the next minute or so I need to join them. Everyone looks so smart, so efficient, so completely and utterly professional, and I'm going to stand out like the sorest thumb in history. Willing just about every part of me to keep it together, I throw myself into the tide of bodies, pushing my way through the revolving doors and into the lobby.

Immediately, I find myself at the centre of a huge atrium that's filled with plush leather chairs and coffee tables and pot plants. I've been here once before, of course, last Friday when I was whisked off to a quiet room, interviewed by Mrs Kavanagh and offered a job in the Finance department. But I'm still overwhelmed by it all. Snapping myself out of my reverie, I make my way over to the reception desk where two perfectly turned out women, one blonde and one brunette, are currently talking to visitors. I stand there for a moment or two, clutching at the handles of my handbag and waiting to be noticed. At last, the blonde receptionist glances up at me. She looks me up and down, taking in my too-short skirt and my too-tight blouse, and then she homes in on my face. I'm just glad I found a chemists at Waterloo. A few minutes in the ladies' toilet and I'd removed every trace of Lucy's make-over.

'Can I help you?'

'Hi, my name's Maya Scotton.'

The receptionist stares at me blankly and I feel immediately inferior. She looks like she's just stepped off the cover of a magazine: perfect hair-do, perfect outfit, perfect make-up. Nothing at all like me.

'I'm new here,' I help her out. 'I'm supposed to be meeting Mrs Kavanagh at nine.'

The receptionist checks her computer monitor. 'It's only ten to.'

'I know. I'm early.'

'Well,' she sighs, 'while you're waiting, you'd better fill out the form.'

She thrusts a sheet of paper at me, attached to a clipboard. A pen follows suit, skimming its way across the marble counter. I study the form. The logo of Fosters Construction is plastered across the top, and beneath that, I find spaces for all the information they need from a new employee: National Insurance number, date of birth, bank details, address, phone numbers. I shuffle to one side, pick up the pen and begin the task. I'm busy trying to remember my National Insurance number when I hear a murmur.

'Oh Lord.'

I glance back up at the blonde receptionist to find that her attention has wandered. She's fixated on something behind me now, mouth open, eyes wide, as if she's just seen the most incredibly delicious cream cake in the world and she's determined to take a bite. The brunette is suddenly by her side.

'Are you okay?' I ask, turning from one to the other.

They ignore me and continue to stare.

'Oh God, I'll never get tired of looking at that,' the brunette whispers.

'Me neither,' the blonde bombshell agrees.

'At what?'

I turn, just in time to catch the back of a tailored black suit disappearing into a lift. Whoever he is, he's certainly got an incredible physique. He's tall, broad shouldered with neat, lean hips. I wait for him to swivel round, but he doesn't. Instead, he simply turns his head to one side, reaches out and hits a button with his left hand. I get the briefest of peeks at his profile but from this distance nothing's clear. The lift doors slide to a close.

'Who is he?' I enquire.

'A sex god,' the brunette breathes.

'And a womaniser,' the blonde frowns. 'And if you think he looks good from behind, you should cop a load of him from the front.'

'And then leave it at that,' the brunette adds quickly. 'Besides, he never mixes business with pleasure.'

I'd like to probe them further on the womanising sex god, but I don't get a chance. A new voice cuts across the conversation.

'Maya.'

I turn quickly to find myself presented with Mrs Kavanagh.

'Good to see you again.' She shakes my hand. 'Have you filled in the form?'

'I have.' I take the sheet from the desk and thrust it towards her.

'Excellent. Well, let's get you settled in then.'

I nod mutely, glance back at the receptionists who've only just about managed to gather their senses, and follow Mrs Kavanagh into a lift. Standing by her side, I watch as she punches the button for the fourteenth floor. The doors close and the lift begins to move.

'Well, Maya,' Mrs Kavanagh smiles at last. 'There's been a slight change of plan.' She clasps her hands together, watching as the floor numbers flash above our heads. 'As you know, we were intending to place you in Finance. However, an opening has come up in Personnel. It's all a bit last minute and Mr Foster wants the position filled today. It's the same sort of work we discussed. If you're okay with all of this, then I'll get your contract amended.'

'I'm okay with it.'

'Good. You'll be based in a rather specialised section of the department. You might find it a little strange for a start, but I'd just go with it if I were you.'

I nod. The lift comes to a halt.

'And one more thing,' she adds as the doors open. 'You might want to bring in a good book.'

'A good book?'

'All will become clear.'

We make our way out of the lift and down a corridor and so far it's pretty much what I expected. Offices to the left and the right, filled with people in suits speaking on phones, or gathering around desks, or staring at documents.

'Here we are.'

She pushes open a glass door. It gives way into a small office that seems to be fairly cramped, even though there's hardly anything in it: two desks, complete with computers and telephones; a filing cabinet in one corner; in another corner, a glass table that's littered with a kettle and a selection of mugs; and beneath the table top, a fridge. There are no pictures on the cream coloured walls. There's nothing but a large window that gives out over a neighbouring office block.

'This is Jodie.' Mrs Kavanagh waves a hand at a pink-clad teenager who's currently lounging at the desk nearest to the fridge. 'And this is your desk. And I'm afraid this is as far as I can go. Jodie will tell you more. I'll check in on you later in the week. I'm just down the corridor if you need me.' And with that, she's gone.

I stand next to my desk, glance down at the computer monitor, the keyboard and the wireless mouse, and then back at Jodie. Yes, she really is a teenager. She can't be any more than seventeen. She must be here on an apprenticeship in office administration. With her blonde hair bunched up on top of her head, she's dressed in a pink T-shirt, pink shorts and pink Converse. Chewing frantically on a mouthful of gum, she stares up at me.

'Do you want a cup of tea?' she asks, deadpan.

'Tea? Yes please.'

'Well, the kettle's there.'

Realising that I'm being invited to make my own tea, I drop my handbag on the floor and sidle over to the glass table.

'Do you want one?' I ask.

'Yeah. Loads of milk. Three sugars. The milk's in the fridge.'

I nod, pick up the kettle and ascertain that there's enough water before I switch it on and listen as it gurgles its way towards the boil. Finally, I reach down and grab the milk from the fridge, noting that alongside the single carton of UHT semi-skimmed, there are several bottles of water and a selection of chocolate bars. The staple diet of a teenager: they must be Jodie's. At last, when the kettle's finally boiled, I pour out our drinks, place Jodie's tea in front of her, just next to a biro and a Sudoku book, and settle myself in behind my own desk. Ploughing through the seemingly endless minutes of silence, I take a few sips of my tea. At last, I can't take any more.

'Jodie?'

Her head turns. 'Yes, Maya?'

'Should I be doing anything?'

'Doing anything?'

'Yes. I mean, I've been employed as a secretary, and I really should be doing something. And I'd like to do something but I really don't know what to do.'

'Well,' Jodie sighs, finishing off her own mug of tea and slamming it down onto her Sudoku book. 'Norman's the boss and he can tell you what to do, but he's not here yet.'

'And will he be here soon?'

'Probably.'

'And this is Personnel?'

'Sort of.' Jodie sighs.

'Sort of? How can it be sort of Personnel?'

'It just is.'

I pause for a few seconds to take in the information. I sort of work in Personnel, and I work for a man called Norman.

'And what does Norman do?'

'Whatever Mr Foster wants him to do.'

'Which is?' I hold out a hand, begging for just one answer that makes sense.

'Oh, you know, this and that.' She picks up the biro and swings it about in mid-air as if this and that are actually in the room.

'And what happened to the last secretary?'

'She went to Finance.'

'Finance?' I'm gawping now, and I know it. That was my bloody job. 'Why did she go to Finance?'

'Dunno.' Slipping the biro between her teeth, Jodie sets about thinking hard. 'She was pretty good at Sudoku,' she says at last. 'Maybe that's it.'

I lean forwards in my chair and wonder what sort of mad-cap place I've landed myself in. It's only the first hour of day one and I'm already suspecting that I should start to look for another job.

'So what's Mr Foster like?' I ask tentatively.

Jodie shakes her head. 'A complete shit.'

And probably at least fifty years old, my brain muses. He's the owner of a building company, for God's sake. He'll be fat and bald and wheezy to boot.

'A complete shit?'

'Yup.'

I'm clearly going to get precious little else out of the pink one on this particular matter. She's already back into the Sudoku so I spend the next few minutes trying to switch on my computer. At last, Jodie lets out another sigh and comes to join me.

'It's here.' She reaches around the back and presses some invisible button.

I stand up, lean round the monitor and raise an eyebrow.

'Where did you work before?' she asks, eyeing me suspiciously.

'Oh, I temped for a bit. You know, moving about all over the place.' I bite my lip. There really is no way I'm going to tell her the truth: that this is my first secretarial job. And as it happens, I don't have to. Norman saves the day.

'Ladies!'

A huge mountain of a man barrels his way through the door. He's at least six feet tall, with legs like tree trunks and a belly the size of a barrage balloon. I stare into the face of what I can only describe as a colossal teddy bear. He's a mass of wrinkles and smiles ... and he really is quite old.

'Welcome, Maya!' While his brown eyes dance with pleasure, two huge, oversized arms reach themselves out to greet me, and I have no option but to step inside them and have the breath squeezed out of me. 'I'm Norman.'

'Hello, Norman,' I whimper into his tie. At last, he lets me go and I stagger backwards, trying my best to gather my wits. 'Maya,' he grins. 'Such a beautiful name. I'm going to say it over and over again. Maya. Maya. Maya. Maya.' He sings my name into the air as if he's become enraptured by it. 'Now, Maya, let me induct you.'

Into what, I wonder. And will I actually know what I'm doing after this?

'This is your office.' He swipes his massive hands through the air. 'And that's Jodie.' He points a finger at the pink one. 'The kettle's over there.' He motions towards the corner. 'That's the fridge. And that's a filing cabinet.' The big hands sweep through the air again. 'Most of our stuff is either on that thing.' He points at my computer. 'Or in here.' He taps his own head. 'And my office is through here. Come along. Let me show you.'

Okay. So, I'm still no clearer on anything. I follow the man-mountain and find myself in the most incredible space: an enormous room, complete with a glass wall giving out over the Thames. It's a thoroughly modern office with a thoroughly modern, massive desk that's buried under a mound of paperwork. To my right, there's a leather sofa and a coffee table, and to the left, a book shelf and an exercise bike. While Norman begins to rummage around on his desk, my eyes scan the contents of the bookshelf: empty mugs; empty glasses; a selection of knick-knacks that wouldn't look amiss in an old lady's sitting room; and finally, one single framed photograph. I step forwards and find myself staring at a younger Norman, still huge but much leaner and suntanned. Standing in front of a Georgian country house, he's flanked by a kindly looking man, and an even kindlier looking woman.

'That's Mr and Mrs Foster,' he smiles appreciatively. 'I started out with them almost fifty years ago. I used to be tea boy. Then I worked my way up.'

'They started this company?'

'Yes, my love. From nothing. It was a simple building firm for a start. Old Mr Foster was a builder by trade. The company specialised in council houses and then we widened out into private housing. In the last few years, we've expanded again. Office blocks, car parks, shopping malls. You name it, we build it.' He winks. 'And now we've branched out abroad. We have contracts all over the place. And we have a couple of factories too.'

'So, that's Mr Foster there?' I point at the photograph. 'The man upstairs.'

Norman chuckles and then his face straightens out into a frown.

'No, my love, old Mr and Mrs Foster aren't with us any more. Their son took over ...' He coughs. 'Eventually. That's the man upstairs. The big cheese. The big kahuna. He who must be obeyed. Daniel Foster.' He glances down at his watch. 'And I've got to nip up and see him.'

I gaze around the room, searching for more photographs, but there aren't any.

'Norman,' I venture. Really, I ought to be calling him Mr Whatever, but I suddenly realise that I don't even know his surname. 'Don't you have a photograph of the man upstairs?'

He raises an eyebrow.

'The big cheese?' I prompt further.

'No.' He dismisses the question immediately, and I understand. For all that he loved old Mr and Mrs Foster, he clearly isn't quite so keen on their son. 'Now then,' he smiles. 'Let's give you some work to do.' He picks up a handful of crinkled sheets from his desk and offers them to me. 'I'm going to need this typed up as soon as possible. It's a report on a factory we own up in Tyneside. Can you get it done this morning?'

I nod.

'Good. Good. Well, I'll see you later. Better go.'

While the big teddy bear slopes off to see the big kahuna, I return to my desk and set about deciphering Norman's spidery handwriting. It's anything but easy. After ten solid minutes of squinting at the first paragraph, my eyes are on the verge of becoming permanently crossed and my brain is crying out for a good lie down in a darkened room. But at least I've managed to work out the secret key to the scrawls. Feeling distinctly pleased with myself, I glance up to find that Jodie's busy with the Sudoku book.

'Bloody hell,' she scowls, scribbling a line through one unfinished puzzle and making her way onto the next.

'Haven't you got any work to do?' I ask.

The pink one's mouth falls open, yet again.

'Work?' she breathes, flabbergasted. 'I don't do any work.'

Shrugging my shoulders, I go back to the task in hand. It's obvious that I've just asked a completely ridiculous question ... and I won't make the mistake of asking it again. It's all incredibly odd, but then again I shouldn't be surprised. After all, Mrs Kavanagh did warn me. Just keep your head down, I tell myself. Get on with the job and question nothing. Take the money and run.

Chapter Three

Half an hour after he disappeared, Norman returns, looking distinctly flustered. He glances down at me and disappears into his office. At last I finish the report, print off a copy and take it in to Norman before I return to my own desk with precious little more to do. I spend the next hour gazing at my telephone, willing it to ring. I check my office emails, willing anyone to send me a message. Just give me a job, my brain screams out. Anything to pass the time. But nothing happens. Tomorrow, I decide, I'm going to take Mrs Kavanagh's advice and bring in a good book.

'I'm off to do a bit of shopping,' Norman announces at half past eleven. 'I won't be long.'

I stare after him in disbelief. He's only been in work for two hours and he's already decided to take himself off for a spot of retail therapy?

'When's our lunch hour?' I ask the pink princess.

'Twelve 'til one,' she grunts in return.

I settle in for another half an hour of nothing. It's almost midday when my telephone buzzes. I gaze at it in amazement, wondering what the hell's going on. Somebody's actually calling me? No, that can't be happening. They must have got the wrong number. After a few seconds of buzzing, I pick up the receiver.

'Mr ... er ....' Shit, I still don't know Norman's surname. This really is totally unprofessional. I fumble through my brain for the right thing to say, but nothing right comes to mind. 'Norman's office. Can I help you?'

'You took your time,' a voice growls.

I give a start. Whoever it is, he's definitely none too pleased about something.

'Sorry?'

There's a silence. I hold the receiver away from my head and look at it, as if this is actually going to help matters. The silence continues.

'Hello?' I pull the phone back to my ear. Is he actually still there? Has he hung up?

'Who is this?' the voice demands. It's rich and deep and velvety and if its owner wasn't quite so rude, you might even say that it was sexy. But the owner of it is rude, and he's making me feel uncomfortable.

'Maya Scotton.'

'Maya Scotton,' the voice repeats slowly, as though it's trying out the name for size. 'You're the new girl in Norman's office.'

Girl? Nobody calls me a girl. Before I can help myself, my mouth is firing off.

'Actually, I'm the new secretary in Norman's office.'

'Like I said,' the voice fires back. 'The new girl.'

And that really has got me going. Mr I've-got-a-sexy-voice-but-no-bloody-manners is a sexist pig to boot. I need to put him straight.

'I'm twenty six,' I blurt. 'And I think that entitles me to be called a woman. Do you actually want anything?' I wince. That's definitely not the right way to go about things.

'Yes, I do,' the voice snaps.

After a few more seconds of silence, I sigh. I'd better say something else now, and I'd better sound professional.

'Well, would you actually like to tell me what it is that you want? Only my psychic abilities are a little off today.'

I wince again. That wasn't professional at all. I hear a sigh at the other end of the line.

'I'm sorry to hear that, Miss Scotton. Now, I understand you've typed up a report this morning. Would you be a good woman and email a copy up to me?'

The phone goes dead and I stare at it. I'm in shock.

'But who the fuck are you?' I virtually spit.

'What's the matter?' Jodie glances up from her latest puzzle.

'Some rude fucker's just told me to email a file up to him? Email it up to where?'

'Well, there's only one up from here,' Jodie smiles. She turns her face to the ceiling. 'Mr Foster's office.'

'Oh shit.'

No. No, no, no, no. I smack my hand against my forehead. Now that does make sense. If my brain had been in gear, then I would have done the sums. There's only one floor above us, and that must be where Mr Foster has his lair. That was the boss I was just talking to, the boss I was just extremely rude to. But then again, he was rude to me. He deserved everything he got. With a shaking hand, I call up the file and email it straight up to the big kahuna.

***

It's nearly two o'clock when Norman finally returns, laden with two shopping bags and a stick of French bread. He staggers into his office just as his phone begins to ring. I watch through the doorway as he drops the bags to the floor and loses the French bread under the desk. He scrambles for the phone and picks up the receiver.

'Hello? Yes, I'm here. I'll be up in a minute … I had to get some bits.' He pauses, listening intently, and when he finally speaks again, his voice sounds different, uncertain. 'Yes … Okay … Yes, I'll do that.' He replaces the receiver. 'Maya!' he calls. 'Can you come and join me for a minute?'

I glance over at Jodie. With a sigh, she opens a drawer in her desk and retrieves a nail file and a bottle of varnish. Leaving the pink one to her manicure session, I step into Norman's office.

'Sit yourself down, my love.'

His voice comes from under the desk where he's busy rescuing the French bread. I shift myself onto the edge of the leather sofa, listen to it squeak beneath me, and wait for Norman to position the bread on his desk and plonk himself back down in his chair.

'The factory up in Tyneside,' he wheezes. 'The one you've just typed the report on.' He picks up a file, smiles warmly at me and slaps it back down on the desk. 'We've got a big meeting about it this afternoon.'

'Okay.'

He continues quickly, as if he's running out of time.

'The factory's been running for years. It currently employs two hundred and twenty five people. It makes machinery that we use in the building trade. Concrete mixers, that sort of thing.' He wafts a hand about. 'Only it's been cutting a loss for a couple of years now. It's a weak link in the chain, Maya. And Mr Foster is thinking of shutting it down.'

'Okay.' I really don't know why he's telling me all this. After all, I'm just a secretary. But I can't help the next question that comes tumbling out of my mouth. 'And they'll all lose their jobs?'

'If it goes ahead.'

Suddenly I'm thinking of my dad, of all the heartache and the anguish that came our way when redundancy hit. 'Can't you convince him to keep it?'

Norman's thick lips pucker themselves up into a smile. 'I don't think so. The company can't afford to prop up a failure, not in this day and age.'

'This is awful.'

'It is, my love.'

'Norman?'

'Yes?'

'Why do I need to know this?'

'Oh.' He waves his hand again. 'Background information. A quick briefing. Just so that you know what's going on in the meeting.'

'In the meeting?'

'Yes …' He pauses and seems to swallow some kind of lump. 'Well, Mr Foster just called. He … er … wants you up there.'

My world jolts to a stop.

'Me? Why me?'

'Oh, I don't know.' He pulls an I'll-be-damned-if-I-know sort of a face. 'Maybe he just wants someone to take notes.'

Well, that's obviously a load of bollocks, my brain calls out. You know exactly why Mr Foster wants you up there. He's going to give you your come-uppance for not knowing your place … and then he's going to sack you.

***

Ten minutes later, I step outside the strange bubble that's Norman's department into the normal, business-like operations of Fosters Construction. As soon as we've sidled our way into the lift, Norman pushes a button and we're rising, but not for long. Moments later, the lift doors open onto the fifteenth floor. I half expect to emerge into a corridor, just like on any other floor, but instead I step out into something from a Hollywood movie: marble floors, plush sofas, a huge glass desk and, behind it, the most perfectly preened receptionist I've ever laid eyes on. I gaze around at the walls to find that they're adorned with massive canvas photographs of massive buildings, mostly swanky skyscrapers, and obviously all the products of Mr Foster's company. Jesus, I didn't think it would be like this. Suddenly, I'm feeling intimidated, all the more so because I can hear a rich, velvety voice in the background. It's deep in conversation and it still doesn't sound too pleased. My eyes follow the direction of the voice, to the left, where there's a huge oak door, obviously the entrance to the big kahuna's cave.

'Is he ready for us?' Norman splutters.

'Yes, Norman,' the receptionist smiles. 'In you go.'

'Mood?' he enquires, passing by the desk.

'Code red,' she grimaces. 'Take care.'

Following in the wake of Norman's huge body, I walk into a silent room. Norman moves to one side, revealing a glass table, around which are seated at least ten extremely serious looking people.

'Sit yourself down next to me,' Norman whispers.

I settle myself onto a chair, with Norman on one side and an empty space on the other, at the head of the table. I stare at the sumptuous black leather chair. It's currently waiting for the final bottom to be lowered into it. But where is that bottom? Turning to the window, I find it, along with the rest of Mr Foster. Now, that doesn't look like a big fat sweaty fifty year old at all. In fact, it looks distinctly like the back of the man at the lifts this morning. Shit, my brain cries out. Mr Foster's a sex god and you've gone and pissed him off! With his back to the room, and his arms folded in front of him, he's looking out over the Thames. I take in the back of his fair, ruffled hair, his tall, lean frame with its broad shoulders and slim waist. And then, finally, I allow myself a quick peep at his backside. He's not wearing a jacket now and it's on full view, and my goodness, it's a real stunner. All trim and hard and pert. No, he's not bad from the back, not bad at all. And suddenly I'm remembering the receptionist's words. 'You should cop a load of him from the front.'

'So you finally made it, Norman?' A rich, velvety voice fills the room, the same rich, velvety voice that was snapping at me earlier.

'Sorry, Mr Foster. I was waylaid.'

'Dan.' The voice cracks through the air, like a whip. 'Call me Dan.'

'Sorry, Dan.'

The arms are lowered and he turns slowly. I hear myself gasp. That's the first thing that happens, shortly before my adrenal glands decide to go on the rampage. Something flutters wildly in my stomach and my heart valves begin to flap like a line full of washing in a force ten gale. Fucking hell, my brain gurgles, that receptionist was one hundred percent right. The man is a sex god! He's absolute, fucking perfection! Doing my level best to cover up a serious case of the jitters, I quickly try to take it all in: the tousled blond hair, the strong, clean-shaven jaw, the sensual lips that are parted slightly, and finally the eyes. They're bright blue and they're mesmerising, and they're looking straight at me. I'm beginning to blush, and I know it. And my lungs seem to have contracted because my breath is suddenly coming in short, uneven spurts. Look away, my brain screams out. You're making an idiot of yourself. Just pack it in! He moves away from the window and before I'm aware of what's going on, he's already seated in the chair at the head of the table, the chair that's right next to me. Oh shit, I can smell him now. He's all fresh and cleanly washed with no hint of aftershave, just the quietest undertone of some expensive body wash. Oh God, it's gorgeous. Closing my eyes, I drink in his scent, knowing full well that this really is no way to behave in some high-powered business meeting that I have no business being in.

'Miss Scotton.'

My eyelids flick open and as I turn to face the voice, something quakes deep down inside. Bloody hell, he really is handsome. In fact, I don't think I've ever clapped eyes on anyone this good looking outside of a magazine. He'd be gloriously perfect if he wasn't exuding arrogance from every pore.

'Maya Scotton. Welcome to the organisation.'

His lips snap into a straight line, his eyes seem to harden into steel and I realise that there's no trace of a real welcome in his expression.

I falter. 'Thank you, Mr Foster.'

'It was nice talking to you earlier.'

The air is heavy with sarcasm. I almost choke. He really isn't that pissed off about the phone call, is he? Maybe I should apologise for that right now. I really should, but there's something about this man that renders me speechless. I let my mouth fall open and gawp at him. He gazes back at me for a moment or two, then shrugs dismissively and glances down at an iPad. So that's it then? No sacking?

'So, Norman, you need to fill us in on the latest figures for Tyneside.'

'I do, Mr Foster.'

'Dan.'

'Yes, Dan. Well, I've come up with the following ...'

While Norman's voice begins to drone on, laying out a seemingly endless stream of facts and figures about sales of concrete mixers, I stare at my notepad, wondering yet again why on Earth I'm in this room. And all the time, a curious spark is jumping its way around my body, returning again and again to my crotch. Oh bugger, this really isn't good at all. I already have it on good authority that this man is a womaniser and a complete shit, and yet my thoughts are running amok like naughty little children, and like an over-indulgent parent, I'm quite happy to sit back let them get on with it. I glance down through lowered lashes to find his left hand laid flat on the table top, palm downwards, his fingers splayed slightly. There's no wedding ring. He's not married? Someone this bloody gorgeous should have been snapped up long ago.

I let my eyes travel up his arms, past the rolled up sleeves of his uber expensive shirt, and the obviously ripped biceps that are lurking beneath the cotton, up to his collar and his perfectly knotted black tie, and then I risk a peek at his face ... only to jump clean out of my skin. He's looking right back at me. And coldly too. Oh God, I want to die. He's been watching me all the time. And while I've been ogling him like a dirty, old pervert, he's been taking it all in and probably still musing over that phone call. He's just biding his time, I decide. He's been waiting for the perfect moment to tell me to sling my hook. Shit, my mouth has gone completely dry. I turn away quickly and pick up a glass of water that's on the table top in front of me. Taking a swig, I tip the glass too quickly, spilling most of its contents down the front of my blouse.

'So ... to ... to sum up,' Norman stutters. 'In the current market, I'm afraid there's simply no hope.'

'That settles it then,' Mr Foster murmurs absently, glancing at the wet patch on my chest. 'We'll shut it down.'

I hear myself choke. What? In one fell swoop, and without the slightest trace of emotion, he's decided to put an end to an entire factory? I sense a knot of anger in my stomach. I'm thinking about my dad.

'Norman, you're in charge of liaison.'

'Of course,' Norman sighs.

I know that I'm staring at him, and I know that it's probably the worst thing I can possibly do, but I just can't help it because suddenly I'm wondering how a man who seems to be so completely perfect on the surface could be so completely cold and heartless beneath it all. I watch as he flips from one document to another on his iPad. Finally, he looks up, straight back into my eyes and I'm caught. I should turn away now, but I really can't. I'm locked in by his blue irises, and I'm beginning to tremble. He knows the effect he's having on me. I can see the corners of his lips begin to curl up, ever so slightly.

'So, tell me Miss Scotton. What's your opinion on the matter?'

My body jolts. Why is he asking me?

'Me?'

'Yes. You.'

'I ... er ...'

God, this really isn't my territory. I can type a letter and send an email and sort a file, but I really can't comment on the financial viability of a concrete mixer factory. But he's got me fixed with those bloody eyes and I know exactly why. He's giving me a mauling, teaching me a lesson for daring to be rude back to him. And when he's finished mauling me, he'll sack me. Quickly, I put down my glass, hoping to all that's holy that he's not noticed my shaking hand. He begins to tap the table with his index finger.

'We haven't got all day, Miss Scotton.'

Norman coughs into his chest.

'Maya's a secretary, Mr Foster.'

'Dan,' he snaps.

'Sorry. Dan. Maya's a secretary and she's only just started to work here. I don't think it's very fair to ask for her opinion.'

'Why not?' he growls. 'I'd like to know what everyone thinks.'

'You're going too far,' Norman mutters.

Quickly, I glance around the table, at the suited, high-powered men and women who all know exactly what they're doing in their jobs, and I notice that they all seem to be distinctly uncomfortable. What's just happened here? Did Norman really just dare to tell the big kahuna that he's going too far? I turn back to find that Daniel Foster doesn't seem to be the slightest bit fazed by the fact. Instead of losing his temper with Norman, he's simply staring at me some more. And I can feel something begin to quake inside, just between my thighs.

'Well?' he demands.

'I ... er ... I ...'

'Surely you have an opinion, Miss Scotton.'

'I ... I do. But I'm not sure it's of any use.'

God, the man is a bastard. He's putting me right on the spot, toying with me before he bares his teeth.

'I'd like to hear it, whether it's of any use or not.' He lays his hand flat on the table in front of me, and like an idiot, I stare at it. It's big and firm and strong and Lord above, I bet it would feel really bloody good on my skin.

'Well ...' I squeak. 'If you close down the factory, then that's two hundred and twenty five jobs down the drain.' I take a look at Norman. His head seems to have slumped to his chest and I suddenly realise that my suspicion is correct: I'm talking a load of bollocks. But well, hey, in for a penny, in for a pound. 'That's two hundred and twenty five families affected by the closure, and that will have a terrible effect on the community.'

Taking a deep breath, I will myself to stop talking. I've said enough, and showed no business acumen at all. Wishing that the floor would open up and toss me back down into the Norman bubble,

I stare out of the window. The silence is never-ending, and when I finally gather enough balls to look back at the sex god, I find him smirking. I hate you, a voice calls out from the back of my head. You may be eminently fuckable, Mr Foster, but the pink princess was completely on the ball: you are a complete shit! I pick up my glass of water and, remembering just in time that my hands are shaking, plonk it back down again.

'Thank you, Miss Scotton.' He gets to his feet and makes his way back over to the window. God, he's got a sexy walk. It's all effortless and graceful and self-assured. 'A pithy summary of the effects of our decision. Two hundred and twenty five jobs. Two hundred and twenty five families. Just think of all those lives that are about to be ruined.'

My mind shoots out an expletive and I catch it just in time.

'Unfortunately, the factory isn't turning a profit. It's turning a loss. A huge, fuck-up of a loss. We'll close it. You all know what you need to do. Get on with it.'

Norman shoves himself up from his chair and waits until the suits have all left the room. And now it's just me and Norman and the delectable shitbag.

'I have some matters to discuss with you, Dan,' Norman says quietly. And now I'm wondering why he's not calling him Mr Foster any more.

'Not now.'

'But ...'

'Off you go, Norman. And you, Miss Scotton, I'd like a word please.'

Feeling like a condemned woman, and certainly not a girl, I stay exactly where I am, watching as Norman waddles his way out of the room.

'So, it's your first day here?'

I watch as he circles round to the back of his desk, knowing that my mouth has fallen open once again. Dear God, I'd love to see him without that shirt on. I'd love to run my hands all over those perfectly toned shoulders and right down that obviously taut chest. And, oh shit, I'd love to rip those expensive trousers off him and see what lies beneath. I tear my thoughts out of pervert mode and straighten myself up. Resting a long index finger on the glass top, he pins me down with his come-to-beds.

'Yes. It is.'

'And how are you finding it?'

'Interesting.'

His eyes soften.

'I'm glad to hear it.' He pauses, glancing down at my skirt. I feel my temperature rise and my legs begin to shake. 'I kept you behind, Miss Scotton, because there are a couple of things I'd like you to know.'

Oh great. So, here it comes. Number one, nobody talks to me like that. And number two, you're sacked.

'The first thing is that your blouse is soaking wet.'

I practically hear myself swallow. 'I know that, Mr Foster, but thank you for reminding me.'

'No problem.'

'And the second thing?'

He taps his finger against the glass.

'Well it's sort of linked to my first thing, really.' His lips part slightly and he lifts a hand, pointing a finger directly at my chest. 'I can see your bra.'

He shoots me a grin, and while half of me wants to leap across the desk and brain the sexist bastard right now, the other half wants to snog his ruddy gorgeous mouth off. But either of those things would be a little over the top. Instead, I decide to make a hasty retreat, to run away back to my desk and write my resignation letter.

Chapter Four

As soon as I get home, I run a bath, wriggle out of the tight skirt and the even tighter blouse, and soak for half an hour. My mind is whirling from the strange day I've just had. Fosters is a huge company, and every part of the headquarters is professional and business-like ... apart from mine. So, what exactly is Norman's role in all of this? And if Mr Foster isn't willing to prop up an ailing factory on Tyneside, then why is he willing to put up with an old man and his pink teenage sidekick? And more than that, why wasn't I sacked? After all, the big kahuna doesn't seem to be the kind of man who'd take any sort of crap lying down. And yet he took it from me today. Well, I muse, dunking my head under the water, perhaps that was his idea of a come-uppance: belittling me in front of a room full of suits and pointing out that he could see my underwear through my wet blouse. Perhaps he's finished with me now.

At last I'm out of the bath, pulling on denim shorts and a camisole top. It's unbearably hot, but that's Camden in the height of summer. Even the pigeons are wilting. I lie on my double bed for half an hour, gazing up at the flowery curtains as they drift lazily in a light breeze, listening to the upstairs neighbour's music. By seven o'clock I'm ready to join Lucy in our pokey excuse for a kitchen.

'Finally.' She turns and smiles, leaving the net curtains to dangle to a close. She's wearing a short dress, all flowers and girliness. 'Dinner's nearly ready.'

'What are you looking at?'

'There was a motorbike out there earlier.'

'It's a road, Lucy. Sometimes it's used by motorbikes.'

'But this one was out there for ages.' She points at the window. 'For ages,' she repeats, narrowing her eyes, as if this is really going to ram the point home. 'And there was a bloke on it. All in black. And he was staring at our front door.'

'What did he look like?'

'How am I supposed to know? He had his helmet on.' She blows out a good lungful of air. 'Anyway, he's gone now.'

'That's interesting. How was your day?'

'Crap.' She picks up a wooden spoon and waves it in the air, spattering something brown all over the work surface and the hob. 'In fact, it was a bloody nightmare. We've started setting up for the exhibition. Big Steve wants this layout, Little Steve wants that layout and I run around like a blue-arsed fly.' While she sucks in a breath, I laugh quietly to myself, thinking of Big Steve and Little Steve, the owners of Slaters, a swanky art gallery in the heart of Soho. 'They're driving me mad,' Lucy complains. 'Perhaps I should start looking for a new job.'

I smile at her, sympathetically, knowing full well that she's never going to hand in her notice. She loves it too much. She's managed Slaters since graduating from Edinburgh with a degree in Art History, at the very same time that I graduated from the art school with honours, and sank into oblivion. 'We've had an artist pull out, you know,' she says tentatively. 'They've gone and had a nervous breakdown and burned all their work.' She arches an eyebrow and I know what's coming next.

'I'm sure you'll find someone.'

'There's enough space for two canvases. If you get going, you could knock something out. There's still a couple of weeks to go. Big Steve and Little Steve would love to see your stuff. You know that.'

I hang my head. Lucy's been at it again, informing the owners of Slaters that Maya Scotton's shit hot with the oils, that she's wasting her life away, that she just needs a little nudge in the right direction to get herself back on track.

'No inspiration, Lucy. You know the deal.'

'And there's not likely to be any inspiration while you're knocking out letters instead of knocking out paintings.'

I laugh at that. If only she knew the truth, that apart from a deathly dull report, I haven't knocked out a single thing all day.

'So, come on then, how was it?' she demands. She's got her back to me now, stirring the contents of a huge pan. I really ought to ask what she thinks she's cooking tonight, and then I ought to suggest we get a take-away. It smells distinctly strange.

'Give me wine first.' I slump onto a kitchen chair. 'So, what are we eating?'

'Chilli.'

I swallow back a groan. From bitter experience, I know that Lucy's chilli doesn't taste remotely like chilli. In fact, it tastes more like mud. But I shouldn't complain. She's absolutely useless when it comes to cooking, but I'm even worse ...

'Tell me you got some wine.'

'In there.'

She points towards the ancient fridge that frequently makes strange noises and doesn't seem to keep anything cold. I get up, shuffle over to the fridge and yank open the door, helping myself to a bottle that's been trying its best to chill on the top shelf, noting with delight that there's a second bottle lounging next to it. Picking two glasses out of the cupboard, I line them up on the tiny table and fill them to the brim.

'Steady.' Lucy holds out a hand. 'I've got another full-on day tomorrow.'

'And I've got another full-off day,' I moan, downing half the glass in one go.

'What's a full-off day when it's at home?'

'Don't ask.'

'I am asking. What's it like? Come on.'

'Well,' I muse, pausing to down the second half of the glass. 'I think I've landed myself in a nut hole.'

'A nut hole? I thought it was a building company.'

'It is a building company. And most of it's perfectly normal, all professional and that.' I pour my second glass. 'But not the bit I've got landed in.'

Lucy checks on the chilli, turns down the heat, and joins me at the table. She pulls out a chair and takes her own glass of wine.

'I thought it was Finance.'

'It was supposed to be Finance but they moved me at the last minute. I've been dumped in some weird Personnel department with a teenage Sudoku fiend and some old bloke called Norman. And there's nothing to do. And that's not the worst of it. The woman who used to work for Norman was given my job in the Finance department.'

Almost immediately and pretty much as I'd expected, I can hear Lucy laughing. Picking up my glass, I take another glug of wine. Today, life has become seriously strange and it's going to take a serious amount of blotting out. What does it matter if I end up with the mother of all hangovers in the morning? I'll be amazed if I'm given any work to do.

'Well, I'd just go with it.' Lucy manages to squeeze the words out at last. 'I mean, it's a job. What does Norman do?'

'Whatever Mr Foster wants him to do.'

'And Mr Foster?'

'The owner, the man upstairs, the big cheese, the big kahuna.'

'And what's he like?'

'Fucking gorgeous.'

'Married?'

'No ring.'

'Girlfriend?'

'A womaniser, according to the receptionist downstairs.'

'Rich?'

'Probably. He owns the company.'

'Sexy?'

'Eminently.'

'Get stuck in.'

'What? No. He's horrible.' And while I try my best to pull an I'm-completely-disgusted-by-this-bastard type of face, my body temperature seems to soar by a few degrees and out of nowhere there's a strange quivering sensation between my thighs. 'He summoned me up to a meeting today for absolutely no reason. And then he put me on the spot and made me look like a twat. And then he kept me behind and told me he could see my underwear.'

'Oh, my God!' Lucy squeals. 'I told you! A rich businessman on the prowl.'

'I don't care if he is on the prowl. He's horrible.'

'Mmmm ...' Lucy's eyes have glazed over now. She takes a huge gulp of wine. 'So Mr Foster's all mean and hot and moody. And maybe you'll be the one to tame him.'

'And maybe you're talking shit.'

Lucy shrugs her shoulders, leaves the table and goes back to tending the so-called chilli. She really does read far too many romances. But then again, I've started digging into her collection in recent months. And that reminds me: before the night's out, I need to find a good book to get me through tomorrow.

'It's not what I thought it would be, Lucy. I think I might jack it in.'

'And then go back to painting?'

'No.' I stop her in her tracks. 'Don't go on about that again.'

I turn the wine glass around in front of me, admiring the way the evening sunlight fragments itself against the glass, spilling little shafts of light across the table.

'It's about time,' Lucy grumbles.

I know she's right. It's been five years since I last picked up a brush. Somewhere along the way I lost my confidence, my inspiration, everything. And more than anything, I want it back.

'I'm not ready.' I tap the table, wondering exactly when I will be ready.

'You know, you're not going to just wake up one day and feel like it. You've got to get started, whatever you feel like. You've just got to get on with it.'

I nod slowly. She's right again. I should just get on with it. But then again, she doesn't realise how deep this goes. She has no idea about my all-consuming fear that somewhere along the way I've lost my talent. And without my talent, I'm nothing. At least, if I keep on putting off the moment I start to paint again, I'll never have to find out.

'I could go for another secretarial job,' I suggest.

'You're wasting yourself.'

'It'll do for now. Until … you know …'

I stare at Lucy and she stares back at me. Eventually, her head bobs to one side.

'There it is again,' she whispers. She's up on her feet in a flash, scurrying over to the window and pulling back the net curtains. 'He's back.'

'Who?'

'Motorbike man.'

I join Lucy by the window. There, outside our ground-floor flat but on the opposite side of the street, is a man on a motorbike. He's clad in black leathers. He has his helmet on, the visor down, but there's no doubt about it. He's staring back at us.

'Who is he?' Lucy breathes. 'And what the fuck is he doing?'

'Just close the curtains. He'll go away.'

'I'm going out there. I'm going to give him a piece of my mind.'

'No! Luce!'

Before I can stop her she's out of the front door, flying down the road in her tiny dress, with her boobs wobbling about all over the place.

'Oi! You!' she shrieks. 'Motorbike creep!'

The motorbike revs into life and roars away into the evening.

Chapter Five

I wake early the next morning, haul myself out of bed and stand by the open window, gazing out at the gardens of Mornington Place. Heat has wrapped itself around the city, closing itself tight against every single building, every single street, every single living being. I glance up at the sky and wonder when it's all going to break. The morning is a blur. I've hardly slept and I'm too tired to think straight. Under Lucy's supervision, I'm squeezed into a fresh set of work clothes that seem just as tight as yesterday's outfit, and ordered to put on at least a slither of eye shadow, eyeliner and mascara. I comply, just to keep her quiet.

I'm silent on the walk through Camden and I'm silent on the tube. While Lucy reads yet another celebrity magazine, I stare out of the window, watching as one station after another slides its way in and out of my consciousness. I say goodbye to Lucy at Tottenham Court Road, remembering just in time to eject myself from the carriage at Waterloo where I lose myself in the crowds. I don't know how I get there, but by some miracle I find the Jubilee line. I'm on the platform, hovering by the safety line and sensing the crackle in the air that signals the arrival of the next train when I hesitate, almost swivelling around on my heels and returning to the flat. I don't know what makes me change my mind. I don't know what takes me by the hand and guides me onto the next train. Whatever it is, it takes me down to London Bridge and straight back to the imposing tower on the south bank.

Twenty minutes later, I'm back in Norman's strange department. While Jodie opens up her computer and updates her Facebook status at least twenty times, I make endless cups of tea for Norman and help him tidy his office, which consists mainly of moving the exercise bike from one side of the room to the other, and then back again.

When I offer to sort through the piles of paperwork on his desk, I'm told to leave well alone. He knows where everything is, and that's enough. Finally, Norman busies himself with reading the paper.

'Can you close the door on your way out, my darling?' he mutters, fumbling his way through the massive pages of the *Daily Telegraph*. 'I need to focus on the business section.'

By ten o'clock, I've typed and re-typed my resignation letter at least five times but I just can't seem to find the right words. I know I'm pretty lucky to be paid for doing almost absolutely nothing, but there are several really good reasons to get out of here. Number one: I feel guilty being paid for doing almost absolutely nothing. Number two: I'm bored. And number three: I really don't understand that man upstairs and I don't ever want to run into him again … ever. Just thinking about him makes my pulse quicken and my heartbeat accelerate, and a twinge of desire flare into life between my thighs. But while my body seems to love him, my brain detests the man. I push the keyboard away, reminding myself that the rent needs to be paid. Maybe I should just keep my head down and do as I'm told. After all, if I'm careful, I should be able to minimise contact with him. I blow out a breath and wonder where Jodie's got to. She left the office almost an hour ago, under orders from Norman to replenish the teabag supply, and there's been no sign of her since.

Absent-mindedly, I pull a large blank notepad towards myself and begin to doodle. I start with the outline of a face and barely know who it belongs to. Out of nowhere, features begin to appear, and I'm hardly aware of them. Eyes, ears, nose, a mouth. I begin to shade, to add detail, including a mop of hair, and before long the doodle has developed into a full-blown sketch. I know who it is now, and I have no idea why I'm drawing him, but I'm determined to finish it off. I move on to the finer details, adding more definition to the lips, wondering idly what they'd feel like against my body. I shade the hair a little more, imagining that I'm running my fingers through his tumbling locks. I strengthen the jaw and shade the firm cheek bones. And finally, I return to the eyes. There's something not quite right about them. They're too vulnerable. I've got it all wrong.

'That really is quite a remarkable likeness.'

A rich, velvety voice shakes me out of my dream world. Caught in the act, I slap my hand over the sketch and look back over my shoulder only to find him standing directly behind me. How did he do that? How did he get into the office without me hearing the door? And how long has he been standing there? I notice that he's wearing an expensive black jacket and that his hands are thrust into his trouser pockets. My eyes travel up his chest, growing wider at what they see. Behind that crisp white shirt, there's clearly a perfect six pack. I catch my breath and look up further, past the loosened black tie, pausing at his neck, noting that the top button is undone. I wonder momentarily what it would feel like to run my lips across that skin. Finally, I take a breath and raise my eyes to his face. He's smiling at me with those steely blue eyes, only now they don't seem to be steely at all. They're softer somehow, and they're twinkling. I watch as the eyes move from the picture and fix themselves on my own face. A spark of electricity kicks off in my stomach, flinging itself about my body like the Tazmanian Devil. Suddenly, I'm breathing far too quickly and my hands have begun to shake.

'I ... don't know why ...'

His lips curl up into a smile and my God, he has a lovely smile. I want to reach up and run my fingers across his lips but that really would be out of order.

'You have a talent there, Miss Scotton.'

'But ...' And anyway, why is he smiling? The man hates me.

'But,' he mimics me. 'I wonder why you've chosen to sketch my face?'

He leans further forwards, reaches out and takes hold of my hand, repositioning it slightly to the left so that the sketch is on full view again. It's only a second or two of physical contact, but all sorts of mess is kicking off in my body. I'm a quivering wreck.

'It's not ...' Oh shit, why am I even trying to claim that it's someone else? It's certainly his face. It's exactly his face ... apart from the eyes.

'And you've done this from memory?'

'Yes.'

'But we've only just met.'

I shrug my shoulders and turn back to the sketch. He's leaning in closer again. I can almost feel his breath on my neck. And now I'm picking up on his scent. I love it. I could drink it in. I want to turn back around and dig my head into his firm chest, but that would be completely unprofessional.

'And you already know me so well,' he says softly. 'I must have made quite an impression on you.'

Yes, you did make quite an impression on me, and you know it, my brain screams out. In fact, you make quite an impression on all women, and you know that too. And this particular woman may currently want to dig her head into your chest, but you're an arrogant twat, and she's not about to forget that. While my brain complains, my mouth refuses to work. Somewhere along the line, something has been disconnected. I remain silent. Turning over the notepad and hoping to God that he's moved away, I get up from my chair. But he hasn't moved at all. As soon as I take a step to the side and turn around, I slam straight into him and catch my breath. My face is right up against that chest and good Lord, he smells even more divine up close. A hand clasps me on each shoulder and I'm held in place by his grip. I find myself gazing up into his eyes and for a moment or two, I'm lost.

'Steady now,' he whispers.

'I ... er ... need to ...' I point towards the kettle.

'Of course.'

I'm released. He takes a step backwards, holding out his hands in apology. I'd like to move at this point, but I can't. All I can do is stand rooted to the spot. He smiles again and I register a flutter in my stomach, followed by a delicious twinge down below. Oh God, he's playing with me, manipulating me. It's wrong on every possible level. He's a complete shit and a womaniser. He's a dangerous drug. I can tell that even now. Don't even get started, my brain warns me. Before you know it, you'll be hooked. Now snap out of this.

'Can I get you anything?' my mouth asks and I shake my head, wondering what I could possibly get. A cup of tea perhaps? A word-search book from Jodie's desk? A bottle of nail varnish out of her drawer?

'Water.' He nods towards the fridge.

'Please.'

I swallow hard, realising that I've just demanded manners from Mr Mean and Hot and Moody. Yes, something has definitely come loose in the circuitry. At some point, I really should have a good rummage through my brain, find that loose wire and plug it straight back in again.

He smiles slowly. His lips part. 'Water, please.'

I make my way over to the fridge and lean down to retrieve the bottle of water, knowing full well that his eyes are fixed on my backside. There's some grade A sexual harassment going on here, and I really should just get my bag and leave. And while I'm at it, I should lodge some sort of complaint with some sort of complaints department. I kick the fridge door closed, swivel round, approach him cautiously, and pass him the water with an extremely jittery hand.

'Thank you.' He takes it from me and I wonder, for a split second, if I've just seen a little shake in his hand too. 'I wanted to talk to you.'

Without taking his eyes away from mine, he unscrews the lid and takes a gulp. 'About our little phone call yesterday.'

'Oh, that.'

'Yes, that. I must say, I was quite taken aback that Norman's new girl would dare to be so rude to me.'

'I'm not a girl. I'm a woman.'

'Of course you are. I keep forgetting.' He takes another swig of water, gives me another long stare. I feel my temperature rise. I glance back down at my desk. Oh God, I wish I had some work to get on with.

'So, what about the phone call?' I ask.

'I just wondered if you'd like to apologise.'

Apologise? And why would I want to do that? Well, the sensible part of my brain reminds me, because it's an easy way out of a tricky situation. But I ignore the sensible part of my brain. Maybe it's because I'm exhausted and feeling distinctly prickly right now, or maybe it's because there's just something about this man that makes me want to wind him up. I don't know exactly why it happens, but it does. My mouth opens and I hear the words fly out into the air.

'I don't think so.'

And you can sack me if you like, I want to add. At least that way I won't have to finish off that bloody resignation letter.

'You don't think so?' He raises an eyebrow.

'No, I don't think so.'

He stares at me for a moment, and I'm pretty sure this is the point at which I'll be instructed to pack my bags and leave. Instead, he simply shrugs his shoulders and changes the subject.

'Well, let's have another look at that picture.'

Before I have time to react, he steps forwards, swiping the sheet of paper away from the desk.

'I like this a lot.' He straightens up with the sketch in his hand. 'May I keep it?'

What? So he can admire himself more than he already does?

'No.'

'You don't want to give it to me?'

Pardon? I'm not entirely sure he means the picture any more. His eyes are suddenly hooded.

'It's just not very good.'

'It's extremely good.'

'It needs to go in the bin.'

'Well, I don't want to put myself in the bin. And if you don't want to give it to me, you can always sell it to me.'

No, please. He's not just said that. He's not just made me sound like a tart!

'Take it if you want it,' I blurt. Oh, no, please, I've not just really made myself sound like a hussy!

He holds up the sketch and smiles.

'Thank you, Miss Scotton. I will.'

Lowering the picture one more time, he begins to study my face. What the hell's going on now? The smile fades, only to be replaced by a frown and he's staring at my lips. Shit, this is all getting a bit sexually charged, or at least I think it is. I mean how would I know? I've never been in a sexually charged situation before. All I know is that he's staring at my lips, and I'm wavering a little under his glare and there's something pulsating between my legs and my skin seems to be on fire.

'Teabags!' Jodie announces, exploding her way through the door.

While Daniel Foster breaks himself out of his reverie, the pink one skitters across the office and slings a huge box of teabags onto the table next to the kettle.

'I'd better get going,' the big kahuna murmurs. 'I'll see you later.'

With that, he takes the picture and makes his way out through the door. I flump back down in my chair and take a few good deep breaths, battering my heartbeat back into submission. What the hell was that all about?

'That looked a bit intense,' Jodie muses, pulling off a fluffy pink gilet. 'What did he want?'

'I don't really know.' I pick up my book.

'Well, can I give you a bit of advice?'

Advice? I gaze, dumbstruck, at the pink princess. 'Feel free.'

'If he comes on to you ...' Her plucked eyebrows struggle to raise themselves. 'Run a mile.'

***

I spend another hour trying to read the first chapter of my book, but it's next to impossible. I can barely focus on the words. My brain's too busy mulling over Daniel Foster's little visit and Jodie's priceless nugget of advice. By half eleven, I reach breaking point. I'm in serious need of something to do. I could try another sketch but that might only land me in more trouble. Instead, I spend half an hour drafting out another letter of resignation but I still can't seem to find the right words. As strange as it seems, I don't want to upset Norman. I twiddle a pencil between my index finger and my thumb and decide that I've had enough. Closing down the computer, I shove the pencil to one side and shrug myself out of my chair.

'I'm going out for a coffee,' I announce.

'But we've got coffee here.' Jodie nods towards the kettle.

'And I don't want a coffee here. I want to go out.'

'But it's not lunchtime yet.'

'So what?' I hear myself rant. 'Nobody's going to miss me anyway. I mean, I don't actually do anything. Nobody actually does anything. Why am I even here? Why are you here? Why is Norman here? I'm going out for a coffee and if Norman doesn't like it, then Norman can bloody well sack me.' I glance at Norman's door. Thank God it's still closed. 'I'm off.'

Before Jodie can object any more, I'm out of the office and waiting for the lift. It seems to take an age but when it finally arrives, it's empty and I give out a huge sigh of relief. Right now, I couldn't face a single one of those suited types with their meaningful jobs. As soon as the lift reaches the ground floor, I'm off, making my way through the massive revolving doors and breathing in the hot, summer air. It's close, very close … and I shiver. There's a storm coming on. Glancing up at the sky, I pray that it won't happen any time soon, and then I set off down the embankment, half running, half walking, without the slightest idea where I'm going. All I know is that I need to get away from the midday crowds. Dodging the tourists and the workers out on their lunch breaks, I take a right, heading away from the river, searching for an oasis of peace and quiet where I can gather my thoughts. At last I find it, half way down a side alley, a deserted backstreet coffee shop that's definitely seen better days.

I push open the door and make my way to the counter. The young woman behind the counter stares at me, and then she stares at something behind me. Her eyes seem to double in size.

'A latte please,' I demand.

'Uh?'

'A latte please. Small.'

'Two pounds fifty,' the young woman gasps, still looking beyond me at something else.

'I'll get this.' Out of the corner of my eye, I see an arm, and then a hand reaching out. 'And I'll take a cappuccino.'

I turn slowly, already knowing exactly who's standing behind me. His voice is unmistakable. And I can smell him too, now that I've gathered my senses. I turn slowly to find him standing close behind me. He smiles down at me. His blue eyes seem to twinkle.

'Thank you, Mr Foster,' I gulp.

'Dan,' he mouths back at me, and suddenly I'm a wreck. And worse than that, he seems to have noticed. His smile broadens and he puts a hand to my back. At his touch, a flood tide of chemicals crashes its way through my body, tearing at my foundations, ripping away every last scrap of logic and sense. I'm a shambles, a shivering, quaking muddle of sexual want. He leans forwards slightly and whispers into my ear.

'Go and get us a seat. I'll bring the drinks over.'

My heartbeat falters and I feel queasy. No, no, no, no, no. He can't be coming on to me. He's a top notch bastard, a heartless, hollow piece of shit, and he may be filthy rich, and he may be the most agonisingly handsome man I've ever laid eyes on, but I'm not having this.

'Okay,' I breathe.

Shit. Shit. Shit. I'm in trouble. Why can't I just say no? Why can't I just tell him I'm getting a take-out? And why the hell is he telling me to call him Dan? Nobody calls him Dan, not even Norman, and Norman's clearly allowed to call him Dan. In a fog of confusion, I find myself staggering through a maze of mismatched tables and chairs, desperately trying to muster my thoughts. But it's not easy. After all, a womanising sex god has just bought me a coffee and touched me on the back. My thoughts are simply in no mood to be mustered at all. Think, brain, think, I will myself, glancing round at the empty coffee shop, trying to pinpoint the best place to sit. Apart from a few tables and chairs, there's a sofa by the window, and I can't sit there. If I sit there, we could end up with an uncomfortable body contact situation. No, it has to be a table. I've got to keep some distance between me and Mr Mean and Hot and Moody.

'The couch will do fine.'

His voice hits me from behind and suddenly he's overtaking me, a mug of coffee in each hand, aiming for the bloody sofa. So, I have no choice in the matter. Daniel Foster is placing the mugs on the coffee table, his lovely pert backside in the air, and now he's shrugging off his expensive jacket and lowering himself down ... gracefully. He waves me over without a trace of an expression on that wonderfully perfect face. He knows what he's doing. But why is he doing it to me? That's the question. I try my best to ease myself down with equal grace onto the sofa but it's far too low. I hear it squeak beneath me and I seem to sink further.

'Are you okay?'
'Pardon?'
'Are you okay?'
'Yep.'

'Only I saw you running through the lobby and I was worried. I followed you here.'

Followed me here? He bloody followed me? But why did he follow me? Questions are zinging about in my head, and they're finding no answers.

'I'm fine,' I half whisper. Is that all you're going to say, my brain screams. Aren't you going to ask exactly why he followed you?

'You don't look it.'

'It's nothing.'

He picks up his coffee, surveys the sprinkling of chocolate and places it back down again. 'So, how was your first day?'

'Fine.' Is that it? Fine? Is that the only word I'm going to be able to utter? Why am I currently in possession of a sorely limited vocabulary?

'You've settled in?'

'I think so.'

He picks up his mug one more time, takes a sip of his coffee and grimaces.

'Well, that's shit,' he mumbles under his breath, and I'm not sure whether he means the coffee or the fact that I'm claiming to have settled into my new job, whatever that is. I watch as he places the mug on the table. He leans back, snaking his left arm across the back of the sofa, just behind my head, and gazes at me, his eyes still twinkling.

'Has Norman been keeping you busy?' he asks.

I want to tell him the truth. I want to tell him that up until now I've done precious little. In fact, I want to ask him why Norman even needs a secretary. After all, he's the big kahuna and he should know. But then again, I don't want to land Norman in trouble because when all's said and done, Norman's a good man.

'Yes,' I whisper.

And shit, he's smiling at that. He's actually smiling. Does he really know that the Norman department does nothing at all, that while one of Norman's extraneous secretaries buries her head in Sudoku puzzles, the other one makes endless cups of tea or reads romantic novels? And as for the head of the department, well, apart from flapping over a factory in Tyneside and reading the paper and moving his exercise bike from one side of the room to the other, I'm not sure what he gets up to at all.

'So, have you finished that book yet?'

Oh great, so he does know that I do sweet Fanny Adams.

'What book?'

'The one on your desk. That romantic thing you've been busying yourself with?'

'Ah ...'

'Ah ... You like a happy ending then?'

'It's just ... escapism.'

'Of course it is.'

I shake my head and wish that I could disappear in a cloud of smoke.

'I was quite taken with your artistic abilities.'

'It was nothing. Just a doodle.'

He's frowns at me, his lips curling ever so slightly at one side of his mouth. 'I think it was more than that.'

More than that? What on Earth is he getting at now? I have absolutely no idea. It's time to change the course of the conversation.

'I didn't think someone like you would come into a place like this.'

'I wouldn't ...' He reaches up and loosens his tie. 'Normally. But you came in here, so naturally I had to follow.'

'You had to?'

He nods. 'I couldn't leave you on your own.'

'But ...'

He says nothing more, just stares at me, straight in the eyes and runs his fingers down the length of his tie, slowly, lazily. With a quivering hand, I take a sip of my drink and stare resolutely out of the window. I'm feeling distinctly uncomfortable now because I know that those eyes are still examining me, and because my breath is faltering and my stomach has begun to churn. I want to look back at him but I can't. I can't look into those eyes. He'll have me mesmerised before I can say 'rip my bloody knickers off.'

'It's interesting isn't it?' he asks. 'Seeing how the other half live.'

Arrogant bastard! My brain explodes. He's so up himself. I glance at his expensive shirt, his gold cufflinks, his Rolex watch, and I desperately want to tell him that he's currently wearing a year's worth of salary for one of those poor bastards he's about to make redundant.

'So,' he says quietly. 'Tell me about yourself.'

What? Why do you want to know about me? I'd like to ask him if he's making a move because I'm slightly suspicious that he is. And then, if he is making a move, I'd like to inform him that he's wasting his time because I don't date bastards. I open my mouth and my lips falter. At last, I look up to find a flicker of amusement in those eyes.

'For example, where did you grow up?' he helps me out.

'On the East Coast.' My words jitter through the air. 'A small town called Limmingham.'

He nods slightly. 'Family?'

'Er ... yes.' I swallow.

He tilts his head forwards, prompting me to elaborate.

'Mum and Dad still live there.' In a tiny house, on a tiny pension, seeing as my dad lost his job when the local factory was shut down by a rich pig-head like you. 'I've got an older sister. She's in Oxfordshire now. Married with kids.'

'How old is she?' he asks and I'm wondering why he's so interested.

'Thirty-five.'

'Same age as me. And you're twenty-six. That's quite a gap.'

Good grief. He remembered my age.

'I think I was an accident.'

'A quirk of fate,' he smiles.

My breath catches. I'm a quirk of fate? Does that make me a good thing or a bad thing? And what's he getting at now? And why is he smiling again? And oh God, in spite of the fact that he's a complete bastard, he really has got a gorgeous smile. But then again, it's probably fake.

'What's your sister's name?' he asks.

I watch his face. The smile dissolves into nothing, his features becoming a mask. There's a slight twitch of his right eyebrow. Nothing more. Why does he want to know that tiny, irrelevant detail? I dismiss it all. He's just making small talk.

'Sara.'

He stares at me now. And that eyebrow has definitely twitched again.

'And how about you?'

'What about me?'

'You're not married?'

'No.' Stupidly, I wave my left hand in the air. Why the hell am I doing that?

'Relationship?'

What? Stop asking stuff like that. I'm not going out with you, you pig.

'No.'

And is that really any business of yours, my brain seethes. And anyway, why do you want to know? Surely, you're not going to ...

'Come out for dinner with me on Friday night.'

Oh shit, he is. And he has. And now my brain is turning cartwheels, displacing all sensible thoughts in every possible direction. No, a voice screams out inside my head. This is not the man for you. He places a hand on my arm and I fizzle. My brain has shot into orbit and I want it back. After all, I need it to make a sensible decision.

'I know what you're thinking. You're thinking I'm a nasty piece of work.'

'I ...' Of course I am. A completely arrogant, smarmy, up-your-own-arse, nasty piece of work. 'No, I'm not.'

'Is that because of the meeting?'

'No, not at all.'

'But it is what you're thinking?'

'Yes.'

What? Yes? Why did I have to blurt that one out?

'So, why am I a nasty piece of work?'

I scan the crappy coffee shop, as if I'm going to find any answers here.

'It's okay,' he adds, and the smile is back. 'I know I have a reputation and believe me, I deserve it. To keep a company like mine on its feet, it's actually a requirement to be a nasty piece of work.'

'But those jobs. That factory.'

'Those jobs need to be sacrificed to save the company. Do you know how many people work for me in total?'

I shake my head, feeling ridiculously stupid.

'Five thousand, give or take. That's not to mention the contractors and the sub-contractors around the world. If Fosters doesn't function with efficiency, then there's much more at stake than two hundred and twenty five jobs.'

'Oh.'

'Remember the bigger picture, Maya. The company is everything.'

'To you?'

Yes, definitely to you. You wouldn't be wearing expensive bloody suits and expensive shirts and bloody off the radar, expensive watches if it wasn't for your profit margin, you git.

'To everyone who works for it,' he says quickly. 'Now, about that dinner.'

Oh God, he's not going to let it go.

'I don't know.'

'I do.'

His eyes skim me up and down, taking in my too-small blouse and too-short skirt. I curse myself for failing to go shopping last night. I really do need to sort myself out and stop relying on Lucy's work clothes.

'I'll pick you up at eight.'

I should be shaking my head by now. I should be whispering a quick 'No thank you.' In fact, in all probability, I should be screaming a huge 'No thank you.' But instead, I sit silently, watching as he stands up and shrugs his body back into the expensive jacket, giving me just enough time to admire the ripple of muscles beneath his shirt.

'But you don't even know where I live.'

'I'm your boss.' He straightens the cuffs and twitches the jacket back into shape. 'Of course I know where you live. Eight o'clock. Wear a dress.'

As he begins to make his way towards the exit, my heartbeat flicks up another gear. I don't even own a dress. And anyway, who the hell does the bastard think he is ordering me around? And more than that, why on Earth have I gone all hot? I turn to tell him that he can stick his dinner up his arse, but he's already gone.

Chapter Six

I let my shoulders sag and stare at my reflection in the full-length mirror. I'm dressed in one of Lucy's trademark short, flowery dresses with a deep V-neck. My hair tumbles down over my shoulders. I've managed to keep Lucy at bay with the make-up bag and I've sorted myself out: a quick application of eyeliner, mascara and pale eye shadow. Nothing more. And then there's the jewellery: a silver chain and a Yorkshire jet pendant, with matching dangly earrings, all left to me by my grandmother, the only jewellery I love to wear.

'I told you this would happen,' Lucy drawls from the bed. 'You've bagged yourself a rich, powerful businessman.'

Turning away from the mirror, I scowl in Lucy's general direction.

'No, I bloody well haven't.'

'Mr Mean and Hot and Moody has asked you out. It's perfect. It's that skirt.'

I turn back to my reflection and glance down at my legs. They're far too scrawny. If anything, the strip of material that Lucy calls a skirt should have put him off.

'Mr Mean and Hot and Moody has not asked me out. He's virtually ordered me to go out with him.'

'And that's sexy.'

'How on Earth is that sexy?'

'All that power.'

'All that arrogance,' I laugh and then I shake my head. Good God, Lucy really does need to get a grip on reality. And more than that, she'd do better to concentrate on her own pathetic love life instead of living vicariously through mine. I can't remember the last time she dated anyone. I catch a breath. Shit, is this a date?

'Stuff this,' I hiss. 'I'm not going.'

'Why not?' Lucy sits up quickly. I can see her face in the mirror. She's looking distinctly panic-stricken.

'This whole situation. I just don't like it.'

And that's a lie. I like it very much. I'd be an idiot if I didn't. A thoroughly gorgeous, thoroughly rich, thoroughly powerful man seems to have taken some sort of interest in me, and I'm loving it. But you shouldn't love it, the sensible part of my brain complains. He's a shit. And besides, you've sworn yourself off men. After Tom, you need to get yourself back on track. You need to start painting again, and that's never going to happen if you let another man into your life because if you do, the only thing that's going to happen is heartache, especially if the man in question is an arrogant womaniser.

'I fancy him but I don't like him.'

'Fair enough. If you get the chance, just shag him and be done with it.'

'You know I'm through with that sort of stuff.'

She nods mutely, knowing full well that casual sex is off the menu in my world.

I've been there, done that and worn the T-shirt ... several times. I shiver involuntarily, recalling the after-effects of the break-up: the stream of men picked up in bars; the seedy, drunken one night stands conducted in one soulless flat after another; the cold morning-afters, walking unknown streets with tears in my eyes, searching desperately for the nearest tube station.

'And besides,' I add. 'I don't think it's quite as simple as that.'

'Why not?'

'Well ...' I wonder what I can say now. Why isn't it as simple as that? Is it because he's fuck-off gorgeous? Is it because my body seems to be completely incapable of resisting him? Or is it that my mind seems to chuck reason out of the window every time he's anywhere near me?

'I think ...' I muse, 'if I have anything to do with him, I'll end up getting hurt.'

'How?'

'I could get wrapped up in a man like that. I could become addicted. And that's not good.'

'Why not?'

'Can you think of anything that's addictive that's actually good for you?'

'Cigarettes,' Lucy mutters to herself. 'Booze. Heroin. Cakes ... No,' she announces at last. 'You're right.'

'I'd get wrapped up in him, and he'd just use me.'

'There's always something, isn't there?' she sighs. 'Why can't they just be perfect?'

'No man is perfect. And this man is far from it. He shuts down factories without batting an eyelid, he treats his staff with utter contempt, and he's so far up his own arse, he can't have seen daylight in a month. He's an arrogant bastard and I'm not ready for this.' In one swift move, I pull the dress up over my head.

'Oh come on, Maya. He's your boss.'

'Meaning?'

'He might sack you and we need the rent money.'

'God.' My chin sags towards my chest. 'I can do without this. I feel like a prostitute.'

'How come?'

'How come? If I'm going out with this man to stop him sacking me, then I'm going out with him to make sure I get a pay packet, which means that I'm going out with him for money, which makes me a prostitute!'

Lucy's on her back now, howling with laughter.

'Come off it. You're going out with this man because he makes your lady parts do a special dance.'

'Shit.'

She's right. I could easily have backed out on this before now, but I didn't. I could have gone straight back to my ridiculous office and fired off an email to Mr Mean and Hot and Moody, telling him to sling his ridiculously mean and hot and moody hook.

'Put the dress back on.'

'I can't.' I drop it to the floor. 'I can't go through with this. Yes, he makes my lady parts do a special dance, but he's a bastard.'

'He owns a massive company, Maya. The man's got to be a bastard. Have you ever heard of a business magnate who's a complete teddy bear?'

'Alan Sugar.'

'Oh, come on. You can't back out. You haven't even got his mobile number. You agreed to go out with him.'

'I didn't.'

'You didn't say no.'

'I didn't get a chance.'

'Look, just go out to dinner with him and be boring. He won't come back for more. And don't get feisty. He'll probably like that. He'll see you as a challenge if you get all feisty with him, and then he'll definitely want to fuck you.' She turns on her back and stares at the ceiling, dreamily. 'Oh God. He's a rich, powerful business magnate, and he's going to fuck you.'

'Stop it. He's getting nowhere near my ... thing.'

'I bet he's one of those control freaks. Oh God, he'll definitely want to dominate you. Shit!' She shoots out the word and rolls onto her front. 'I bet he'll tie you up and everything.'

'Nobody's tying me up. I don't need controlling. Not after what I've been through.'

'Oh bloody hell, Maya, I'm sorry.' Suddenly earnest, Lucy pushes herself up onto her knees. 'I wasn't thinking. It's just that I thought you were over that, what with Tom and everything.'

She stares at me in silence, knowing that she's touched on a subject we rarely discuss.

'Tom helped me forget for a while.' Leaning down, I pick up the dress. 'He didn't make it go away. Let's not talk about Edinburgh.'

'You can't just block it out.'

'I think you'll find that I can.' I gaze at myself in the mirror and a demon raises itself in my brain. 'If Mr Mean and Hot and Moody thinks he's going to control me, he's got another think coming.' Throwing the dress at Lucy, I skitter over to my wardrobe, delve through its contents and pull out a pair of jeans.

'You can't go out in those,' Lucy snarls.

'Why not? I'll do what I like.'

My mobile pings, announcing the arrival of a text. Retrieving the phone from the clutter on my dressing table, I open up the message. It's from a number I don't recognise.

Don't forget the dress. And store this number. The name is Dan.

What? How has he done that? My brain wheels for a second before landing on the obvious answer. I already know that he's taken the trouble to go through my file. Why wouldn't he take my number?

'He's got your number?' Lucy's eyes are agog. 'How did he get your number?'

'He's my boss, shit head.'

'Oh my Lord. This is serious.'

Of course it's serious. He knows my number, my address, and plenty about my past. He's got all the details he needs to stalk me good and proper.

'Tell me about it. I'm texting him now. I'm backing out.'

Leaping up from the bed, Lucy grabs the mobile out of my hand.

'No, you're not.' She waves the phone in the air. 'Just one night! See how it goes!'

'No, Luce!'

'Promise not to bail.'

'Why are you so eager for this to happen?'

'Because it's about time you started dating again. Even if it is with some sort of sociopathic sex fiend.'

'Look. I'm not going to bail. Just give me my phone for God's sake.'

At last, she hands it me back to me. I read the message again, everything bristling at his arrogance. I'm certainly not about to follow his orders. For a start, I won't bother storing his number because after tonight, he won't want to see me again. I'm going to be queen of boring. And who the hell does he think he is, ordering me about like this? He may well be my boss between nine and five o'clock, but right now he's just a man who seems to have asked me out on a date. I will not be ordered around. I text him back.

I'll wear what I like, if you don't mind.

My fingers quiver at my own audacity. He won't like that. I'm pretty sure he's not told to back off all that often. The reply comes quickly.

Of course I don't mind, as long as it's a dress.

Jesus. What's this all about? Is he after easy access? A quick fuck somewhere up an alleyway. Is that his thing? Well, no way am I giving in to any demands from this man, boss or not. I chuck the mobile onto my bed and decide once and for all that he's not getting his way. The mobile begins to vibrate and then it begins to ring. I lurch forwards, snatching it up before Lucy can get anywhere near the bloody thing. If that's Mr Foster insisting that I dress appropriately for a quick one up an alley, then I'm going to tell him that he can get stuffed right here and now. I check the screen and register a surge of disappointment. It's Mum.

'Hello, darling,' she purrs.

'Mum. I haven't got much time. I'm going out.'

'Ooh, have you got a date?'

Should I tell her? No, I'll keep that one to myself. Ever since my life with Tom fell to pieces, she's been on at me to get back on my bike.

'No, I'm going out with friends.'

'Well, you should really think about it sometime soon, darling.'

Lucy's coming at me now with a make-up bag. 'No!' I snap, batting her away.

'Oh Maya, don't be like that.'

I sigh. I can't be bothered to explain who the 'No' had really been aimed at.

'You've left it too long. You need to get back on your ...'

'Mum! I'll date when I'm good and ready.'

'You'll be good and ready when it's too late,' she complains. 'When all your bits are starting to sag and your egg timer's run out ...'

'Is there a purpose to this call?' I demand, rummaging through my cupboard for a T-shirt. The first one that comes to hand is a plain white thing. 'Only I'm in a bit of a rush.'

'Well, it's your dad.'

I slam to a halt.

'Is he okay?'

'Of course he's okay. He's out in the garden cleaning out the fish pond. No, it's about the party.'

Party? What party? I rifle my way through my mind, only to find that it's a complete mess. Somebody's been through it like a whirlwind, chucking stuff all over the place. Nothing's where it's supposed to be, and I've got the distinct feeling that it's all down to Daniel Foster.

'Your dad's sixtieth.'

'I haven't forgotten,' I lie. Bugger it, I need to buy him a present, and a decent one at that.

'Two weeks tomorrow, Maya. You'll be there, won't you? Sara's coming with that disgusting husband of hers and the kids. The whole family's going to be there: Auntie Betty, Uncle Brian, all your cousins. Why don't you bring Lucy? She's always a laugh.'

'I'll do that, Mum. I'll call you nearer the time.'

Chapter Seven

He's standing in the doorway, twiddling his car keys, and my God, he looks gorgeous. His fair hair is freshly styled. Slightly overlong, his fringe curls down over his forehead, giving him the appearance of a naughty schoolboy. He's obviously taken the time for a shave and he's wearing an expensive black suit with a crisp white shirt. His black tie is loose, his collar unbuttoned at the top. I don't care if he is a complete bastard who's about to ruin the lives of over two hundred people, he is so fucking fuckable. Reminding myself that all of this lust stuff can land you in no end of trouble, it takes every last remnant of my self-control not to gawp at him like an idiot. I clamp my mouth shut and will my body into submission. It's not easy. At the very sight of him, just about every part of me has decided to tremble.

He frowns slightly and his eyes travel up and down my outfit. 'You're not ready yet.'

Oh God, what do I say? Open, mouth! Open!

'I am ready.'

'But I told you to wear a dress.'

Okay, I remind myself. Whatever you do now, don't get feisty. 'I don't own any dresses.'

'You could have bought one.'

'I don't wear dresses.' I'm really quite pleased with how I'm handling this. Not feisty at all.

He glances down at my faded jeans, back up at the white T-shirt, his gaze resting on my breasts, and I squirm.

'At least go and put on a skirt and a blouse. And don't tell me you don't have any. You wear those for work.'

Jesus, this is going to be hard. I need to force the words out in the most unfeisty manner possible.

'I don't want to,' I explain. 'It's Friday night and I don't want to wear my work clothes.'

'Maya.' His harsh tone startles me. His eyes have travelled up to my face now. 'I want you in a skirt.'

What the hell? Did he really just mean what I think he means? Well, if that's his intention, he can bugger off.

'I'm wearing this, and if you don't like it, then I guess you won't be taking me out to dinner.'

He sighs an audible, pissed off sigh. He seems to think for a moment or two and finally, he holds out a hand.

'Okay,' he breathes at last. 'You can have your own way this time.' I place my hand in his and feel a tremor of electricity running straight up my arm. It flings itself through my body and hits me straight in the heart. 'But I have to warn you,' he says darkly. 'You'll regret this later.'

Shit. I'll regret this later? How will I regret this later? If he is one of those all-powerful domineering types then he'll only want to tie me to his bed and spank me. And no way is he doing that because I'm going nowhere near his bed in the first place.

He leads me away from the front door, quickly, giving me just enough time to shut it behind me. He practically drags me to his car and I gasp. Well, I could have predicted it. A black Mercedes-Benz. Opening the passenger door, he lets go of my hand and motions for me to get in. I comply, sinking myself into the leather seat and gazing round in awe at the surroundings. The door is slammed shut and I start. A good beginning to the evening. I've pissed off my date.

'So …' He lowers himself into the driver's seat and pulls the door shut. 'Would you like a little music on the way?'

'Music?'

'Music. It's that stuff people do with guitars and drums and things.'

'Oh that. Yes I'd like a little music, please.' At least that way I won't have to talk to you.

'So, what can I give you?'

His eyebrows arch. Oh bloody hell. That was definitely a double-entendre.

'I don't know. What have you got?'

Oh shit, no! That was definitely a double-entendre returned. I'm being too flirty by far. I wince, hoping to God that he's not going to pick up on it. But when I look up at his utterly handsome, completely ruddy gorgeous face, my heart thuds with panic. He's smiling across at me and there's a mischievous glint in his eyes.

'Plenty.' He fixes me again with those blue eyes. And I realise that he could lean over and take me right here, and I wouldn't really mind. 'How about this? He flicks a button on the steering wheel and as the engine roars into life, the car fills with the sound of violins.

'What's the song?'

'You Don't Know Me. Ray Charles.'

I listen for a moment or two, taking in the melancholic rise and fall of the strings.

'It's sad.'

'It is.' He keeps his eyes fixed on the road. 'Listen to the words. He's utterly in love with the woman he's singing to. He can barely speak, his heart's beating so fast.'

I take a peek at his chest, trying to work out if this is an intentional choice, to see if his heart really is beating so fast he can barely speak, but I can't make out a thing. His black jacket covers everything. And anyway, I'm being ridiculous. It can't be a message. It's just a random choice of a random song.

'But he's forced to hide himself from her,' he adds.

'Why?'

He chews at his bottom lip. 'Because he has no choice.'

I gaze at his profile. What's he thinking about? I couldn't even begin to work it out. Instead, I swim away into a curious blur as the streets of North London flash by. Just go with it, a voice urges me from somewhere at the back of my head. Just let go and lap it up, woman. Enjoy! I'm in a daze, but at some point, I'm vaguely aware that Regent's Park has flashed past us. But where are we now? Is this the Bayswater Road? Are we in Kensington? I have no idea. All I know is that the buildings to either side of us look distinctly intimidating now, and the car has slowed to a whisper.

'We're here.' The car draws to a halt at the kerb. He casts a glance at me. 'I've booked a table.'

His eyes flicker momentarily, and he nods towards a building on my side. I turn to take it in. It all seems pretty expensive. A uniformed valet waits patiently beneath a canopy and behind him, a second figure stands guard by a black door. To the right of the door, there's a single gold plate on the wall. Daniel Foster gets out of the car, hands over his keys to the valet and circles round to the passenger door. It's pulled open and a big, strong hand appears in front of my face. I put my hand in his, feeling a shimmer of excitement run through my arm at the physical contact. I'm trembling as he gently lifts me from the car. I straighten up. He's still holding my hand, gazing down into my eyes and I wonder if he's going to kiss me right here on the pavement. He snaps his eyes shut, flicks them open again, and the moment's gone. In silence, he guides me up the steps and through the doorway.

My mouth falls open as soon as we're inside. My brain struggles to take it all in. In front of me, a sea of tables stretches out beneath a vaulted ceiling that's clearly been hand-painted. I gaze up in awe at the delicate flowers that intertwine above me, and then back down at the tables, each one covered with a crisp white tablecloth, adorned with silver cutlery and cut glass. It's only then that I'm able to take in the rest of the room: a set of high windows to the left, edged with thick curtains, complete with huge swags and tails; three vast chandeliers hanging from the centre of the ceiling; walls that are decorated with vast mirrors; and here and there, in an alcove, a marble statue or a man-sized fern nestling in a golden pot. Opulence just isn't the word for it.

'Where are we?' I gasp, cursing myself for not bothering to read the sign outside.

'Carlton's,' he says curtly. 'It's one of the most expensive, exclusive, elite restaurants in London.' He catches the attention of the maître d'. 'And I called in some favours to get us a table here tonight, but don't let that bother you.'

I stare at the floor, shame washing over me for my childishness.

'So, are you regretting your choice of outfit yet?'

'I might be.'

'There is, of course, a dress code in this place, but I'll see what I can do.'

'Mr Foster.'

A small, black-suited, black-haired, black-moustachioed man approaches us. The maître d'. He takes Dan's hand and shakes it, and then turns to stare at me in horror.

'Good evening, Raoul. Can I have a word?'

He moves away with the maître d', talking into his ear, smiling here and there, shrugging his shoulders, frowning at one point, and I realise he's doing his damnedest to use his reservation. I could kick myself for being such an idiot. At last, the maître d' looks me up and down, a slight scowl appearing on his face and I could sink to the floor with embarrassment. So, he wasn't demanding a dress for easy access after all, but the idiot could have told me the reason for his demands.

'Is he letting us in?'

He nods.

'What did you say?'

'I told him that you're a filthy rich American heiress with connections to the Mafia.'

'You didn't?'

'I did. I told him that you're a little eccentric, but utterly determined to have dinner here tonight. I told him that if he were to throw us out, then you'd be highly likely to see to it that he sleeps with the fishes.'

'No.'

He takes off his jacket and drapes it over my shoulders.

'At least we can hide a little of the crime scene with this.'

And then the hint of a grin appears at the corner of his mouth. His eyes seem to twinkle with life for a moment and I realise that he's actually enjoying my discomfort. Is this a sense of humour? He leads me to a table, a table right at the centre of the room, and the maître d' pulls out a chair. Well-dressed women and well-dressed men are seated all around me, and I can feel their eyes on my clothes. It's not long before I sense the beginnings of anger in my gut. It's curled up into a ball for now, but I know it won't take much to set it free. After all, is this really necessary? He didn't have to insist on keeping this reservation. He could have taken me somewhere else, somewhere a little less up-market, a little more fitting to my current choice of clothing. But he seems to be determined to belittle me. I look up to find that the smile has disappeared again. He's deep in thought.

'It's not nice, is it?' he asks at last.

'What?'

'Wearing the wrong clothes?'

I can feel a frown coming on. What on Earth is he going on about now?

'No, it's not,' I scowl back at him. 'So, why are you doing this to me?'

He leans back, examining me closely, and then his face seems to relax.

'You did this to yourself.'

'If you'd told me why I had to wear a dress, I might have worn a dress.'

'I thought you didn't have any dresses.'

'And I would have bought one if I'd known you were bringing me here.'

'So you were simply defying me for the sake of defying me?'

'Defying you?' I gasp. Oh Lord, he really is one of those tie-you-up-and-dominate-you types. 'That's control freak talk.'

'Maybe it is.'

'And maybe I don't like control freaks.'

'Really? Why ever not?'

'Maybe.' I pick up the menu. 'Maybe,' I sneer. 'It's because this is the twenty-first century and women are generally viewed as equals. Maybe it's because I actually have a brain and I don't need to be controlled.'

'And maybe you should relax and let someone else make the decisions for a change.'

'And maybe I shouldn't.'

'And maybe I shouldn't have brought you here,' he whispers, knocking me off balance for a split second. Was that remorse?

'No, you shouldn't. But seeing as we're here now, we'd better get on with it.'

I snap open the menu and stare at a bunch of things that I don't really understand.

'May I order for you?'

'I think you'd better. I don't have a fucking clue what any of this is.'

'You know ...' He leans forwards and rests his chin in his hand, allowing a twinkle back into his eyes. 'You may be angry with me right now - and I'm angry with you too, just for the record - but you really don't have to swear like a builder. Not here.'

'I'm so fucking sorry,' I sneer back at him, and there's that twinkle again. Shit, I'm being feisty, and that's exactly what men like him enjoy. I remind myself of Lucy's words. I'm presenting myself as some sort of challenge, although why he's interested in it, I have no idea. No, this definitely isn't the way ahead. I shake myself into action. It's time to get all boring on his ass.

'So, tell me about yourself,' he says after an age.

'I already did that in the coffee shop.'

'And is that all there is to you?'

'Yep.'

I fold my arms and stare across the room at an expensive dress.

'Oh cut the crap, Maya.'

'You know, you don't have to swear like a builder,' I admonish him.

'And you don't have to be difficult with me.'

'You asked for it.' I mentally slap myself for my feisty tone. Be boring, woman! Be boring! It shouldn't be too hard. After all, you are boring.

'Come on, tell me about yourself.'

'There really is nothing to know.'

'What does your dad do for a living?'

'Nothing,' I snap. And then I can't help myself. 'He worked in a shoe factory but some rich, up-his-own-arse twat shut it down.'

'You say that as if you think I'm responsible.' He runs a finger up the stem of a wine glass. 'Can I remind you that this particular rich, up-his-own-arse twat has never owned a shoe factory in his life.'

I glare at him and find the twinkle has returned. For God's sake, I don't know where I am with this man. Twinkle or cold stare? Just pick one and stick to it, please.

'No, but you do own a concrete mixer factory.'

'I've explained about that.'

'Whatever.' I seethe for a few minutes, staring at anything and everything. Finally, I stare at Daniel Foster only to find that he's pushed himself back in his chair, folded his arms and stretched out his legs. And he's staring back at me, a grin playing across his face. Instead of desperately trying to move the conversation on, he's simply been sitting there enjoying my discomfort.

'Why did you insist that I come to that meeting?' I hear myself ask.

'I like to meet my staff.'

'That's not what I've heard.'

'Somebody's been spreading rumours.'

'And why have you asked me out to dinner?'

He chews his lips and gazes around the restaurant, as if he's trying to find inspiration. At last, he sits up straight, draws his chair back to the table and finally leans in towards me, his face perfectly serious.

'Because I think you're beautiful.'

I can't help myself at that. I begin to laugh. Not a quiet chuckle. No. A loud belly laugh. The clatter of cutlery comes to a halt. But Daniel Foster doesn't seem to mind.

'I am not beautiful.'

His forehead creases. He seems genuinely confused.

'You don't think so?'

'No.' I suppose I'm alright. But beautiful? Come on.

'Well, you've turned heads in here tonight.' He waves his hand around the restaurant.

'That's because of this,' I hiss, pulling at my T-shirt.

'Oh no.' He tuts. 'It's because of your long blonde hair, your incredible green eyes, your amazing figure and, of course, your stunning little ass.'

'Excuse ...'

'You're quite a catch.'

'I'm not a bloody fish.'

'And before you accuse me of being a sexist pig, I'll throw in the fact that you're obviously a talented, intelligent and spirited woman. I could go on.'

'Please don't.'

I don't like blowing my own trumpet, and I certainly don't like anyone else doing it for me.

'You studied at the School of Art in Edinburgh.'

I stop full on in my tracks. I'm blindsided. Where has that come from?

'I said don't go on. And how do you know that?'

'I'm your boss. I've seen your CV.'

'Well, fine ...'

'But what stumps me is this ... you get the highest accolades from Edinburgh, and then you end up working as a secretary.'

'There's nothing wrong with working as a secretary.'

'Of course not. But wouldn't you be happier if you were making use of your talents?'

'I'm fine as I am.'

'Are you?' He stares at me for a moment or two and I'm lost in his eyes. And worse than that, some sort of fluttering sensation seems to have kicked off in my knickers. Damn the man. How is he doing this to me? 'You're twenty-six. You left art college at twenty-one and you seem to have been drifting ever since.'

'I've not been drifting.'

'Really?'

'Really. I was in a relationship.'

'But you didn't paint.'

'How do you know that? It's not on my CV.'

'A quick look on the internet ...' He takes a swig of water. 'I see no mention of Maya Scotton the artist, Maya Scotton the talented oil painter.'

No, you wouldn't see that, I muse to myself. Because Maya Scotton the artist and Maya Scotton the talented oil painter ran away from a controlling bastard and fell in love with a twat. And somewhere along the way, she pushed the painting to the side. And now ... now ... she can't seem to get back to it.

'How did you know about the oils?'

'A quick call to your old tutor at the School of Art.'

'You're stalking me?'

'Researching you.' He leans forwards and begins to sketch out the last few years of my life. 'After Edinburgh, you disappeared off the face of the Earth. At some point, you undertook a little secretarial training. Typing. The basics.'

'And?' I virtually spit. He has no business poking his nose into my business. This is beginning to feel like a job interview, and I've already been through all of that. I don't need to justify myself again.

'And then you took on a lowly job as a secretary at my company.'

Jesus, he's not about to give up. And I'm not about to make it easy for him.

'Do you do this with all of your new employees?'

'No.'

He smiles, a self-satisfied sort of a smile and takes another sip of water.

'So why me?'

'I've told you. I think you're beautiful.'

'And I think you're wrong.'

I reach out, grab hold of a ridiculously heavy piece of cutlery and begin turning it in my hands.

'So, why don't you tell me about you?' I gripe, laying the fork back down. Yes, go ahead! Why don't you tell me what made you the biggest fucking arrogant prick to walk this planet?

'There's nothing to know,' he says.

'Cut the crap.'

An eyebrow twitches.

'Where did you grow up?' I demand.

'Surrey.'

'Brothers and sisters?'

'Only child.'

'Parents?'

'Dead.'

Shit, I'm stupid. Stupid. Stupid. Stupid. I already knew that. The conversation could come to a crashing halt right now. I need to indulge in some damage limitation.

'I'm sorry.'

'It's okay.'

'What do you do when you're not at work?' I ask.

'I'm always at work.'

'Oh, come off it. Not now, you're not. You must have hobbies.' I should really shut up now because I'm sure he's frowning. 'Come on, what are your hobbies?'

'Knitting,' he grins.

So, there is a playful side to him after all. I laugh out loud and he seems to smile appreciatively. And then I groan to myself. I'm clearly not going to get a straight answer to any more probing questions. But I carry on regardless.

'Women?'

'Yes.'

'What do you mean yes?'

'I mean yes.'

'Relationships?'

'Not sure.'

'What do you mean not sure?'

'Not sure.'

'This is pointless,' I growl.

'Then allow me to take over.' He leans forwards, picks up a fork and mirrors my actions. 'Do you get on with her?'

'Do I get on with who?' I sigh.

'Your sister?'

My sister? Why is he asking about her again? And what is it with the strange question? Wouldn't it be better to ask how many children she has, or how often I see her?

'What's it to you?'

'I'd like to know everything about you. Do you get on with her?'

It's clear that he's not backing off. I think of Sara. She's mellowed with age, but when she was younger she could be a right cow. An 'it' girl, the leader of the pack, all self-assured and sassy right from the start. She always knew that she was superior and she was never slow in letting the world know.

'We're fine now.'

Oh, shit, where did that come from?

'What do you mean now?'

I shake my head and glance towards the door. This conversation is throwing me all over the place and I'm feeling way too hot in his jacket. I really could do with getting out of here now.

'Maya.' His voice snaps me out of my thoughts and I look him straight in the eyes. He seem earnest now. He really wants to know. 'I've touched a nerve. I'm sorry.'

Yes, he has. I have no idea why he's getting in so deep so quickly.

'Aren't you supposed to talk about music and films and holidays on a first date?' I ask.

'I'm not entirely sure. All I know is this. Music and films and holidays are just the window dressing. I'd much prefer to start at the centre and work my way out. And now I know I've touched a nerve, I want to know more. You can tell me about your sister.' He lays down the fork. 'I'd like to know.'

I stare at him. My lips twitch. My eyes begin to sting. He examines my face. A hand slides its way across the table and covers my own. It's a small action, and it's clearly intended to be comforting. And it works. I can't help myself. There's something about those eyes, something about that touch. Everything around us seems to have fizzled away. I can hear nothing, see nothing, apart from this man in front of me. And suddenly, I just want to open myself up.

'When she was younger, she wasn't particularly pleasant to be around,' I explain, and I don't know where this confession is coming from. 'She was better looking than me. She was better at sport, better with the boys. She had more friends. She was just ... better. The only thing I was good at was art. I used to sit in my bedroom painting and drawing for hours, sometimes all night. I got into art college and that's all there is to know.'

His hand squeezes mine. He stares at the table cloth, deep in thought.

'Dan, I don't want to talk about this any more.'

He looks up at me and smiles, a full on, warm-me-to-my-soul smile, and I think that I might just like this man.

'Why are you smiling?' I ask.

'Because I've just peeled back a layer.' He lets his fork drop to the table, pushes back his chair and stands up. 'Come on,' he says, holding out a hand. 'Enough of this dinner crap. I'm taking you home.'

Chapter Eight

So, he's had enough already. He's given up on wining and dining me, and he's simply going to take me home. Oh well, it's my own stupid fault. I set out to be queen of boring and it seems that my mission has been well and truly accomplished. So, he'll dump me back on my doorstep and I'll slink back inside and throw myself into an evening of Lucy and wine and slushy DVDs. I'm slumped in the passenger seat, feeling distinctly disappointed when I notice we're heading south and I seem to be listening to Bob Dylan, telling his lady to lay herself across his big brass bed. Another message? Or simply another random choice of song? I peek at his face. His eyes are fixed on the road again and there's no hint of emotion, no trace of a clue.

'This isn't the way back to mine,' I murmur, nudging myself into action.

'I know.'

Trafalgar Square gives way to Whitehall.

'I live in Camden.'

'I know.'

'You said you were taking me home.'

'I am. I'm taking you to my home.'

'Pardon?' Now, that must be adrenalin pumping its way through my body because my heart begins to thud and there's a distinct fluttering in my stomach. Yes, he does want me to lie across his big, bloody brass bed. And I'm not entirely sure I'm ready for those sorts of shenanigans. Suddenly, I'm in fight or flight mode. Blood is pumping. I'm on high alert. 'But I don't want to go back to your house.'

'Actually, it's an apartment.'

'And I don't want to go back to it.'

The Cenotaph flashes past us in a blur.

'And I think you'll find that you do.'

'But why are we going back to yours?'

He sucks in a breath and keeps his eyes firmly fixed on the road. His big hand reaches down and changes gear. We speed up slightly as we pass by the Houses of Parliament. The thudding has increased threefold, and I'm currently wondering if my heart is going to burst its way straight through my rib cage. I can barely hear the next words, but I'm pretty sure of what he's just said.

'Because I'd like to fuck you.'

'I beg your ...'

My mind is a mess. Less than twenty minutes ago, I was sitting at a dining table in a posh restaurant with an apparently caring and sensitive man. He listened patiently to my story and pulled all the right faces, made all the right noises. And now that man's gone. He's mutated once more, back into an arrogant, albeit eminently sexy bastard. The big hand moves from the gear stick and lays itself gently on my leg, sending a shimmer of warmth skittering up my thigh and straight into my special bits. I grit my teeth against the sensation. Oh Lord, this is bad. He only has to touch me and I'm an overheated, brainless, horny mess of sex. I really need to get out of here.

'This is a bit quick,' I snap.

'You want me to slow down?'

He takes his foot off the accelerator.

'That's not what I mean. You know what I mean.'

'Of course I know what you mean. But what's the point of waiting?'

I can feel my breath coming in short gasps. Good God. He's gone from first to third base without so much as a by-your-leave. I scowl at him and he must know that I'm scowling at him because now he's grinning.

'Take me home.' I growl. 'To my home. I don't want this.'

'Oh yes you do.'

'I ...'

The car rolls to a stop at a red light. Removing his hand from my lap, he turns and gives me a full on dose of his glorious face. And it's amused. Yes, very amused.

'Listen, Miss Scotton. I've been watching your every move and you've already given yourself away. Your cheeks have been flushed all evening and you've been shaking like a leaf. Every now and then you've even had to catch your breath. And you must have seen a similar reaction in me.'

A similar reaction? I've seen nothing of the sort. His bloody face has been playing with me all night. He's a master of self-control.

'And let's face it; you drew a sketch of me. I think that says something.'

I wince and feel the heat rising in my skin. Oh God, I'm blushing.

'Normally I wouldn't even bother with dinner, but you're a special case.'

'A special case?'

He nods. 'Very special. So, let's just get on with it. It's my full intention to take you back to my apartment and fuck you in every possible way I can imagine.'

'And what if I don't want you to ... do that.'

'Then you should persuade me to turn this car around now. But just to let you know, it's going to take quite a bit of persuasion.'

'You don't even know me.'

'I know plenty about you.'

'Is that why you just grilled me in the restaurant? Was that another job interview?'

His lips turn up at the corners. 'Isn't a date always a job interview of sorts?'

'Was that a date?'

He shrugs his shoulders.

'Not sure.'

'You should get to know me some more before you ... you know.'

'I'd prefer to 'you know', and then possibly get to know you some more.'

'Possibly?' I shout. I can hardly believe what's going on now. 'You're an arrogant shit!' I splurt out the words and regret them instantly. Bugger it, I've just insulted my boss. And yes, he deserves to be insulted, but I really shouldn't have done that because now he's going to give me my marching orders. There really must be more diplomatic ways to sort this out. 'Oh God,' I mumble. 'You're going to sack me now.'

'No, I'm not,' he laughs. 'You're perfectly right. I am an arrogant shit. And you're not the first woman who's told me that.'

'And I bet I won't be the last.'

He revs the engine as the lights change to green, but I can still hear the words.

'You might be.'

He turns his head and raises an eyebrow. I might be? Any woman who's ever gone out with this man must have told him exactly the same thing. And there'll certainly be more. How could I possibly be the last? Unless ...

'Oh, don't tell me you're after a relationship,' I gasp.

We're moving again now. He swings the Mercedes into the left hand lane, flips on the indicators and turns onto a bridge. Keeping his eyes fixed firmly on the road, he seems to think for a moment or two before answering.

'I'd simply like to see if you meet my needs.'

'I can't believe this.'

'Just think about it.' He flashes his blue irises at me. 'You wouldn't buy a car without a test drive. And I want a test drive. I'd like to run my hands over your body and feel your curves. I'd like to get inside you and find out how comfortable it is. I'd like to rev your engine and listen to the sound.'

I squeeze my legs together. God, he's being crass and I'm turned on. And I can't help the next words that spill out of my mouth.

'I'm afraid I can't help you, sir. There's nothing on this forecourt that's going to interest you.'

'I disagree. I very much like the look of this particular model. And I'm thinking she's going to be a nippy little number.'

Now, that's enough.

'Turn the car around.'

'No can do.'

'Turn the car around.'

'No chance in hell.'

Panic stations. Send up a flare and unhook the lifeboats!

'Mr Foster, I'm pleading with you. Turn the car around. The next lights you stop at, I'm getting out.'

'I'm afraid not. And call me Dan.'

I tug at the door, even though the car's still moving.

'Don't try to open the fucking door here,' he barks. 'You'll hurt yourself.'

'Then stop the fucking car and let me out!'

The Mercedes screeches to a halt. I pull at the door again, frantically trying to make an escape, but nothing seems to happen. Letting go of the handle, I flop back in the leather seat, crossing my arms and staring resolutely out through the windscreen. I can barely believe what's going on now. If I'm not very much mistaken, I'm being kidnapped. The only thing I can do is shut myself off.

'What are you scared of, Maya?' His voice sweeps across me, sending a shiver of lust through my groin. 'Look at me.'

I sense a movement by my side, feel the touch of his fingers against my chin. Gently, he turns my face towards his and before I know it, my head is swirling. I'm lost in those pools of blue.

'I'll take you home to Camden, if that's what you really want. But you need to know that you shouldn't be afraid of me. I'm not going to force you into anything you don't want to do.'

'But you've locked me in.'

'It's a temporary measure. Just until you calm down and see sense.' He tips his head towards me. 'What's your problem?'

'I don't have a problem,' I lie.

'Then let me take you to bed.'

Now, this is a bad idea and I know it. But while my brain is trying to drag me off in a sensible direction, my body has other ideas. A wave of something warm pulses its way from my stomach and up through my chest, sending me dizzy for a split second. And before I know it, I'm nodding.

'And you'll stay the night,' he informs me.

'Why?'

'I'll let Bob do the talking.'

Letting go of my chin, he flips the car into first gear and revs the engine. Before long, we're moving again, flying across the bridge, circling a roundabout and turning right onto the south bank. He's clearly finished with talking for the time being. And so am I. Leaning my head back against the seat, I will my heartbeat to behave, but it's having none of it. In fact, it's having some sort of a tantrum. I try my level best to tune back into the music. But Bob Dylan has barely managed to inform his lady that he longs to see her in the morning light when the Mercedes pulls in to the left, and waits for a garage door to open.

Chapter Nine

I'm leaning against the counter in a huge kitchen, and he's leaning back against a wall. I've only just got my breath back after being hustled out of his car, into a lift, out of a lift, and into his massive penthouse apartment. He touches his head back against the wall, his hands in his pockets and his feet crossed. He looks for all the world like he's about to break out into a whistle.

'What are you doing?'

'Admiring the bodywork.'

'You're a horrible man.'

'You might be right about that.' He pushes himself away from the wall and stalks towards me. 'But then again.'

As I watch him move closer, I begin to quiver. His eyes are glimmering now beneath their lids.

'I want to go home.'

'No, you don't.'

'I'm saying the words.'

He leans forwards, placing a hand on the counter top to either side of me, and he looks down at my lips.

'And you don't mean them.'

'How would you know?'

'I can tell.'

He leans in towards me. His lips brush against mine, setting off a firework display in my groin. Shit, he's right. I don't mean those words at all. I'm burning up from the centre outwards and now all I want is to feel the touch of his hands.

'I'm going to kiss you now,' he murmurs. 'And let's be clear about this. By the time I've finished, you really won't want to be going anywhere.'

'Arrogant prick.'

His lips are on mine in an instant. He kisses me deeply, his tongue entwining itself with mine, slowly, lazily, languidly. After the initial onslaught, he seems to be in no rush at all. And his lips are so soft and warm, so bloody perfect, reacting to mine, moulding themselves against me. With immediate effect, I'm a mess, an overly-sexed, frustrated, agonising mess. I thrust my hands into his hair and draw him closer, hardly aware that his hands are round my back, tracking their way across my skin. He pulls himself away and in a split second, my T-shirt is over my head and slung onto the floor.

'Enough of that thing.'

He runs a hand across my shoulders, taking his time, across my throat and down to my chest. All I can hear is the sound of my breath. I'm starting to gasp. Any more of this and I'll be hyperventilating. But again, he's in no rush. He leans back slightly, sucks at his top lip as if he's thinking deeply, and finally reaches up to my bra. He slips his finger inside the right cup, gently easing it downwards, revealing my nipple. He glances up at me and gives me a boyish grin before he leans in and begins to suck gently. I feel a hand at my back, pushing me forwards and holding me tight, and I gasp at the edge of pleasure that cuts through my body, right to my centre. Taking his time, he repeats the process with my left cup and my left nipple, and I hear myself groan.

'So ...' He nuzzles his mouth into my neck. 'Do you still want to go home?'

'No,' I pant. 'Shit. No, I don't.'

He tilts his head back and gives me a dose of his gloriously blue eyes.

'Well then,' he smiles. 'It's time for round two.'

Without any warning at all, I'm swept up from the counter and flung over his shoulder. He strides purposefully across the kitchen, through some sort of lounge area that I can barely make out, partly because I'm upside down in a fireman's lift and party because of the dim lighting. I'm carried up a flight of stairs and down a hallway. A door is kicked open and I'm landed on my feet. He takes a step backwards while I try to regain my balance. I could pass out already, and I'm struggling to see straight, and he's not even out of breath.

'Are you alright?' I hear his voice in the darkness.

'I'm fine.'

I turn slowly, adjusting my eyes to the gloom, trying to take it all in. I seem to be standing in the middle of a huge bedroom. It's edged on one side by a floor-to-ceiling window that gives out over the river. To the right, I can clearly make out the Houses of Parliament and Big

Ben, lit up against the night sky, but to the left it's all alien to me. I'm aware of a tapping sound. I peer up at a massive skylight and realise that raindrops are softly dripping against the glass.

'I'll put the lights on, Maya. I'd like to see what I'm doing here.'

He flicks a switch somewhere and the room is suddenly bathed in a soft, unassuming glow. I turn away from the window, finding myself faced with an entire wall's worth of walk-in wardrobes. A chaise longue sits in a corner of the room and beneath the skylight, draped in a soft, cream-coloured throw, the mother of all beds. I stare at it, mesmerised. You could lose yourself in that thing ... literally.

'Don't be nervous.'

My eyes flick away from the bed, over towards the door, and my heart begins to race. He's standing there, staring at me. His lips are parted and his eyes glimmer. As he begins to move forwards, every single muscle in my body becomes tense. He's in front of me in an instant and while I gaze at his chest, I feel his hands close around my back.

'Where shall we start?' he whispers.

I look up at his face. My eyes are about level with his nose. I'm about to suggest another kiss because the last one was just about the best thing I've ever experienced, but then I realise that he's not waiting for an answer. He sinks to his knees and smiles up at me, locking me into his gaze. And I'm helpless. I'm incapable of looking away, but at the edge of my vision, I'm vaguely aware that he's reaching out, unbuttoning my jeans with slow, masterful moves, peeling them open, pausing for a moment to lay his palm flat across my stomach. I sense a flutter in my groin and I let out a moan. His smile broadens. He knows exactly what he's doing to me. The jeans are drawn downwards. Gently, he manoeuvres them over my hips and down my legs, pausing here and there to wrap a big hand around my waist or run his fingers across my thighs. At his bidding, I lift my feet, one at a time, so that he can take my jeans off. He skims his hands up the outside of my legs until he reaches my crotch before sliding a finger into my knickers. And then he sets about the same slow removal process, this time landing light kisses along the length of my right leg on the way down and then back up my left. A strong arm comes around my buttocks, holding me in place, and his kisses slowly circle my stomach. He eases my legs apart, his lips working their way downwards, across my pubic hair. A finger strokes lightly across my clitoris, lighting me up with a thousand watts of sexual energy.

'Oh fuck.'

'You're so responsive.'

'Am I?'

'Oh yes. I'd better get you horizontal. I don't want you passing out on me.'

He pushes himself up to his feet and runs his hands down my arms. I should do something now, say something, but I'm hypnotised by his touch, mesmerised by his eyes. I'm in a stupor.

'Are you sure you're alright?' he asks, lowering his face to mine.

I nod weakly while he reaches round to my back and unclasps my bra, slipping it gently from my shoulders and dropping it to the floor. Suddenly, I realise that while I'm now completely naked, he's still fully dressed. Snapping myself out of my torpor, I reach up and push his jacket from his shoulders.

'Now ...' He leans in towards me. 'Get your backside onto that bed, Miss Scotton.' He presses a thumb against my lips and my heartbeat judders. 'I think it's about time to take you out for a spin.'

My brain wants to tell him to fuck right off but instead I clamber onto the bed and lie on my back watching as he unfastens his tie. He pulls it away from his neck and tugs it tight between his hands. Oh shit, he is one of those 'look at me, I'm so powerful and I'm going to tie you up' types. I should run a mile but I can't. My legs have turned to jelly. He throws the tie onto the bed and proceeds to undo his shirt. Slowly revealing himself to me, he draws it from his shoulders, staring at me all the time. And then he unbuckles the belt and throws it onto the bed right next to the tie. Oh shit. I really ought to go now. How on Earth am I going to cope with this?

'Are you going to ...'

'Tie you up?' he grins, unzipping his trousers and shrugging them to the floor. 'Probably.' He pauses, standing there in nothing but a pair of white pants that must have some expensive designer label on them. Bloody hell, he's ripped. There's not an ounce of fat on him.

'I'm not sure that I ...'

'You'll just have to go with it, Maya. It's my modus operandi.'

I prop myself up on my elbows, gazing in disbelief at his toned body: the broad shoulders, the rigid six pack, the firm lines of the muscles that descend neatly in a V shape towards his crotch. He smiles mischievously as he inserts his fingers into the waistband of his pants and slowly edges them down, performing a strip tease for me. My eyes must be the size of saucers as his pants drop to the floor, releasing an erect penis that springs out into the open threatening to cause all sorts of mayhem. Jesus, he's well-endowed. How the hell is that going to fit inside me?

'Put your arms above your head.'

'I ... I don't really think I can do that sort of ... thing,' I stutter.

He bites his lip and frowns.

'Why not?'

'I just can't ...'

He climbs up onto the bed and settles himself beside me, propping up his head with his hand. The warmth from him radiates through my body. He gazes into my eyes, waiting for an explanation. But what can I tell him? That I ran away from a man who tried to control every single aspect of my life? That I lost myself in my last relationship. That in the aftermath, I buried myself in months of sleeping around? That now, I'm determined to be in control of everything in my life, and this just seems to be the wrong way to go about it? And besides, I've never done this sort of thing before. A warm finger glides across my stomach and I convulse inside.

'Let me tell you something.' The same finger travels up my chest, pauses briefly between my breasts and then catches the bottom of my chin, turning my face gently towards his. 'You should try it first.'

'I'm really not sure ...'

He smiles a slow, languid smile.

'Trust me. It's nothing sinister. It's just sex. You simply allow me to restrain you. You give control to me. You do exactly what I say ... and then you simply lie back and enjoy.'

'But I don't want to lose myself.'

The smile broadens.

'You're not going to lose yourself, Maya. In fact, you're more likely to find yourself if you trust me. Give me a chance to show you how good this can be.' I feel his hand around the back of my neck, holding me in place while his lips hover over mine for an age, waiting for my answer. At last, in spite of everything, I nod uncertainly. Shit, what am I doing?

'Good choice.'

His body moves over me, his arms enveloping me, and his lips clamp down on mine, kissing me deeply, transforming me into a mess. I have enough time to run my fingers through his hair before he grabs my wrists, his fingers tightening against my flesh. He manoeuvres my arms up towards the headboard.

'Keep them there. Do exactly as you're told.'

I quake inside. This doesn't come naturally to me. But suddenly I just can't help myself. There's something about this man that makes me want to give in. He raises himself up above me, kneeling back on his haunches.

'Good God, woman, you're beautiful.'

Leaning forwards, he patiently skims his palms across my hips, my waist, my breasts and then up to my neck, leaving a trail of heated flesh in their wake. I moan out loud at the waves of pleasure that his hands send through me.

'I love the upholstery. It's so soft.'

'You can stop with all the car talk now,' I whimper. 'It's naff.'

A finger lands quickly on my lips.

'No talking. Close your eyes now. Just feel it.'

I do as I'm told and he proceeds to explore my body. I feel a warm hand on my right breast, gently cupping it, sweeping a finger round my nipple. He takes the nipple in his fingers, slowly drawing it out. And then his lips close over it, sucking gently, sending a storm of sensations running through my breast and down the centre of my body. I moan in appreciation. He does the same to my left breast. Moving again, he begins to trace kisses down my sternum, across my stomach, his lips landing lightly like a thousand butterflies, churning up a myriad of sensations. I'm becoming hyper-sensitive. He could touch me anywhere now, and my skin would goose pimple at the slightest contact.

'Oh God …' I breathe. 'That's so good.'

'Did I say you could talk?'

I shake my head and clamp my lips shut.

'I mean it, Maya. You do exactly as I say.'

Or else what? I wonder. You'll punish me? I feel both of his hands on my stomach, holding me firmly around my midriff.

'Now, open your eyes and look at me.'

I do as I'm told and find him sitting back on his haunches, smiling down at me. He's got me right where he wants me and good God, he's pleased with himself. But then again, he's got every right to feel that way. The man is physical perfection. And what he can do with his lips and those hands. I can only shudder at the thought of what he can do with his cock.

'Have you ever come during penetration?' he asks.

Why? What are you? Some sort of amateur gynaecologist?

'No,' I admit and now I feel small. I almost want to apologise, but then again why should I? It's not my fault if nature made me this way. I place my hands on my stomach. Right now, I'm totally uncomfortable, completely exposed, and I know that my subconscious has just fired out an order to protect myself.

'That's a shame. I'll have to see what I can do.'

He leans across my legs, chooses the tie, throws the belt onto the floor and motions for me to return my hands above my head. I look up to find that he's not the owner of a big brass bed after all. In fact, it's a big wooden bed, complete with a thick, slatted headboard. Oh shit. This really is going to happen.

'It's okay,' he says gently. 'I'll look after you. And we'll start small.'

He takes my hands in his, loops the tie gently around my wrists in a figure of eight and pulls them together.

'Feel alright?'

I nod.

'I don't want to cut off your blood flow.'

'It's fine.'

He takes the ends of the tie and secures them to the headboard. So, that's it. I've gone and done exactly what I vowed I wouldn't do. I've let a power-hungry, super rich control freak tie me up. And now he's going to go and fuck me senseless. Oh, shitty, shit, shit. I'm in trouble. And I'm squirming too at the very thought of it.

'Lie still,' he orders me. 'I need to make sure there's oil in this engine.'

'I said enough of the car talk. It's naaa ….'

The final word disappears into a haze as he slides a single finger inside me. I don't know whether it's the shock, or the sudden ripples of pleasure that are pulsing through my abdomen, but I can barely breathe. His lips are lowered to mine and while his finger circles gently inside, his tongue begins to explore my mouth. At last, I gather together at least some of my senses.

'Oh Lord,' I mutter around the edge of his mouth, 'you've had a lot of practice at this.'

'Lots,' he confirms. 'Now shush. Don't make me gag you.'

I stare up into his eyes, marooned in the swirls of blue.

'You wouldn't,' I gasp.

'I would,' he says darkly.

***

And then all hell lets loose. A clap of thunder. A flash of lightning.

'Shit!' I scream. 'Shit!'

'Maya! What's wrong? Am I hurting you?'

'No, you twat. It's a fucking storm.'

'And?'

'I fucking hate thunder and lightning. Untie me now!'

'What?'

In an instant, he leaps up and frantically loosens the tie. By the time I push myself up on the bed, he's standing next to me, his eyes wide with confusion.

'I'm so sorry,' I gasp. 'I can't do this! Not while it's thundering.'

He runs a hand through his hair and shakes his head. And then there's another almighty crash.

'Shit!'

Instinctively, I curl up into a ball. I feel the bed dip, the warmth of his skin as he wraps himself around me.

'Maya, you're shaking. You're petrified.'

'Of course I'm fucking petrified you fucking dickshit.'

Oh Lord, I've just called my naked boss a dickshit. I really shouldn't have done that. I half expect him to kick me right off the bed and sack me on the spot, but he draws me closer, resting his palm across my chest.

'Fuck me, your heart's thudding.'

'I'm not putting this on, Dan. I don't like storms.'

'Why not?'

'Because they're scary!' I shout.

Another flash of lightning cuts across the window. I cringe, waiting for the next crash of thunder to tear its way through the air. It's not long in coming. Two seconds.

'I'm sorry,' I whimper.

He plants a kiss on the top of my head.

'No need to be sorry. Just tell me what I can do.'

'Nothing. Just hold me. Please.'

He strokes my head slowly. Another crash of thunder rips through the sky. My body wants to jolt, but I'm held firmly in place against him, clasped tightly by his arms. And there's something strangely reassuring about being restrained like this, something curiously relaxing about letting him take control.

'Have you always been like this?' he asks.

'Ever since I can remember. When I was little, my mum used to make me a tent. Two chairs and a blanket draped over them. She promised it would keep me safe. She'd get in it with me and we'd ride out the storm in there. I'm a bit too old for that now.'

Several seconds of silence pass between us, broken only by the sound of rain crashing down against the skylight.

'You're never too old for anything,' he says at last. 'Stay where you are. I won't be long.'

He peels himself away and I turn to see what's going on. He opens a wardrobe door, disappears for a moment and returns with a sheet and a duvet. Throwing them onto the chaise longue, he sets about dragging it across the room, positioning it right next to the bed. He shakes out the sheet, draping it half over the back of the chaise longue, the rest over the side of the bed, pinning it into place with a pillow. He takes the duvet and disappears inside the makeshift tent.

'Chuck me the pillows,' he calls. 'Now.'

I pull the pillows from the bed and throw them onto the floor. One by one, they disappear inside the tent. Finally, he emerges, looking distinctly pleased with himself.

'Will this do?'

There's another crash of thunder. My muscles turn rigid.

'Well, it'll have to. Get in,' he orders.

I crawl inside his thunder tent and find myself on the duvet. He slides in next to me and positions himself on his side.

'Come here,' he murmurs.

I smile weakly and crawl into his arms, feeling them close around me.

'This isn't exactly what you had in mind tonight, is it?' I ask stupidly.

'Not exactly.' He kisses the top of my head and pulls me into his chest. 'But it doesn't matter. I'll have to check the weather forecast next time I see you.'

'There'll be a next time?'

'Of course.

Chapter Ten

I hardly know where I am when I wake up. Above my head, I can see sunlight dancing against a white sheet. It takes a moment or two for the previous evening to filter through into my memory, another moment or two for me to realise that I'm lying against a warm chest. I turn my head slowly, carefully taking in the smattering of hair, realising that I'd like nothing more than to run my hands up and down that chest right now. I'd like to take it all in: the tight definition of his pecs; the taut lines that lead my eyes down towards to his crotch; the firm muscles that curve across his abdomen. This man does some serious workouts. That much is obvious. But what else do I know about him? Very little, is the answer. Apart from the fact that he owns a construction company and drives a German car, that he's a serial womaniser and a control freak to boot, I know absolutely zilch. Taking a slow, deep breath, I remind myself that I've had enough warnings. Whichever way I look at the situation, nothing good can ever come of it. I'll only end up falling for this man and in spite of all his words, he'll drain me of what he needs and then move on to his next conquest before my tears have dried. I gaze up at his face, relieved to find that he's still fast asleep. I can tell that from the deep rhythm of his breathing, the steady rise and fall of his rib cage. He seems so innocent now, so completely at ease. But he isn't innocent at all. In fact, he's far from it. And I certainly shouldn't give him the benefit of any sort of doubt. Instead, I should simply get the hell out of here before he wakes up and challenges my common sense.

As quietly and as gently as I can, I crawl out of the tent. My pulse is racing as I retrieve my clothes from the floor. I tiptoe my way downstairs, skitter through the living area and fumble to dress myself in the kitchen. Any minute now, he'll wake up and find me gone. Any minute now, he'll be thundering down those stairs demanding that I get my backside back up to his bed. I have to act quickly because I know I'd comply ... and that would be the mother of all mistakes. I take no time to examine my surroundings because there really is no point. I'm never going to come here again. Tugging open the door, I make my escape, my heart pounding like a pneumatic drill as I enter the lift, frantically punching the button for the ground floor. I turn and watch as the doors close, encasing me in mirrors, leaving me to stare at my tousled hair and faded make-up while I wrestle my breathing back under control. A few seconds later and the lift opens onto a small lobby. I'm almost there now, almost free of the danger. Launching myself out of the lift, I push my way through a set of heavy glass doors and stumble out into the early morning sunlight.

It takes me forever to find the nearest tube station, but soon I'm scurrying down the steps at Vauxhall. I hardly know how I make it to Waterloo, how I manage to navigate my way back onto the Northern Line. Seeing as I can barely focus on the real world, it's a complete bloody miracle. I sit bolt upright, rigid, watching the tunnel walls as they slip by. Before I even make it to Camden Town, there's a ping from my mobile. With a shaking hand, I pull it from the depths of my handbag. Sure enough, it's him. Still just a number ... and no name.

Where are you? Are you OK?

Really? Why are you asking? Do you really care? My fingers hover across the keypad. So what should I say? Actually, Mr Foster, no. I'm not alright at all. You see, I'm severely attracted to you and really, bloody scared of what you might do to me if I spend any more time in your company. I've only spent one night with you so far, and that's reduced me to some sort of quivering, indecisive mess. So, if you don't mind, I'd like to call it a day. Finally deciding that it's best to simply ignore the text, I thrust the phone into my handbag and go back to staring into the blackness. Finally, the tube draws in to Camden Town. With my head down, I make my way along Camden High Street, silently ashamed of myself. I've done it again. I've caved in to a one night stand. And that's all it was ever going to be. Well, at least we never got round to the sex. That's a plus point. I turn the corner into Mornington Crescent, slope past the last few houses and finally come to a halt in front of our flaking front door. I push the key into the lock and head for the kitchen where I find Lucy, dressed and ready for work, knocking back a morning cup of tea.

'What are you doing here?' she demands.

'I live here.'

'Yes, but ...'

'Yes, but nothing. Are you working today?'

I sling my bag onto the table, flick on the kettle and grab a mug from the cupboard.

'Yes, I am. But only until three.'

She stares at me expectantly. And I stare back.

'Well, what happened?' she asks.

'Nothing much,' I lie.

'Oh come on. Tell me everything ... now.'

'Okay.' Opening another cupboard door, I take out a box of tea bags. 'We went for dinner in an expensive restaurant, only we didn't have dinner because before we'd even ordered anything, he dragged me back out of the restaurant and took me home to his apartment.'

'Oh my God. Did he roger you?'

I shake my head and Lucy's face is spattered with confusion. I decide to be pithy about this.

'We had that thunder storm and I got scared.'

I pull a teabag out of the box.

'Oh God,' she groans, looking distinctly panicky now. She knows exactly what I'm like in storms. I've lost count of the times I've watched her faff about with sheets and chairs while I count the gaps between the thunder and the lightning bolts. 'I thought about you last night. I knew you'd lose it.'

And I did lose it. In fact, I lost it big style.

'I called him a dickshit, Lucy. I called him a dickshit and he made me a tent and I fell asleep.'

'He made you a tent?'

'Yep.'

'You called him a dickshit and he made you a tent?'

I chuck the teabag into the mug.

'I didn't make him do it. I told him about it and he just did it.'

'Well, that's sweet.'

Sweet, my arse, I want to scream. Because what you don't know is that he spent most of the evening ordering me about or interrogating me. Is that sweet? Really? There's another ping from my mobile. I glance at my handbag and decide to ignore it. Lucy, on the other hand, seems to have other ideas. I watch in despair as she swoops down and claims the phone. As soon as she opens the message, her bottom lip takes a dive.

'Look at that!'

She turns the screen towards me.

Did I upset you? Are you home?

'Is that him?'

'Yes.'

'And? Don't tell me you ran out on him.'

'I left this morning. He was still asleep.'

'Oh, for fuck's sake,' Lucy whines. 'Why did you do that? What's the problem, Maya?' Her eyelids tremble. 'No! Don't tell me! He's got a little willy!'

'Anything but.' I watch as the kettle rumbles its way towards the boil.

'So, he's just boring then?'

'Not in the slightest.'

The kettle clicks itself off. I pick it up and fill my mug.

'So, he's got a girlfriend?'

'No, I don't think so.'

I rummage in a drawer for a clean teaspoon.

'Then what?'

'Oh, I don't know.' I slam the teaspoon down on the counter. 'I like him, Lucy. I like him a lot. I just don't trust him and that's the problem. I can see myself falling for him big style and I can see him shitting on me.'

My mobile pings again.

Lucy opens up the latest message and stares in awe at the screen. 'So, you like him a lot. And he obviously likes you back.'

I shake my head. 'I don't know about that.'

'Well, I do.'

She holds up the mobile, displaying the message for me to read.

I'm on my way to yours.

'Shit!' A surge of panic explodes in my gut. I can't bloody deal with this. I just can't. I'm really not in the mood for a confrontation. I can't risk seeing him today, and that's all I know. 'Lucy, I've got to get out of here.'

'Why? What? Where are you going?'

'I'm coming into work with you.'

I'm changed in record time. A fresh pair of knickers, combats and a strappy T-shirt. Teeth brushed, a quick wash, a smattering of deodorant, and I'm ready. I practically drag Lucy out of the front door, leaving her to scurry behind me back down Mornington Crescent and up the High Street. Scanning the traffic for a black Mercedes, I feel like a member of the SAS on some sort of special operation. And my heart's thumping the whole way. By the time we reach the tube station, Lucy's totally out of breath and I'm a nervous wreck. As we descend into the station, I'm overwhelmed with relief.

If he's prowling the streets of North London and seeking me out, then he's going to be severely disappointed. There's no way he can find me now.

'So, what makes you think he's going to shit on you?' Lucy asks, finally breaking the silence somewhere between Warren Street and Tottenham Court Road.

I stare at the empty seat in front of me. 'Oh, just everything.'

As the tube draws into Tottenham Court Road, Lucy springs up from her seat. I follow her blindly through the tunnels and out onto Oxford Street. It's still early and the crowds haven't formed yet. It's not long before we hang a left, winding our way towards Soho Square, past the strange, tiny, mock-Tudor gazebo at its centre, veering to the right and further down into Frith Street. After another couple of minutes, we finally arrive at the gallery.

'Maybe you should just give him a chance.' She places her hand against the glass door. 'He's hot and he's rich. He's got a big willy and he's not boring.'

'For God's sake, leave it out,' I grumble.

'You can't hide in here all day,' she grumbles back.

'You just watch me.'

With a huff, Lucy pushes open the door and we enter the rarefied atmosphere of Slaters. As the door swings to a gentle close behind us, the constant noise of Soho is blocked out. I make my way over to the window where a pair of deep red sofas face one another across a glass coffee table. Throwing my bag onto the floor, I slump into one of the sofas, satisfied that at least for now I've escaped the wrath of Daniel Foster. With a deep breath, I take in the ground floor of the gallery: the pot plants and the padded seating; the oak flooring and the clean white walls; the canvases, landscapes and portraits. That's all that Little Steve and Big Steve are interested in, and for the last thirty years, it's kept Slaters going. All sorts of influences fly around the place: impressionism, expressionism, realism, abstract. You name it, it's here. But whatever the picture, whatever the influence, there's always talent, and real talent at that. Over the years, the two Steves have built up a reputation for discovering new artists, for encouraging them, for helping them make their names. And now, younger artists than me are exhibiting ... and I often wonder if my time has already passed.

'I'll put the kettle on. And then you can help me. I've really got to sort that bloody basement out today.' Lucy totters across the wooden floor, disappearing into a room at the back.

I hear the tapping of footsteps, a puffing and panting, and I realise that someone is climbing the stairs, making their way up from the basement. After what seems like an age, a small, grey-haired man appears at the top of the stairs. He's no more than five feet tall, and distinctly overweight. He looks like Santa. Dressed in his customary check shirt and brown corduroys, it's Little Steve.

'Maya! It's good to see you. What are you doing here?'

I force myself up from the sofa, move forwards, and let him throw his podgy arms around me. 'I've got nothing to do today. I thought I'd give Lucy a hand.'

'Where is she?'

'In the kitchen, making tea.'

'Thank fuck for that.' Little Steve motions towards the sofas. 'I'm about ready for a cuppa. I've had a hell of a morning.'

As we lower ourselves down at opposite sides of the coffee table, a second set of footsteps clomp their way up the stairs. A few seconds later, Big Steve emerges from the basement. In a matching check shirt, this time paired with jeans, Big Steve is tall and trim. In direct contrast to his partner, he's clean shaven and dark haired, although seeing as the pair of them are in their mid-sixties, I'm pretty sure that the hair has been helped along by a good dollop of dye.

'Maya,' he grunts, seating himself next to Little Steve. 'Good job you're here. It's all hands on deck. Me and him have been falling out big time this morning.'

Lucy pokes her head out through the kitchen door. A few moments later, she joins me on the sofa with a tray of mugs. While we each pick up a mug and begin to sip at the tea, Big Steve scowls at Little Steve and Little Steve scowls back.

'So, what's the problem?' Lucy sighs.

'We've just sold both of those seascapes downstairs,' Little Steve explains. 'Some weird bloke with bad breath and an ugly shih tzu. Big Steve's fucked up the books.'

'I did not fuck up the books.'

'You did too. He's gone and put everything in the wrong columns. And we've got to arrange delivery for Monday because weird bloke wants them pronto. And he's gone and moved everything round downstairs.' He shoots a look of death at his partner. 'It's not right, Lucy, but he won't have it. And we haven't even started on the invitations yet.'

'Calm down,' Lucy snaps. 'I'll sort it all out.'

'And you're here to help, Maya?' Big Steve arches an eyebrow at me.

'She's here because she's avoiding a man,' Lucy intervenes. 'He's a rich, sexy bod but Maya's scared she'll fall for him and he'll shit on her.'

'Oh, give him a chance,' Little Steve advises. 'This one here changed his ways. It can be done.'

I take a look at Big Steve. Now this pair have been an item for over thirty years. The typical married couple, always in each other's pockets, frequently arguing, forever making up. I can't imagine that Big Steve ever played the scene.

'I tamed him.' Little Steve grins. 'And he's been all mine ever since.'

'Not all men can be tamed,' I grimace.

'Oh, they can.' Big Steve frowns. 'It just takes the right person. Now, shall we get some work done here?'

That's all it takes. A frown from Big Steve is like an order from up above, a commandment set in a tablet of stone. The tea is finished, Lucy clears up and we set about sorting out the basement. While Lucy disappears into the office to fix the mess with the books and arrange delivery of two paintings to a man with halitosis and a questionable dog, the two Steves argue incessantly and I take on the job of rearranging the paintings one more time. I order them about and they scurry here and there, practically falling over each other. By lunch time, we're all pooped. Big Steve takes himself off to a local deli to get sandwiches while Little Steve fetches two bottles of white wine and a collection of mismatched wine glasses from the kitchen. At last, we all collapse back onto the sofas, and settle in for food and beverages.

'We'll be doing no more work today after this.' Big Steve raises a glass. 'But never mind. Here's to the ladies! They've sorted us out good and proper.'

I squirm at the phrase. Suddenly, I'm thinking about Daniel Foster again, and his threat to sort me out good and proper. Eyeing up my handbag, I'm on the verge of checking my mobile when I hear the door wheeze open. I'm facing away from the door, lifting a glass of wine to my mouth, but from the expression on Big Steve's face, I know that it must be a welcome visitor.

'Well, hello stranger!' He springs up from his seat.

Little Steve chokes on his sandwich, spraying chunks of half chewed chorizo across the table. With a jittering hand, he lays his lunch back inside its wrapper and peers over my shoulder. 'What are you doing here?' he asks.

'Just passing.'

At the sound of the velvety voice, my own sandwich decides to jitter about in my hand. I glance across at Lucy to find that she's gazing over the back of the sofa, her eyes wide with astonishment.

'We haven't seen you in a while, darling.' Little Steve wipes his mouth. 'Have you been busy?'

'You could say that.'

'Ladies,' Big Steve calls. 'Come and meet Daniel Foster.'

I glance again at Lucy only to find that she's staring back at me, open mouthed, and I rather suspect that she's already put two and two together and come up with the right answer. Her mouth begins to open and close, something like a goldfish, and I will her to stay silent.

'Dan,' Big Steve goes on, 'this is Lucy, our manager. And this is Maya, her friend. Come on you two!'

As I raise myself up from the sofa, I wonder how the hell he's managed to track me down to Slaters, and then, very quickly, I wonder if my legs are about to give way. Unwillingly, I turn, and it hits me straight away: the full-on impact of the sex god in all his glory. He's dressed in black this morning: jeans that hang loosely from his hips, matched with a T-shirt that shows off the contours of his upper body to perfection. There's not an extra ounce of body fat anywhere on this man, and fuck me it's hot. He smiles down at me, his eyes shimmering in a ray of sunlight. He looks good enough to eat. I'd like to pounce on him right now and demand to be fucked good and proper. I catch my breath at the very thought of it, and then I hear myself begin to pant. Shit! No! Don't do that, my brain complains. Don't go acting like a prize idiot in front of your friends. Remember, this can't end well!

It's Lucy who sidles forwards first to greet him.

'Hi,' she simpers, holding out her hand.

'Hi back.' He takes Lucy's hand, kisses it quickly, and lets it go. And then he turns to me, full on. 'And you are?' He smiles broadly. 'Sorry, I've forgotten.'

'Maya,' I mutter.

I can see that my hand is quivering as I hold it out. His fingers lock themselves around mine and immediately, I feel it, that super-heated charge of energy that shoots around my body every single bloody time he touches me. I'm a quivering wreck as he leans down and brushes his lips against the back of my hand.

'What a beautiful name. It's good to meet you, Maya.'

'Maya's a talented artist,' Little Steve announces. 'Shit hot with the oils.'

'Is she?' Keeping a firm hold of my hand, he turns away.

'Well, she would be,' I hear Lucy pipe up, 'if she actually had any paints.'

'A painter with no paints?' He homes back in on me and I'm done for. All manner of sensations kick off into action and my brain takes its customary Daniel Foster holiday. 'Well, that's not good enough.'

'So, why haven't you been round in a while?' Big Steve demands.

'Too much on at work.' Slowly, he unwraps his fingers and turns away. 'But I'm looking to acquire something. I thought I'd come and take a look at what you've got to offer.'

'Well, let's have a browse. Glass of wine? It's good stuff.'

'That would be wonderful.'

While Big Steve picks up a spare glass and fills it with white wine, Daniel Foster gazes down at me. Now what's that look on his face? As far as I'm concerned, it's unfathomable. Big Steve thrusts the glass at him. The big kahuna accepts it, shoots me a dark glance, and finally allows himself to be manoeuvred into the main space of the gallery.

I catch hold of Little Steve's arm before he can make a move.

'How do you know him?' I whisper.

'He's one of our best customers. He spends thousands in here.'

Thousands? In here? Completely out of nowhere, I'm knocked flat on my backside in a metaphorical kind of a way. This can't be true. Daniel Foster? An art lover? I shake my head. No, it can't be true at all. In fact, it's impossible. No way does this arrogant, self-satisfied, sexist pig of a womaniser admire the finer things in life. I'm not falling for that.

'Ooh, I love it when he comes in,' Little Steve gurgles dreamily. 'I can't get enough of that man. Look at his arse!'

'How come I've never met him?' Lucy demands.

'We usually we do private showings for him, darling. He works long hours so we open up at night, and he makes it worth our while. You must have seen his name in the books, Lucy.'

She shakes her head, but I'm not surprised. Lucy's brain is a colander at the best of times.

'But this is strange.' Little Steve gawps at Daniel Foster's backside. 'He's never come in at the weekend before now, and certainly never without prior arrangement. He's got a good eye and he knows his art. He's very picky though. I'd better go and help. This could fund our new camper van.'

While Little Steve scurries off to join the other men, I shake my head again. So, it is true. He knows his art.

'That's him?' Lucy gasps. 'Mr Mean and Hot and Moody?'

I drop my head.

'For God's sake, he's sex on legs. And he's into art. And look at that! He's a gay icon to boot. Why don't you want any more to do with him?'

'I told you, Lucy. He'd break my heart.'

'Well, I think it's worth the bother. And you saw him in the buff?'

'Yes.'

'Fuck.'

'Lucy!'

'I'm not on your side any more,' she scowls. 'You're going to have sex with that man if it kills me.'

While Lucy rushes off to help with the viewing, I slump back down into the sofa. In one fell swoop, I knock back my glass of wine. Refilling it, I gulp down a second. Every now and then, I risk a peek at the happy crowd of art lovers. They're admiring a landscape here, laughing together there. The two Steves take every opportunity to touch their favourite client on the arm or on the back and finally, after at least half an hour, they return to the sofas.

'Sit down, Dan.' Lucy points at the space next to me.

I wince.

'No, I can't stay.'

He's staring down at me now, his blue eyes dancing in the sunlight. He leans forwards, taking his time, positioning himself deliberately close to me, and I drink in his scent as he places his empty glass back onto the coffee table. When his head is next to mine, he turns and looks me directly in the face. He's so close now I can practically feel his breath on my lips.

'Have you seen anything you fancy?' Lucy asks mischievously.

'Yes, I've spotted something I want.'

He doesn't move. Without a care in the world for what's going on around him, he continues to stare into my eyes. And then he turns his attention to my mouth, his lips parting slightly for a moment. At last, he seems to gather his wits and straightens himself up.

'Shall we reserve it for you?' Big Steve enquires.

'No need.' He reaches into his pocket, pulls out his mobile and begins to enter a message. 'I always get what I want in the end.' He pushes the mobile back into his pocket. 'Thanks for the wine,' he smiles. 'I'll be back to seal the deal. See you soon.'

I stare at my handbag. Amongst the sound of polite goodbyes, I hear yet another ping. I wait until the door closes before I reach down for my phone. There's another message waiting for me. With a

jittering hand, I open it up. I swallow hard. It's one word. And one word only.
Monday.

Chapter Eleven

Sunday begins with an inevitable hangover. Drinks at the gallery were quickly followed by drinks at various bars in Soho. And all of this culminated in the usual taxi drive home, during which I propped up Lucy's semi-comatose body and reassured the taxi driver more than once that there'd be no vomiting. Finally, just after one o'clock in the afternoon, I return to something close to consciousness and check my mobile. Nothing. Not one single message from Daniel Foster. Obviously, he's already said everything he wants to say, and there's no need to say any more.

I peel myself out of bed and stagger into the kitchen. As soon as I make it through the doorway, I come to a halt, amazed at what I find. Not only has Lucy managed to rouse herself and get dressed, but she's also decided to take it upon herself to prepare a full Sunday roast. I sit down on a rickety chair, my mouth hanging open in astonishment at the sight. A panful of potatoes is busy simmering on the hob, right next to a second panful of Brussels sprouts. And there, hunched over the sink, struggling to wash a chicken under the tap, is Lucy.

'Afternoon.' She flips the chicken over, wrestles with its legs and dowses it some more.

'Afternoon,' I mutter back. 'You've not used soap on that, have you?'

'I'm not a complete idiot. How are you?'

'Gruesome. I feel like the walking dead. And you?'

'Fine.'

Fine? Well, that's a bloody miracle, considering the industrial quantities of wine that were downed last night, along with the endless shots … and the cocktails.

'Do you remember anything about last night?'

Lucy shakes her head.

'Not much.' She turns, waving the chicken about in her left hand. 'Did we go dancing?'

'Sort of.'

'And did we get chatted up by a load of Elvis impersonators?'

'You did. I couldn't be bothered with it all.'

'Well, of course not.' The chicken is raised and lowered again, and already I'm worrying about hygiene matters. 'You've got Mr Sex on Legs.'

I let out a loud sigh.

'I've not got Mr Sex on Legs.'

'Yes, you have.' She slaps the chicken down onto a baking tray. 'The way he was looking at you in Slaters, I'd say you've got him.'

'Pphhh.'

I gaze at the kettle, wondering whether or not there's enough energy in the reserves to force myself back up onto my feet, cross five feet of linoleum and make a cup of tea.

'He's seriously into you, Maya.'

'He'd seriously like to get into me. He wants a quick shag and that's about it.'

'Well, if I were you, I'd let him get on with it. Bloody hell, that'd be a ride and a half. Did you see the bulge in his jeans?'

'I didn't bother looking.' I shake my head, trying my best to sound all complacent about the matter. It's not in the slightest bit easy. Just thinking about the bulge in his pants has set my pulse racing. 'I've already seen it all.'

'Lucky bitch.' She turns away for a moment, prods the chicken with her forefinger and then turns back. 'So, are you seeing him again?'

'Only at work.'

'But he came into the gallery on purpose.'

Oh God, she's not going to leave it alone, is she? In fact, I'm pretty damn sure that there's a Lucy inquisition on the way, and I'm not in any fit state for that. I'll just have to bat it away with some heavy duty nonchalance.

'Whatever,' I sigh.

'To see you.'

'Yeah, yeah.'

'That wasn't a coincidence.'

'Uh huh.'

'I just can't work out how he tracked you down.'

'Yada yada yada.'

'But the thing is this.' She puts her hands on her hips. 'If he is just out for a quick shag, then he's going to a hell of a lot of trouble to get it. And looking like that, I'd say he doesn't need to go to a hell of a lot of trouble to get it at all. All of which suggests to me that he's really got the hots for you and he's not just out for a quick shag at all.'

'Brilliant deductions, Lucy. Now let's change the subject. I'm bored.'

'You will have sex with him,' she grins, unfurling a length of tin foil. 'I'll bloody make sure you do.'

While Lucy begins to shroud the chicken in aluminium, I stumble to my feet and focus my eyes firmly on the kettle. It's nestled in amongst a mess of potato peelings, calling out to me. I might have the mother of all hangovers but I must have that cup of tea now. I've just about managed to stagger a full three feet across the lino when the doorbell rings.

'Get that, will you?' Lucy mumbles, tucking the chicken in.

'Oh, bloody hell.'

With another huge sigh, I veer away from the kettle, lose my balance for a split second, and then drag myself out into the hall. I open the front door to find a strange man on our doorstep. I squint at his name badge, only to discover that he's called Dave and that he's a delivery man, but then again that much is pretty evident because sitting in front of him is a huge wooden crate. I stare down at the crate in bewilderment. This has got Lucy Godfrey stamped all over it. The woman's an internet shopping fiend. But what the hell has she gone and ordered now?

'Luce!' I call out. 'It's for you!'

I'm about to turn away when the delivery man pipes up.

'Actually, it's for someone called Maya Scotton.' He thrusts a clipboard at me. 'And I'll need a signature.'

'For me?' How can it be for me? I don't remember ordering anything. I never order anything. I just don't have the spare money to buy stuff at the minute. I stare blankly down at the crate.

'Look,' he complains. 'It's definitely for you, so can you just sign for it and take it off my hands? It weighs a ton.'

Reluctantly, I sign a slip and watch as the delivery man trundles off back to his van. Before long, he's gone and I'm left alone with a gigantic box. Leaning down, I slap a hand on either side of the crate, and try to pick it up. But it's impossible. The delivery man was right. It does weigh a ton.

'Lucy!' I call out. 'I'm going to need some help here!'

A couple of minutes later, after a good deal of swearing and a fair amount of bruising, we finally manage to manoeuvre the crate into the hall. Another two minutes later, and the crate is wedged into my bedroom, stuck half way between the door and the wardrobe.

'I'm fucked!' Lucy gasps. 'What is it?' She's totally out of breath from the exertion. But then again, so am I.

'No idea. Go and sort the dinner out. I'll open it.'

With a shrug of the shoulders, she's gone. I sigh at the crate. Whatever it is, and whoever it's from, I'm only going to have to return the bloody thing. It takes me a few minutes to work out how to open it. Finally, I resort to prizing off the top with a knife. At first, I'm presented with a layer of foam packaging. I pull it out, scatter it across the floor, peer back inside the crate ... and freeze. Straight away, I can see the edge of two canvases and beside them, some sort of wooden contraption which I already know is an easel. I tug the easel out of the box and lean it against the wardrobe, still folded up. Next comes a palette, quickly followed by a clear plastic bag that's crammed with tubes of oil paint in every possible colour: burnt sienna, aquamarine, deep umber, magenta, midnight blue ... I catch my breath at the sight of them. It's a long time since I've seen my old friends. I've kept them at arm's length for far too long. The clouds part for a brief second and I catch a glimpse of my former self: determined, committed, fulfilled. I empty out the bag, arranging the tubes across the floor, co-ordinating the colours before reaching back inside the crate. At the bottom, I find two bottles of linseed oil alongside a palette knife and a selection of brushes in a wooden presentation box. It's all top of the range material and it must have cost a bomb. For a moment or two, I rummage further, searching for a card, anything to give me a clue to the identity of my mystery benefactor. I find nothing.

And then it hits me. There's no need for a card. No need for any evidence at all. I know exactly who's responsible for this. Picking up a tube of paint, I turn it slowly in my hands. I'm trembling. He's known me for less than a week and already he's researched me and pursued me, and now he's hit me right where it hurts. I glance across at my mobile. There's been no contact all weekend, not since the last text at Slaters. But should I text him now? Should I simply re-pack the crate and tell him in no uncertain terms that he needs to take it all back? Or should I thank him, accept the gift and make it totally clear to the man that he's not just bought himself a passport to my nether regions? Or should I accept the gift and simply go with it? Throw caution to the wind, climb back into bed with him and see where it goes? Because when all's said and done, that's what I really want to do. Before long, my eyes are stinging with tears. I curl up into a ball, my mind tumbling its way through the possibilities. I don't know how long I spend like that, but at last, I hear Lucy's voice.

'Oh God.' She kneels down on the floor next to me and clasps her arms around me. 'Who's sent you this lot?'

'Who do you think? You told him I had no paints.'

'Daniel Foster? Jesus, this lot must have cost an arm and a leg.'

I hear myself laugh.

'It's nothing to a man like him. It's just his way of getting into my knickers, Lucy, and I'm not having it. He can take it all back.'

'You can't give it back.'

'Why not?'

'You just can't.'

'Then it can go to a charity shop.'

'Maya,' Lucy says sternly. 'You need to keep this stuff. You can't afford to replace it and at some point, you might even get painting again. It's got to happen one day.'

I nod silently.

'Anyway,' Lucy mutters, 'dinner's ready.'

I nod again. Pushing myself up from the floor, I return to the kitchen where I'm presented with a plate full of pink chicken that's been carefully arranged alongside a mound of undercooked roast potatoes. The whole thing is finished off with a mountain of Brussels sprouts that are so al dente they could easily pass for concrete. I suppose we could put this right somehow, but I'm so exhausted by this point I can't even begin to think my way through an eminently simple situation. Instead, very gently, I inform Lucy that pink chicken is a death wish … and fortunately she agrees. With immediate effect, we give up on the Sunday roast. It's scraped into the bin, shortly before we set about creating a well-loved back up: beans on toast.

***

And then I'm back in my super-heated bedroom. I spend an hour or so staring at a blank canvas before I lie down on my bed and fall asleep. Waking just after six, I stare at the canvas some more. Perhaps it's fatigue, perhaps it's the hangover, or perhaps it's the heat that envelops me. I've no idea what causes it, but I soon begin to see the outline of a tree. Nervously, I unfold the easel, prop the canvas up against it, take a pencil in my hand and sketch out a few lines. Before long, the tree appears in front of my eyes. And then it's joined by another … and another. Their branches twist and curl through the air, forming an intricate lacework against the sky. The basic sketching is soon complete. It's time to take out the oils. I retrieve the palette, select a handful of brushes and set about choosing my colours: raw umber, a deep venetian red, ochre, a touch of raw sienna. Unscrewing the tubes with a shaking hand, I squeeze a blob of each colour onto the palette and make a start. By the time I've laid down the darker colours, the nerves have gone and my hands are no longer shaking. Right in front of me, tree trunks emerge out of nowhere, taking their shape, branches lacing their way out across the canvas. I watch in awe, as if it's somebody else's hands working here. I have no idea why I've chosen to start with this place, but I know exactly where it is. I'm painting a stretch of woodland back at home in Limmingham. A place I visited often when I was younger. It's my place of sanctuary.

It's nearly midnight when I'm finally done for the evening. I return from my trance, clean up and climb onto my bed, exhausted. Still in my shorts and strappy top, I inhale deeply, taking in the welcome scent of oil and linseed, gazing up at the ceiling, quietly satisfied that after years in the wilderness, I've finally found myself again. My heart begins to thud at the thought of it. I've found inspiration, and I have no idea how that's happened. All I know is that a button has been pressed somewhere. And now I've set myself back on a path. I click off the bedside lamp and watch the curtains as they flutter lazily in a breeze. It's hot again tonight, so hot that sleep won't come easy. My eyelids grow heavy and finally I begin to drift off into a fitful sleep. And I'm dreaming of paint, and colour, and heartbeats pounding. And I'm wondering if that's the sound of a motorbike I can hear ...

Chapter Twelve

I almost fail to go into work on Monday morning. But the rent's due and I've got to pay my way. And although I've made my decision about Daniel Foster, there's still something drawing me back into the building. When I arrive, I'm a nervous wreck. Scanning the lobby, I hope that he's come in early, that I won't be confronted by him. I just want to make it up to my office safely. And I do. Pushing open the glass door, I find Jodie already at her desk, busying herself with the task of painting her nails bright red.

'Maya!'

At the sound of Norman's voice, I dump my handbag on my desk and venture straight into his clutter.

'What can I help you with, Norman?'

He gazes up at me from behind the piles of paperwork. 'What's going on?' he asks, wafting a sheet in the air.

'Nothing much.'

'I mean with the Tyneside factory.'

'Why are you asking me? I thought it was being shut down. Two hundred and twenty five lives shattered.'

'It is being shut down,' he confirms, holding the sheet out in front of him. 'But every single one of those employees is being offered a transfer to another part of the company, or an extremely generous redundancy payout.'

'I beg your pardon?'

'He's never done this before. Whenever he's had to close anything down, he's always sent them on their way with the bare minimum. These payouts are ridiculous.'

I walk over to his desk, take the sheet from Norman's hand and run my eyes down the figures. They are, indeed, ridiculous.

'Is this anything to do with you?' He stares up at me.

'Of course not.'

'But that little speech of yours ...'

'He paid no attention to that.'

'Maya, he paid full attention.' With a sigh, he scrabbles around in the mess, grabs a handful of papers and thrusts them at me. 'I've drafted some letters. I need you to type them up, and then I need to check them with the Legal department. Can you get them done quickly?'

'Of course.'

I take the letters back to my desk and stare at Jodie for a moment, wondering yet again why Norman doesn't just ask her to do something every once in a while. And then I stare at my desk. Right next to my telephone, there's a jam jar filled with sweet peas in a whole host of colours: pink, red, white, blue, purple. Tiny petals, curling in on themselves. It's a simple display, but I'm moved. It's transported me straight out of the greyness of the city, back to my childhood home, to our garden and my dad's vegetable patch.

'What's this?' I ask quietly. Shoving my handbag onto the floor, I pick up the jar and take in the scent.

I catch sight of Jodie as she shrugs her shoulders.

'Dunno. They were here when I got in.'

'Maybe it's Norman,' I tell myself. It seems the sort of thing a sweet, clueless old man would do.

'Could be the cleaner,' Jodie suggests. 'He's a bit of an idiot.'

I place the jam jar back down on the desk. I don't care if he is a bit of an idiot, if it's the cleaner who's done this, then it's a sweet, simple little gesture and I love it. In fact, I'm inspired and I wish, for once, that Norman hadn't provided me with a pile of work. I'd love to pull out a blank sheet of paper and sketch them.

'I'd better get on with this then,' I say loudly. 'I'll just do some work, shall I?

Jodie shrugs her shoulders again and blows onto the nails of her left hand. Clearly unbothered by my sarcasm, she's got far more important things to see to.

I'm just getting into typing the second letter of the day when I'm disturbed by a trousered leg on my desk. I look up to find Daniel Foster staring down at me, his eyes glimmering, a frown lining its way across his forehead. Immediately, my heart decides to launch itself into some sort of manic dance.

'Jodie!' he snaps.

The pink princess seems to jump clean out of her seat.

'Yes, Mr Foster?'

'Sling your hook.'
'Eh?'
'Get out,' he growls. 'Now.'
'Oh. Okay.'

Shoving the bottle of varnish back into the drawer, Jodie gets to her feet and begins to sidle out of the room.

'How long should I be?'

'Long enough. Here.' He reaches into his jacket pocket and pulls out a note. As he thrusts it towards her, I'm pretty sure I catch sight of a twenty. 'Go and get yourself a coffee.' Without batting an eyelid, she takes the note and scurries out of the office. My God, that girl has some gall, brazenly taking money off her boss like that. He watches the door swing to a close before he turns back to fix me with his gaze.

'So,' he whispers, leaning forwards and pushing the jam jar to one side. 'Tell me. Why, exactly, did you run?'

'I ... er ...'

'I ... er ...' he mimics me, 'woke up on Saturday morning to find an empty space next to me in my little two man tent.' His eyes flash with anger. 'And I ... er ... was not amused.'

Good God, I hardly recognise him. The gentle, caring man who held me in his arms on Friday night, the man who soothed me while I was in an agony of fear, has totally disappeared. He's back to the abrupt, rude bastard I met last week. I wonder for a moment if the gentle version was only a charade. If it was, he obviously couldn't keep it up for long. Sod you, my brain screams out. You don't get your own way and your true colours come out, don't they? Well, I'm not having that. Later on, I'll finish off my resignation letter, and then I'll be out of here before you know it.

'Oh, why? Because you didn't get your fuck?'

'No,' he seethes. 'I ... er ...' He falters. 'I wanted to talk.'

His words knock me off balance. To talk? Surely not. And what the hell would this man talk about? Exactly?

'Oh.'

'Oh,' he mimics me again, and that's enough to set a spark to the anger in my gut. 'And while you're at it, would you care to tell me why you ignored my texts?'

'My phone was out of battery.'

He leans down and breathes into my face.

'Cut the crap, Maya.'

'There is no crap to cut.'

'We're going to sort this out.'

'Oh really? Are you going to sack me then?'

He sits up straight. 'Of course not,' he scowls, looking more than slightly offended.

'Good, then get off my desk. I've got work to do.'

'It's my desk.' He taps the latest romantic novel to one side. 'And I very much doubt the claim about work.'

'Well then, just get off your desk and leave me alone.'

'That's not very nice. Not after what I did for you on Friday night.'

'Oh, so I have to pay you back for that, do I? And while we're at it, I suppose I'm expected to pay you back for the paints as well.'

'Absolutely not.'

'You shouldn't go around sending ridiculous presents to total strangers.'

'We're not total strangers. I've had my hands all over that beautiful body of yours. And it wasn't a ridiculous present. A gifted artist with no paints is a travesty. I simply rectified a bad situation.'

'So what do you want in return? A fuck? Do I owe you one?'

He points at me, and out of nowhere he's seething. 'Nobody owes anybody anything around here. Now, I suggest that you get your act together because I'm going to take you for lunch.'

'Take me for lunch?' I simmer. 'You're going to take me for lunch?'

'Yes, I'm going to take you ...' he pauses to make his point, 'for lunch.'

Oh bugger, he's not talking about food, is he? He actually is going to take me ... for lunch. And now there's all sorts of stuff kicking off down below and that's not good. There's absolutely no way I can deal with this. If Daniel Foster gets inside my knickers one more time, I think I might be lost. And I don't want to be lost, because being lost is inevitably followed by having your heart broken. No way am I letting this man take me for lunch. No way. No how.

'I'm working through lunch.'

'Norman!' he calls out.

There's no answer. He calls again, louder.

'Norman!'

The door opens. Norman scurries out of his office.

'What is it, Mr Foster?'

'Norman, enough of the Mr Foster crap.'

'Sorry, Dan.'

'Are you making this good woman work through her lunch hour?'

'No. No, of course not, Dan.'

'I should hope not. We don't pay her nearly enough for that kind of dedication.'

'Is that all you wanted?' Norman asks, glancing from Dan to me, his face puckering up with confusion.

'Yes it is. You can leave us now.'

I wince at his tone of voice. I know he's angry with me for putting a spanner in the works with his plan to fuck me senseless, but there really is no excuse for talking to Norman like that. I wait for Norman to close the door before deciding to pull up the big kahuna on his manners.

'I don't care how angry you are, you don't need to be so rude to people, you know.'

He sits up straight, obviously stunned.

'These are my employees, Maya. I can speak to them how I like and I don't need any lessons from you.'

'Well you clearly need lessons from somebody. You're about the rudest bastard I've ever come across. I actually started to like you on Friday night, but I'm glad I bailed. I'm glad I didn't let you screw me. You'd just walk all over me like you walk all over everyone else.'

He stares at me, open-mouthed, for what seems like an age. At last, he shakes his head. Go on then, I silently urge him. Sack me now!

'I'll pick you up at twelve,' he murmurs, shoving the jam jar back to its original position.

He pushes himself up from the desk and saunters over to the fridge. Slowly, he leans down and opens the fridge door, pulling out a bar of chocolate. He's taking his time, and I know it. He's showing me his wares, the arrogant git. Well, I don't want his wares. He stands up straight, turns around, unwraps the chocolate and takes a bite, staring at me all the time.

'Nice and sweet,' he sighs, licking his lips and chucking the wrapper into the bin. 'I'll see you later.'

Chapter Thirteen

At eleven fifty-five precisely I launch a getaway. I'm more than pleased with myself as I collect my handbag and scurry off down the hallway. I punch the lift and wait, but not for long. Almost immediately, the doors open to reveal no one ... apart from him. A typhoon of spasms set off in my groin and my heart begins to do some sort of tap dance. My body's doing exactly what it always does when I'm in his presence. It's going on the rampage. And I'm not happy with it.

'You're not taking me for lunch,' I mutter.

'Oh yes I am.' He flashes me a smile and waves a hand. 'Get in.'

A ripple of lust makes its way up my body. Go on, a voice cries out, go and get some.

'No.'

'Oh, for God's sake.'

He steps out, grabs me by the arm and drags me back into the lift, holding me up close to him as the doors slide shut. I close my eyes and drink in his smell. It's bloody wonderful. Does he ever smell bad, this man?

'We're going up,' I grumble.

'Indeed we are.'

'To your office?'

'There's nothing else up there.'

'For lunch?'

'Absolutely.'

I open my eyes and find his bright blue irises staring into mine. They're filled to the brim with desire. Yes, I'm absolutely certain of it now: he's not talking about sandwiches and a bag of crisps at all.

'This is going no further.'

'It takes us to the top floor, Maya. That's enough.'

'You know what I mean.'

'Of course I do.'

As the doors open, I falter. There's got to be some way out of this, because I strongly suspect that if I let this man do what he wants with me, then I'm going to be smitten. I glance over at the receptionist and decide that I'll have to be very careful about this. Whatever else happens today, I don't want his secretary earwigging what I'm about to say.

'I'm on my period,' I whisper, leaning my head in towards him.

'No, you're not,' he whispers back.

'We've got no birth control.'

'You're on the pill.'

'How do you know?'

'Lucky guess.'

'I've got a sexually transmitted disease.'

'Maya,' he sighs. 'You're perfectly clean.'

'You don't know that.' I point a finger at him.

'You are though, aren't you?'

'Well.' I fold my arms and shrug my shoulders.

'I knew it. And for the record, I'm perfectly clean too. I've been tested. I can even show you my certificates.' He raises an eyebrow and grins. 'Oh come on, Maya. You want this and so do I. So, come on.' He holds out a hand. The grin widens. 'Let's go for a spin.'

I'm in a daze now, and I must have been hypnotised by those eyes because somehow I've raised my hand to his. It's gripped firmly and I'm yanked out of the lift into the clean, bright reception area of Daniel Foster's office. I watch as it passes me by in a blur, catching sight of the receptionist for just long enough to register the stunned look on her face.

'No calls, Carla. No interruptions at all for the next hour.' What? An hour? He's going to have me at it for the whole of lunchtime? 'This way.' He guides me into his office, kicking the door shut behind him.

'There's no lock,' I gasp.

'Never needed one before. Don't worry. She won't come in.'

He swings me to a halt in the middle of the room and releases my hand. I stand still, trying desperately to calm my breath but it's next to impossible.

'So?' he begins, stalking round me. His whole demeanour has changed now and I'm all at sea. A few minutes ago, he was almost playful and now that he's got me here, a cloud has descended over him. 'Are you going to tell me why you bailed?'

'No.'

'I made you a tent and you bailed on me.'
I begin to tremble. He really is angry.
'I'm so sorry.' I can't help the edge of sarcasm in my voice.
'So, what's the problem?'
I shake my head. Can I really tell him the truth? That in spite of all his shortcomings, and those seem to be legion, I actually quite like him? That I could imagine falling for him big time, and then he'd break my heart? That in spite of everything he says, I just don't trust him? Perhaps not.
'You're very sexy and all that, but I'm afraid I just don't like you very much.'
'And that's because I'm an arrogant shit?'
'By your own admission.'
He raises a finger.
'You don't ...'
'Yes, I know,' I snap. 'I don't know you. But I know enough about you to know that this is just a bloody bad idea.'
'You don't know anything about me.'
'No, I bloody don't. You peeled back my layers on Friday night but I found out nothing about you. You gave me nothing.'
'How about this then?'
He stalks back to his desk, grabs hold of a silver frame from his desk and turns it around to show me. I hear myself gasp. He's had my sketch framed and it's on his desk. So, what is that supposed to prove? That he's a narcissistic prat?
'So, you like looking at yourself?' I laugh. 'I could have guessed that.'
'No.' Slowly, he places the frame back into position. Slowly, he turns around and steps back towards me, homing in for the kill. He reaches out and I flinch momentarily. 'I'm not that hung up on myself,' he says quietly, skimming his index finger down my cheek. I feel myself begin to cave in at the sudden contact. I close my eyes, my breath coming in shorter spurts, and I lean in towards his touch. 'The reason I like that picture is because of the eyes.' His voice is soft now, low and gentle, and it's melting me. He runs the finger under my chin, tilting my head up so that I have no choice but to lock eyes with him. 'It's because you've seen something in them that no one else can see.'
'I don't understand.'
Through a haze of confusion, I remember. They're too vulnerable.
'You see the real me.'
'I don't ...'

It was an accident. Surely. I hadn't drawn for a long time. I simply got it wrong. He moves closer.

'I want to peel back my layers for you,' he whispers into my ear. 'You just need to give me time.'

I feel a hand come from behind, cupping me softly around my waist. I smell his freshness as he nuzzles his head into my neck, his lips touching gently against my skin, sending a tsunami of tingles through every last corner of my body. I'm losing my ability to speak, my ability to think. The last few ounces of sense that I had in my possession have been wrenched from my grasp and now I'm at his mercy. I could stay here forever, held tight in his embrace.

'I need to have you.' Pulling back, he places a hand on either cheek and stares intently into my eyes. 'This feels so right.'

I just about manage to nod in agreement, and that's all I can do because my mouth is refusing to budge. He's rendered me dumbfounded. He's having his way. I'm being womanised ... and suddenly, out of nowhere, I just don't seem to give a damn.

He lowers his lips to mine and kisses me deeply, his tongue exploring my mouth, encouraging my own tongue to dance with his. He wraps his arms around me and begins to kiss me harder, his lips moulding themselves around mine, firmly and possessively. I want to reach up and hold him. I want to run my hands across his shoulders, around his back and through his hair, but I'm held firmly in place by his grip. He presses his crotch against me and I sense the hard edge of an erection. Oh God, this is going to happen. He's going to fuck me, right here in his office.

I'm vaguely aware that I'm being manoeuvred away from the desk now and before long, my legs are halted by something. He begins to ease me down. Releasing me from the kiss and then from the embrace, he lays me flat on my back on a huge, plush leather sofa. My pulse is racing at the sight of him arched above me. Breathing quickly now, his eyes filled with determination, he pushes my legs apart and kneels between them. Urging my hips upwards, he works on arranging my skirt, hitching the material up towards my waist.

'There's no getting out of it this time, Miss Scotton,' he grins. 'I'm going to fuck you good and proper.'

'Oh,' I gasp, and I really don't know what else to say. 'Okay.'

'Hands up.'

Without arguing, I comply. I can't help myself. There's something about his tone, mixed with that fucking gorgeous face that just makes me want to cave right in and be his slave. In one fell swoop, he slides a finger inside my knickers and tears them away. Shit! Where did that come from?

'My knickers!'

'You'll have to go commando for the afternoon.' He tosses the ruined underwear onto the floor. 'Ah.' He smiles appreciatively down at my crotch. 'I've been here before, only last time I was rudely interrupted by a set of severe meteorological conditions.'

Without warning, he thrusts a finger into me. I cry out at the sudden intrusion and silence myself immediately. What on Earth is Carla going to say? She must have heard that, but the big kahuna doesn't seem to be the slightest bit bothered. Instead, he simply readjusts his position. Moving his left leg to the outside of my thigh, he lowers himself down on top of me, one hand holding my forehead, the other continuing to work me up into a storm of sexual want. The finger is withdrawn for a split second, and then he breaches me again, this time with two, stroking me on the inside with a gentle, unhurried pulse, while all the time his thumb slowly circles my clitoris. He watches me constantly, gauging my reactions, adjusting his fingers until he's finally satisfied that he's found the right spot. And then, he picks up the pace. Bringing his face down to mine, he slips his tongue into my mouth and seals his lips around my own, soaking up my moans.

It's not long before the pressure builds, forced on by the constant thrumming of his fingers. Clenching deep down inside, muscles begin to spasm. I try desperately to turn my head to one side, to free my mouth and gasp for air because I don't seem to be getting enough of the bloody stuff through my nose, but I'm held firmly in place by his hand and his mouth is still securely locked onto mine. In an instant, I come apart at the seams. A rush of heat spills its way through my vagina and every single muscle down below clenches and pulsates. I cry out into his mouth and shudder my way through the most intense orgasm I've ever experienced. At last, he lifts his head, leaving me to gasp and pant.

'Goodness me, Miss Scotton. You've come over all flustered.'

I gulp, swallow, try desperately to stop myself from trembling, but I get nowhere near to achieving my goal. His fingers are still slowly massaging me inside, taking in the slowing contractions. At last, they're removed. Raising himself up on his knees, he slides the same fingers into his mouth, watching me mischievously as he sucks on them for a moment.

'Nice and sweet. I knew you would be.'

'So that was your lunch then?'

'I think it's called an *amuse bouche*, Maya.'

I gaze up at him, knowing that the edges of my lips are curling up into a smile. Good God, this man is all manner of crass. But I seem to love it.

'I'm going to skip the starter.' He moves his left knee back between my legs, reaches down and begins to unbutton my blouse, taking his time like a child on Christmas Day, prolonging the enjoyment of unwrapping a present. 'I'm ready for the main course now. Keep your arms where they are.' At last, when every single button is undone, he gently lifts the edges of the blouse and parts them. His smile deepens as he runs a finger across the cups of my bra. 'You are too fucking beautiful,' he whispers. 'I want you to come like that when I'm inside you.'

Unfastening his trousers, he pulls them down over his hips, taking his underpants with them. When his cock is finally freed, my heartbeat jitters and my breathing falters. In the cold light of day, it seems even bigger than it did on Friday night. He must have seen the panic in my eyes because he smiles down at me.

'Don't worry. I'll break you in gently.'

He lowers himself again, planting a hand on the couch to either side of my chest. I feel his penis nudge against my opening, once, twice, and then it's eased inside me, stretching me, filling me completely. I suck in a breath and hold onto it for a moment, wondering just how far this is going to go. He withdraws slightly, giving me a chance to adjust to the intrusion, and then he pushes his way inwards once again.

'Shit, you feel so good. Enjoying that?'

Well, what to say? I close my eyes, shutting myself off to everything else but the sensation of his warm, erect penis as it pulses inside me, probing further still until he's fully immersed, completely buried inside me. Oh yes, I'm enjoying that. In fact, I don't think I've ever enjoyed anything quite so much in my entire life. I'm pinned down by a hunk of lean muscle, and he's deep inside me, and I can feel every inch of him, throbbing with desire.

'Oh God yes.'

'And I've not even started yet.'

He changes his position now, propping himself into place on his left elbow. Reaching up with his right hand, he grabs hold of my wrists, pinning them down against the leather. He pulls back out of me, right to the rim, and then slowly pushes in again. I open my eyes to find his face right in front of mine. He's watching me closely, his lips parted, moistened slightly, his eyes glazing over with need. I sense a shimmer of electricity as it tickles its way through my groin.

'Now, let's get some ground rules sorted out here.' He brushes his lips against mine.

'Ground rules?'

'Ground rules.' Withdrawing again, he gazes down at me, completely serious now. His fingers tighten around my wrists. 'No talking unless I ask you a question. And you don't come until I tell you to. That's the deal. You control yourself until I'm ready. Is that understood?'

I nod breathlessly. He's obviously forgotten that I've never come during penetration so this really doesn't seem like it's going to be a problem at all. In fact, in a couple of minutes' time, he's probably going to end up feeling severely disappointed in me ... but never mind. He pushes his way in again, readjusting his position one more time, and somehow, somewhere inside, a warm glow sparks into life. I hear myself gasp. God knows how he's doing this, but he seems to have found a spot that no one's ever found before. And fuck, I might just have to control it after all. Staring down at me intently, his eyes hooded, his lips still parted, he begins to pick up the rhythm.

'So, how do you want this?' he breathes.

'How?' I swallow. Just like this seems to be doing the trick.

'Slow and gentle, or fast and hard?'

'Oh, the second one,' I grin. Shit. Why have I said that?

'And what's the magic word?'

I'd like to say 'now', but I'm not entirely sure he's in the mood for humour. Instead, I go for the blatantly obvious. After all, it's going to get me what I need.

'Please!'

Almost before I've finished speaking, he draws back and slams himself into me. Shocked at the sudden onslaught, I cry out. Again, he withdraws and pounds forwards. I sense an edge of pain in the depths of my body, alongside a tightening of muscles I never knew I had. Maintaining eye contact, he slams again. And something builds inside me, a fizzling pressure right at my core. On a fourth pound, I'm thrust back against the couch and the pressure increases. I gasp to catch a breath. My lungs seem to have been squashed, driven upwards by a slowly expanding tension that's threatening to explode any moment, sending me into freefall. I bring myself back from the edge for a second or two, listening to him, focusing my eyes on his face. And I realise that he's struggling too. His breath is coming in short, ragged spurts. His forehead is moist and he's biting his bottom lip. He's on the verge of being torn apart by this, just like me.

'Fucking hell, Maya,' he growls. 'You feel so fucking good.'

I moan and that's all I can do. His cock slams into me again. I feel it running against the inner walls of my clitoris, increasing the pressure one more time. I sense a spasm deep inside and I know I'm already close to losing control.

And then he stops, still throbbing deep inside me.

'Are you ready for some kink?'

My eyelids flutter.

'Kink?' What the hell's he going on about now? How much more kink can the man want? I'm already under orders to control my orgasm, and if I'm not very much mistaken he's got my hands in some sort of vice-like grip.

'If you like.' I push the words out, staccato, deciding that the bloody man can have anything he likes as long as this carries on.

Raising himself up, he tugs down my bra, revealing my left nipple. He leans down and begins to suck while he pounds at me again. And then suddenly, without warning, he grips onto the nipple with his teeth, biting viciously, sending a surge of excruciating pain throughout my body. It scrambles my brain with immediate effect.

'Fuck!' I scream.

'Quiet.'

He sinks into me again, latching his teeth onto my nipple, and I'm lost in a second surge of pain. Shit. That really is kink. And shit, I think I like it. Pleasure and pain, all mixed into one. Oh yes, I like it. The problem is I have no idea why. All I know is that I want more. And it's not long in coming. He bites again and I scream, and the pressure inside increases tenfold. My climax is close now. It's going to be a bloody miracle if I can hold it back. I cling on for all I'm worth, fighting back a floodtide of spasms in my vagina, grateful when he picks up the speed again, ramming into me relentlessly. At last, his fingers tighten on my wrists, squeezing me hard.

'I'm going to come, Maya. Let go.'

On a final surge, I'm ripped apart. And so is he. He thrusts into me one last time and he's spent, emptying himself out inside me, his body juddering and twitching as he buries his face into my neck. At last, my hands are freed. Instinctively, I wrap my arms around his back. I lie panting beneath him, loving the sensation of his big, exhausted body draped over me, the quick rise and fall of his chest, his warm breath against my throat.

'Fucking hell,' he mutters. 'It's never been like that before. I don't have a fucking clue what's going on here.'

He raises his head and stares at me, as if he's searching my eyes for an answer to his puzzle.

'Well,' I sigh, reaching up and touching his chin. 'As far as I can see, you just fucked one of your employees senseless on a sofa.'

'I think it might be something more than that.' He kisses me gently on the forehead.

And then we lie coiled up in each other for an age. While he strokes the side of my face, gazing into my eyes, my hands are allowed to roam freely. For the first time, I run my fingers across his broad shoulders, down the side of his glorious face, along the edges of his soft lips. It's strange but right now, without knowing the first thing about this man, I feel like I'm a part of him … and he's a part of me.

'Don't bail on me again,' he murmurs at last.

Again? It's going further than this? Daniel Foster, the disgustingly good looking womaniser is after more? With me?

'I won't.'

'You'd better not. I'd only track you down.'

I stare up at him, realising that he's deadly serious.

'Like you tracked me down on Saturday?'

'Exactly. You've got a very talkative neighbour, you know. She told me where Lucy works. I'll always find you.'

'And I don't get a choice in this?' I smile as innocently as I can.

'I'm afraid not. Not any more. I've had my test drive and I've decided to keep you.'

He digs his head back into my neck. His breaths are slowing now. 'I knew it would be like this,' he mumbles into my neck.

'What do you mean?'

Without looking up, he shakes his head, refusing to elaborate.

'Are you alright?' he whispers.

'Of course,' I laugh. I've just had the most mind-blowing sex of my life and he's asking me if I'm alright.

'Did I hurt you too much?'

'Hurt me?'

Oh that. He's talking about the nipple business. My mind rolls around on itself wondering what to say.

'No. Well yes. But it was kind of …'

He raises his head and smiles at me.

'You've not done the pain thing before?'

'No.'

'I'm sorry.' He lands a gentle kiss on my nose. 'I got a bit carried away there. I should have asked first. I should have been specific.'

'Is that the normal way?'

He pushes himself up further.

'The normal way?'

'Well, I'm assuming you're all BDSM.'

He chews his lip.

'I've dabbled,' he says casually. 'I'm just making it up as I go along.'

'So why did that come to mind? Causing me pain?'

'No idea.' He stares down at me, all uber serious. 'Like I say, I just got a bit carried away. You seemed to like it though.'

I smile coyly. I've never in my life tried any of that kind of stuff. But my first taste of it could well have got me hooked.

'Looks like I've bagged me a filthy kinkpot,' he grins.

He withdraws from me slowly, kissing my nipple one last time before tucking my breast back inside my bra. At last, he stands up, pulling up his trousers and rearranging his shirt. He's perfect again, completely unruffled, which is more than I can say for myself. Glancing down, I decide I'm a brazen hussy, a post-coital disaster zone. I push my skirt back down and button up my blouse. When I'm ready, he holds out a hand, waiting for me to slip my fingers into his before he draws me up to his chest, wraps his arms around me and kisses me softly, gently, so that I really could melt. At last, he pulls away.

'Bathroom. Now.'

I'm led through a door at the far end of his office, finding myself in a sleek, modern bathroom. An entire wall is edged with a vanity unit, complete with two sinks and a huge mirror. Alongside that, there's a toilet and a walk-in shower.

'Sometimes I run into work,' he nods towards the shower. 'It's handy to be able to freshen up.'

Spotting a box of tissues, I pull out a handful. I'm fully aware that there's something dribbling down the inside of my right leg, and I really need to clean myself up before I go back to an afternoon of reading my book and making endless cups of tea. I've hardly begun when he comes up behind me, takes the tissues out of my hand, curls one hand around my stomach and leans down, wiping his cum away from between my legs. Oh God, this should be a moment of severe embarrassment but strangely, it's not. While he digs his head into my neck, kissing me tenderly, running the tissue up my thigh and along my clitoris, I hear a moan escape from my lips.

'Turned on again, Miss Scotton?' he whispers into my ear.

'Bloody hell, yes.'

He must have dropped the tissue now because all I can feel are his warm fingers slowly massaging me back into a frenzied mess. His hand tightens around my waist forcing me back into his erection.

'Me too.'

I look up at his reflection, finding him staring at me, a smile playing at the edges of his lips. He presses his crotch into my backside, slowly, rhythmically, and before long I'm on the verge of climaxing, my muscles quivering at his delicious touch. Apart from the sound of shallow breathing that's coming from both of us, the room is silent. He removes his fingers from my crotch, gently pulls my skirt up one more time, and I hear his zip. Oh God, we're going in for round two. At this rate, I'm not even going to have the energy to switch the kettle on this afternoon. I feel a knee between my legs, urging them open.

'Again?' I gasp.

'Oh yes.' He frowns at me. 'I want my dessert. Is that a problem?'

'No.'

'Then brace yourself.'

I lean forwards, placing my hands on the counter, and gaze up at him in the mirror, my entire body tingling with anticipation. He studies me for a moment or two, as if I'm some sort of complicated document he can't quite understand, and then he reaches down, tracing his fingers from my backside, down to my clit. He parts my lips and guides his cock into me, filling me in one slow, satisfying move. I moan out loud.

'Oh God.'

'It's good isn't it?' He pulls out to the edge and then forces his way in again, slowly. 'Really fucking good,' he breathes, staring back down at me, his eyes heavy with lust, his mouth perfectly serious. 'And for the record, it's never felt like this for me either.'

Oh come off it, I want to laugh. You've screwed hundreds of women, if not thousands. You're going to have felt this way more times than you can shake a stick at.

'And that's a fucking fact,' he confirms, before I can say anything.

He skims a hand up my spine, resting it on the nape of my neck, gripping me tight and holding me in place. Again, he withdraws. Again, he drives his way gradually back into me, adjusting his angle this time so that a wave of warmth rolls its way through my muscles. Oh God, I hope he's not planning on keeping this up for long because if he does, then I'm not going to see the end of lunchtime.

'Dan, please. Go faster. Go harder.'

The seriousness fades in an instant.

'Did I say you could talk, Maya?' he smiles.

'No, you fucking well didn't,' I growl. 'But if you carry on like this, you're going to kill me off. Faster, now! Harder!'

To my surprise, he follows through with my orders. While one hand stays at the nape of my neck, the other grips me by the waist. My arms grow taut, waiting for the onslaught and it's not long in coming. He withdraws and slams back into me immediately, sending a fierce heat through my insides. Again he withdraws, picking up the pace, ramming into me again and again.

'I'm going to ...'

'Wait.' His hand tightens against my neck, a warning, as he slams into me another four or five times before he growls, 'Now.'

I come to pieces immediately, every muscle in my groin contracting and convulsing, while he throbs inside me, filling me with his hot cum. I'm about to collapse onto the counter top when he slaps me once, on my right buttock. I jolt at the shock, and then I convulse again.

'What was that for?' I cry out in confusion.

I'm pulled upright. Still buried inside me, he wraps one arm tightly around my stomach while his free hand comes up and takes my chin, pinning my head back against his chest.

'Remember who's in charge here,' he warns me sternly. 'Don't think you can order me about when it comes to sex. I want complete control.'

I shake my head out of his grasp.

'Well, I'm so sorry,' I sigh, spraying out as much sarcasm as I can gather.

He tightens his grip one more time and grinds himself into me. Even though he's just coming down from one orgasm, I wouldn't put it past the man to work himself up to another before he's even out of me. He leans down and nips my ear lobe.

'Don't get feisty with me, woman. It only makes me want to fuck you more.' He licks me gently at the back of my ear and I tingle with pleasure. 'And just for the record, I'm quite capable of fucking us both to death so don't give me the excuse.' He withdraws from me, watching me all the time in the mirror. At last, he lets me go and spins me round. 'Time for something to eat,' he grins, tucking his penis back inside his trousers. 'I can't have you going back to a tough afternoon with Norman on an empty stomach. You'd better clean yourself up this time.' He plants a gentle, chaste kiss on my nose. 'If I do it, we'll never get out of here.'

When I return to the office, he's already on the sofa with his feet up on the coffee table, a lunch laid out in front of him: a selection of sandwiches, a bowl of posh crisps, two bottles of water. I have no idea where it's come from. He taps the space next to him and I sink down by his side. Picking up a sandwich, I turn it around in my hands. The truth is I'm not that hungry at all. My stomach is all over the place.

'So, you've decided to keep me then?' I venture.

He turns towards me, mid chew, and takes in a deep breath.

'Yes.'

'Which means?'

'I'm not sure.'

He shrugs his shoulders while I take a half-hearted bite out of my sandwich.

'Well, that's cleared things up a bit,' I mutter.

'Don't be a smart alec.'

'Why not?'

He motions down to his crotch where I can clearly see the beginnings of another erection.

'I've got a meeting in half an hour. How the hell am I going to discuss progress on a multi-storey car park with this thing kicking off in my pants?'

Choking on a mouthful of bread, I gaze down at the bulge and wonder if this is an avoidance tactic. Well, if it is, then it's not going to work.

'I'd just like to know what you want out of me, that's all,' I push on. 'I mean, I'm not getting into some sort of kinky contract with you.'

'What on Earth makes you say that?'

'You want to tie me up. You like to order me about. You just spanked me in there.' I nod towards the bathroom. 'Put me straight if I've got this all wrong, but I'm guessing you're one of those dominant types.'

His face breaks out into a smile. 'I have preferences. That's all.'

'And you want me to be your submissive?'

'I'd like you to submit.'

'In everything?'

'Wherever necessary.'

'That's a bit too vague.'

'Well, I'm sure we can firm things up as we go along.' He smiles mischievously. Leaning his head back against the sofa, he stares at me for a moment or two. 'Listen,' he says at last. 'I'd like you to paint something for me. I love that sketch.'

He points the remnants of his sandwich back at the framed picture on his desk before popping it into his mouth and finishing it off. I shake my head, suddenly heavy, as if my body has been flooded with molten lead.

'I haven't painted properly. Not for a long time.'

'You haven't opened your present yet?'

'Yes, I have. I started something but it's early days.'

He stares at me some more, his eyes glimmering with interest.

'So, why didn't you paint for so long?' he asks.

I lean forwards and put my sandwich back on the plate.

'Lots of reasons.' I clasp my hands around my knees. I'm not happy about this, not happy about him rummaging around in my weaknesses.

'If you're not painting, then you can't be happy,' he says, his voice softened, almost tender. 'And if you're not happy, then I can't be happy.'

Releasing my knees from their grasp, I lean back and turn to him.

'Why would it bother you?' I demand. 'You've barely known me for five minutes.'

'I've known you for long enough.' He places a hand on my thigh, and somewhere deep inside my stomach a fluttering sensation kicks into action. 'You're a stunning woman, Maya. Intelligent, sexy, gifted, incredible. Every time I'm with you, I'm a mess. And you feel the same way about me.' He holds me with his gaze. That wasn't a question, but he's still waiting for confirmation. I nod. 'Good. Then this is going to carry on. And because this is going to carry on, I need to see you happy. And I need to know why you didn't paint.'

I throw my head back, stare at the ceiling and suck in a lungful of air. I'm being put on the spot, yet again, and he's clearly not going to give up until he's got an answer. But where to start with it all? Not with Edinburgh. That's all I know for certain. I can never tell him about Edinburgh. I'll start later on into the story.

'I was kind of caught up in my ex. I thought we were going to get married and have a family. I just dropped the painting and invested everything in him.'

'And he didn't encourage you?'

I shake my head, suddenly ashamed of myself. Why have I been so weak? So directionless? And why did I abandon my dreams? Closing my eyes, I hope to God that I'm not about to cry, but I rather suspect I am. I'm half expecting a barrage of follow-on questions from him now, all on the subject of the ex. But it doesn't come. Instead, he begins to speak quietly.

'I'm not the greatest expert on the matter. All I know about relationships is what I saw in my parents. And I saw that they loved each other deeply, that they invested in each other and encouraged each other. They were equals. My mother backed my father in his business. She understood that he had to work long hours and she supported him. And in return, my father encouraged my mother.' He squints towards the windows. 'She painted.'

'She did?'

'Only amateur. Nothing like you. She was a watercolour woman. But my father encouraged her all the way. And your ex-boyfriend should have done the same. He should have supported you.' He bites his lip and seems to think before he fires out the next question. 'Are you over him now?'

'Yes, I am.'

'Good. Any other exes I should know about?'

He watches me closely, picking up on the hint of a squirm. Oh great, so he's sensed my unease. Don't ask about that, I will him silently. Because I've already made my decision, and I'm seriously not going to tell you.

'It's okay.' He squeezes my leg. 'We can peel back that layer another time.' He reaches forwards, grabs hold of a bottle of water, unscrews the lid and takes a giant gulp before he speaks again. 'I'd like to see you tonight.'

I grin like an idiot, reach up and wipe a crumb away from the side of his mouth. He raises an eyebrow at me.

'What should I wear?' I ask.

He thinks for a moment, as if he's weighing up his next words.

'That's entirely up to you.'

***

When I'm finally ushered back out into the reception area, I find myself confronted by a distinctly confused-looking Carla and a distinctly pissed-off looking stranger perched against her desk. I stop in my tracks and take in the stranger, noting that he's tall, lean, dark-haired and in his mid-thirties at a guess. And judging by the hint of a snarl that's currently spreading itself across his lips, he's taken an instant dislike to me.

'Dan,' the stranger sighs. 'Finally.'

'Clive. What are you doing here?'

'I thought I might come for a little catch up over lunch.' He stands up and straightens his jacket. 'But when I got here, Carla informed me that you were busy. She said we weren't to bother you under any circumstances. Apparently, she was under orders not to open your door. All very strange.'

'I was ... discussing something with ...'

I watch in amazement as Mr Mean and Hot and Moody seems to swallow hard and fumble for an explanation. Abruptly, all of his cocky self-assuredness evaporates, leaving nothing but an anxious frown in its place, and for the life of me I really can't figure out what's going on. Okay, so I might have that just-fucked look about me. My skirt is creased, my hair is ruffled and my blouse seems to be crumpled to within an inch of its existence. And while Dan seems to be as perfectly turned out as ever, I'm pretty sure that this strange man, who's apparently called Clive, knows exactly what we've been up to. But why would that bother the big kahuna?

'This is Maya.' He waves a hand at me. 'Maya, this is my good friend, Clive Watson. He's the head of the Finance department here.'

The head of the Finance department eyes me suspiciously then takes a step forwards. Taking my hand in his, he stares at me, coldly.

'Do you work here?' he asks.

'Yes.' I smile weakly. I'm getting the distinct feeling that this man isn't warming to me at all.

'Maya's working in Norman's office,' Dan explains.

'So what is she doing up here?'

I watch as Daniel Foster glances from me to his friend, and finally fixes his eyes on the lift door. He's shut himself off.

'She just brought some papers up.'

'Interesting.' The edges of Clive Watson's lips are lifted a little, but his eyes don't catch the smile. 'Can you spare me a few minutes, Dan?'

'Of course.'

'I'd better get back downstairs now,' I say quietly. 'Lots to do.'

And with that, I'm gone.

Chapter Fourteen

After a less than busy afternoon, I make my way back up to Camden. It's unbearably hot again after the weekend's rainfall and I'm soon close to overheating on the tube. While the train judders its way up the Northern Line, I fidget about in my seat, glancing down at the too-short skirt, reminding myself that I'm wearing no knickers and hoping to God that the man in the opposite seat hasn't noticed. Keep your knees together, for God's sake, a voice cries out at the back of my head. You can't go flashing that about at all and sundry.

While the train slows to a half-expected halt in the middle of a tunnel, I close my eyes and allow my thoughts to rake their way back over the lunchtime rendezvous. His big hands are back on my body now, his lips skimming across my skin, his eyes fixed on mine in the bathroom mirror while he gently massages me down below. At the sound of a moan, my eyelids flip back open. Jesus. That must have been me. Glancing anxiously round the carriage, I take a few good, deep breaths, deciding that it's about time to get a grip on myself because the Northern Line is no place for a mental sexual odyssey. Dear Lord, I'm in trouble. In fact, I'm in five star, top-of-the-range, it-doesn't-come-any-bigger-than-this trouble because I already like him far too much and I'm already beginning to worry that it's all going to come crashing down round my ears. Before I can pursue my thoughts any further, the train jolts back into action and within minutes, I'm caught up in a tide of bodies washing its way up the escalator at Camden Town.

I'm home well before Lucy. Leaving the bath to run, I stand in front of my full length bedroom mirror and undress. Fully naked now, I gaze at myself, wondering what it is that he finds so irresistible. Giving up on the puzzle, I head back to the bathroom and slip into the tub. I spend the next half an hour languishing in the water beneath an open window, enjoying the occasional waft of cool air from outside. I dry myself off and take a look through Lucy's wardrobe. Sometime soon, I really am going to have to go clothes shopping but for tonight I'll just have to make do. And for some reason, I want to wear a dress. I pick a short, flowery number and pull it on. I dry my hair, pin it up and apply my usual bare minimum make-up. Finally, I'm ready. Returning to the kitchen, I search through my handbag for my mobile and stare at it for an age. Do I dare a text? At last, just after seven, I summon up the confidence.

I'm all ready and I'm wearing a dress!

There. That should do it. Not too eager, but just eager enough. Clutching the phone in my hand, I sit back and wait ... but nothing comes. My mind begins to race. Perhaps he's in the shower. Or he's gone for a run. Perhaps he's busy with some last minute work. Whatever's going on, he can't have seen the text. He may well be the biggest, arrogant bastard that London's currently got to offer, but after everything he did and said at lunchtime, I'm still pretty sure he would have sent a reply. After half an hour, I wonder if I should send a second text. I'm about to start on it when the front door swings open and Lucy launches herself into the kitchen. She stops in her tracks, drops a bag of shopping onto the floor and gapes at me.

'Wow!' she breathes. 'You look great in that dress. What's going on?'

'I've got a date.' I gaze back down at the phone. 'I think.'

Taking a bottle of white wine out of the bag, she stands up straight and pins me down with a frown.

'You think?'

'Yep.'

'With Mr Mean and Hot and Moody?'

'Yep.'

Her face breaks out into a huge grin. She grabs two glasses out of the cupboard and fills them with Pinot Grigio.

'He talked you round?'

Suddenly, I'm thinking about the sofa, and then I'm thinking about the bathroom, and now I'm blushing.

'Kind of.' I reach out for a glass.

'You go, girl!' She perches on a rickety chair. 'Is he picking you up?'

'At eight.' I look back down at the phone. Still nothing.

'Well, get plenty of grape juice in you. Fortify yourself.'

I smile weakly and take a sip of lukewarm wine.

'Good day?' I ask.

While Lucy stands up, rummages in the shopping bag and begins to run through the painful details of yet another day with the Steves, I watch as the minute hand on the kitchen clock creeps its way up towards the twelve.

'The man with the shih tzu came back,' she rattles on. 'His breath stinks like a blocked drain ...'

She cuts an onion, slices a red pepper and chops up a handful of mushrooms. By a quarter past eight, she's finished with the preparation, slinging the ingredients into a frying pan along with a can of chopped tomatoes.

'Oh,' she sighs. 'I think I was supposed to fry stuff first.'

I take a deep breath and decide that it's time for the second text.

Are you running late?

I sit in silence, watching as Lucy sets about boiling the crap out of a panful of pasta. By the time she lumps everything together onto a plate without the slightest regard for presentation, it's just gone half past eight. I wait for Lucy to settle down at the table before I shoot off a third text.

Are you OK?

I stare at the screen for what seems like an age.

'Isn't he coming?' Lucy splutters through her final mouthful of something vaguely Italian and distinctly undercooked.

I shake my head. Still no reply.

'I don't think so.'

Without another word, I pour a second glass of wine and take myself off to the living room. Somewhere deep inside me, a cloud seems to have formed and I'm in no mood for a chat. I curl up in the corner of the sofa, stare blankly out of the window and listen to the rattle of plates and pans being washed up in the kitchen. At last, the rattling comes to an end and Lucy joins me on the sofa.

'Why isn't he coming?' she demands.

'I've no idea.'

She checks the time display on the DVD player. Five past nine. We both know what that means.

'Have you texted him?' she asks.

'Three times.'

'Any answers?'

'Nothing.'

She turns and gives me one of her overly compassionate specials, and I wish that she'd stop it.

'Well ...' She takes a gulp of wine and pushes out a belch. 'He's either stood you up or he's been in some sort of horrific car accident.'

'Don't.'

'Or he's had a heart attack.'

'Lucy, he's stood me up. It's perfectly obvious. He's had what he wanted out of me, and now he's moved on.'

'He's had what he wanted?' she gasps, spilling wine all over the sofa.

'Yes,' I hiss. 'At lunchtime. He had what he wanted in his office. Twice. Now, get over it and shut up.'

'Fuck! What?' Her eyes widen to almost cartoon proportions and her bottom lip drops so low, it very nearly comes into contact with her breasts.

'I should have seen this coming,' I mutter, ignoring Lucy's state of near hysterical disbelief. 'He's that sort of man. He's not going to change the habit of a lifetime, is he?'

'So, that's it then.' She shakes her head, picks up the remote and begins to flick through the channels.

'Looks like it, Luce.'

'Bastard. You're better off out of it.'

'I'm fully aware of that.'

'Anyway ...' She shakes her head again. 'Life must go on. *Bridget Jones* is on at half past and I've got another bottle of wine.'

I pull a cushion over my lap and hold it tight. I need comfort right now, and *Bridget Jones*, wine and cushion will do just fine. Slugging back a mouthful of Pinot, I lean my head into the sofa, wishing that Daniel Foster would get the hell out of my mind.

Chapter Fifteen

The following morning, it comes as no surprise to find myself slumped at a desk, drowning in exhaustion and feeling distinctly tetchy. It's all my own fault, of course. After Bridget Jones had finally managed to bumble her way to a happy ever after, I just couldn't help myself. Back in my bedroom, I must have spent a good two or three hours adding a few more layers of colour to the canvas before trying to grab a snatch of sleep underneath the fug of a London heatwave. And now, with my energy reserves depleted by too much wine, a good dose of creativity and way too little rest, all I want to do is bite somebody's bloody head off.

In fact, to be rather more specific, all I want to do is bite Daniel Foster's bloody head off because, as it turns out, he's in work today. And that means he wasn't involved in a horrific car accident at all, and he certainly didn't suffer a heart attack either. And that leaves only one alternative. The bastard *did* stand me up. I pull the jar of sweet peas towards me and come to a decision: I've been an idiot. I should never have let a man like that come into my life in the first place because, true to form, he only went and did what he was always planning to do. He pursued me, sweet talked me, and then he got exactly what he wanted. And now he's lost interest. In fact, in all probability, he's already moved on to his next conquest.

Still, stupidly, I check my mobile for messages ... only to find a single text from Lucy.

Keep your pecker up, kid. And jack in that job. We can cope.

No, Lucy, we can't, my brain complains. That bloody flat is costing us a bomb. As soon as we possibly can, we need to move out of Camden and find somewhere a little more affordable, and until then I'm stuck right here in this stupid excuse for an office, in a stupid excuse for a job, one floor down from the womanising shitbag of the year. I plant my gaze on the computer screen, knowing full well that there's only one way to make myself feel better. I need to tell him straight what a complete bastard he's been, even if he does sack me off the back of it. Before I know what I'm doing, I've repositioned the keyboard, logged into my email, and I'm typing:

'Mr Foster. Actions speak louder than words. In spite of everything you said, you've obviously had second thoughts. Just to let you know, I feel thoroughly used. I don't need to tell you that you're an arrogant piece of shit who goes around taking what he wants without a care for the people he hurts. You already know that. Miss Scotton.'

I click the send icon, lean back in my chair and glance across at Jodie only to find her staring right back at me as if she's trying to fathom the innermost workings of my mind. Letting out a sigh, I go back to pretending to read Lucy's ridiculous chunk of romantic sludge while another sixty minutes drag their heels and I spend every single one of them with my stomach in knots. Every now and then, I turn a page of the book. Every now and then, I check my computer screen. Every now and then, I sigh.

Still no reply.

'I'm going out for lunch,' I announce at last.

Jodie's head pops up from a magazine.

'But it's only half eleven.' She reaches for her mobile.

'And I don't give a shit. I'm going out for lunch right now.' I pause for dramatic effect. 'And I might not come back.'

Snatching my handbag from beneath my desk, I storm out of the office and make for the lift, riding it down to the ground floor and blustering my way out of the building. I'm on auto-pilot now, taking a right and stomping my way along the embankment like a stroppy diva on a bad day. And yet again, I have no idea what I'm doing or where I'm going, but after wandering the streets and alleyways of Southwark for at least half an hour, I find myself in exactly the same coffee shop where he asked me out in the first place, sitting on exactly the same sofa and glaring out of exactly the same window. Knowing full well that I'm more bothered about Daniel Foster than I care to admit, I take a sip of my latte. On a second mouthful, I finally come to a decision, the only sensible, logical decision that I can possibly make. I need to leave the south side of the Thames behind me. And to hell with the bills. I need to go home. Deciding that I'd better let Lucy in on my plans, I dig through my handbag in search of my mobile only to find that it's not there. For a split second, I panic, wondering if I've been the victim of a pickpocket, and then I remember: I've left it on my desk. But I need my phone. And that means one last foray into the dangerous world of Daniel Foster. Taking several deep breaths, I steel myself for the task ahead.

***

A few minutes later and I'm back in the lift, staring down at a selection of over-polished shoes and trying to keep my pulse under control. I have no idea why I'm so nervous about a simple thing like picking up a mobile phone and walking out of an office but here I am, nevertheless, tucked into the back of an elevator with a bunch of well-dressed professionals, struggling to take in a decent breath. I'm admiring a pair of stilettos when I become aware of a familiar scent tickling its way up my nose. Slowly, sensing that my heartbeat has begun to accelerate, I raise my eyes and take in the back of a pair of black, tailored trousers that are directly in front of me. My eyes climb further, up past an expensive, black jacket, finally coming to a halt at the back of a head that seems to be topped with a mop of ruffled, blond hair. In an instant, my knees begin to wobble. Oh shit. This is just perfect. He's here, right here in the lift with me, standing right in front of me, and he's blanking me completely. I swallow hard, discovering that my mouth seems to have dried up, and even though I know he's just not worth it, my heart begins to thud. At the thirteenth floor, the last of the lunchtime traffic spills out into a corridor, leaving nobody else but me and him. When the doors close, he stays exactly where he is, rooted to the spot with his back to me. It takes a few seconds for the lift to rise to the fourteenth floor. As the doors open once again, I make a move, but find myself suddenly held back by a strong arm.

'This is my floor,' I complain.

'Not today, it's not.' He nudges me backwards, waiting for the doors to close. 'You're coming with me.'

'I thought you've already had what you wanted,' I snarl and I realise that I'm shaking now. 'I mean, you've stripped my assets and now it's time to move on, isn't it?'

He turns quickly, so quickly I don't have time to see it coming. Grabbing both of my hands, he pins them against the wall, pushing his body up close and grinding his crotch into mine. Immediately, a wave of heat floods its way through my groin. I close my eyes and hear myself moan. Now, that wasn't in the plan. I've been ambushed and already I seem to be reaching for the white flag.

'This is not asset stripping,' he breathes into my face.

I suck in a deep breath, open my eyes and decide that it's going to take every last molecule of grit and determination to get out of this one. He grinds into me again, sending a bolt of lust right to my core.

'You stood me up last night,' I choke.
'Something came up.'
'Did it now?'
'Absolutely.'
'You could have texted me.'
'It was impossible.'

I laugh. Really? You didn't have a single moment to explain yourself?

'And you didn't reply to my email.'
'I didn't like your email. It didn't warrant a reply.'

The doors open and I'm released. I've had just enough time to lower my hands when my wrist is grabbed and I'm yanked out into reception. I'm stunned. If his secretary sees this, then the gossip is really going to fly around the building. I half expect to be dragged into his office, just like the last time. After all, he's probably just feeling a tad randy and in need of a lunchtime booty call. Instead, I'm pushed behind Carla's desk and shoved down onto her chair.

'What are you doing? Where's Carla?'
'Gone home sick. I need a PA for the afternoon.'

He straightens up and scowls at me. Jesus, he's in a mood. And Jesus, he looks as hot as hell. And Jesus, even though I've spent the last few hours of my life trying my damnedest to reason the sodding man out of my head, he could take me right here if he wanted to ... and I really wouldn't complain.

'You'll do,' he growls.
'Me? But I don't know what to do.'
'There's the diary.' He motions towards a huge black, leather-bound book. 'The computer's still logged in. That's a phone. If it rings, answer it. And try not to be rude.'

Open-mouthed, I watch as he strolls off into his office. Well, what the fuck's going on now? After ignoring me for the best part of a day, he launches a surprise attack in a lift and then he orders me to answer his phone? The man's a complete fruit loop. Get out of here this instant, the sensible half of my brain screams out. And I'd go along with it too, if only the idiot half wasn't currently musing over the possibility that Daniel Foster just can't stay away from me. I shake my head and will my mouth to close. This is all too intriguing. It's as if he's thrown down a gauntlet and all I know is that I'm sorely tempted to pick it up.

Before I can follow him into his office and demand to know what the hell he's playing at, the lift doors slide open, revealing a pair of extremely serious-looking men. As they approach me, I know that my mouth has begun to open and close in panic. I must look like a goldfish.

'We've got an appointment with Mr Foster,' one of the men announces.

I open and close my mouth some more. And then I find myself opening the diary, scrabbling through the pages until I arrive at today's date. Running my finger down the page, I stop at one o'clock. Mr Ross and Mr Chapman from some company or other. Desperately trying to compose myself, I get up from my chair.

'One moment please.' I edge my way past them into the big kahuna's lair.

I find him sitting at his desk, jacketless. He's staring at his iPad now, deep in thought.

'Mr Foster,' I announce crisply. He looks up at me, his face expressionless.

'Mr Ross and Mr ... er ...' Shit, I've already forgotten the second man's name. 'Mr Whatsit are here.'

I catch the slightest hint of a smile at the corner of his lips.

'Please show Mr Ross and Mr Whatsit in,' he says politely. 'And Miss Scotton.'

'Yes?'

'Coffee for three.'

'Coffee for three o'clock?'

'Coffee for three people, Miss Scotton. Please do your best not to behave like a complete moron.'

'But I am a complete moron, Mr Foster,' I inform him. 'After all, I'm still here, aren't I?'

Without waiting for a reaction, I turn my back on him and take my time sauntering out through the open doorway. Doing my best to smile winsomely at Mr Ross and Mr Whatsit in the process, I show them both into the inner sanctum and while a conversation strikes up between the men, I turn my attention to a closed door that's just to the right of my desk. Tentatively, I push it open, finding myself in a small kitchen where I discover a kettle, flick it on and set about rummaging through the cupboards. With a great deal of effort, I manage to locate cups and saucers but when it comes to anything that vaguely resembles coffee, I'm not so lucky. I'm bending down, checking out the contents of the fridge when the sound of his voice causes my body to jolt.

'Will you be bringing us drinks any time soon?'

Straightening up, I bang my head on an open cupboard door. Before I know it, I'm dazed and a pair of big, strong hands is gripping me by the shoulders.

'Careful. You might knock some sense into yourself.'

I rub the top of my head and glance up into his bright blue eyes. No, don't go there, my brain screams out at full volume. He'll have you hypnotised before you bloody know it!

'Get off me.'

'Are you alright?'

'Of course I'm bloody well alright.' I shake myself free of his grip. 'Where's the fucking coffee?'

He struggles to suppress a smile. Taking a step past me, he opens up a cupboard, one that I've already been through at least twice, and pulls out a bag of filter coffee. And then he motions towards some sort of contraption that looks like a prop from a science fiction film.

'I ...' I falter, rubbing my head some more. 'I don't know how to use one of those.'

'Better learn then.'

He shoves the packet of coffee into my hands, swivels on his heels and in an instant, he's gone. I stare in dismay at the coffee machine. What the hell am I supposed to do with that thing? I've just about managed to work out where the coffee should go when another voice startles me from the doorway.

'We're off now!' It's Mr Whatsit. 'Thanks for the coffee.'

He winks at me and for a split second I toy with the idea of kicking him in the nuts. Instead, I smile sweetly and go back to the wretched coffee machine, grabbing a glass jug from underneath a stainless steel spout and staring at it, dumbfounded. According to the diary, the big kahuna's got another four meetings this afternoon and I'd like to provide refreshments for at least one of them, though I have no idea why. Maybe I'm just enjoying the game. And maybe I just don't want to be beaten.

'Maya!' I hear him calling me.

Dumping the glass jug onto the counter, I scurry back through reception and almost trip through the doorway into his office. He doesn't notice. He's busy flicking his way through a file.

'What is it?' I snap.

'Bring my diary in,' he mutters. 'I've got a date to add.'

'Do it yourself. I'm making coffee.'

I watch as he licks his finger, turning another page or two, apparently unbothered by my rudeness. He spends the next few seconds examining a graph before he finally looks up at me.

'Miss Scotton,' he smiles slowly. 'Let me remind you that I'm in charge around here. Now do as you're told.'

I feel a twinge of something down below, right between my thighs. And somehow I just can't help myself. I hurry back out to reception, retrieve the diary and a biro, and return to him immediately. Without a word, he waves me into a chair that's been positioned right next to his desk, watching me closely as I sink down into the leather.

'Now,' he says. 'Thursday the thirtieth. I've got an on-site meeting at the Rowley shopping centre.' He watches me some more, and I watch him right back, my temperature rising at the sight of his bloody wonderful face and his ruddy gorgeous eyes and his stonkingly perfect lips. He taps a finger against the desk and sighs. 'Well write it in, woman.'

'Screw you,' I breathe.

I know exactly what I'm doing. I'm being feisty, and it's working too.

His lips twitch.

'The thirtieth,' he repeats himself. 'Write it in.'

'Write it in,' I mimic him. Opening up the diary and turning to the correct page, I scrawl the word *Rowley* as messily as I can. 'Is that it?'

'No, it's not. Have I got anything on tonight?'

I flip my way back to today. There's a huge list of meetings during the day and his next one is due any minute, but the evening is empty.

'Nothing.'

'Good. So, write this in. It's just a little reminder to myself.'

I poise my pen, ready for the next messy entry.

'Fuck my secretary.'

Oh, good Lord. What's happening now? It's as if some demented sex fairy is on the loose, tweaking me over and over again down below. Willing it to stop, I clamp my lips together and stare at him.

'Good and proper.' He points at the diary. 'Make sure you add that bit.'

'And what will Carla think when she gets back?' I scribble the words *fuck my secretary* large across the bottom of the page, noting that he leans forwards anxiously as I do it. 'I mean, she is your secretary, isn't she?' I add *good and proper* in capital letters, underscoring them a few times for good measure.

'Not this afternoon, she's not,' he frowns. 'This afternoon, you're my secretary. You need to rub that out.'

He waves a hand at the diary.

'No can do,' I smile and I'm pretty sure he's repressing a smile in return. 'It's in biro, and besides, you told me to write it. And anyway, why don't you just fuck your secretary right now? Over there.' I nod towards the sofa. 'Like you did yesterday? And then why don't you just ignore her afterwards and make her feel like an insignificant piece of crap?'

'I'd love to fuck her right now. Over there.' He nods towards the sofa. 'I'd like to fuck her so hard she can't speak for a week.'

'Of course you would. I mean you're not interested in a word she's got to say. In fact, why let her talk at all? Why not just gag her?'

He leans further forwards.

'What a wonderful idea. I'll bear that in mind for later.'

'There is no later.'

'We'll see about that. Now go and find some correction fluid and sort that diary out.'

'I've got a better idea. Why don't you go and find some correction fluid and shove it up your arse?'

'That's very childish of you, Miss Scotton.'

'Sack me then.'

I glare across the desk at him, while he glares back at me, all mean and hot and moody. I watch as his lips twitch, his fists clench, and I'm silently satisfied that I've just given him the mother of all hard-ons. In fact, I'm almost certain that he's about to leap out of his chair and shove me backwards over the sofa one more time when I'm disturbed by the sound of a phone.

'That's your phone,' he glowers. 'Go and answer it.'

I push back my chair, storm out to reception, and grab the receiver.

'Mr Foster's office,' I announce at the top of my voice. 'What do you want?'

'Who's that?' a male voice demands and I recognise it instantly. It's Clive, the evil friend.

'Mr Foster's secretary.'

'You don't sound like Carla.'

'That's because I'm not Carla.'

'Who are you then?'

'I'm Mr Foster's piece of skirt.'

'Maya!' I hear him call through the doorway. 'Behave yourself!'

'Well, Mr Foster's piece of skirt,' Clive Watson grumbles. 'Would you mind putting me through to him now?'

I buzz through the call.

'It's your twat of a friend,' I explain. I'm so proud of myself.

There are a few seconds of silence before he speaks.

'Put him through ... and Maya?'

'Yes?'

'Shut my door for me, please.'

Holding the phone to his ear and obviously waiting for privacy, he watches me as I pull the door to a close. While I make my way back into the kitchen and stare at the coffee machine, my mind begins to sift through the possibilities of what's going on inside that office. Why on Earth doesn't Dan want to talk within my earshot? And what on Earth could he be talking about? Well, I'm pretty damn sure it can't be company matters because if it was, then the big kahuna wouldn't be quite so bothered about secrecy. All I know for sure is that the evil friend took an instant dislike to me yesterday, and that following on from his visit, I was unceremoniously dumped for a few hours. I come to the only conclusion I can. Clive Watson thinks I'm a worthless gold-digger. And perhaps, right now, he's doing his level best to talk my prospective sugar daddy out of having anything further to do with me. I'm back at the desk when the door opens and Daniel Foster steps out into reception, a scowl plastered right across his face.

'Did you and Clive have a nice conversation?'

He dismisses my question with a shrug and disappears into the kitchen. A couple of minutes later, he returns, slams a cup of coffee down onto the desk for me and takes himself back inside his office. I'd like to go and ask him what's got him so riled but the lift doors open one more time to reveal the most stunning woman I've ever seen. Eyeing her closely as she approaches my desk, I take in the facts: she's brunette, maybe early thirties at a push, a couple of inches shorter than me, and really incredibly slim. She seems to have no backside at all, and barely any breasts. Not like me. I'm well-endowed in both directions. And as for the clothes, well this lady is the polar opposite of Maya Scotton in every possible way. For a start, her tiny frame is draped in a designer dress and I'd bet a week's wages that those are Manolo Blahniks on her feet.

'Maya,' she smiles. 'So nice to meet you.'

'Pardon?' I gulp. I want to ask her exactly how she knows my name, but Dan's already standing in the open doorway.

'Lily.' He holds out a hand. 'I've got a few minutes before my next meeting. Come on in.'

I stare in disbelief as skinny Lily allows him to embrace her and plant a kiss on her perfectly made up cheek. Obviously gauging my reaction, he shoots a glance in my direction. I smile sweetly back at him. And that's a bloody miracle, seeing as I'm already halfway to being on the boil. Is this really why he's lured me into his office for the afternoon? To make it perfectly plain to me that I'm not the only woman in his life? And this woman has got 'sexual deviant' written all over her flawless little face. In a heartbeat, I decide that she must be one of his BDSM buddies, and if not that, then maybe one of his subs. Perhaps he's going to take her into his office right now, tie her up and fuck her good and proper, just to make it absolutely clear how little I mean to him.

He motions her into his office, looks back at me one more time, and closes the door behind him. It's a good half an hour later when she finally re-emerges. And while I've spent the time grudgingly answering the phone and scribbling out countless messages, I have no idea what she's been up to. She looks just as immaculate now as she did when she went in. And no, the make-up hasn't been smudged.

'So,' she breathes. 'You'll definitely be there.'

'Without a doubt.' He smiles. 'Black tie?'

'Black tie,' she confirms. 'It was nice to meet you, Maya.' She turns to me. 'I hope we meet again.'

What? So you can include me in one of your kinky threesomes? No way, lady! That's never going to happen. He shows her to the lift, his hand on the small of her back and I sense a surge of jealousy.

'Who was that?' I demand when we're finally on our own.

'Lily.'

'Lily who?'

'Lily Babbage.'

I snigger.

'It's her name, Maya. And she's my friend. It would be nice if you could show a little more respect.'

'Lily Babbage,' I murmur, leaning back in my chair. That's a madam's name if ever I've heard one.

The conversation is cut short by a group of new arrivals: a whole bevvy of people from Finance, including Clive the evil friend, who scowls down at me as he enters the inner sanctum. Screw you, a voice shoots out in my brain. You really don't like me at all. Well, guess what! I don't like you back!

Three meetings later, and I've pretty much had enough. I've managed to make coffee and even serve coffee, spilling it onto his carpet by accident only once, and across the huge glass meeting table twice, both times on purpose. I've witnessed more men and women in suits than I care to remember, and I've answered more phone calls and taken more messages than I care to forget. The last visitors left twenty minutes ago. I waved them off with my feet up on the desk before leaving him with a pad of badly scrawled, almost illegible messages and his telephone. I glance up at the clock. It's nearly seven and I must have done my time by now. This game of silly buggers needs to come to an end. After all, I certainly didn't let him beat me. But then again, I'm not entirely sure that I won.

It's quiet now. Standing up and taking in a deep breath, I smooth down my skirt and decide that it's time to call it a day on the whole charade. I find him sitting behind his desk, clutching the note pad, gazing out over the Thames where just about every inch of water seems to be bathed in the early evening sunlight.

'Dan.'

He turns at the sound of my voice, fixing me with a long, unfathomable stare. 'I'm going home.'

His forehead creases.

'No, you're not.' He slides the pad onto the desk top. 'You're coming back to mine.'

'I'm not, Dan. I don't want to be messed about any more.'

He runs a hand through his hair.

'I'm not messing you about.' He looks up at me. His eyes are tired, his hair's a ruffled mess, but oh God, he's still incredibly handsome even when he is worn out. Pushing himself up from his chair, he comes round to my side of the desk, leans back on it and folds his arms across his chest. 'I'm sorry. I should have contacted you last night.'

'Then why didn't you?'

He shakes his head, bites his lip.

'I can't explain. Please just let it go.' His eyes bore into me, melting me, sending a delicious quiver right up my spine. He's waiting for my reaction, and even though I'm not too happy about giving up, I just can't help myself. I nod. Unfolding his arms, he allows the smallest of smiles to play across his lips. 'Your email knocked me for six,' he admits at last.

'You deserved it.'

'I know.'

'So, why this?' I wave my hand at the doorway. 'Why the game?'

He shrugs his shoulders.

'I needed to keep you here. I didn't want you to run.' He pauses. 'And you nearly ran, didn't you?'

'How do you know?'

He takes in an almighty breath before launching into a confession.

'I followed you at lunchtime. I watched you sitting in the window at that shit awful café. You sat in the same seat that we sat in the other day.'

'You followed me?'

'I did,' he confirms. 'What were you thinking about?'

'How I should never let another man hurt me again in my life.'

He stares at me for a moment or two.

'I hurt you.' It's not a question. It's a statement. He lowers his head. 'I'm sorry I hurt you. It's not going to happen again. Forgive me.'

He gets up from the desk and takes a step forwards. He's close to me now, so close I can feel his breath against my face.

'So you followed me back here and got in the lift with me?' I ask.

'I did. You were in a world of your own. You didn't notice.'

'And was Carla really ill?'

He shakes his head.

'I gave her the afternoon off. I couldn't risk letting you go. This was all I could think of. I panicked.' He smiles a small, lop-sided smile. A lock of blond hair falls across his forehead. He looks for all the world like a naughty schoolboy, and I just want to nuzzle my head in his neck. 'So,' he sighs. 'I had an afternoon with the world's worst secretary, but never mind. You didn't do too much damage.' He glances at the coffee stain on the carpet. 'And at least you're still here.' I feel a hand at my back and I'm drawn in close. The other hand cups the back of my head, gently. He gazes down at my lips. 'Come home with me tonight.' He runs his lips over mine. They feel like silk.

'I don't think I can do this, Dan.'

'Why not?'

Oh God, I'd better get this sorted in double quick time. I'm already starting to lose my mind. Any resolve, any determination is quickly disintegrating at the touch of his lips, the tightening of his hands. Fight back, my brain screams. Counter attack!

'I can't do a quick fling.'

He pulls his head back, fixing me with the come-to-beds.

'Is that all you think I want?'

'Men like you ...'

'There are no men like me. I'm a one off. And you're a one off too.' He leans forwards and his lips close around mine, firmly. He kisses me slowly at first, slipping his tongue into my mouth. I close my eyes, groaning at the intrusion and I just can't help myself. My own tongue begins to explore, curling against his. The pressure of his lips increases. His fingers clutch at my hair. Oh God, I know where this is going. 'I want you,' he breathes. 'I just can't fucking help it.'

'Dan.'

I open my eyes, finding myself locked in by his gaze, lost in the blue irises.

'Shush, Miss Scotton.' He brings a hand round to the front of my face and brushes a finger against my lips. Cocking his head to one side, he smiles. 'You need to make amends for this afternoon.'

'Make amends?' I gulp. 'How am I supposed to do that?'

'I'll give you one guess.'

And with that, he begins to guide me backwards, one determined step at a time, his eyes still fixed on mine. I'd like to turn round, to see where we're headed but I'm held so tight, it's impossible. Four steps is all it takes before I'm brought to a halt by a wall of glass. Shit, my brain calls out. He's going to fuck you up against the window. You're in big trouble here, lady!

'Excuse me?' I gasp. 'People can see.'

'Only if they've got binoculars.' Releasing me from his grip, he reaches up and begins to unbutton my blouse. Making quick work of it, he pulls it from my shoulders and drops it to the floor. 'Or superhuman vision. This is the fifteenth floor.' He snakes his hands round my backside and unfastens my skirt. 'And besides, the glass is tinted on the outside.' The skirt falls to the floor and he gazes at my body in admiration. Reaching out, he traces a finger down my stomach, slowly working his way outwards to my hip bone and then back again, down towards the apex of my thighs. I struggle to control my breathing while he hooks a finger into the top of my knickers, gently easing them down my legs. Taking his time, he crouches in front of me, motioning for me to lift my feet so that he can remove the knickers completely. He takes a moment to smooth his fingers across my hair, sending a delicious wave of pressure rippling through my abdomen, before he raises himself back up to his feet.

'You are a work of art, Miss Scotton.' Kicking off his shoes, he gives me a cheeky smile and reaches round to unfasten my bra.

Well, if he's going to have me stark naked against his floor-to-ceiling window, then he's going to have to lose a few items of clothing himself. I begin to unbutton his shirt. I've barely managed to get it off his shoulders when he tosses my bra to the floor. He helps me out with his belt, trousers, pants and socks and for a few magical seconds, I get the full impact of his body, the glorious contours of his muscles, the six pack, the broad, strong shoulders, the perfectly proportioned biceps. God, I could look at that body all night. But I get little chance to take it all in. Without any further ado, he thrusts himself against me and I gasp at the sudden contrasts: hard, cold glass from behind; the heat of his taut body in front.

I run my hands over his shoulders, across his muscles. And while I explore his body, his lips work their way around my neck, under my chin, finding my left ear lobe, nibbling and licking for a moment before he trails them round to my mouth and locks me into a deep kiss. He presses his crotch against mine, his hard, hot erection rubbing against my clitoris, and I light up in anticipation. Delicious sparks are sent flying through my muscles, and every last one of them begins to clench.

'Shit,' he breathes at last. 'What the fuck are you doing to me?'

What am I doing to you? I want to laugh. Shouldn't that be the other way round, I'd like to ask, but I can barely breathe let alone talk. A hand moves between my thighs, coaxing them apart. I convulse with a groan as his fingers enter me, two of them, checking urgently that I'm ready for him. And I am. I'm so ready. He takes them out, leaving me a second's worth of respite before I feel his cock edging its way inside me, his hands under my buttocks, grasping them firmly, lifting me off the ground. He pushes further, moaning at the sudden pleasure. Moving slowly, he works his way at one angle, and then another until he hits just the right spot and I squeal in delight.

'Too much?' he asks.

'Bloody hell, no! Get on with it, man!'

He smiles darkly and begins to thrust, sending me squeaking my way up the glass. I cry out in pleasure, my muscles are tingling. He withdraws and thrusts again, picking up the pace, pounding into me, forcing my body up the glass with each new onslaught. And each time, I sense a wave of pleasure in my groin, growing in power with each new lunge, ebbing away as I slide back down in his grip.

'I fucking own you, woman.' Another thrust, another pounding thrum of contractions inside. 'Never forget that.'

My brain is scrambled. I can barely take in what he's just said. But there's no point in arguing over it right now. He can fucking own me. If it means that I get this on a regular basis, then I'm fine with that. Out of nowhere, on the next thrust, my insides begin to contract.

'I'm going to come,' I moan.

'Not until I say so, Maya. You know the deal.'

His arms tighten across my back and I wrap my legs around his firm waist, concentrating for all I'm worth, squirming in his hold, trying to fend off my orgasm. I feel him thrust and ram harder now, fast and relentless. His lips covers mine, his tongue pushing its way into me as he grunts his appreciation against my mouth.

'Now.' He pulls back. 'Look at me.'

I lock eyes with him as he rams into me one last time, and I let go, allowing my muscles free rein. A final wave of contractions surges its way through my vagina, while he spills himself into me.

'Fuck,' he cries out, slowing his rhythm and digging his face into my neck. 'Fuck.' He slows further while the aftershocks of my own orgasm clutch at him greedily.

Finally, he comes to a halt, still holding me tight. I skim my hands across his shoulders. They're covered in sweat now, and I must be covered in sweat too. Along with the obscenities I've scrawled in his diary, there are going to be some pretty questionable smear marks on the window come tomorrow morning. What on Earth is Carla going to think? He raises his head and grins at me. A wide open, boyish grin.

'That was fucking wonderful,' he sighs.

'I'm with you on that one,' I whisper, slowly gathering my senses. 'But just for the record, I'd like to get something straight.' He raises his eyebrows. 'I fucking own you too.'

Chapter Sixteen

The short drive along the south bank begins in silence. I gaze out of the window of the Mercedes, wondering what the hell's going on. After starting the day hating the man, I'm about to finish it off in his bed. It's an unspoken fact. And it feels like the most natural thing in the world.

'Are you okay?' he asks.

I bite my lip. Well, how do I answer that?

'You're very quiet.'

'I've had a strange day. I still can't work out why you blanked me last night.' I hear him take in a deep breath. 'Can't you just explain it?'

'I'm sorry and that's all you need to know. I'll make it up to you.'

'You'd better.'

We swing by a roundabout and out onto the embankment. Almost immediately, he takes a left, down into the basement of a huge apartment complex. He waits for the garage doors to open and then manoeuvres the Mercedes inside, pulling into his own space. I stay exactly where I am, taking in a few deep breaths of my own. Whatever happens tonight, something tells me there'll be no turning back from this, at least not without some major heartbreak. The door opens and I look up to find him standing there, holding out his hand to me. He's spent the entire afternoon treating me like crap, followed by taking his fill of me in full view of anyone on the south bank with superhuman vision, and now that's all swept away by an old-fashioned gentlemanly gesture. I can't help but smile as he draws me up and gathers me into his arms. Holding me tight, he touches his cheek against mine. His hard body is up against me and I can feel a thudding, a real honest to God thudding. And for once, it's not my heart. It's his.

'Thank you for this,' he whispers into my ear.

I lean my head back.

'Thank you for what?'

'For being with me.'

He smiles, and there's not a trace of the arrogant man from earlier. His eyes are vulnerable now, exactly like they were in my picture, and I find myself wondering just how long it's going to last, because I want this Dan tonight: the tender, caring, quiet gentleman.

'Come on.'

Unwrapping me, he takes hold of my hand, guiding me away from the garage and into a lift. He pulls me in close to his side as he punches in a code for the top floor. For a few seconds, we ride the lift in silence. When the doors open again, I step out into an entrance hall I barely remember from the last time I was here. I'm surrounded by white marble, and in front of me there's a dark wooden door. Letting go of my hand, he opens the door, gesturing for me to enter first. I find myself in a huge, open plan space that I can only vaguely recall: a kitchen, lined with sleek, grey cabinets, and beyond that, a living area. All I can see from here are two vast, cream-coloured sofas facing each other across a heavy, wooden coffee table and beyond that, an open fireplace.

'Wine?'

He puts his briefcase down and takes his mobile out of his jacket pocket, making a show of switching it off and throwing it onto the counter.

'Yes please.'

'I've got a Sancerre on the chill. Will that do?'

I nod, drop my bag to the floor and heave myself up onto a leather stool, one of four that are arranged around a granite breakfast bar. Watching as he shrugs off his jacket, throws it over another stool and saunters over to a stainless steel fridge, I decide right here and now that I'll never get enough of ogling that backside. And yes, it may well be pervy, but I just can't help it. The man's got the perfect ass. He pulls out a bottle of white, kicks the fridge door shut, grabs a couple of glasses from a cupboard and comes over to join me. I watch as he uncorks the bottle, fills my glass and hands it to me with a smile. I know that my fingers are shaking again as I grip the stem. I take a sip, examining my surroundings, and notice a pile of paperwork on the counter top.

'The factory closure in Tyneside,' he says quietly, sinking onto the stool next to mine. 'Redundancy deals. Nothing interesting.'

'I'll have to disagree with you on that one.'

His eyes widen for a moment before he fills his own glass.

'And why's that?'

'Because I happen to know you've organised some pretty generous redundancy packages.'

Nudging the glass to one side, he frowns.

'And how do you know about that?'

'Norman.'

'Bloody man.' He shakes his head.

'You didn't want me to know about it?'

'Of course not.'

'I thought ...'

His features soften. His mouth twitches slightly and then, while his face breaks out into a wide smile, he points a finger at me.

'You thought I did it just to get in your knickers.' He bites back a laugh. 'Well, I didn't. I was going to get in your knickers come what may. And besides, that's a pretty expensive way to woo a woman.'

'So, why did you do it?'

He rubs his chin. 'Because you made me think.'

While he turns his wine glass around, I fidget uncomfortably on my stool. I'm just not satisfied with his explanation. I need a bit more of an answer than that.

'But it's a bit out of character. I mean, for a mega-rich, power-hungry businessman like you ...'

Oh shit, I've gone and said the wrong thing there. That much is obvious because the frown to end all frowns has just spread itself across his face. I'm about to apologise when the clouds finally break.

'You really shouldn't go judging people before you know them, Miss Scotton.'

'No, I shouldn't. But these deals are out of the ordinary, and they're eating into your profits. I bet your head of Finance isn't too pleased about it.'

'Spot on.'

He takes a mouthful of wine and stares at me. So, that's it then? The real reason why Clive Watson doesn't like me? Because I've inadvertently persuaded the big kahuna to find a speck of humanity in himself? Well, that explains everything.

'I don't think he's too keen on me.' I've got my theory but I'd still like to gain some confirmation here. 'I just can't work out why.'

'I wouldn't worry about it. I'll deal with Clive. Now, why don't you go and have a look around?' He nods towards the lounge. 'It's time to start peeling away those layers.'

I glance around the apartment before turning back to face him.

'Go on,' he urges me. 'Go and have a nose.'

Picking up my glass, I make my way through to the living area. Ignoring everything else, I'm drawn straight towards the huge window that stretches the entire length of the room, reaching from the wooden floor right up to the high ceiling. It gives out over the Thames just like the window in his bedroom upstairs. To the right, I can see a bridge and across the river, the Houses of Parliament and Big Ben. A little further along I can just about catch the edge of the London Eye, while to the left, a forest of cranes spreads its way along the south side of the river bank. I turn and examine the room. It's simple and beautiful, made all the more so by the five huge oil paintings displayed around the walls. I hear myself gasp. Why didn't I notice those before? In a trance, I take a step forwards, gazing up at the pictures, one after the other. Landscapes and seascapes. All by different artists. Exactly the sort of thing I'd choose for my own home.

'Do you like them?'

I tear my attention away from a painting to find him standing nearby, glass in hand.

'I didn't notice these the other night.'

'I didn't give you much chance.'

He moves towards me.

'They're beautiful,' I murmur.

'They are. The one on the left there is by Phillipa Green.' He motions his glass towards a painting. 'I'm a fan of hers. I love the colours. And this one is by David Grant. You must know these people.'

'I know of them. I've seen their work in Slaters.'

'Which is where I bought these.'

He watches my face, gauging my reaction.

'You really are an art lover.'

'I guess it's my mother's influence.'

I shake my head in disbelief and he laughs.

'And you thought I was just some glorified builder.'

'An arrogant, sexist, glorified builder.' Oh shit, why did I have to say that? Wishing that I could suck the words back in, I take a look at him. Am I getting this right? Does he actually look wounded?

'Sometimes,' he mutters, 'people put on a front.'

And why would you need to put on a front, I'd like to ask. But I really shouldn't probe any further. The expression on his face tells me that.

'I don't know you, do I?' I ask instead.

'Not yet.'

I raise my glass again and hide behind a gulp of wine. Not yet? My mind is on the verge of spinning over what he means by that when he saves me from the bother.

'Why don't you go and slip into something a little more comfortable?'

'Slip into what?'

'One of my shirts. Go on. You can rummage through my wardrobe. I've got nothing to hide.' He nods towards an open wooden staircase that twists its way up towards some sort of balcony. 'First door on the left, remember?'

Placing my glass on the coffee table, I make my way up the stairs, knowing that he's watching me as I go. I can feel the heat of his eyes on the back of my body.

'And Maya,' he calls out as I reach the top step. I turn round and look back down at him. 'Just a shirt.' He winks. 'Nothing else.'

I waver for a moment, wondering whether or not I should tell him to get stuffed because nobody tells me what to wear, but yet again, my body seems to have broken ranks with my brain. Instead, I simply throw him a coy smile and nod before turning away to find myself confronted by a corridor: two doors on the left and two on the right. I'm sorely tempted to have a nosey round, but that would be going a little too far. Instead, I head straight for the first door on the left, right back into his bedroom.

After taking a moment or two to reacquaint myself with the room, I slowly undress, arranging my clothes on the chaise longue. At last, completely naked, I make my way across to the huge built in wardrobe, pulling open a door and discovering a range of perfectly ironed shirts in a myriad of colours, from white on the left, through greys, black, pale blue, pink and shades of purple on the right. I opt for a plain white shirt, shrugging it off its hanger and over my head, smelling its freshness, feeling its expensive quality. I'm about to close the wardrobe door when I notice a set of drawers to the right. So, how does he arrange his socks and his pants, I wonder. Just how anal is he about these things?

As soon as I open the first drawer, I suck in a breath and my heart decides to do a quick jig. The drawer doesn't contain socks and pants at all. Instead, it's lined with a black silk-like material, and it's filled with a strange collection of objects that I've only ever heard about before. I hold my breath, wondering what the hell I've got myself into.

My eyes have fallen straight onto a pair of leather cuffs.

'Is everything alright?'

His voice comes from behind me, pinning me into place, and I know he's close by. Another few seconds and I feel his chest against my back. My pulse has quickened now.

'I thought you said you had nothing to hide.'

The next few seconds drag by in silence.

'I don't,' he says at last. 'You already know something about my sexual preferences.'

Of course I do. But this?

'So, you keep these here for your women?'

'You're the first woman I've ever brought back to my apartment. And these are brand new.'

Brand new? Well, that can only mean one thing.

'You bought them for me?'

'I did. I picked them up on Saturday.'

Good God, he went straight from Slaters to a porno store.

'You were that confident?'

'Not confident. Just hopeful.' His body remains pressed against me, the heat of his chest coursing its way through my spine. 'I wasn't planning on introducing this tonight.'

Of course not, my brain whirls, because tonight you're playing the gentleman, not the dominant. But suddenly, I'm not entirely sure that I want the gentleman any more. At the sight of the cuffs, I'm beginning to tremble ... and it's not with fear.

'Close the drawer, Maya.'

My heart pounds in my chest. 'I don't want to close the drawer.' With an unsteady hand, I reach out and touch a leather cuff. His left arm snakes around my stomach, holding me fast, while his right hand covers mine for a moment or two before moving on. He picks up the cuff.

'Two for your wrists and two for your ankles. They attach to straps on the bed.'

'What straps?'

'Already in place. Just out of sight.' He places the cuff back down. His hand moves across the drawer to a strip of black silk. 'A blindfold, obviously.' His fingers move further, coming to rest against a piece of leather. 'And this is a basic gag.'

Jesus. All that talk about gagging me wasn't just talk after all?

'Why would you gag me?'

I feel him shrug. 'I like to have complete control. It's just my thing. To know that you can't speak, even if you want to, it turns me on.'

'Why?'

A silence descends over us and I realise that I'm not going to get an answer, not tonight.

'If you're not happy with it, then we don't go there.'

'I might ...'

'Just think about it.'

Nervously, I scan the drawer, my eyes landing on what seem to be two silver pegs attached by a length of silver chain. Each peg, I notice, has its own silver screw.

'Pain,' I breathe, sensing a twinge down below.

'If it's your thing, then it's your thing. If it's not, then so be it. I'll only go as far as you want me to. Those are nipple clamps. You enjoyed it the other day. I bought them just in case you wanted to try it again. They can be adjusted to whatever you want to take. All of this can be pleasurable.'

'You've used all of this stuff before? Your modus operandi?'

'My preference. I didn't hide that from you.'

My heartbeat starts to pick up in pace.

'You said that you'd dabbled. BDSM.'

'I did.'

'Tell me about it.'

His grip tightens. His breath becomes shallow for a moment, and then he seems to regain control. I wish I could see his face now. I need to work out what's going on in his mind. But it's impossible. I'm held firmly in place against his chest.

'It doesn't matter,' he says at last. 'I've done some pretty hard core stuff, but that's all over now. All you need to know is that it was always done with consent.'

'And what did you get out of it?'

'A level of gratification at the time, but it never lasted. This is all pretty soft to be honest with you, but it can bring intense pleasure.' I feel his lips against my neck. Brushing a trail behind my ear, they send a spark of anticipation right down to my groin. 'It's too soon.'

As he reaches down to shut away the contents, I watch in surprise as my own hand shoots out to stop him.

'No,' I whisper. 'It's not too soon.'

His hand hovers in mid-air, wavering there for a few seconds, waiting for me to change my mind until finally, when I don't, it returns to the cuffs. He rests a finger against the leather, and I listen to his breathing. It's sharper now.

'Maya, don't blunder into something you're not sure about.'

'I'm not blundering. I want to try it.'

For a few seconds more, he holds me exactly where I am, his left arm tight around my stomach. I feel his heartbeat pounding against my spine and all I can hear now is my own nervous breathing, jittering, each breath catching against the next.

'So be it. Give me your hand.'

I raise my left hand, watching intently as he takes it in his fingers, slowly wrapping the cuff around my wrist. One by one, he fastens the buckles, checking that the leather isn't too tight against my skin.

'Other one.'

Repeating the process, he motions for me to present my right hand. Sliding the leather around my skin, he fastens the buckles and checks for comfort. When he's finally satisfied, his fingers close around the cuffs, pausing there for a moment before he reaches out and picks up the blindfold. I watch as he straightens it out in front of my eyes, as the black silk is brought closer to my face. And then I'm plunged into darkness, the fabric soft against my skin. He knots it at the back of my head, just tight enough that it won't move.

'Does that feel okay?'

'Yes.'

The next thing I know, the shirt is pulled over my head. I'm lifted up in his arms and carried over to the bed. He lays me down gently, sweeping my hair out of my face and running a finger down the side of my cheek. I'm left where I am for a minute or so, but judging by the sounds I can hear now, he's taking off his clothes.

'Put your hands up, Maya.'

I do exactly as I'm told, my mouth drying up with anticipation. The bed lowers as he climbs onto it, settling himself by my side. Within seconds, I feel his warmth next to me, his skin against mine. One hand is manoeuvred into place behind my head, and then the other. He repositions himself above me, and I hear a clink of metal, the shifting of straps. My wrists are tethered into place, my arms pulled tight as the cuffs are adjusted. He takes his time, making sure that everything is perfect, that I'm completely comfortable.

'You look beautiful like this.' He traces a finger from my neck, down the centre of my torso. The finger pauses at my stomach, swirling its way lazily around my belly button before travelling further downwards, skirting the insides of my thighs. I let out a groan as flickers of electricity travel throughout my body.

'Spread your legs. Further.'

Again, I do as I'm told. Again, the bed moves. I hear his footsteps padding away from me, then back again.

'I'd like to restrain your legs. Are you okay with that?'

Am I? I have no idea. I'm already blindfolded with my hands pinned down by cuffs and straps. Well, what difference is it going to make? I nod mutely and immediately, a strip of leather is wound around my left ankle, and then another around my right. I sense the sudden resistance as the straps are attached and gradually tightened until he's happy with my position. With another movement, he's back by my side. His lips touch against mine and then close over my mouth, his tongue swirling slowly, lazily around mine for an age. A hand cups my cheek before working its way around my neck, a warm palm here, fingertips there.

'You need a safeword,' he breathes against my mouth. 'Something you're going to be able to drag out of your head when you can't think straight.'

Fingers stroke their way slowly down my neck, across my right breast, pausing to explore my nipple. They move on, downwards across my stomach, sending tingles of pleasure throughout my body, and then further, patiently stroking my crotch over and over again before his hand closes around my clit, pressing in on me, setting off a flood tide of spasms. I strain against the cuffs, wanting instinctively to bring my legs together.

'Safeword, Maya,' he reminds me. 'You say it, I stop.'

I can barely think straight as it is, but he seems determined to get a safeword out of me. I fumble through the jumbled mess that is my mind, and all I can think of is that stupid, bloody machine in his office.

'Coffee!' I splurt.

I hear him chuckle.

'Coffee, it is.'

His lips travel downwards, kissing my throat, my chest, working their way slowly, languidly in towards my nipples. He takes the left nipple first, sucking and lapping at it tenderly, sending waves of electricity coursing through my body, right down to my stomach, and further to my clitoris. I hear myself moan like some sort of wanton hussy as he moves on to my right nipple, repeating the same process, slowly, patiently cupping my breast with his hand, gently massaging it as he sucks and licks and nips.

'You enjoyed the pain yesterday,' he whispers.

'I did.' Jesus. Where did that come from?

'Do you want it again?'

'I do.'

What? Did I really just say that? Before I can take it all back and ask if I can possibly have a little time to think about the whole pain thing, he latches onto my nipple, gripping it between his teeth. I cry out as I'm hit by a wall of agony. My mind is emptied of doubt in a split second. He bites again, holding my stomach down with his hand. I cry out again, tugging at the cuffs, holding onto my breath, waiting for it all to subside.

'No more,' I manage to gasp, my breath coming in shorter spurts, my entire body quaking at the after effects of his onslaught. 'Not yet.'

Somewhere at the back of my head a voice screams out at me. And I know it's my own voice, my reasonable, logical voice. And it's doing its utmost to be heard. You need time to think your way through this, lady! Why the hell did you just enjoy abject pain? Are you a masochist? Because if you are, then Jesus, you must be really fucking screwed up!

'No more,' he confirms, lapping his tongue against my nipple, soothing it before he begins to run his lips slowly downwards.

Adjusting his body above me, he comes to rest between my legs. I'm still trying to control my breathing when his big hands wrap themselves around my waist. He skims his palms up and down my sides, over and over again, finally bringing them down to my legs. Closing his fingers tight around me, he digs his thumbs into the insides of my thighs. I tense immediately, unsure of where he's going with this. He keeps me there for a few seconds before finally releasing his hold. I feel his warm breath against my stomach, and then his lips, gently fluttering against my skin, sending tiny tremors through my nerves. I hear myself moan. I try to writhe about. It's instinctive, but he stops me immediately, pushing me back into place and digging his thumbs into my thighs one more time. It's almost uncomfortable, but strangely pleasurable. It's his silent command and I stop moving immediately. Those thumbs are going to send me into a spin if he does that one more time. Another movement. And finally, his tongue trails lightly along the length of my clit, once, twice. On the third run, it pauses to lap at my labia. I moan again. My muscles spasm.

'Please,' I groan. 'I need you inside me.'

'No talking.'

A hand curls around my thigh, squeezing a reminder into my skin. His tongue returns to my clit, gently circling, working me up into a frenzied mess. I try to squirm but my legs won't budge and a hand comes to rest on my stomach, holding me firmly in place.

'You'll do this my way.'

Almost immediately, a finger is thrust into my vagina. It's withdrawn and replaced with two. I cry out, not with pain, but with shock at the sudden change of tactic. The tongue returns to my clit while the fingers work at the front of my vagina, finding that magic spot and slowly massaging me out of my mind. He must be able to feel the spasms, to judge when I'm about to come because just as I'm about to implode, he stops.

'Let's keep you on the edge for a while.'

I know that he's above me now. The mattress dips at either side of my head. I feel his warm breath against my face.

'Taste yourself.' A finger enters my mouth and I suck greedily. He takes it out, running it along my lips, and then he kisses me again, lowering his body onto mine, his hand cupping the back of my head, gripping a handful of hair and holding me still while he rubs his erection against me. This alone is going to send me wild. I can't grind back. It's impossible.

'What do you want, Maya?' he whispers into my mouth, his voice loaded with desire.

'I want you.'

'Not good enough.'

He presses another kiss into my mouth, forcing his cock against my groin. I could scream already.

'What do you want?'

'I want you to fuck me,' I pant.

'What's the magic word?'

'Please.'

He sits up. I feel his hands on my clit again, probing at my opening, examining my lips, slowly separating them, sliding a finger part way in and then out again. Oh God. He's having a good look at me. I know he is. If I wasn't restrained, I'd squirm with embarrassment. He seems to pick up on my unease.

'Relax,' he murmurs. 'It's nothing to be shy about, Maya. You're beautiful, every last bit of you.'

The fingers return to my vagina, working slowly. And they're joined this time by a third, on the outside, working at my clit. He's still kneeling up between my legs and, oh God, he's watching me. I know it. It seems to go on for an age. Nothing is said. I listen to my breathing as it grows faster, more shallow. He doesn't seem to tire. Keeping up the same rhythm, the same pace, he waits patiently as the pressure rises deep inside me. I'm on the verge of exploding when the fingers are removed.

'No!' I cry out. 'Why? Let me come now.'

I struggle against the bindings. In an instant, he moves again and I'm gripped by the chin.

'When I say.'

The fingers return, more this time, maybe three, and they thrust deeper, stretching me, probing, exploring, feeling out for my reaction. At last he gets what he wants. Somewhere deeper inside, he's found another spot. He focuses on it now, taking his time, working at it slowly so that the pressure inside me builds to the point of explosion. I try to writhe again. His hand push me down again.

'No,' I gasp. 'I can't take much more.'

'You know what to say.'

His tongue returns to my clit, working me towards the edge, from the outside as well as the inside. My brain has emptied itself out now. I'm in a stupor. And I'm covered with sweat. I can barely catch my breath.

'This is fucking beautiful.'

'Please ... let me ...'

'Shush.'

I can barely think any more. I certainly can't string a sentence together. Why can't the fucking man just let me come?

'Do you want me to finish this, Maya?'

'Yes ...'

His fingers come to a halt.

'Maybe I will,' he whispers. 'But then again, maybe I'll keep you going like this for an hour or so.'

'No,' I groan. 'I'll die.'

I hear him laugh gently.

'Then all you need to do is say you'll give yourself up to me.'

'What? Why?'

Is that it? Is he torturing me into true submission?

'Because it's what I need. Complete control. And you haven't given that to me yet.'

'But, I ...'

His fingers edge inside me one more time, moving slowly, picking up where they left off. I sense the beginning of contractions deep inside, delicious, aching. And already, I know he won't let me see them through unless I give him what he wants.

'Give yourself to me.'

'Yes,' I splutter. 'But only in bed. In bed. Only in bed.' I may be a mess right now, and shit this really is pleasure on a grand scale, mind-fucking pleasure, but I'm not about to give up on any of my basic human rights.

'Or wherever else I decide to fuck you senseless.'

'Okay!' I shout. 'Yes! Yes, I do!'

The fingers are withdrawn.

'No,' I cry. 'I said yes! Don't stop!'

'I'm not stopping. You wanted me to fuck you. Remember your word.'

I barely have time to choke back a cry before he's inside me, hitting the back wall of my vagina, knocking the breath clean out of my body. He withdraws, right to the hilt, before ramming into me again ... and again, relentlessly, viciously, like a machine. Before long, the pressure is back, every single muscle down below on the verge of an explosion. My body can't cope with much more of this.

'Dan! For God's sake!' I scream.

'Make as much noise as you want. No one can hear you.'

He picks up the pace now, the strength of his blows remaining hard, moving at a frenzied speed. I hold on, trying desperately to find something, anything to keep me from being torn apart. I can barely make it when he finally cries out.

'Now, Maya!'

I implode, and while I gasp and claw for breath, convulsion after convulsion rips its way through my insides, electric shocks shimmering across my nerves. I moan incoherently as he collapses on top of me, his body straddling mine. Struggling for breath, he buries his head in my neck.

'Fucking hell,' he mutters. 'Fucking perfect.'

He stays inside me for an age, his penis throbbing its way down from his orgasm. At last, I feel him move, steadying himself while he takes off the blindfold. I blink a few times and I'm rewarded with a beautiful, full on smile. 'My woman likes it kinky,' he grins.

'I think I do,' I pant. 'Shit, why has it never been like that before?'

'You've not lived.'

'And this is soft?'

'Believe me, it is.'

'So, what's hard core?'

The smile dissolves.

'I told you. I don't want to talk about that. I've left that world behind.'

He brushes his lips against mine, kissing me softly before he pulls himself out of me. I'm still twitching and pulsing inside. He cups my clitoris, patiently massaging me down, staring into my eyes the whole time. At last, he reaches down and releases my legs, then leans over and releases my arms. I manoeuvre myself into his embrace, my back against his chest, feeling his cooling sweat. His arms close around me. His right hand slides over mine and he begins to interlace our fingers.

'I need to tell you something,' he whispers.

'What's that?'

'I'm never going to get enough of you.' He runs a hand gently across my breasts, down to my stomach and I grin like an idiot. 'This isn't asset stripping.'

I want to turn my head and examine his expression, to see if it's as serious as the tone he's just taken on, but I'm held tight against him, as if he's scared to let me go.

'What is it then?' I ask.

'Mergers.' He pauses. 'And acquisitions.'

Another silence cloaks us while I try to soak up what he's just said.

'Who's acquiring who?' I ask.

He doesn't answer.

'Are you hungry?'

'Starving.' I yawn. My eyelids are heavy. 'And I'm knackered too. I actually had to do some work today.'

I hear him chuckle.

'You're a hard task master, Mr Foster,' I murmur.

'I've not even started yet,' he murmurs back and although I know he's smiling again, I'm not entirely sure that he's referring to office work, and I'm not completely certain that it's really a joke. 'Close your eyes for a while. Have a rest.'

I do as I'm told. And I'm fine with that, because right now all I really want to do is sleep. And I want to sleep in his arms.

Chapter Seventeen

When I open my eyes again, I stretch out a hand, only to find that the bed's empty. He's not here. Noticing that I've been covered up with a silky, cream coloured throw, I lean up on my elbows and gaze out of the window. Now, either that's a sunset or it's dawn. And considering the fact that I feel thoroughly refreshed and distinctly ravenous, I'm willing to bet on the latter. Heaving myself out of bed, I make my way over to the window and peer at the clock face on Big Ben. Yes, it is dawn. In fact, it's nearly half past four and streaks of red are already beginning to nudge their way across London's rooftops.

I glance around the bedroom, discovering that he's tidied up. Even my own pile of clothes on the chaise longue has been refolded, only neatly this time. I smile to myself. So, the man's used to control and order and tidiness. Well, if he's letting me into his world, then he's got an awful big shock on the way. Moving over to the wardrobe, I open it up and select a fresh, white shirt. I pull it on and make my way downstairs to find him. The kitchen and living area are empty, but the glass doors that lead out from the kitchen onto a verandah are open, and I can see him out there. Dressed in a pair of jogging bottoms and a grey T-shirt, he's leaning against a low wall, gazing out across the Thames. I tiptoe my way to the threshold and pause, careful not to let him know that I'm nearby. I want a glimpse of Daniel Foster unguarded, and I want to know what the hell he's up to, dragging himself out of bed at this time in the morning. To his left, there's an expensive looking set of outdoor furniture: two sunbeds, one raised into a sitting position, and a low, black marble table where a laptop has been left open next to a coffee cup. I edge my way forwards now, close enough to see that his hands are clasped on the wall in front of him, that his lips are parted slightly, and that his eyes seem lost. The moody, overworked businessman is gone. And so is the controlling, arrogant sex fiend. All I can see now in front of me is loneliness, and all I want to do is wrap my arms around him.

'Dan?'

He gives a start and turns. Immediately, a smile spreads across his face, masking the loneliness, shutting it away from view.

'What are you doing?'

'Watching the sun come up.' He holds out an arm, beckoning for me to join him. I shuffle forwards into his embrace. It's warm and cosy and comfortable. He wraps an arm around me and pulls me against his chest, turning me towards the river.

'I didn't want to wake you,' he nuzzles into my ear. 'I had some work to do.' His arm tightens and it's a good couple of minutes before he speaks again. 'Look at that. It's beautiful.'

The morning sun begins to pour its warmth across the rooftops.

'It is beautiful,' I whisper back.

'You should paint it one day. Capture the light.'

I shrug my shoulders.

'Do you watch the sun come up every morning?' I ask.

'In the summer, yes, most days. I love the way colour comes back into the world.'

'Very poetic,' I laugh. He rewards me with a pinch.

'Every day is a new beginning.' I turn back to find him squinting across the river. 'This is the first time I've shared this view.'

I feel a rush of warmth in my heart, and suddenly I'm brave. 'Just now ... I was watching you. You looked a bit ... I don't know ... lost.'

His arms grow tense. I hear him sigh. 'I'm fine.' He turns me round. Fixing me with a grip on either arm, he locks me in with his eyes. 'Promise me you won't run again.'

So is that it? He's worried that he's going to lose me?

'I'm not going anywhere.'

He nods slowly, lowers his face to mine and kisses me gently, sweetly. When he pulls back, he gazes into my eyes.

'So, what have you been up to?' I nod towards the laptop.

'Finalising a presentation. We're bidding for a project in Scotland. I need to go up there for a couple of days. I'm leaving this afternoon.'

'Okay.'

My heart slumps. Already, I'm wondering how on Earth I'm going to survive more than a few hours apart from him. But that's the nature of his job and the nature of his business. If I'm going to be sticking around, then I guess I'll just have to get used to it.

'I didn't say anything before,' he goes on. 'I didn't think I needed to. But now ... well.' He reaches up and moves my hair back from my face. 'What are you doing this weekend?'

'Nothing planned.'

'Then you're spending it with me.' He squeezes my arm. 'I get back early on Saturday morning. Give me a chance to get changed and then I'll come and pick you up.' He kisses my forehead. 'Wear jeans and a T-shirt.'

I scowl up at him and he digs me in the side, causing me to giggle. He smiles for a moment, then leans down, softly touching his lips against mine, coaxing them to open. I groan in pleasure as his hands skim over my shoulders and around my back. My own hands travel up his back, feeling their way across his shoulders, down to his waist and his firm backside.

'You need some food inside you,' he whispers.

'I need some you inside me.'

'Filthy woman. Are you demanding sex?'

'I think I am. Does that get me a spank?'

'Not this morning.'

Before I can ask if he's sure about that, he lifts the shirt over my head and drops it to the floor. He sighs contentedly and cups my right breast, working his hands round and round, stopping every now and then to pull gently at my nipple. I glance around, anxiously checking for nosy neighbours.

'Don't worry, Maya. No one can see.'

He leans in for a long, deep kiss and a shimmer of excitement runs through my veins. Moving his right hand to my crotch, he begins to circle a finger slowly against my clitoris, while his tongue works its way around my mouth. I feel his left hand on my back, surprised by its warmth. I pull his T-shirt over his head while he shrugs off his joggers, revealing a huge morning erection.

'Somebody's pleased to see me,' I smile.

'He's always pleased to see you. And he wants you from behind. Right here, holding onto this wall.'

He spins me round and while I rest my hands against the wall, he gently eases my legs apart. Clamping one arm around my stomach, he begins to massage my clitoris, circling his finger slowly in exactly the right spot. I close my eyes and moan into the cold, morning air, sensing that familiar thrum of pleasure as it sparks into life. I feel the warm palm of his free hand as it touches the base of my spine and then tracks its way up towards my neck. He leans forwards, his erection pressing against my backside. I'm getting goose bumps, and

I don't know whether it's from the building excitement, or the chill in the air. His lips dance across my skin, warm by comparison, and silky soft.

'Ready?' he asks quietly.

'Ready.'

Both hands are removed from my body and I miss them immediately. He guides my legs further apart and his fingers slip between my thighs, running lightly down the space between my back passage and my vagina. He pushes a finger inside, making sure that I'm as good as my word.

'You're so wet, Maya. Do I excite you that much?'

'Yes, you bloody well do,' I groan.

'And you excite me too. I can barely control myself when I'm with you. Do you want me to fuck you now?'

'Yes, please!' I half shout.

The end of his cock nudges at my opening and he enters me, slowly, edging his way inside, moving his hands to my hips and holding me firm.

'Hang on to that wall,' he warns me.

I pull my hands back, holding on to the edge of the parapet. And then he begins, driving all the way in, filling me up completely. My breath comes in short gasps as he withdraws and pushes again. He picks up the rhythm, pulling out and thrusting back inside me, never missing a beat. And oh God, the pressure builds quickly until I don't know if I can bear it any longer, but I know the deal now. I have to hang on until he tells me it's time. He wants us to come together, and I'm going to see that it happens. He grips me harder and the thrusting comes to a halt. What the hell's going on now? Slowly, he grinds himself around. It's agonising, but wonderful. The pressure subsides and a new, deeper sensation takes its place. I cry out and tighten my grip on the wall. My insides must be lighting up like a Christmas tree now. He's dragging this out, prolonging the pleasure for both of us. At last, just when I'm at the point of screaming out for him to finish me off, he launches back into his relentless pounding, ratcheting up the speed and the power.

'Now!' he cries out.

I let go for all I'm worth, and while he explodes inside me, I'm blown away by an onslaught of sensations. Everything is pulsating now, everything quivering. My arms are weak and my head is light. My knees buckle beneath me and his hands tighten around my hips, steadying me.

'Woah, woman!'

He withdraws and pulls me upright, holding me close against his chest.

'Are you okay?'

'Yes,' I gasp. 'You nearly fucked me unconscious.'

Still panting, still trying to wrestle his breath back under control, he laughs.

'I told you, you need some food inside you. I bet you haven't eaten since yesterday morning.'

I scramble through my brain, only to find that he's absolutely right. In almost twenty four hours, I've had nothing but a slice of toast.

'Look at that.' He waves a hand at the scene in front of us.

I gaze out over the river to where a sheen of soft, bright sunlight tumbles across the rooftops. Gently lifting London back out of the shadows, it winks its way across the windows, casting a soft, golden glow against stonework.

'A new beginning,' he murmurs. 'The colour's back.'

The sunlight tumbles further, over the water, dancing and flipping its way from the north bank to the south. So, what does he mean by that? A new beginning for us? And is this a relationship? I'd like to ask, but it's probably too soon. I turn to find him gazing out over the river, a smile on his soft lips, and I feel new sensation in my heart, as if it's swelling, as if my rib cage isn't going to be able to contain it for much longer. It can't be possible. This must be some sort of chemical reaction because it's way too soon for the L word. And how long have I known him now? It's hardly long enough for that.

'I need a shower.' I lean my head back into his chest. In actual fact, I don't want to move at all. A curious calm has descended over me and I just want to stay here all day.

'A shower?' he grins down at me. 'I've got one of those.'

He leads me inside, back upstairs and into the en-suite. He turns on the shower, checks the temperature and then motions for me to enter. As soon as I'm under the warm rush of water, his hands circle my waist, gently feeling their way across my contours. He turns me round and tips my head upwards so that my eyes meet his, landing a soft kiss on my lips before he reaches for the body wash. Squeezing out a handful, he begins to massage my shoulders, working his way downwards, covering every single square inch of my torso, working from my back, round to my front, smoothing his palms up my stomach and out over my breasts. Finally, he washes between my legs and I'm on fire immediately, groaning like a hussy. His free hand cups the back of my head. Pulling me in towards him, he covers my lips with his mouth, grinding his kiss into me as he kneads his palm against my clitoris. His hard body is against mine, his taut muscles pressing against me firmly. He urges my legs further apart and I feel him against my opening. Jesus, he wants more? Well, he can go ahead, because I definitely do. I open wider and he enters me, pushing me back against the cold tiles.

He thrusts deep inside me and I clasp my arms around his shoulders, clinging on for dear life. He's clearly in the mood for hard. He thrusts again and I yelp at the force. He's pounding me now, right up to my limit. Picking up the pace, he thrusts again and again, sliding me up the tiles and then back down, finding a spot immediately, his cock moving over it, working me up into a pulsating knot inside.

'Hold on,' he growls into my ear.

He withdraws to the hilt and pauses, staring into my eyes. Just that look could send me over the edge. I try my damnedest to control myself, but a wave of heat is already rising in my groin. He thrusts deeper this time, withdraws and thrusts again.

'Shit ... I ...'

He covers my mouth again, pounding harder while I clutch at his shoulders, trying to gain some sort of hold. At last, he pulls his mouth away and locks eyes with me. And I don't know how it happens, but I know instinctively that he's right on the edge. He holds his breath, his mouth open, every muscle in his body tightened in pleasure. I let go with all my might. My muscles spasm and clutch at his cock, holding on to him greedily as he comes inside me.

'Bloody hell,' he breathes, digging his head into my neck. 'I'm never going to get into work at this rate.'

He holds me against the tiles, still twitching inside me

'Well that's your own fault,' I taunt him.

'I only meant to wash you down. As soon as I touched you, I had to go the whole fucking way.'

'You should exercise a little more self-control.'

'That's impossible when you're around.' He pulls himself out of me. 'Come here.'

He turns me to face away from him and begins to massage shampoo into my hair.

'Don't let me see your boobs again, or I'll want another go.' He rinses my hair and then steps under the water himself. 'You'd better get out. Dry yourself down and get dressed quickly, before I get another hard on.'

I dry myself off with an unbelievably huge, luxurious towel and then I wrap it around myself. He's out of the shower quickly. I'm just about to squeeze toothpaste on my finger and run it around in my mouth when he signals for me to stop. Rummaging around in some space age bathroom cabinet, he takes out a spare toothbrush. I use it. He takes it from me and places it in the holder, next to his own. While he shaves, I return to the bedroom and drag a comb through my hair, cursing its length and promising myself that I'm going to get it cut soon. He produces a hairdryer and I set myself to the task of getting my locks into some order. Finally satisfied that I'm vaguely presentable from the neck up, I put on yesterday's clothes and take myself down to the kitchen. I find him seated at the breakfast bar, looking delectable in one of his trademark black suits. He watches me over the rim of his coffee cup.

'What can I get you to eat?' he asks.

'Toast, please.'

'But you've barely eaten anything.' He gets up from the stool. 'What you need is a full English fry-up.'

'Toast will do just fine.'

Shrugging his shoulders, he sets about retrieving bread from a cupboard and popping it into a toaster. It's the most mundane act in the world, but Jesus, I could get used to this, watching a sex god making me toast first thing in the morning.

'Coffee?'

I nod, ogling his backside as he takes a cup from a cupboard, places it under the spout of a coffee machine and presses a button. 'I'm afraid it only does Americano, unless I recalibrate the fucking thing and kick it a few times.' I avert my eyes quickly when he turns and brings the coffee over, positioning it on the worktop in front of me. He kisses me gently on the cheek and a shimmer passes right through my body. Oh yes, I could definitely get used to this. 'I'll take you up to Camden,' he says. 'We've got time. You'll need a clean pair of knickers.'

'That's thoughtful of you.'

'If you were a man, you'd just turn them inside out and wear them for another day.'

'Yeuch.' I screw up my face. 'That's disgusting.'

'You know, you could always leave some clothes here.' He glances away, out of the window. Looking distinctly uncomfortable, he unfastens the top button of his shirt.

'I could do.'

'I mean ... if you're going to be round here on a regular basis ...'

If I'm going to be round here on a regular basis? My heart skips several beats. Now, I'm pretty sure that's not womaniser talk. In fact, I'm absolutely sure that's relationship talk.

Chapter Eighteen

An hour later, I lower myself into the leather passenger seat of the Mercedes, safe and cosy in its sumptuous luxury. It's early and we make it to Camden in good time. He parks the car right outside my flat, in spite of my warnings about killer traffic wardens. Inside, I lead him to my bedroom where he settles himself on my bed, leaning back against the headboard with his legs stretched out in front of him and his arms crossed lazily behind his head. I stare at him for a moment, taking in every last bit of his male perfection, wondering how I've managed to land a man like this. And as if he's read my thoughts, he narrows his eyes back at me.

'Knickers,' he snaps. 'No more sex.'

'Selfish bastard.'

I click my tongue in disgust and set about finding clean underwear. While I'm at it, I change into the clean skirt and blouse that Lucy's left for me. When I've finished, I turn back to find him staring intently at the family photographs that I keep on my bedside table. He reaches over, selecting one in particular, and picks it up for closer inspection.

'Who's this?'

He turns the photo and I shake my head.

'Who do you think?'

He turns the photo back towards himself. His lips seem to twitch.

'Your sister.'

'The one and only. She was about ten in that picture.'

He stares at the photograph for a long time, running his index finger across his lips, deep in thought.

'You said she was better looking than you,' he says at last.

I open my underwear drawer and search through its contents, finally settling on a pair of black, lacy knickers. Once he sees me in these, he might just change his mind about the 'no more sex' thing.

'She was, and she still is,' I mutter. Pulling off yesterday's pair, I sling them into a corner.

'You're wrong,' he says quietly. Suddenly, his tone has changed. When I look up, I find his eyes fixed on me, examining me. 'You're the beautiful one.'

I don't know how it happens. In a heartbeat, my happy mood is swept aside, replaced by emotions I thought were dead and buried long ago. I'm the beautiful one? No way is that statement correct. I'm inferior to my sister in just about every possible way. Salt water stings its way into my eyes. Oh no, I will myself, do not cry in front of him.

'Just leave it.'

'Maya, it's true.'

I shake my head again. He's skirting far too close to my weak spot, and all I want him to do is back away.

'You said she was better looking than you. She's not. You said she was more popular than you. I'm betting that she wasn't.'

Oh God, he's not giving up on this any time soon. If he's not careful, he's going to ruin a perfect morning, good and proper.

'She had friends. Lots of friends,' I explain. 'I'm telling you, Dan. She was the Queen bee where we lived.'

'And why was that?'

'Is this important?'

'It could be.'

I pause.

'I don't want to talk about it,' I say tartly, bending over and stepping into my fresh underwear.

He frowns at the photograph. 'She was probably confident. That's all. Over confident, in fact. And most of those friends only hung around with her because she had a certain power over them.'

I pull the knickers up and turn my back on him. First the coffee shop. Then the posh restaurant. And now here. It's one thing to show a passing interest in someone's family but this is beyond the pale. For the life of me, I can't work out why he's so intent on dragging this particular demon out of the shadows.

'Please leave it,' I whisper.

Teardrops begin to gather. They're queuing up now, waiting impatiently to cause a scene. And finally he seems to have noticed.

He turns to one side, replaces the picture on the table, and when he looks back up at me, a new softness has crossed his features.

'I'm sorry,' he says gently. 'I've gone too far.' Getting to his feet, he edges his way around the bed and draws me into his arms. 'It was wrong of me to say those things.'

And that's all it takes. One simple, tender act and I begin to sob. Digging my head into his jacket, I feel his arms close protectively around me. I have no idea how long I spend there, but when I finally tilt my head back, there's a huge wet patch on his shoulder.

'What's that?' he asks, nodding towards the corner of the room.

Evidently, while I've been crying my heart out into his tailored suit, he's been busy thinking about something else. Releasing me, he moves away, leans down and retrieves the canvas from behind the crate. He stands it against a wall, positions himself on the edge of the bed, and stares at it.

'I started again.' I wipe the last of the tears from my cheek.

'Where is it?'

'It could be anywhere, I suppose. But in my mind, it's a place on the outskirts of the town I grew up in. It's not finished yet.'

He motions for me to sit between his legs. Obediently, I manoeuvre myself into place and feel his arms around me, his chin resting on my shoulder.

'It's beautiful. You need to finish it.'

I suck in a shaky breath.

'I will.'

'Tell me about this place.'

'It's just woodland, that's all. It's pretty near the primary school, but not many kids went in there. They all said it was haunted ... but I knew it wasn't. It was a kind of sanctuary for me.'

'A sanctuary?'

I try my best to swallow back a sob. This is a part of my life that I've always managed to keep closed away from prying minds. Even Lucy has no idea what I was like as a child. But Daniel Foster is about to find out because just about everywhere he treads, he manages to open me up. I simply have no choice in the matter.

'From feeling different,' I say at last. 'I was a dreamer. I used to paint and draw. I used to read a lot too. The other kids thought I was weird. I never felt comfortable around them.' I point at the painting. 'I used to go there when things got too much for me.'

'Sanctuary,' he murmurs.

The next few seconds drag by in silence, and while my cheeks are tickled by yet another handful of tears, he holds me firmly, brushing his fingers against my arm in slow, reassuring movements. At last, his right arm releases me and I turn to find that he's pulled his mobile from his jacket pocket. He gazes into my eyes as he begins to speak.

'Carla, this is your boss. I'll be in late this morning. As soon as you get this message, clear my commitments until eleven o'clock. If anyone asks why I'm not in, tell them to mind their own fucking business. Oh, and Carla, just ignore anything strange you find in the diary.'

He scowls at his phone and touches the end-call icon.

'What's going on?' I ask.

'You heard me. I'm not about to leave you alone when you're all upset, and especially not when I've caused it. We'll drop the car back at my place. I'll get the concierge to taxi my things over to the office, and then we'll walk in. Slowly. Stopping off for coffee. I need to make sure you're alright before I leave.'

***

After a record-breaking drive back to his apartment, I find myself leaning against the wall of the south embankment, staring out across the water at the Millbank Tower. And right by my side, Daniel Foster is propped up on his elbows, arms crossed, quietly examining my face. I'd half expected to be dragged back up to his apartment for another dose of sex. But true to his word, he arranged for his briefcase and suitcase to be taken over to the office, and then he guided me straight outside.

'Are you sure about this?' I ask.

'Of course.'

'But your work ...'

'Sod work.'

In the morning sun, his eyes are brighter than I've ever seen them before. I take a moment or two to get lost in them, staring at the dark blue circles that edge their way around his irises. Fraying here and there, they bleed inwards through a paler blue, towards the tiny flecks of gold that are gathered round his pupils like iron filings around a magnet.

'So, what shall we talk about?' he asks, tugging me out of my swoon.

I shrug.

'No idea.'

'How well do you know this side of the river?'

'I know bits of it. I'm a north side girl really.'

'Woman,' he corrects me quickly.

'Woman,' I laugh.

'Well, we'll have to change that. I'm going to transform you into a south side woman. What do you think about that?' He nudges his arm against mine and my heart valves malfunction for a split second. Relationship talk, my brain calls out. That was definitely relationship talk!

'Try your best.' I'm going to be cool about this if it kills me.

'Okay, I will. In fact, I'm going to give you a guided tour, starting with where I live.' He turns and leans back against the wall. 'This is the Albert Embankment and that …' he nods up at his penthouse apartment, 'is Lambeth House. Store that away in your head for future reference, Miss Scotton. You'll be coming here a lot.'

There's a ping from his mobile. With a deep sigh, he takes it out of his pocket and opens up a message. He frowns, bites his lip, shakes his head slightly and then drops the phone back into his pocket. The message has bothered him. That much is obvious.

'Who was that?'

'Nobody worth bothering with.'

He shrugs off my question, distracted by the sight of a young couple who stroll past us in the morning sun, holding hands. He watches them for a few seconds before he stares down at his right hand, lifting it slightly, examining it as if it doesn't really belong to the rest of his body. Finally, he thrusts the hand out towards me. With a smile, I place my fingers in his, feeling them close around my skin, sending a warm, delicious tingle right to my centre.

'Come on then,' he says. 'We'd better get moving.'

With my hand firmly clasped in his, he leads me on. We cross a road and continue down a walkway that's dotted with wrought iron benches.

'Lambeth Palace.' He waves a hand to the right. 'I don't know what it's for. And that's a bunch of nut jobs.' He points out across the river, towards the Houses of Parliament.

'This is really informative, Mr Foster. Thank you. Just like a real guided tour.'

'Don't be sarcastic. Remember the situation.'

He points down at the bulge in his crotch.

'I'm sorry.'

'If you get cheeky with me this morning, Miss Scotton, I'll have to cancel my trip to Edinburgh, take you back home and fuck you senseless. And that would be one hell of an expensive fuck.'

'Edinburgh?' I stop in my tracks, wavering next to a bench and gazing up at a streetlamp. Even now, after all this time, the mere mention of the place sends a shiver skittering its way up my spine. 'I didn't know you were going to Edinburgh.'

His eyebrows dip into a frown. 'Is that a problem?'

'No, of course not.'

'It's where you studied. It should hold some fond memories for you.'

It does, I want to tell him. And some bad ones too. But there are just some doors that you're never going to open, Mr Foster, so don't even ask about it. He studies my face for a moment, and I know that he's suspicious.

'Another time.' He squeezes my hand and leads me further on down the embankment.

We cross Westminster Bridge, moving on past the old County Hall where the first queues of the day are beginning to form.

'Load of boring fish.' He waves a hand to the right, at the Aquarium. 'Big round thing.' He points up at the London Eye. 'Fancy a ride?'

I come to a halt beneath the huge, metal stays of the Eye and gaze up at the wheel. Just looking at the bloody thing sends me into a spin. In an instant, my legs turn to jelly and my heart begins to pummel at my rib cage. If I look at it any longer, I'll throw up.

'Not right now, thanks.'

'Scared of heights?'

I nod pathetically, and he nods in return before we move on again, in silence, making our way past Jubilee Gardens and under Waterloo Bridge, passing one landmark after another until he finally comes to a halt.

'Gabriel's Wharf,' he announces, guiding me away from the river. 'My favourite place to stop off for a coffee.'

He steers me down a set of steps into a courtyard that's littered with metal tables and chairs. Letting go of my hand, he pulls out a chair and motions for me to sit down. I find myself gazing straight ahead at a wooden pagoda that seems to have seen better days. In fact, the entire place seems to have seen better days. To my left, the South Bank Tower pops its head out of a clump of trees and to the right, a faded mural covers the wall. Obviously intended to jazz up the place, it's flaking now, and cracked. The whole area is encircled with small, shack-like buildings, tiny outlets.

'This is your favourite place?' I ask. We've passed all manner of upmarket cafes and he's chosen this? 'I mean, it's not what I expected.'

'You mean it's not all swish and posh?'

'Exactly.'

'Well, maybe I'm not all swish and posh,' he smiles, tapping the side of his nose. 'And that place there,' he nods towards a small coffee shop that's nestled in between a jewellery store and an independent gallery, 'does the best coffee this side of the Thames.'

Without asking me what I want, he disappears off into the shop, leaving me to examine my surroundings. There's barely a soul around at this time of day. The tourists are still pretty thin on the ground, and every last one of them seems to have decided to give this place a miss. In the quiet, I can hear the sounds of laughter coming from the coffee shop. I narrow my eyes, trying to see what's going on, only to find that it's Dan, deep in conversation with the owner. A moment later, he returns to the table, pulls out a chair next to me, and sits down. I hear another ping from his mobile.

'Aren't you going to read it?'

He shakes his head.

'Could be important,' I push.

'And it could be a load of bollocks.' He smiles warmly at the waiter as he brings us our drinks. The waiter deposits the drinks on the table, takes a good look at me, and touches Dan on the shoulder.

'*Bella*,' the waiter beams. '*Avete scelto bene.*'

With a nod, he disappears back inside his shack.

'What was that all about?' I demand.

'No idea.' Picking up his mug, he takes a sip of coffee.

'But you nodded at him. You speak Italian?'

'A little. Do you?'

'No.'

He smiles, and I know full well that he's just understood every last one of the waiter's words, completely. *Avete scelto bene*. I commit the words to memory. As soon as I get to a computer, I'm logging straight onto a translation site.

'So,' I murmur, 'thank you.'

'For what?'

'Spending time with me this morning.'

'I wanted to do it, Maya. And for once in my life, I'm going to do things I actually want to do. And besides, it's been enlightening.'

'Has it?'

'Oh yes. I've learned that you're scared.'

'I'm not scared.'

'Really? I beg to disagree. I already knew you were scared of thunder and now I know you're also scared of heights. I wonder where this all comes from.'

'It's not important.'

'I'd say it is. And just for the record, I will drag it out of you.'

And how? By tying me up and torturing me with pleasure? Alright then, mister. If you think you're going to have some fun dragging this out of me, I'm simply going to undermine you and spill the beans straight away.

'My sister.'

'Sara?' He's suddenly serious. 'I thought you didn't want to talk about her.'

'I don't, but seeing as you're determined to drag it out of me, we might as well just get on with it.'

He slips an arm around my back, waiting for me to elaborate. Taking in a good lungful of air and then blowing it back out again, I launch into my pathetic little story.

'When I was little, we slept outside one night. We had a little wooden playhouse down at the bottom of the garden. We pleaded with Mum and Dad to let us sleep in there. In the middle of the night, there was a thunder storm and she told me that the house was going to catch on fire. She told me the lightning was going to get me.'

'Which you now know is rubbish?'

'Of course I do,' I snap. 'It's just hard to shake off the after-effects. That's all. I was stuck in that bloody shed all night. She wouldn't let me out.'

'And the heights?'

'She made me climb a tree once. I got stuck. She had her friends with her. They all thought it was hilarious. They left me. I fell out of the tree and broke my arm. It's stupid.'

And that's done it. Stifling a sniff, I curse myself for my weakness. Whenever I begin to talk about Sara and my childhood, it's always the same. I begin to well up.

'She's caused a lot of damage,' he mutters.

Okay. Time for a tactical withdrawal. If he pushes any further into Sara territory, there's going to be another embarrassing scene.

'I'm scared of thunder and I'm scared of heights. I wouldn't say that's an awful lot of damage.'

'No, it's not. But I think there's more.'

I pick up my cup. 'Why do you say that?'

'Just a feeling.'

I shrug, take a sip of my drink and gaze up at a bunch of trees.

'I have a theory,' he adds.

'Already?'

'Do you want to hear it?'

'Go ahead,' I sigh. I'm sure he's going to foist it upon me anyway.

'You grew up believing she was better than you, even though that simply wasn't true. And I'm betting this made you unsure of yourself, even though you had nothing to be unsure of.'

I look up into the whorls of blue. He's hit the nail right on the bloody head there. But how the hell has he done that? I should be sensing the first sparks of anger right now, but I'm not. Instead, I just want to cave in.

'I'm right, aren't I?' he probes.

I shake my head, too weakly.

His lips curl upwards, but I can see that there's no trace of a smile in his eyes, only anger.

'I'm guessing you escaped her influence in Edinburgh, but the damage was already done.'

'Damage?'

'A crippling lack of self-esteem.' He pauses, letting the words hang in the air between us, watching my face for the slightest trace of confirmation. And he must have found it too, in a wobbling lip or a second's worth of a micro-expression, because before long he's talking again. 'You shone while you were in Edinburgh. That much is obvious. But it didn't take much for you to be knocked back down again.' He takes a sip of his coffee. 'Now I have no idea why you never pushed your talent in the art world, but I'm certain of one thing. Your sister is the root cause of all this.'

'She was young.' Tears prickle their way into the open. 'She was an idiot. She's alright now.'

'And you've forgiven her?'

'Why not? People change.'

'They do. But do they change that much?'

The first slither of salt water dribbles its way down my cheek. With a frown, he reaches up and wipes it away.

'Too far, too soon. I'm sorry.'

He lowers his head, searching my eyes for forgiveness and with a faint smile, I give it to him.

'So, yet again, you've found out plenty about me,' I whisper. 'And I've found out bugger all about you.'

Placing his cup back on the table top, he lets out a sigh.

'Fire away then.'

'Let's discuss your childhood.'

'There's nothing to discuss.'

'I beg to differ. Come on. What were you like?'

'Like every other kid.'

'But rich.'

He taps the table and turns away. Catching sight of a pigeon underneath a neighbouring table, he watches its progress as it scavenges for crumbs.

'I was given opportunities,' he says at last. 'For which I'm grateful. Apart from that, what else is there to know?'

At the sound of a ping, he reaches into his jacket pocket for his mobile. Opening a message, he frowns and shoves the phone back into his pocket before spending the next few seconds chewing his lip.

'Who was that from?'

'Nobody important.'

'But it's irritated you.'

'It has.' He checks his watch. 'I can't avoid it any more. I'm sorry. I need to get into work.'

Without warning, he pushes back his chair, pulls me up to my feet and draws me in to his chest. Held firmly against him, I feel his hand under my chin. He tilts my head back and kisses me gently, before skimming his lips across mine.

'How does this feel?' he asks.

'What do you mean?'

'Just tell me, Maya. How does it feel having my arms around you?'

I shake my head. I'm not really sure what he's after.

'It feels good,' I murmur.

'I need more.'

'I don't know, Dan. I feel relaxed, comfortable. I don't feel anxious when I'm with you. I like it.' I hesitate, not knowing whether or not it's a good idea to tag on the next bit. But, what the hell. 'I love it.'

'Good.' He brushes a finger against my lips. 'Remember that feeling while I'm away. Know that you can trust me. And no running. No matter what happens.' He pauses, as if the next words are finding it difficult to form themselves. 'No matter what people say.'

'No matter,' I promise unevenly, wondering what on Earth people could say that would make me run for the hills.

'Remember this.' He kisses me gently one more time. 'Because this is your sanctuary now, Maya. Right here.'

Chapter Nineteen

'Ready to go in now?'

I nod. His hand is still clasped firmly around mine, just as it has been all the way down here from the Albert Embankment. We're standing together on the broadened walkway right outside Fosters Construction and even though he's spent the entire morning either fucking me senseless or psychoanalysing me, somewhere along the way, that pesky little word has crept its way back into my brain. I've wrestled with it and shown it the exit, more than once, only this time, it's digging in its heels, shaking its head and resolutely refusing to go. So, am I already in love? Can it really be possible? Because if I am, then what am I in love with? I still barely know the man.

'Dan?'

'Yup?'

'If you keep hold of my hand, all of your employees are going to know there's something going on here.'

His grip tightens again.

'Let them. I like this hand holding business. If they can't deal with it, that's their problem.'

Without another word, he leads me in through the revolving doors, shooting a brisk 'good morning' at the doorman and half dragging me across the lobby. There's just about enough time to catch sight of the gawping receptionists before the lift doors open and I'm hauled inside. For a few precious seconds we're alone. He locks eyes with me, smiling mischievously and I begin to quake. But it doesn't last for long. From the first floor upwards, the doors open time and time again, and we're joined by one unsuspecting employee after another. In turn, each one registers the hand that has me in its grip, steps dubiously inside the lift, and sets about staring at their shoes.

'And don't forget Saturday. Ten o'clock. Be ready.'

I realise that he's talking to me. Here and there, a head twitches, an eyebrow bounces up and down. Oh God, this is excruciating, knowing that they just can't wait to get to their respective offices and start spreading the news. Mr Foster's broken the habit of a lifetime. He's dating an employee. And more than that, it's a simple office girl. I can just imagine all the gaping mouths and the bitchy comments. *What? The secretary in Norman's office? What's she got that we haven't got?* We reach the fourteenth floor and I'm jolted out of my thoughts by a hard squeeze of my hand.

'Wear jeans and a T-shirt.' He grins, flashing his eyes, and I've forgotten all my worries about the soon-to-be-spreading rumours. 'That's an order.'

I'm released from his grip and sent on my way with a tap on my backside.

I open the door to Norman's bubble to find that Jodie's already busy sharpening a pencil, while through the open doorway, Norman's deep in conversation on the phone. Throwing my bag onto the floor, I settle into my chair and gaze at the desk. There's my mobile, exactly where I left it yesterday, languishing between the romantic novel and the jar of sweet peas. I pick it up and check my messages: two from Lucy, both asking if I'm okay, and one from my sister. I deal quickly with Lucy, telling her exactly where I've been, imagining the squeals of delight as she realises that I've had another good seeing to. And then I open up the message from Sara.

What are you doing this weekend?

Oh great, that's all I need. Sara hardly ever bothers to contact me, only when she's had an argument with the gruesome husband, only when she expects to be propped up by the faithful little sister. Well, I'm doing no propping up this weekend because I'm spending it with the most amazing man I've ever met. I have a mission to peel back his layers, and there's no way I'm going to jeopardise that. I text back.

I'm busy. Sorry. How about another time?

For a few moments, I feel guilty and then I wonder what I'm feeling guilty for.

'Maya.'

Norman's voice jolts me out of my thoughts. I glance up to find the big teddy bear standing in front of me with a handful of scrunched up papers. At first, I'm stunned that he's actually got any work for me to do at all, and then I'm overcome with dread. Oh great, another hour or so wrestling with hieroglyphic scratchings. And I'm distinctly worried about the way he's looking at me when he approaches my desk.

'I need you to type up a few bits for me today.'

'Great!'

'It's the Tyneside redundancy deals.' He pauses for a moment. The creases in his face pucker up. 'I don't really know what's going on.'

Well, don't ask me, I'd like to shoot back at him. I'm just a plain and simple office girl who's secretly a kick-ass artist, and who's currently not-so-secretly dating your boss. If you can call it dating.

'Maya, I'm a little concerned.'

'What about?'

'About how things are going.'

'Things are fine, Norman.'

'It's just that I've heard a little rumour.'

Wonderful. So, it's less than half an hour since we were spotted together in the lift, and the gossip has already spread around the building.

'Oh.'

'Are you ... is there ... are you ... are you seeing?'

It's definitely time to put him out of his misery.

'I think so, Norman.'

'Oh.'

'You don't sound very pleased.'

'I'm surprised, that's all.' The creases gather together one more time. 'Well, actually, I'm a little worried.'

I'd half expected this, I suppose. Norman must know something about Dan's reputation and he's obviously grown to like me while I've been sitting in his office doing absolutely bugger all. I suppose it was pretty inevitable that he'd want to dish out a few words of completely unnecessary advice. I'll just let him get on with it.

'I'll be fine, Norman.'

An eyebrow struggles to raise itself. It's not that easy on Norman's forehead, not with all the wrinkles getting in the way.

'It's not you I'm worried about,' he says quickly before disappearing back inside his office.

My mouth has fallen open. I know it has. But there's precious little I can do about it. Gaping at Norman through the open doorway, I'm temporarily wrapped in confusion until at some point, my brain finally manages to re-boot itself. Norman's worried? And he's worried about Dan? But what can he possibly be worried about? At last, I manage to close my mouth. The world comes back into focus and I find the pink one sucking on her freshly sharpened pencil, inspecting me closely as if I'm some sort of alien species.

'You and Mr Foster?' She slips the pencil out of her mouth.

'Kind of.'

'Bloody hell.' With a shrug, she opens a drawer and produces a Sudoku book. 'Well, don't say I didn't warn you,' she mutters, diving in for the first puzzle of the day.

***

By twelve o'clock, I've managed to decode just about every last one of Norman's scribbles. Knowing that Dan's already left for Edinburgh, I make my way out for a solitary lunch. And maybe that's just what I need. After all, I could do with a little time on my own to take stock of the strange new direction my life seems to be taking. I'll try Borough Market perhaps, get myself a takeaway dish and sit in the grounds of the cathedral. But I don't get a chance. As soon as I'm out of the revolving doors, I'm stopped in my tracks.

'Maya.'

With frightening speed, he moves in front of me, blocking my way. Wobbling on my heels, I look up into the face of Clive Watson.

'Jesus,' I gasp, taking in the fact that he's got a black eye.

'Any plans for lunch?'

'I was just …' For no apparent reason, I point at a random tree. But bloody hell, excuse me. Why has he got a black eye?

'No plans then,' he scowls. 'You can come with me.'

'I …'

Oh Jesus, that's Dan's work. I'm pretty sure of it. They've had some sort of almighty ding-dong. But what about? I stare at the scowling face, and wonder why on Earth he should be so determined to take me out for lunch. An idea edges its way into my head. It's entirely possible that Mr Watson has his own designs on me. And maybe that's why he's standing right in front of me now, demanding that I go to lunch with him. But that's ridiculous. I'm no Elizabeth Taylor, for fuck's sake. Men just don't fight over me. No. This black-eyed, scowling man simply wants to spread his venom. Just like Norman, he's convinced that I'm bad news for the world of Daniel Foster. Well, let him. I'll go out to lunch with this sly piece of work and I'll put him in his place.

'Let's go then,' I say briskly.

In silence, he leads the way through the cobbled backstreets, away from the river and finally down a narrow alley where the shadows quickly gather. Here, out of the sunlight, I'm chilled. I have no idea whether it's down to the air temperature or the fact that I have a serious sense of foreboding about this situation. Whatever it is, before long, he comes to a halt outside a bar. Pushing open the door, he stands back and waits for me to enter. I'm ushered straight through the main section of the bar, past a smattering of lunchtime punters, into a gloomy back room that hasn't been renovated in years. We settle ourselves into a booth where red leather bench seats curl their way around a dark, ebony table. He picks up a menu and studies it. Almost immediately a waitress appears by his side.

'I'll have a whisky.' He makes his order without looking up.

'Water,' I murmur, although I could really do with a huge glass of wine. On the surface, I'm fairly sure that I'm managing to hold it together, but underneath it all, I'm a gibbering mess.

'So,' he sneers. 'You're seeing Dan.'

He snaps the menu shut and fixes his eyes on me, his face coughing up just about every bad-tempered expression it can muster. Well, I decide, if he really wants to be a first class arsehole, then he can put up with some first class apathy in return. I lean back in my chair. I'm going to wind this idiot up, good and proper.

'I think so,' I sigh.

'There's no think so about it.' He scrunches up his nose. 'He was in late this morning and so were you.'

'Is that really any of your business?'

'I'd say it is.' He reaches up, touches the edge of the bruise and winces. 'The gossip's all over the building. You were seen holding hands in the lift.'

'Is that illegal?'

'He's known you for less than a week and he's already making a public display of it. Wouldn't you say that's a little quick?'

'I'd say he's a grown man and he can do what he likes.'

Running a thumb across his lips, he studies me closely.

'He's a grown man who's in charge of a multi-million pound company, Maya. A grown man who cancelled an important meeting this morning to hang around with you.'

Before I know it, I'm leaning forwards, arming myself with a scowl of my own. In the light of this new revelation, any hint of apathy has just been tossed right out of the window. I'm ready to explode.

'So that was you then?' I seethe. 'You were texting him this morning? Because he took a couple of hours off work?'

'No. I was texting him this morning because he was with you.'

Now, that's it. I've well and truly had enough of the twat friend. He's clearly taken some sort of a dislike to me, for no good reason, and I'm just not having it. It's high time for a rant.

'So what?' I glare across the table at the black eye and it glares right back at me. 'What are you so worried about? Do you really think I'm going to distract him from his work? Is that it? He was late in this morning and now Fosters is going to go bankrupt? Or is it the fact that you can't stand the idea of losing your best friend to a woman.' Somewhere above the black eye, a section of skin seems to flinch. 'Oh yes, that's it. You've lost your partner in crime. No more working your way through the women of London like a dose of salts.' He folds his arms and stares down at the table top. I've got him on the ropes now. It's time to go in for the kill. 'Or is it because you think I'm some sort of heartless gold-digger?' I point an accusing finger at his nose, feeling fairly satisfied that I've just covered all the bases. 'You think I'm after him for his money.'

I come to a sudden halt because suddenly, out of nowhere, Clive Watson's mouth is smiling. Now, why is it doing that? I can't work it out and this really isn't on. Every single tactic I pull out of the bag is falling flat on its face. When the waitress gets back, there are no two ways about it, I'm going to order that massive glass of wine and slug it back in one go.

'None of the above,' he replies at last. Unfolding his arms, he leans back in his chair and glances out of the window, as if he's searching for inspiration. At last, his expression seems to soften. Oh shit. Perhaps my first theory was right after all. He does want me for himself.

'None of the above?' I shift about in my seat. 'So, what is it then?'

He shakes his head.

'You're not going to tell me?' And maybe it's better that he doesn't, not if my theory is correct. He throws back his head and stares at the ceiling. 'Well then,' I grumble. 'This is bloody pointless. If you're not going to talk to me about it, perhaps you should talk to Dan.'

He shakes his head again.

'I can't do that.'

'Why not?'

'We've fallen out.'

'The black eye?'

'He hit me. I hit him. He's gone to Edinburgh with a split lip.'

'But why? Why did you hit each other?'

'Because we had a discussion that got a little heated.'

'A discussion about me?'

He nods. 'You should stay away from him. You don't need to know the reasons.'

'I'll have to disagree with you on that one.'

'Trust me, Maya.'

I laugh again.

'Trust you? I'd never trust you.'

'Well, you should.' He levels his gaze at me. 'I've tried my best to get him to back off but it hasn't worked.'

My brain jolts with the realisation. Monday. That was the reason Dan stood me up. He'd listened to the evil friend and decided that I wasn't good enough for him. But what made him change his mind back again?

'What makes you think I'm so bad for him?'

'Nothing.'

'Nothing? You warned him to back off for nothing?'

'You've got it the wrong way round. I wasn't trying to protect him.' He takes a deep breath. 'I was trying to protect you.'

Now, hang on a minute. Trying to protect me? This is making no sense at all. I know that my mind's fried from a week of contact with the man, and I'm totally knackered from a night and a morning of incredible sex with him, and I'm all over the place at the minute. I can barely make sense of anything.

'I don't get it.'

He turns his glass in his hands, his brain obviously whirring inside his skull.

'I'll be blunt about this. I warned him to stay away from you because you're not his usual type of target. Women who want nothing more than to be tied up and fucked and abused. Women who expect nothing more out of him than a quick fix. Women who conveniently disappear off the radar once he's had his fill.'

'How can you talk about him like this?'

'I'm just being honest. That's all. You need to question his motives.'

'Why?'

'Because he's latched onto you for a reason.'

'Which is?'

He shakes his head. He seems troubled now.

'You're a beautiful woman, that's for sure. And you're an artist which appeals to him. But there's more to it.'

'Which is?'

'I can't tell you that.' He pauses for a moment, running his tongue across his bottom lip. 'You're a decent woman.'

'I wouldn't be so sure.'

'This isn't a joking matter. You're hardly innocent, but you're no match for Daniel Foster.'

'Why not?'
'You know very little about his past.'
'I know enough.'
'Trust me. You don't.'
'Well, why don't you fill me in then?'
'It's not for me to give the details. All I can say is this. I've known Dan for over twenty years. I know him better than anyone else. And one thing I know for certain is that he's going to hurt you.'

There's something about the look in his eyes that's seriously giving me the willies now.

'Why would he do that?'
'Because he can't help himself.'

While the drinks arrive, I stare into space, past the table, into nothingness.

'What do you want out of this?' I hear him ask and I don't want to answer, because I'll sound like an idiot. After all, I want what most people want. And for a moment there, I thought I'd found it. 'Let's get this out into the open. You want him to say those magic words.' He takes a sip of whisky. 'But he's never going to say them, Maya, because he's incapable of saying them. You'll fall for him hook, line and sinker and he'll break your heart. That will happen, I promise you. But right now, he's obsessed with you and that's not a good thing. Believe me. If you've got any sense, you'll get out of it.'

I stare at Clive Watson, and he stares right back at me. He seems pretty honest now, and that nagging doubt is back in my mind. Has he got the hots for me? Is he competing with Dan for me? Is he playing dirty? Or has he really got my best interests at heart? I can hardly believe that he has. All I know for sure is that I'm deflating like a cheap balloon, and I feel sick.

'I need to go now,' I whisper. 'Excuse me.'

Chapter Twenty

I spend the afternoon back at my desk, staring at the jar of sweet peas, turning it around every now and then to admire the delicate flowers. They're so simple. If only Daniel Foster could be the same. But he's not. In fact, he's anything but. I pick a flower out of the jar and hold it in my hand - a pure white bud - and remind myself of his words. 'Know that you can trust me. No matter what people say.' Over and over again, I replay the words inside my head, hoping that somehow if I hear them enough, I'll finally believe them. Eventually, they might even become some sort of talisman, protecting me from the poison. But they don't. No matter how hard I try, the warnings creep back, refusing to be banished, dragging a whole hoard of questions in their wake. What seemed to be so simple first thing this morning, now seems so bloody complicated. There's just no way I can begin to untangle the mess in my mind. Not right now. I need to talk to Dan. I need to ask him straight. And he needs to stop being so bloody evasive about his life. Because there's no way I'm pulling out of this. It's beyond impossible. It's far too late for that.

Finally, I'm roused from my trance by the familiar ping of my mobile. It's Lucy.

Swing by the gallery on the way home. I need a drinky poos and a catch up.

I sigh heavily. She wants to grill me on the Mr Mean and Hot and Moody situation, and right now I really don't feel like being grilled. She's bound to pick up on the fact that everything isn't quite right in the world of Daniel Foster, and that's going to lead to a heavy duty conversation. But there's no way that Lucy's going to settle for a rain check. I'll just have to grin and bear it. I text my reply.

I'll walk up. See you about half five.

After work, I make my way along the embankment. I cross to the north side of the river, taking the Golden Jubilee footbridge, weaving through the crowds at Trafalgar Square and heading vaguely towards Soho. Even though I've walked these streets before, I've never quite managed to sort out my sense of direction when it comes to central London. I've got lost a thousand times in this area and today, seeing as I'm in a daze, it's a miracle that I actually make it to Frith Street at all. I push open the door to Slaters and find Lucy right in front of me.

'I won't be long!' she chirps. 'Sit down. There's a glass of wine for you! I've got tomorrow off. I'm going to get wasted tonight.'

'Oh God,' I groan. This doesn't bode well. Whenever Lucy announces that she's going to get wasted, she's always as good as her word. I was under the impression that this was going to be a civilised drink after work. And now it's turning into a full-blown session. 'I've got work tomorrow.'

'Oh, come on. You can do it!'

I nod, watching as Lucy skitters off down the stairs to the basement. I throw my bag onto the floor and flop down onto a sofa. Hearing a ping from my mobile, I take it out of the bag, and open up the message. Somehow, I already know that it's from Dan.

Missing you.

I stare down at the text, realising that my hand has begun to shake. I should text him back and tell him that I'm missing him too, but my fingers refuse to move. I want to ask him what's going on. I want to ask him exactly why he's latched on to me. But this isn't the time. Letting my shoulders slump, I gaze out of the window, catching sight of an Italian coffee shop across the street and realising that I never got round to translating the barista's words from earlier. With a few quick flicks of my finger, I'm logged into a translation package, typing in the words: *Avete scelto bene*. It's not long before I find myself staring down, open mouthed, at the result: *You have chosen well*. Fuck. What the hell does that mean? Well, if the Italian barista is a secret member of the BDSM crew, then it can only mean one thing. Dan's chosen me because he knows that he can manipulate me, because he can lure me into his seedy little world with his lies and make me his next submissive. As if, a voice cries out in my head. This train of thought is ridiculous, woman! Get a grip. I chuck my phone back into the bag, shaking my head as if that's going to help. Fortunately, before I can dig myself further into a pit of confusion, I'm joined by Little Steve. He throws himself down onto the sofa, helps himself to a glass of wine and frowns.

'What's up?' I ask.

'Big Steve is pissing me off,' he says tartly.

'He's always pissing you off.'

'Well, he's gone too far today. He's only gone and deleted a load of files on the computer, including the fucking guest list for the exhibition. I'm telling you, Maya. That man's a complete fucking twat.'

'But you love him.'

'Yes,' he mutters grudgingly. 'I have no bloody choice, do I?'

He swigs back half the glass of wine in one go and fidgets about in his seat. I hear another ping. Reaching down into my bag, I pull out my phone one more time and open up the message.

No reply? Are you alright?

Little Steve begins to cough deliberately.

'Are you okay, Steve?'

'Well, yes. It's just that …'

'What?'

'Lucy tells me you're involved with Daniel Foster.'

Bloody Lucy and her big mouth. I'm surprised she's not put a full page advertisement in the Evening Standard by now, informing the whole of London. I hurl my mobile back into the bag.

'I am, Steve.' I force a smile.

'Oh.'

'Oh? What do you mean oh?'

'Well.'

'Come on, Steve. Spit it out.' A quick check. Yes, the smile's still there.

'How serious is it?'

'I don't know. It's early days.'

'Mmm.'

'What's the problem?'

'Well, he's fucking gorgeous and all that …'

Picking up my glass, I take a huge mouthful of Pinot Grigio and resign myself to the fact that another warning is on its way.

'And me and Big Steve have always found him to be most agreeable. But …'

'What do you mean but?'

'Well, how to say this? We had him round to our flat once, to a party.'

'And that's bad?'

He shakes his head.

'There was a woman there who'd … you know … been with him.'

'He's been with a few women, Steve. I already know that. Look, you don't need to worry about me. I'm not being womanised.'

'It's not that.'

I gaze at Steve, waiting for him to whack me around the head with the next brick of information.

'I just think there's more to that man than meets the eye.'

Oh great. As if I need any more crap to be flung into the pot. Norman's worried that I'll hurt him and Clive's worried that he'll hurt me. What else can there be?

'She met him at a club. BDSM. Bondage. Sadomasochism. You know the sort of thing.'

My cheeks begin to flush. So, Little Steve already knows about Dan's modus operandi, which means that he's already labelled me as some sort of rubber-wearing, stick-anything-up-my-backside, pee-on-me type.

'I'm alright, Steve. I know what he's like.'

'Do you though, darling?' He swigs back another mouthful of wine and watches me closely. 'This woman,' he whispers, leaning in close. 'This woman agreed to a session with him and it was …' He seems to swallow hard. 'It was pretty extreme by all accounts.'

The smile falls from my face. If I'm not careful, it'll be out of the door before I can grab hold of it.

'What do you mean?'

'I mean *he* was pretty extreme.' He takes a deep breath before he mouths the next word. 'Whips.' He raises an eyebrow. 'She didn't go into too much detail. All she said was it was scary, that he lost control.'

'He did?'

Little Steve nods.

'It was lucky there were other people there. Maya, she told me that he's a real sadist, and I mean a *real* sadist. Those were her words. I'm just saying. Be careful.'

'I will be careful, Steve.'

I grapple with the smile, shoving it back into place. It's not easy. On the inside, I'm beginning to quake. How extreme would he want to be with me? So, for now, he's going easy. But who's to say that he won't change his mind after a few sessions? Perhaps he'll grow bored with the light-weight version, and then he'll want to go back to whatever he did before. And who's to say he won't have me trussed up and gagged and totally lose control? I turn cold. Sickness lurches through my stomach. My mind is on high alert now, wondering what the hell I've got myself into. Delving back through every moment with him so far, it searches for confirmation of Little Steve's gossip. There's not been much as yet, just the nipple business in his office, and he actually apologised for that. And then there was the smack. But is he just reining himself in for now, controlling himself for all he's worth? And will he ever lose that control with me? Now this adds a whole new slant to Clive's warning. *He's going to hurt you.* This changes everything.

I sit in a daze, hardly aware of the fact that we've been joined by Big Steve and Lucy.

'What's up with you?' Lucy beams.

'Nothing.' I shake my head.

Suddenly, I'm glad that Lucy's decided to go on a bender, because I need to go on one too.

***

We spend the next hour or so sitting in the window of the Slaters Gallery. By the time Lucy announces that we need to hit the bars, I've already knocked back two huge glasses of wine.

'Good luck!' Big Steve laughs as we stagger our way out into the streets of Soho. 'You'll need it!'

The evening passes in a blur. Moving from one packed bar to another, we slug our way through God knows how many drinks, drivel our way through countless ridiculous conversations, and bat away the attentions of various men who come at us like flies around a cow pat. And while Lucy loves every last minute of the drunken chat-ups and the slurred put-downs, I have no interest in any of it. I just want to go home, have a bath, and do my level best to ponder over the problem in my life. By half past ten, the world is swirling around me and I can barely string a thought together. I've lost count of the glasses of wine. Lucy's really on a mission to get steaming drunk tonight, and it's already a case of mission accomplished. Finally, we find ourselves washed up in some dive of a pub, surrounded by middle-aged men and scraggy dogs. Spotting a table in the corner, we order two glasses of wine that smell distinctly like socks, and hunker down.

'There's something wrong!' Lucy exclaims, pointing a wobbly finger at me.

'No, there's not.'

'Yes, there is. You've been miserable all night. I know you too well. I know when there's something on your mind. And there's definitely something on your mind.'

I squint at her for a moment or two, reminding myself that there's really no point in trying to deny anything. She always manages to squeeze it out of me in the end, especially when there's alcohol involved.

'Should I put an end to it?'

'Put an end to what?'

'Me and Dan.'

'Oh, for fuck's sake, Maya. No! You stay with him. See this through. You're painting again, for fuck's sake. And you're happy when you're with him. What's the fucking problem now?'

I wince at Lucy's foul mouth. I know I can swear, but this woman is a powerhouse of profanity after two bottles of wine.

'Something that Little Steve said.'

'Oh, ignore that fucker!' She swings her wine glass through the air, losing half of its contents across the table. 'What's he said, the fucker?'

'He had some gossip about Dan.'

'Pphhp! Go on!'

'Some woman Steve knows told him that he's a sadist.'

'A whatty?'

'A sadist.'

'Oh.' Her lips form a perfect circle.

'Listen to me, Lucy. He used to go to BDSM clubs.'

And now, her face screws itself up into a knot.

'Whaaaa?'

'He's told me that he's given it up.' I watch as Lucy's face unscrews itself while her eyes light up with excitement. 'But I'm not sure he's being straight with me.'

'Did he tie you up?' she demands breathlessly.

'Lucy, that's not important right now. The fact is, Little Steve knows a woman who met up with him at one of these places, and she reckons he's a sadist.'

'Bloody hell. But he's not done any of that stuff with you, has he?'

'No. Well ...'

'Oh my fucking God! He has!' She slaps a hand across her mouth.

'No, he hasn't. Well, nothing much.'

'What?'

I bite my lip.

'Listen, shit head!' She wags a finger. 'If he's told you he's given it up, and if you know you can trust him, then just get on with it!'

If I know I can trust him. Well, that's the thing, isn't it? When he's got me tied up, and possibly gagged - and God knows he wants to do that, he's mentioned it enough times - can I trust him to control himself? I hardly know him. I have no idea what he's capable of. I wonder if I should ask Lucy for her opinion on the matter, but her head is already on the table and I half suspect that she's passed out. I touch her gently on the shoulder. Her head twitches.

'Come on,' I mutter. 'We need to go home.'

Half an hour later, I'm slumped in one corner of a black cab, my head leaning against the window while Lucy is fast asleep in the other. I check my phone. Three messages from Dan. The first one, apparently, came in at a quarter to ten.

Are you alright?

The second arrived just after ten.

Answer me, Maya.

The third text arrived at half past.

I need to know that you're alright. Answer me.

Oh Lord, I know it's just a text message, but it sounds pissed off. My fingers are trembling now as I try to think of some suitable wording. I'm saved from the bother when my phone begins to ring in my hands. I stare down at the screen, squinting, trying to make the caller identity come into focus. I don't know why I'm bothering. I already know it's him. He's probably calling to give me a good ticking off for not staying in contact. Well, let him try. I'm in the mood for a rumble. My thumb sweeps across the keypad, miraculously finding the accept call icon.

'What's going on?' he demands. Shit, he really is pissed off.

'Nothing,' I slur. 'I've been out with Lucy.'

'Why didn't you reply to my texts?'

'I didn't hear my phone go off.'

He's silent for a few moments, registering everything. I know it. While I'm stupidly drunk, completely incapable of covering up my worries, he's perfectly sober and taking it all in.

'Are you drunk?'

'Maybe.' I hiccough. 'Have you got a problem with that?'

'Not at all.'

'But you have got a problem?'

Another silence. When he finally speaks again, his tone has softened.

'I haven't got a problem with you going out with your friend, but I do have a problem with you ignoring me. Next time, just make sure you check your phone. It doesn't take long to send me a quick text.'

'You don't need to keep watch over me,' I whisper. 'I can look after myself.'

I hear him sigh. 'I'm sure you can.'

'You're angry.'

'You could say that.'

'So, if you were here, what would you do? Punish me?'

'I wouldn't rule it out.'

I freeze. I don't seem to be able to breathe.

'And how would you like to punish me?' I demand.

'What?'

'Tell me. How would you like to punish me?'

'Why are you so obsessed with punishment all of a sudden?'

I'm not about to answer his question. He can fucking answer mine first.

'Come on. What would you do? Would you spank me?'

'If you must know, I'd love to spank you right now.'

Panic sets in. Panic on a grand scale. I could throw up right here in the taxi, and it's nothing to do with the industrial quantities of Pinot Grigio that I've ingested. Is he really suggesting that if I dare to defy him, if I take a step too far, he'll take his hand to me? Or is that just my jumbled, wine-addled mind on the rampage?

'Would you whip me?' I hear myself ask.

'Behave yourself. You're drunk.'

Oh boy, he's just gone and said the wrong thing there. Nobody tells me what to do when I've downed a vat of wine.

'Don't tell me to behave myself.'

'Maya!'

'I never agreed to being punished.'

'Because we haven't discussed it yet.'

'So you were going to bring it up?'

'Absolutely. Compliance, control, defiance, punishment. It's all part of the deal. Maya, what the fuck is the matter with you tonight?'

'Nothing.'

'Something's wrong.'

I try to swallow, but there's suddenly a huge, drunken sob working its way up my throat. Fuck it. I'm about to cry.

'I can't do this,' I blurt.

'What?'

'I can't deal with this.'

'Can't deal with what?'

'You. I can't see you again.'

'Why not?'

'Because ... I don't understand you, because I don't know where I am with you. Because ...' The drunken sob explodes into the open. 'Because you scare me, Dan. Yes, you scare me!'

'Maya!'

I turn off the phone and sling it into my handbag. My head is swimming. I barely know where I am.

***

The alarm bores its way into my head. Reaching out with an unsteady arm, I tap it back into silence, gazing at the display, realising that I can't go into work for two very good reasons: firstly, I'm not convinced that I'll be able to make it through the day without collapsing in a shambolic heap; and secondly, after last night's phone call, I should probably never show my face at Fosters Construction again. But even now, I'm not entirely sure that I'm finished with the big kahuna, and perhaps it would be best to hedge my bets. Deciding to call in sick and spend the next few hours in my bedroom nursing the hangover from hell, I force my head up from the pillow and discover my handbag lurking in the corner of the room. It takes an age for me to crawl out of bed and launch my body in the right direction. When I've finally managed to rescue my mobile, I stumble back over to the bed and collapse onto the covers. Turning the phone back on, I squint at the screen and my stomach turns a somersault. Seven missed calls from Dan.

After giving my excuses to Mrs Kavanagh, I doze for a while before I finally haul myself back out of bed. I tug on shorts and a T-shirt, shuffle into the kitchen, make breakfast and return to my bedroom with a mug of tea and a plate of toast. Chewing on my breakfast and slugging back the tea, I spend a good few minutes staring at the canvas. And then I just can't help myself ...

Pulling out the palette, I choose my colours: cadmium yellow, burnt ochre, raw sienna, umber, copper, bronze, pewter, Prussian blue. I squeeze a blob of each onto the palette, playing with the colours, mixing them, merging them until I'm happy. And then I begin: a daub here, a swirl there, a stroke drawn out across the canvas. Out of the darkness, shapes begin to emerge, colours spring to life, and I'm lost in it all. Time dissolves, the outside world disappears and even though the streets of Camden are rattling with noise, I'm cocooned in silence. Every now and then I lie on the bed, taking stock of where I am. Every now and then, I scurry into the kitchen for a glass of water to keep myself going. Finally, I realise that there's nothing more to do. I'm faced with a woodland landscape, my own sanctuary.

'Are you okay?' Lucy asks from the doorway.

I give a start. I didn't even hear the door open.

'Yes. I've been painting.'

'I knew you were,' she grins. 'I've been on the sofa all day. Daytime television is a pile of shite, you know. Have you eaten?'

'No.' I shake my head. 'I haven't had anything since breakfast. Just water. What time is it?'

'Nearly six.'

'Is it?'

I gaze at the alarm clock in amazement.

'I'm doing the Friday night special. Half an hour. You'd better get cleaned up.'

She nods at my T-shirt which is now smeared with paint in varying hues. And then she notices the finished painting. Her mouth falls open.

'It's done?' she gawps.

'Yes.' I sigh contentedly. 'I think it is.'

She shuffles forwards and sits on the edge of the bed.

'Bloody hell, Maya. It's wonderful! You're back in the swing, lady. And you've got Daniel Foster to thank for that.'

At the mention of his name, a strange, warm sensation skitters its way through my chest, followed quickly by a cold flush of disappointment. Yes, I have got Daniel Foster to thank for all of this. Somehow, he managed to flick on a switch inside me. If only everything about him could be so positive.

'You know, I'd love to show this at the exhibition. It'll be dry by then.'

I screw up my face.

'I'm not sure ...'

'Maya, just let me do it. The Steves are going to go ape over this.'

I gaze at my painting. I'm not really sure I can part with it. But then again, it would really boost my confidence if it was sold.

'Okay,' I breathe at last. 'Do it.'

I take my time cleaning up. Brushes have to be cleaned through with turpentine, the palette has to be scrubbed down and then rubbed with linseed oil. And then I see to myself, removing the smears of paint from my arms and face, and finally jumping into the shower. Finally, near to eight, I join Lucy for dinner: fish finger sandwiches. Even Lucy can't go wrong with those. I find her slumped at the kitchen table with an open bottle of wine in front of her. She offers to pour me a glass and I decline. After a full day of hung-over painting, I decide that I need an early night. By nine o'clock, I'm back in bed.

***

I'm barely awake, but as soon as I'm conscious I know I'm not alone. My arms are being manoeuvred above my head. Fingers curl around my wrists, holding me in place. I can feel the heat of another body against mine. I smell a familiar scent. In a daze, I open my eyes to find the dark outline of a face in front of me. In light of everything I know, I should be panicking right now, but I'm not. He's here, right here in my bedroom, and God knows how that's happened. He's already naked and the sheet has been pulled off the bed. I can see that much in the gloom.

'Dan?'

'Shush.'

With his free hand, he runs his fingertips down the side of my face, my neck, across my left breast and down to my stomach. Nerves come alive. His lips brush against mine while the fingertips trail their way out across my hips and back inwards, towards my crotch. My breath catches at the waves of pleasure that are coursing through me. He takes full advantage of my open mouth, closing in for a kiss, his tongue slipping into my mouth. My brain is in chaos. I just don't have the willpower to stop this. Instead, I accept him and find myself caught in a long, slow, glorious kiss, our tongues twisting silently against each other. I close my eyes and moan into him, while he gently forces my legs further apart. His fingers enter me, his thumb working at my clit. I'm possessed, brain-washed by ecstasy. Finally, his mouth releases me.

'You don't speak unless I tell you to,' he whispers in the darkness, manoeuvring himself on top of me. 'Remember the rules.'

Shit. Why can't my body just obey my brain? After all, a man who's quite possibly some sort of sadist has broken into my bedroom in the middle of the night and now he's pinning me to the bed, and I'm pretty certain that he's about to fuck me senseless. I should be panicking. I should be screaming out my safeword. But my mouth refuses to move. And why is it refusing to move? Because his fucking gorgeous torso is arched above me now and he's reaching down, pressing his palm against my clit. My heart rate zooms off the scale. I'm on fire. This is wrong. On so many bloody levels, this is wrong.

He nudges a knee between my legs, urging them open, and in spite of all my doubts, I find myself caving in immediately. Even if I could get up and bolt for the door right now, I'm not sure that I'd want to. He rubs his erection against my clitoris, firing me up into a mess of want. Taking both of my hands in one of his own, he holds them firm on the pillow above my head.

'No,' I manage to moan at last. 'Don't do this.'

'You know what to say.'

Yes, I do know what to say, but my lips just don't seem to be able to form the word. I moan again. He lowers his head, sealing my mouth with a kiss. His tongue seeks entry and I let him in without hesitation. Why is my body doing this? He certainly knows how to win me back. No talking. Just action. Get straight down to the nitty-gritty.

'What did I tell you, Maya?' he demands softly, rubbing his cock harder against me.

'I don't know ...'

'Of course you know. Think. What did I tell you?'

He inches into me, slowly, feeling his way in, making sure that I give, waiting for me to become wet enough. Deeper and deeper, he edges inwards.

'Answer me,' he breathes.

'Not to run,' I gasp. 'You told me not to run.'

'No matter what people said.'

Another push and he's as deep as he can go. He begins to withdraw, at an agonisingly slow pace. He kisses me again, lapping his tongue around my mouth.

'So you're here to punish me?'

He pushes in one more time, and I begin to tingle. 'Does this feel like punishment?'

Again he withdraws, blanketing my lips with his own. Again he presses inwards. 'You need to trust me.'

'I can't.'

'You don't have a choice, Maya. It's too late.'

He arches his back, adjusting his position slightly, and moves his head down to my chest. Closing his lips around my right nipple, he begins to suck gently. I'm sent into a spin, hurtling away from anything that vaguely resembles logic and reason. After what seems an age, his face is back in front of mine.

'You don't need to be scared of me.'

He begins to quicken, picking up the pace, but remaining gentle. And then, he releases my hands. I can barely believe it. I'm actually being allowed to touch him. If it wasn't currently the middle of a heatwave, I'd think it was Christmas. My hands make an immediate beeline for his shoulders, clutching at the contours of his muscles, running across his back, down his strong arms and finally across his chest. Every square inch of him is defined to perfection, chiselled by hours of workouts, and this powerhouse of masculinity is arching itself above me now, pumping his cock into me and sending my muscles to the point of delirium.

I have no idea how long it goes on for. Spasms gather at my centre, the pressure inside building to the edge of an explosion, and he keeps me there for minutes on end, until I can barely breathe. At last, I can't hold it any longer. I have to let go, and I do it with style, lifting my backside off the bed as my body convulses. He doesn't seem to mind. Instead, while my orgasm clutches at him furiously, one hand slides under my buttocks, holding me in place and he begins to pound out an orgasm of his own, sending me whirling for a second time. At last, he cries out into the darkness, his body jolting as he comes inside me. When he finally manages to gain control of himself, he lowers his body down on top of me, carefully, digging his head into my neck while he steadies the rhythm of his breath. I stroke his hair and begin to wonder what the fuck I'm playing at. In spite of everything I've been told about this man, I've caved in to desire. I'm sleepwalking straight into trouble. And I just can't help myself.

'Dan?'

'Shush.'

He stays inside me. Bringing a hand round to the back of my head and holding me tight, he begins to kiss me, softly at first, gradually working up in intensity, pummelling me with a ferocious passion that I've never known before. And I kiss him back. Reaching up, I run my hands around his neck, clutching at him possessively. It goes on for so long my lips grow sore. At last, he pulls away, withdrawing himself at the same time down below, and I'm shocked to feel his fingers thrusting straight inside me. They swirl about before he removes them, wiping them across my lips, encouraging my mouth to open. He gives me a moment to savour the taste – a curious, sweet mixture, laced with a hint of salt - before he kisses me one more time, his tongue lapping up the contents of my mouth.

'You and me,' he says at last. 'That's the taste of us.'

'You're filthy.'

'And you love it.'

Rolling onto his side, he motions for me to curl up in his arms. I move myself over and nestle against his shoulder. It's a space that feels just right, as if it's been tailor made for me. His right arm closes around my waist.

'How come you're here?' I murmur at last.

I turn my head, taking in the outline of his face. Against the faint glow of the streetlamp outside, I can barely see a thing. All I know is that he's staring at the ceiling.

'Last minute helicopter charter,' he explains. 'They don't come cheap. I got a taxi straight from the airport to here. Lucy was still up. She let me in.'

'But ...'

'Don't be angry with her.' He gives me a squeeze. 'She didn't stand a chance. I can charm the birds from the trees when I want to.'

It takes another moment or two for the enormity of it all to hit home.

'You walked out on the bid because of me?'

'Yep.'

I roll onto my side.

'You lost the deal?'

'Maybe,' he sighs. 'And maybe not.'

'But it's going to cost the company ...'

'Relax, Maya. I had a team with me. After I headed up the main presentation, I left them to it.' He pauses, tucking his free arm behind his head. It may be gloomy in here but I'm pretty sure that he's smiling right now. 'It's probably a good thing I bowed out. I could barely concentrate on what I was saying.'

'And you look like you've been in a bar room brawl.' I reach up and touch his lip. 'Does it hurt?'

'A little.' He takes my hand and plants a kiss on my knuckles. 'But not enough to stop me kissing you.'

'You shouldn't have done this.'

'I had no choice.' Reaching over, he skims a finger down the side of my face. 'My woman was in a tizzy because some git who calls himself a friend decided to stir things up.'

'Oh God.' I collapse back into his shoulders and gaze up at him. 'You know about that?'

He nods.

'I called him after I called you. He owned up to what he'd done, but he wasn't too forthcoming with the details.' He readjusts his head. 'What did he tell you? I need to know.'

I cringe. This is going to be painful.

'He said ...' I falter, rummaging around in my brain for a way ahead. How the hell do I tell him without giving too much away? 'He said I'm not your usual type.'

'True enough.'

I wait for him to elaborate but nothing comes.

'He said you'd end up hurting me.'
'Never.'
'Physically or emotionally?'
He lifts his head from the pillow.

'What's wrong?' he asks. 'Do you think I'm dangerous? Do you think I'd harm you?' He pulls my head against his mouth and whispers into my ear. 'I'll give you pain - whenever you want it - because it turns you on, and that turns me on. But I will never, ever harm you. *Capiche?*' When I finally nod, he lets me go.

'But what about punishment?' I ask, cringing as soon as the words come spilling out into the dark. I hate myself. My voice sounds so small.

'What about it?'

'Orders, compliance, disobedience, punishment. You wanted to spank me the other night.'

'I said I wanted to. I didn't say I would. It's what I'm used to.'

'You want me to submit.'

'You've already agreed to it.'

'In sex. That's all.'

'And maybe we should extend that a little. You doubted me and I need your trust. Punishment goes hand in hand with control in my world. If you allow me to punish you, it means that you submit to me completely. It means that you give me your trust.'

'You want me to agree to this so you can boss me about?'

He laughs.

'I only want to boss you about when it comes to sex ... and anything that affects it. I wouldn't dare boss you about in any other way. I wouldn't spank you for going out with your friend and getting blind drunk without telling me.' He lowers his voice and slows his pace. 'But I would spank you for ignoring me, and I would spank you for doubting me.'

'I don't know ...'

He takes my chin in his hand, turning my face towards him so I have no choice but to look him straight into his eyes.

'This is a learning process for both of us, Maya. The deal's not closed yet. We're still in the negotiation phase. There's got to be some give and take on both sides.'

'I'm not going to let you control my life.'

'I'm fully aware of that. And if you don't want to do something, then we don't do it.' He releases my chin and strokes his thumb across my lips, sending a shimmer of want throughout my body. 'But when I spanked you the other day, you came for a second time which suggests to me that you enjoyed it. So keep your mind open. That's all I'm saying.'

I let my head fall against his shoulder, drinking in his scent while he gently traces a line down my throat, across my breasts, swirling his finger around my left nipple. Along with the talk of spanking, it's enough to set off a flurry of sparks in my abdomen. 'We could try it, I suppose.'

He nods slightly.

'So, that's it then?' he asks. 'That's what put the fear of God into you?'

'No.'

I falter again. I just can't ask him about the whipping. Not now. His fingers have moved down to my stomach and he's clearly in the mood for another go. I'm not about to say something that could slam the brakes on round two.

'So what else did that fucker say?'

'He said you're incapable of …' I pause for a moment, biting back the final word before it escapes from my mouth. This isn't the time or the place to bring up the L word. Instead, I replace it with the first thing that comes to mind. 'He said you're incapable of having a relationship.'

Shifting his body, he draws me into his chest, touching his lips against my forehead. 'I've never run a marathon, but does that mean I never can?'

He moves a hand between my legs, parting them, slowly smoothing his palm against my thighs, moving up further towards my crotch. Closing my eyes, I know I'm done for: my brain is about to be scattered into another whirlpool of ecstasy. I haven't got much time now, and there's a question I need to ask.

'Dan?'

'Uh huh?'

He manoeuvres me onto my back. Leaning over me, propping himself up with one hand, he pushes a finger inside my vagina, as far as it can go, pressing against the inside of my clitoris in a slow, pulsing action. My muscles begin to clench, sending exquisite little ripples of pleasure throughout my groin.

'Why did you choose me?'

'Why do you ask?' He rubs his thumb against the outside of my clit, massaging me simultaneously, inside and out.

'Motives.' I gasp at a sudden rush of warmth. 'I need to know your motives.'

I open my eyes, just in time to catch the hint of a frown. Still patiently massaging me, he's quiet for a while before he finally answers.

'When I'm with you, I feel contented. I feel complete. Is that a bad motive?' He kisses me softly, then takes my bottom lip between his teeth, holding it there for a moment, applying just enough pressure for it to be on the verge of pain. 'Is it?' he asks, releasing me.

'No, of course not.'

'From the moment I set eyes on you, I've wanted you.' He closes his eyes for a moment. 'No. I've needed you.' He withdraws the finger from me and urges my legs apart with his knees. 'Do you really think I could hurt someone who makes me feel this way?'

I shake my head and swallow hard, feeling his thick cock as it nudges against my opening.

'This is all that counts, Maya.' He presses into me, filling me to the hilt. 'You and me. Nothing else. So, just let it go.'

Chapter Twenty-One

I'm woken by a pair of soft, warm lips kissing me. Opening my eyes, I find him leaning over me, a broad smile spread out across his face. The morning sun catches his irises, causing them to glimmer like sapphires. All manner of sensations spring into life between my legs. I want to drag him back into bed right now but the selfish bastard's already dressed and judging by the smell of him, freshly showered.

'Good morning, Miss Scotton.'

'Good morning, Mr Foster. Why have you got your clothes on?'

'Because I've got a job to go to, and I'm pretty sure it's not appropriate to turn up at work stark bollock naked.'

'You could try it. The receptionists in the lobby wouldn't mind.'

'I bet they wouldn't.' He runs a finger down the side of my face. 'I've made you a cup of tea.' He leans back, motions towards a mug on the bedside table, and then gets to his feet, moving over to the full length mirror. He looks delicious in his black trousers and white shirt, but I still feel cheated. He could have woken me up for a morning session before he went and wrapped himself away in his work clothes. But it's too late now, and I suppose I mustn't complain. After all, he did have me at it for half the night. The man certainly wasn't lying when he claimed that he could fuck us both to death. While he turns to fix his tie in the mirror, I gawp at his backside, taking in the way his trousers hang from his waist, the cut of the cloth across his firm buttocks.

'Are we good?' he asks, turning back to face me.

'We're very good,' I practically drool, shuffling up in bed, careful to let him have full view of my breasts. He arches an eyebrow.

'Put those away. I've seriously got to get into work.' I pull the sheet back up and he seems to sigh in relief. 'Seeing as I can't be in

Edinburgh, I'm setting up a conference call later. I'll be busy over lunch, but I should be finished by about five. You're staying at mine tonight.'

'I am?'

'Absolutely.' He winks. 'Now, get dressed. I've got a company car picking us up in half an hour. You can come into work with me.'

He turns and leaves me to gather my senses. It takes a while. After a few sips of tea, I roll out of bed and head for a shower. I dry my hair, apply a quick dusting of make-up and put on today's clothes: yet another of Lucy's miniscule skirts, matched with another of her undersized blouses. I'm scrabbling through my drawers, searching for a sexy pair of knickers when I come across the suspender belt and the black stockings: a gift from Tom a few Christmases back. I've never worn them before. They're still in their packaging. I pull them out, hitch up the skirt and clip the belt around my waist before slipping the stockings on and fixing them into place. Yes, not bad at all, I decide, glancing in the mirror. My own little present for Dan. At last, I head into the kitchen where I find him sitting with Lucy at the rickety table, locked into a conversation that comes to an abrupt halt as soon as I enter the room.

'What are you two talking about?'

'Nothing,' Lucy squeaks.

'It didn't look like nothing.'

'We were talking about art,' Dan smiles. Standing up, he motions for me to take his place at the table. As soon as I've lowered myself onto the chair, he leans down and plants a kiss on the top of my head, before picking up a carton of milk and sauntering over to the fridge. 'I was just asking Lucy about any new stuff they're getting in at Slaters.'

'Yes, that's what we were talking about,' Lucy confirms, sucking at her teeth. 'We were talking about that.'

She's lying. I know she is. Lucy Godfrey is the worst liar on Earth. In all probability, he was grilling her for information on me. Deciding that I'm going to get the truth out of her another time, I shoot her a look of almost certain death, but it's a waste of energy. She's paying absolutely no attention to me now. Instead, she's watching the sex god, perving over his backside while he leans down to put the milk back in the fridge. I can barely believe what I'm seeing here: my best friend eyeing up my sort-of-boyfriend. As he straightens up, Lucy turns away quickly.

'Breakfast,' he says sternly, pointing at the table where a plate of toast is waiting for me.

'I'm not hungry,' I complain.

'I've made it for you. Now eat it. You're going to need plenty of energy for later.'

I stare across the table at Lucy, realising with a jolt that she understands exactly what he's getting at. He's not referring to work at all. Leaning back in her chair and clutching at a mug full of tea, my flat mate begins to smirk like some sort of demented Cheshire cat.

***

As if he's scared I'm going to jump out at any minute, the car journey passes by with me folded up in his arms. More than once, I wonder if I should take his hand and guide it up my skirt so that he can feel the suspenders, and more than once I decide against it. After all, I seriously need to get a grip on my body, because lately it seems to have clubbed my brain into submission and taken the helm, turning me into a raving nymphomaniac. And besides, there's no screen between the back seat and the driver and God knows what would happen if I got Dan turned on enough. We arrive at the back of the building, a roadside entrance I've never noticed before. He gets out first, holding out his hand to me and leading me inside. We're joined in the lifts by others, staring down at their feet again, but somehow today I don't care. The gossip's already spread around the building. So what if they all know? By the time we reach the fourteenth floor, we're alone. He holds out an arm, keeping the lift door open while he kisses me gently.

'I'll see you later,' he whispers into my ear.

***

Back in the office, I spend the morning gazing out of the window with my chin in my hands, day-dreaming about last night. Every now and then, I look up to find Jodie staring at me. Every now and then, I check my mobile, wondering if he's sent a text from up above, but there's nothing. At eleven o'clock, I'm summoned into Norman's office where the big teddy bear paces backwards and forwards a few times, huffing and puffing as he skirts round the exercise bike. Finally, he lets out a huge sigh and waves me away again. I've just about settled myself back on my chair when I jump clean out of my skin at the sound of Norman's voice.

'Maya?'

I look up to find that he's followed me back out to my desk.

'Yes, Norman?'

'He's not supposed to be here today.'

'Who?'

'Mr Foster. I mean Dan.' He wafts a big hand around in the air. 'He's supposed to be in Edinburgh.'

'He is.'

'But he's here. Why is he here?'

I shrug my shoulders. No way am I about to tell Norman that the reason why Daniel Foster returned to London a day early, chartering a helicopter at God knows what cost, was to fuck me back into his life.

'Sweet peas,' Norman mutters, pointing at the jam jar. I follow the direction of his finger to find that the flowers are beginning to wilt now.

'Sweet peas,' I confirm.

'Sweet peas,' he mutters again. His eyes seem to narrow a little, and then expand. His pupils dilate. Somehow, he seems to have been lulled into some sort of a stupor.

'Is there a problem with the sweet peas, Norman?' I ask.

'Not sure.'

He shakes his head before brooding his way back into his office. Collapsing into his chair, he begins to wrestle with today's *Financial Times*. Mystified by his last remark, I stare after him. Okay, so I got it all wrong. Norman certainly wasn't the one who left the sweet peas on my desk. Jodie must have been right all along. It must have been the cleaner. But that's of no interest to me right now. Right now, I want to know exactly how much Dan spent on a helicopter charter. I've just typed the word 'helicopter' into the search bar of my computer when the office door swings open, revealing a delivery man and a gigantic bunch of red roses. He shuffles forwards, heading straight for the pink princess.

'Not for me,' Jodie growls, pointing a pen in my direction. 'She's the one with the rich boyfriend.'

'He's not my boyfriend,' I add quickly, glancing from the roses to Jodie and then back again. 'At least I don't think he is.'

'Well, whatever he is,' the delivery man wheezes, 'this lot is for Maya Scotton and I need a signature before my asthma kicks off.'

I sign for the roses and make space on my desk. As soon as they're plonked down, I dive straight in, searching for a card. Eventually, I find it, open it up and read the message.

I'm glad I've found you.

It's the first time I've ever seen his handwriting: strong, confident, yet stylish. My heartbeat flips and I'm suddenly light-headed. A classic, romantic gesture. Is this his way of telling me he loves me? Well, maybe it is, and maybe it isn't. After all, there's no kiss.

Whatever's going on, all I know is that I need to see him. It's been just over two hours since I last looked at his ridiculously handsome face, and I'm already suffering from withdrawal symptoms. I must be well and truly addicted. Deciding that I'm going to get a fix, and that thanking him for the roses is a good enough excuse, I push back my chair in a flurry of excitement and head out for the lift. My hands are shaking as I tap the button. My legs begin to tremble as I ride the lift one floor up. In a daze, I skitter out into the reception area to find no one at the desk. From the kitchen, I can hear the sound of the space age coffee machine preparing to take off. Hardly thinking about the fact that it's closed, I head straight for the door. I've already opened it, already forced my way through into his office when I hear Carla's voice screeching behind me.

'He's got someone with him!'

It's too late. By the time the message registers with my brain, I'm already through the doorway, gawping at the scene. He's standing in front of his desk. And so is Lily Babbage, the madam. He has his hands clasped on her shoulders, and she's close ... very close.

Caught in the act, my brain screams out. Once a man-slag, always a man-slag!

In an instant, I banish every last ounce of jittery excitement from my body. You've been an idiot, I tell myself. You've let yourself be drawn in by a pair of come-to-beds and a shed load of rippling muscles. Daniel Foster isn't in love with you, you prat. He's just going through the motions. Clive, the evil friend, was right after all: he's incapable of love.

'Maya!' He's surprised, but he doesn't drop his arms. 'What are you doing here?'

I glance from him to her, taking it all in. Finally, he releases the hussy.

'What's the matter?' he asks.

'You can answer my question first. What's going on?' I demand.

Lily Babbage takes a step backwards and smiles archly at me.

'I'd better go, Dan,' she purrs.

He nods and within seconds, Lily Babbage has gone, taking her ridiculous name with her.

'What was she doing here?' I glare at him from across the room. Okay, so I'm probably being unreasonable. I've only met the woman twice and I've already come to the conclusion that she's a BDSM fiend, or a madam, or both. But, nevertheless, I'm fucking furious. He's not going to get away with this.

'You know who she is.' He tips his head to one side, examining my face, and then he begins to stalk towards me. The heat rises in my body. He's got that look in his eyes, as if he wants to pin me down right here and have his way. 'You're jealous.'

My body bristles. I may well be jealous, but I'm not about to have him telling me that.

'What if I am? You need to explain yourself.'

'I'm not getting into this just now. I've got the conference call in ten minutes.'

'Well, stuff you then.'

He's so quick I don't have time to react. Catching hold of my arms, he pulls me in to his chest. I struggle to free myself but the grip tightens.

'Don't be a bitch. It doesn't suit you. I'll explain about Lily tonight.'

I lean my head back and do my best to laugh.

'Tonight's cancelled. You're not fucking me when you're still fucking other women.'

One hand locks around my waist, while the other comes up to the back of my head, forcing my face into position next to his.

'I am not fucking other women,' he growls into my ear. 'I own you and you own me, remember?'

'You're a shit.' He squeezes me hard. 'Get off.'

'Not until you calm down, woman.'

There's no other way out of this. I can see that now. I'm held in his grip and he really isn't about to let go. I'll have to feign compliance, or else I'm going to be found in some sort of compromising position by Carla. I will my body to relax.

'Now, listen to me,' he whispers. 'Lily is no threat to you. Trust me on that one.'

I nod but I certainly don't mean it.

'I like the fact that you're jealous.' He smiles. 'But I don't like the fact that you doubt me.'

'If I'm jealous, then I'm doubting you,' I hiss. 'The two things kind of go together, you prat.'

He pulls me closer. His cock throbs against my groin.

'Smart arse,' he breathes. 'Now, see what you've gone and done. I've got to talk to the Edinburgh team with a massive boner.'

'Poor you,' I breathe back. 'Why don't you just have a quick wank?'

'I've got a better idea. Why don't I just fuck you senseless in my bathroom?'

And that's done it. Even though I despise the man right now, I'm on the verge of squealing 'Okay then! Come on!' I'm so nearly there. I don't know whether it's the twinkle in his ridiculously blue eyes or the electrical charge that's currently zinging about in the air between us, but right now I'm pretty sure I'd agree to anything. It's just as well we're interrupted by Carla.

'Mr Foster?' I turn to find her hovering in the doorway. 'The Edinburgh call's come through a little early. It sounds like things aren't going too well.'

'Put them through, Carla.' Releasing me momentarily, he waves her away before clamping his hand back around my arm. 'I'll pick you up at five, Miss Scotton, on my way down to the car park. You'd better be ready.' He brushes his lips against mine, unleashing a whirlpool of lust between my legs, and then he leans down and whispers into my ear. 'Don't work too hard this afternoon. You'll need all your energy for tonight. I'm going to fuck you rotten.'

We'll see about that, Mr Foster, my brain calls out. If you think you've got the upper hand here, then you've got another think coming.

Chapter Twenty-two

It's a quarter to five and I'm ready to go. I've squared nothing with Norman, but I'm not even sure he'll notice if I'm out before time. All I know is I need to escape before Daniel Foster gets anywhere near me. I need time to think. Closing down my computer, I grab my handbag.

'I'm off,' I announce.

Jodie's head flips up.

'But it's …'

'I know, and I'm going.'

Before she can say anything else, I'm out of the door, scooting into an empty lift and riding it all the way to the ground floor without being stopped once. Down in the lobby, I'm half way towards the revolving doors when a huge, muscle-bound body appears in front of me, halting me in my tracks. My eyes climb up the torso, past a name badge proclaiming that the muscle-bound body belongs to a man called Dave who works in Security, and further up into a pretty stern looking face.

'You can't leave by these doors, Miss,' Dave informs me.

'Why not?'

'Because they're not working at the minute. We're waiting for the engineer.'

'But I need to get out.'

'Then you'll have to go via the basement. The garage doors are open. Take the lift.' He smiles briefly. 'Go on.'

With a huff, I turn on my heels and make my way back to the lift. Punching the basement button, I check my watch. Still only ten to five. I fling myself into an empty carriage and let out a breath of relief as the doors close. He won't be out of his office yet. There's no way he'll manage to intercept me now. When the doors open again, I'm presented with an eerily silent garage. The hairs on the back of my neck stand to attention as I step out and adjust my eyes to the gloom. There's something not quite right here. The doors shut behind me and I take another step forwards, noting the handful of cars: a BMW, a Jaguar, an Audi TT. Another step and I can see the garage doors. They're closed.

'And where do you think you're going?' The voice comes out of nowhere, rich and deep and velvety, and I know immediately who it belongs to. Swivelling round on the spot, I find him standing to one side of the lift, his hands buried deep in his trouser pockets. My heartbeat stalls.

'I was just ...'

I point aimlessly at a wall and he scowls.

'You were just running. Again.'

Taking his hands out of his pockets, he pushes himself away from the wall and begins to close in on me, keeping his eyes fixed on mine, locking me in with a hard, unforgiving gaze. I back up only to find myself stopped in my tracks by the bonnet of a car. By the time he comes to a halt in front of me, I'm a wreck.

'So,' he breathes, 'I'd like to know why you're running.'

'Well, seeing as you're asking, I don't particularly fancy spending the night with a man who obviously hasn't given up on putting it about a bit.'

He folds his arms.

'We've been over this.'

'And I don't believe you.'

'What makes you say that?' he asks.

'You know exactly what makes me say that. How would you feel if you walked into a room and found me draped all over another man?'

'Fucking furious.'

'So, now do you understand?'

He shrugs his shoulders.

'I told you. There's nothing for you to worry about.'

'So explain.'

'Explain what exactly?'

'Lily Babbage. You had your hands all over her.'

'I had my hands on her arms.' He reaches out and grabs me. 'Like this.'

A bolt of electricity thrums its way through my body. My heart begins to pound. My breathing grows shallow. He knows exactly what he's doing.

'Now, sometimes,' he murmurs, 'you might say that this is how one friend holds another, for example when they're trying to talk some sense into them, just like I was trying to talk some sense into my friend earlier. And sometimes, you might say that this is how a man holds a woman when he's about to fuck her senseless against a Jaguar XF, just like I'm holding you now.'

'Oh.'

I take in a deep breath.

'Oh,' he mimics.

'You can't fuck me senseless against this car.'

'Why not?'

'Well, it's not yours for a start.'

'Yes, it is.'

I cast a quick glance at the smooth, black bonnet, and then turn back to face him. Drawn in by the shimmer in his eyes, by the vice-like grip on my shoulders, I'm already submitting, and I know it.

'Any other good reason you can come up with?' he demands.

'Somebody might come in.'

'Not likely.'

'But the main door …'

'Is functioning normally, thank you.'

My mouth falls open at that. He's obviously been tracking my movements, anticipating the fact that I'd try to make a run for it. And he's gone to these lengths to stop me? Half of me wants to reach up and slap him across the face, shortly before storming right out of here. The other half is swooning.

Leaning forwards, he whispers into my ear. 'And before you go on, you might like to remember that this is my building. That lift over there won't open until I say so. And that garage door won't open either, until I inform security. And as for that CCTV camera.' He nods upwards. 'Well, that's switched off until further notice.'

'You've got me trapped?'

'Looks like it.'

'But …'

'Listen.' He releases my arms and takes a step backwards. 'If you really do want to get out of here, then all you need to do is say the word. I'll call security and let you out. But just to let you know, you'd better sound like you mean it.'

He puts his hands back into his pockets. We stare at each other for an eternity. And while he's apparently cool, calm and collected, I'm a quivering mass of nervous energy. At last, the cold stare begins to soften.

'Take off your knickers,' he says quietly.

'What?'

'Take them off.' He motions towards my crotch. 'And do it slowly.'

I gaze at him in disbelief, inwardly gasping at the sudden flood of warmth between my legs. And then, before I have any idea what's going on, I'm hitching up my skirt, slipping my fingers into the top of my knickers and easing them down my legs … slowly. What the hell are you doing now, my brain screams out. Where's your self-respect, woman? Well, God knows where it is. Ignoring my brain, I lean down and step out of my knickers, holding them limply in my left hand as I straighten myself up to find him smiling at me. The warmth returns between my thighs, with a vengeance.

'You know, you really need to cut this running away crap, Maya.' Taking a step forwards, he pulls the knickers out of my hands and drops them to the floor. 'I've got enough to think about without having to rig up elaborate traps.' While he draws up my skirt, arranging it neatly around my waist, his gaze travels to my crotch. 'You're wearing stockings. I approve. Did you wear these for me?'

Yes, I want to tell him, because before I saw you with your friend, it was fully my intention to let you fuck me in these.

'No.'

'Liar.'

Without warning, he reaches out and tugs at my blouse. Ripping it open in an instant, he yanks down my bra cups and pinches my nipples. I let out a moan and close my eyes, hoping to God that he really has switched off the CCTV, because if anyone can see this, I'll never live it down.

'Like that?'

'Yes.'

He leans in towards me.

'It's just as well my woman's in the mood for pain,' he breathes into my ear, 'because she's about to be punished for her errant ways.'

'What?'

I have no time to remonstrate. I'm swung round.

'Hands on the bonnet.'

I comply immediately. He kicks my feet further apart. And then the slap comes out of nowhere.

'Shit!' I scream. My right buttock is on fire. I turn my head. 'What are you doing that for?'

'Punishment, Maya. For doubting me.' Another slap. 'And if you don't like it, you know what to say.' Another slap.

'Fuck it, Dan! I don't like it!'

'Then say the word.'

'No!' I scream as a fourth slap hammers down on the same buttock. I'm not giving in to him. Six more slaps follow. On each one, I grit my teeth and squeeze my eyes together. Tears are flowing now. 'I hate you!' I sob. 'I fucking hate you!'

'No you don't.' I feel a hand between my legs, urging my thighs apart. A finger enters me. 'You're wet. You're loving this.' He withdraws the finger, replacing it quickly with two and I gasp at the intrusion. A hand moves into place on the small of my back, holding me fast while he begins to thrust the fingers in and out with short, vicious movements. My stomach muscles clench while a tornado of sensations blasts its way around my vagina. Jesus, he's being rough with me. And he's totally right. I am loving it. The fingers are removed and I hear the sound of his zip. His cock presses against my opening, and he forces his way into me quickly, burying himself to the hilt, filling me completely. I cry out in pleasure.

'Fuck it, Maya. You're going to drive me mad.'

'And what the fuck do you think you're doing to me?' I shout across the bonnet.

He begins to withdraw and thrust, again and again, hitting the same spot repeatedly with deadly precision, causing my muscles to contract, that familiar pressure to grow inside me. His free hand curls its way under my skirt, holding me in place across my stomach while he smashes into me.

'Please!' I cry out, and I've no idea what I'm begging him for. I'm so close to the edge, I can barely make sense of anything.

At the sound of my voice, he begins to thrash harder, faster than before, so that I struggle to steady myself against the car.

'I'm going to come,' he growls. Immediately, I feel him judder, feel the warmth of his cum inside me. Still holding me tight, he slows his thrusts, bringing himself down from his orgasm, and denying me one of my own.

'I didn't ...' I splutter.

'I know.' He pulls himself out of me. 'This was a fuck for me. You didn't deserve to come.'

'But ...'

I watch over my shoulder in disbelief as he sets about fastening his zip and straightening his trousers. My arms give way and I collapse across the bonnet. I must look like a prize whore, what with my blouse in bits and my backside on show and Dan's sperm dribbling its way down my legs.

'Doubt me and this happens,' he states as if it's simply a fact. 'Have I made my point?'

'I don't really know what your point was.'

He sighs.

'There's only one woman for me and she's currently slumped over the bonnet of my brand new Jag. And I sincerely hope that she's not scratched the bodywork.'

'Well, if she has, then there's only one person to blame for that.'

'Quite right.'

A moment later, a smooth cloth is wiped across my groin. He's cleaning me up again, taking his time, making sure that every last drop of his sperm is wiped away. At last, I'm allowed to stand up straight. He moves my skirt back into place and turns me round to face him.

'You've ripped my flatmate's blouse to bits,' I complain.

'I'll reimburse her.'

'How am I going to get home like this?'

He takes off his jacket and motions for me to put it on. Oh, I get it. The blouse ripping was a tactic, a pre-emptive strike. He knew I wouldn't be able to run any further if my top was in shreds.

'Like I said before, you're coming back to mine.' He runs a hand across my back. 'And you're staying the night.'

'So that you can punish me again?'

'Why would I do that?' Leaning forwards, he smiles into my face while he reaches into a jacket pocket and pulls out a set of keys. 'The job's done. You've learned your lesson and now I want you back in my bed.' He twiddles the keys in his hands. His eyes seem to darken. 'And back in those cuffs.'

Chapter Twenty-Three

'Do you like it?' he asks.

'What?'

'The car?'

'Oh, that,' I huff.

'It's a top-of-the-range Jag, Maya. Show a bit of appreciation. Do you have a driving licence?'

A driving licence? Why is he asking that?

'Yes,' I mutter. I passed a few years ago but the truth is I haven't seen my driving licence in a while now. It must be languishing in a cupboard somewhere along with my passport and every other important document I can never find. 'Why?'

'I've still got the Merc. And now I've got this. A second car. I'll get you included on the insurance. You're welcome to use it.'

'Whatever.'

I'm fully aware that this is some sort of gesture, and I also know that I'm being completely ungrateful, but I just don't care. Somewhere between the Shard and wherever we are now, I finally came to my senses. Lucy's blouse is torn to pieces and I've got a sore backside. And in spite of all his reassurances, I'm currently sitting in the passenger seat of a top-of-the-range Jag with a man who may well be a real sadist.

'Why did you do that?' I ask at last. 'Why did you slap me?'

He flashes me a quick look, then turns back to the road.

'You said you wanted to try it.'

Yes, of course I did. But not like this.

'I thought you might have given me some warning,' I grumble.

'Whatever happened to spontaneity?'

'You just punished me for doubting you. I never agreed to being punished.'

'You could have used your safeword.'

I chew at my lip. Suddenly, I'm in a grump.

'You enjoyed it. You enjoyed slapping me.'

'It's called spanking, and you had the option of getting out of it. But you didn't. So what does that tell you?'

'That I'm a fucking idiot and you get off on inflicting pain.'

'And are you so innocent? You enjoy the pain, Maya. You've already admitted to that. So what's the fucking problem?'

'How far would you go?'

'How far? What's going on here?'

'What are your limits?'

I watch as his forehead creases up. His fingers tighten against the steering wheel.

'You hurt a woman,' I breathe. And yes, I'm going to get it all out now, because I just can't carry on like this. 'At one of those clubs, you hurt a woman. She used her safeword and you just carried on. You had to be restrained.'

He slams his foot down onto the brake and we screech to a halt, causing a flurry of car horns to fire off around us. We're holding up the evening rush hour traffic now, but Dan doesn't seem to care. Taking his left hand away from the steering wheel, he turns to glare at me.

'Who told you that?' he growls.

'It doesn't matter.'

He leans in towards me.

'I'd say it does,' he seethes. 'Who told you that?'

'You don't need to know,' I see the back. 'And I'm the one asking questions here. How far would you go with me?'

'How?' he shouts, slamming a fist against the steering wheel. My body gives a jolt. 'You'll believe stories from God knows who but you'll doubt me?'

His anger sends me into a maelstrom of panic. If he's accusing me of doubting him, then another round of punishment could possibly be on its way. And I'm not having that. Reaching down into the foot well, I grab my handbag and pull at the door handle. Out of the corner of my eye, I see him reaching for the central locking mechanism, but I'm too quick this time. Before he can do anything about it, I'm out of the car ... and running. I have no idea where I am, no idea where I'm going. All I know is I've got to get away from this man. As much as I want him, as much as I try to fool myself that he can give me anything remotely like a normal relationship, I need to escape from him before he strips me of all logic and reason and sanity. Dodging the traffic, I stagger to a pavement and gather my senses. The air is filled with the sounds of car horns and revving engines and angry voices, and somewhere in amongst the chaos of it all, Dan's voice is calling my name.

'Maya!'

My body pumps with adrenalin and I run again, down a side street this time, and then into an alleyway. I keep going until my lungs are on the verge of bursting.

'Maya!'

I duck into a doorway, trying desperately to calm my breaths.

'Maya! Come back! For fuck's sake!'

His voice is distant now.

'Maya! I'm not what you think I am!'

I slap my hands over my ears. Don't believe him, I tell myself. All along, he's been deceiving you, weaving his web of lies around you and luring you into his trap. No matter what he says, you're no different to all those other women he's fucked and abused and abandoned. Now, do the only sensible thing you can do: get the hell out of here.

***

I have no idea how long I spend cowering in the doorway. Eventually, when he's given up calling and I'm convinced it's safe, I step back out into the alley and try to get my bearings. Glancing over my shoulder every now and then, I begin to walk, veering this way and that through a housing estate and a maze of dingy backstreets, emerging at last outside the Globe Theatre. Even though it's early evening, the place is still packed with tourists. Navigating a path through the crowds, I head left along the embankment, moving on in a daze until I finally make it to the Golden Jubilee Bridge. I stagger across the bridge and make my way up Northumberland Avenue, taking a right past Trafalgar Square. I can barely think straight and before I know it, I've deviated completely from my normal route to Slaters. I don't have a clue where I am.

Coming to a halt, I shove my hands into the pockets of Dan's jacket, only to find myself with his mobile phone in one hand and his wallet in the other. Pulling out the wallet, I flip it open, discovering a handful of twenty pound notes and a couple of elite charge cards. I shove it back into the right pocket where my fingers touch something else: a small box. Without bothering to take it out and examine the contents, I continue on my way, telling myself that I'm sure to stumble onto the streets of Soho at some point. Stopping off at a department store, I pick up a cheap blouse. And then I take myself into a bar where I spend five minutes in the ladies, changing into the new top and shoving Dan's jacket into the plastic store bag. I'll dump the whole lot into a bin later. If he wants to teach me a lesson, then I'll teach him one right back.

The next few minutes are spent in a fog of confusion. Wandering through one side street after another, I stop here and there to read a signpost, but Soho doesn't appear on any of them. All I know is I've had enough. At last, I come to a halt at a place I vaguely recognise, where seven roads converge onto one spot. A rickshaw narrowly misses me as I cross the cobbles, heading for the stone column at the centre of the junction. Seating myself at the base of the column, I prop the bags between my feet and break into a full-on, Olympic gold medal-winning sobbing session. Batting away the attentions of concerned passers-by, I take my phone out of my handbag, deciding that it's high time to call for help. Lucy answers immediately

'Lucy, where are you?'

'Still at bloody work. What's wrong?'

'When can you get out?'

'Maya, are you crying?'

'No.' I rub my eyes with the sleeve of my new blouse.

'You *are* crying. Tell me what's wrong.'

'Oh God ...'

'Where are you, Maya?'

I gaze around, taking in the pubs, the early evening drinkers, a theatre.

'That place,' I blurt. 'That place with all the roads.'

'Seven Dials?'

'Yes. Seven Dials. I'm at the middle of Seven Dials. How do I get to Slaters from here?'

'Bloody hell, woman,' Lucy sighs. 'You've gone completely off track tonight. I'll never guide you from there. Stay exactly where you are. I'm coming to get you.'

I press the end call icon and sit in silence, gazing down at the plastic bag that's nuzzled between my feet. I have no idea how long I've spent like this when I'm finally roused.

'Hey.' I look up to find Lucy standing right in front of me. 'What's going on with you? Are you turning into a bag lady?'

I push myself up from the stone base.

'I'm a mess, Lucy.'

'Well, let's get a taxi home.'

My stomach gives a lurch. Adrenalin pumps through my body. That's the first place Dan will look for me, and the last place I want to go.

'No. I can't go home.'

'Why not?'

'Let's go for a drink and I'll tell you.'

Five minutes later, we're sitting in the window of one of the bars at Seven Dials, perched on two high stools with two large glasses of white wine on the table in front of us, and the plastic bag languishing on the floor alongside my handbag. It's a busy evening. We're surrounded by suited, professional types having an after-work drink.

'So what's going on?' she asks.

'It's over. Whatever it was between me and Dan, it's over.'

She stares at me. 'Why's that?'

'Because I think it's true. What Little Steve said.'

Her face is a blank and clearly there's some reminding to be done.

'He is a sadist, Lucy. He gets off on pain. He gets off on hurting people.'

Her eyes seem to expand. Staring at me with a look of pure disbelief, she takes a huge gulp of wine. While her eyes contract to their normal size, a deep frown creases its way across her forehead.

'Did he hurt you?' she demands. 'Because if he did, I'll knee the bastard in the nuts.'

I bite my lip and gaze out of the window. Should I tell her? Should I really let my best friend in on my tawdry secret: that I've willingly subjected myself to a good spanking? With a gargantuan sigh, I realise there's just no other way ahead.

'Yes, he did.'

She leans forwards, staring at me earnestly.

'How? Maya, how did he hurt you?'

'He ...' I falter for a moment, staring at my glass of wine, suddenly washed through with embarrassment. 'He spanked me.' When I look up again, I half expect to find her face spattered with anger and indignation. Instead, she's giggling.

'And you didn't enjoy it?' she sniggers.

'What?'

'Spanking?'

'Why are you laughing?'

'You think because he spanked you, it makes him a real sadist? Jesus, spanking's nothing. Even the local vicar's at it these days.'

'Lucy!'

'I've had it done to me.'

'Lucy! He held me down on the bonnet of his car and gave me ten of the best. Hard. It really fucking hurt! And this, by the way, was shortly after he ordered me to take my knickers off and ripped your blouse to bits.'

'I didn't like that blouse anyway.'

'Lucy, take this seriously.'

'Lord, why can't I meet a man like that? He's a real kinkmeister!'

'Lucy, for fuck's sake. He's got a reputation.'

'It's just gossip. Don't listen to it.' She waves a hand through the air, as if she's swatting a fly.

'You wouldn't be so flippant if you'd seen the look in his eyes. It scares me, Luce. What if he's got me all tied up and he really loses it.'

'He ties you up?'

'Oh shit.'

I slump forwards, throwing my head into my hands.

'I told you, didn't I?' Lucy squeals. 'I told you you'd bump into some rich, power-hungry, kinky control freak. You lucky bastard.'

I pick up my glass of wine and down it in one go.

'You're supposed to be understanding, you fuckwit.' I let out a loud belch. 'This is ridiculous. You know, I thought we were going to have a serious conversation about this. I've just jumped out of his car and run off in his jacket. He'll be out there looking for me.'

'Fucking hell, Maya. Imagine what it's going to be like when he finds you. Jeez, you're in for a right good seeing to.' With that, she drifts off into her own little world for a moment or two. While she finishes off her own glass of wine, her eyes glaze over. 'Look, did he hold you down against your will?' she asks at last.

'Not exactly.'

'What does that mean?'

'He gave me a choice.' I lean forwards and mutter the next bit through clenched teeth. 'I've got a safeword.'

'And you didn't use it?'

I shake my head.

'Maya, why didn't you use it?'

'I don't know. Maybe I was scared he wouldn't be interested if I didn't go through with it.'

'And maybe it's because you wanted to try it out. Maybe you're just as kinky as him.'

I gaze across at Lucy's face and I have no idea what to say. My brain seems to have set itself on some sort of spin cycle. Thoughts, ideas, emotions: they're all over the place. It's just as well that I'm jolted out of the chaos by a male voice.

'Ladies.'

I look up. I swallow. I open my mouth, but nothing comes out of it. Because Clive, the evil friend, is standing at our table.

Chapter Twenty-Four

'I'll get another drink.' Lowering herself to the floor, Lucy examines Clive Watson suspiciously, and he stares right back at her. 'Can I get you anything ... er ...'

'Clive.' He reaches out and shakes her hand. 'No, thank you. I'm not staying long. And your name is?'

'Lucy,' she simpers. 'I'll just ...' She points mutely towards the bar before scuttling away.

Clive Watson leans down, picks up the plastic bag and places it on the table in front of me. And then he perches on Lucy's stool.

'I'm assuming this is Dan's jacket in here.' He taps the bag.

'It is.' I pick up my glass. Remembering too late that it's already empty, I put it back down again. 'How did you find me?'

He smiles knowingly. 'You've got his mobile. It's in his jacket pocket. He has an anti-theft tracking device on it. I used my tablet. Easy really.'

'Is he here?'

Clive shakes his head.

'No, he's not.'

I take in a sweep of the bar. Even though Clive's denying his presence, I'm not entirely sure that Dan would be able to keep his distance, especially not right now. In fact, in all probability, this is just another one of his elaborate traps.

'He's pretty certain you've had enough of him,' Clive explains. 'So he's giving you some space.'

I chew at my bottom lip and check the room again, half suspecting that Daniel Foster's idea of space is nowhere near the normal definition of the word.

'So,' I sigh at last. 'You two are talking again.'

'We are. He came to my place earlier, out of his mind with worry. Apparently, you jumped out of his car. He came after you but you managed to give him the slip. By the time he got back to his car, it had been towed, keys and all. On top of that, he had no mobile and no wallet.'

Good, my brain cries out. He deserves his own punishment for being an idiot!

'Well, you've got them back now.' I motion towards the bag. 'You've done your job. You can go.'

Nodding silently, Clive Watson stares at me. Any minute now, he'll take the bag and disappear off into the night while I continue to drown my sorrows in Pinot Grigio. I shake my head and close my eyes. I should have ended up with Dan tonight, pleasured to within an inch of my life and fucked halfway to oblivion. But now I'll end up crying myself to sleep ... alone. I feel a prick of salt water. Oh great. So I've started already.

'You're crying.' I hear Clive's voice above the din of the pub. 'What's the matter?'

'You were right.' Opening my eyes, I run my fingers up the stem of the wine glass. 'I'm no match for Daniel Foster. He was always going to break my heart. I should have listened to you. I should have stayed away.'

He sucks in a deep breath. 'Well as it happens, my advice was wrong. I'm sorry I interfered. I shouldn't have done that.'

'I beg your pardon?' I stare at him, flummoxed by this latest revelation. It's bad enough that the big kahuna himself has been merrily fucking with my mind for the past few days. I really don't need the accountant side-kick joining in with the fun. 'You said ...'

'I know what I said,' he interrupts. 'And I shouldn't have said it.'

'Care to elaborate?'

He picks up a beermat and flips it over. 'Okay. The first time I saw you with him, I thought he was up to his old tricks. I told him to leave you alone. And he managed it too ... for a few hours anyway.' He leans in towards me, folding his arms on the table. 'But he can't keep away from you, Maya. I thought he was just out to use you, but now ... well ... I think it's more than that.' He squints out of the window. 'I've never seen him like this before.'

'Like what?'

'Besotted.'

In a heartbeat, just about everything that can possibly flap or pump inside my body seems to have kicked into action. Besotted?

Well, if I'm not much mistaken, that's half way to the four letter word.

'He told you that?'

'Good God, no.' Clive shakes his head. 'But judging by the state he was in tonight ...'

'What state?'

He shakes his head again. 'He wouldn't thank me for telling you, and I don't fancy another black eye.' He straightens himself up and readjusts his jacket. 'You'll have to give him the benefit of the doubt.'

'It's not that easy.'

'Why not?'

I examine Clive's face. How much does he know about Dan's preferences, about the way he's lived his life?

'He's got a track record,' I remind him.

'And so have I.'

I shoot him a look of disbelief and he raises an eyebrow in return.

'I know it seems incredible,' he smiles, 'but accountants like sex too.' He glances towards the bar, taking in Lucy's backside. 'You were right when you talked about me and Dan going through the women of London like a dose of salts. We did. But we both got fed up with it and we both put an end to it last year.'

'And how about the clubs?'

He turns back to face me. 'What clubs?'

'You know ... the kinky places?'

'Oh those.' He waves a hand, dismissively. 'That was never my thing. Dan always went to those places on his own. Does it bother you?'

Of course it bothers me, you moron, especially when he splays me out across the bonnet of his brand new Jaguar XF and spanks the life out of me.

'Is he a sadist?' I demand.

'A sadist?' Clive Watson battles against a grin. 'No, I don't think so. He just got a little too close to the edge last year and he knows that. He pulled himself back. He quit the scene over six months ago.'

'But ...'

'Have you been through his jacket pockets yet?' he asks.

'What? Well, yes.'

'And have you opened the little black box?'

For a moment or two, I gawp at the possibly not-so-evil friend, wondering what relevance a little black box can have to anything.

'No.'

'Well, why don't you get it out?' Moving the empty glasses to one side, he pulls the jacket out of the plastic bag. 'Go on.'

Digging into the first pocket, I find nothing but the mobile phone. I try the second pocket. Retrieving the box, I hold it in my hands, waiting for the next instruction.

'Now open it.'

I do as I'm told. My lungs instantly tighten. It's a necklace ... and it's exquisite. The pendant is small and stylised, but it's immediately clear what it is: a tiny white flower, set at the heart of a delicate latticework of silver threads.

'It belonged to Dan's mother,' Clive explains. 'The flower's mother of pearl. And that,' he touches the centre of the flower, 'is a diamond. Just a little one.' He draws in a breath. 'Now taken on their own, these materials aren't too expensive, but when you consider the fact that this is an Art Nouveau necklace made by Louis Comfort Tiffany himself, well ... then you've got a whole new deal on your hands.'

I pick the necklace out of the box and turn it slowly in my hand, watching the pendant as it latches onto the light. A complete one-off. A Tiffany Art Nouveau necklace. And you've been lugging it about the streets of North London, my brain sings out. Not to mention the fact that you nearly dumped it in a bin!

'I have no idea how much it's worth,' Clive presses on, 'but I do know the Victoria and Albert Museum wanted it. Dan couldn't let it go. It meant too much to him.' He leans back on his stool. 'So, ask yourself, Maya, why was this in his jacket pocket?'

Mesmerised, I continue to stare at the pendant. 'He wasn't ...'

'He was. And he is. Now, why would a man want to give a woman something like that?'

I shake my head. This really is a new direction. This really is serious.

'If you ask me, he's lost his mind over you.' I look up to find Clive smiling back at me. 'He deserves some happiness, believe me. Now, just give the man a break.'

I'm vaguely aware that I'm nodding as I return the necklace to its box.

'What's going on?'

Lucy's voice tears me out of my reverie. Still holding the box, I watch as she slides two fresh glasses of wine onto the table top while Clive stands up, making way for Lucy to reposition her backside on the stool.

'I won't be needing that.' I touch the necklace. 'I need to go and see Dan.'

'But what about me?'

'Don't worry, Lucy,' Clive offers. 'I'll help you out with the wine. And then I'll take you home.'

'And I'll get a taxi.' Dismounting from my own stool, I close the box and pick up my handbag.

'No need,' Clive smiles.

'No need?'

'No.' He shakes his head and shrugs his shoulders apologetically. 'I'll be back in a minute.' He winks at Lucy. 'Keep my seat for me.' Picking up the jacket, he motions for me to follow him. 'Dan's outside.'

Chapter Twenty-Five

I smile to myself. Pretty much as I predicted, Daniel Foster's idea of giving me space amounts to nothing more than a few feet. As soon as I step outside the bar, I catch sight of him, standing jacketless by the column with his hands in his trouser pockets. Staring at the pavement and kicking at a piece of rubbish, he's completely oblivious to the fact that I'm approaching him until at last, when I'm no more than two steps away, he looks up. His body freezes. His eyes flicker. His lips part.

'Here's your jacket.'

Clive's voice snaps him out of his torpor. Taking a moment to nod silently at his friend, he reaches out for the jacket and shrugs it on. After spending an evening crumpled up in a plastic bag, it's ridiculously creased.

'We'll be alright now,' he mutters. 'And Clive?'

'Yes?'

'Thanks.'

The two men exchange a second nod before Clive takes himself back inside the pub. And now we're alone. He stares at me for what can only be a few seconds, but it feels like hours.

'I'm sorry,' he murmurs at last. 'I thought it was what you wanted.'

A smile inches its way across my face, and there's a burning warmth in my heart.

'It's always a good idea to ask first,' I inform him.

'You're quite right.'

We go back to staring at each other. His eyes glimmer in the evening sun and I'm caught.

'I need you, Maya. I haven't got a fucking clue what I'm doing here. You've got to help me get this right.'

I laugh. 'You can't teach an old dog new tricks.'

'I'm pretty sure you can.' He smiles. 'And I'm thirty five. Not that old.' His eyes travel down to my right hand. 'You've seen it then?' He takes a step forwards and touches my hand, and I realise that I'm still clutching the black box.

'Yes. I ... er ...'

'This was supposed to be a surprise.' Gently, he takes the box from my hand.

'It's too precious,' I complain. 'If you still want to give it to me, I can't accept it.'

'Turn around.'

'But ...'

'Please just do as I say.'

He takes me by the shoulder and swivels me round on the spot. And although I know what he's about to do, I still take in a little breath when I feel his hands on my shoulders. He gathers my hair and brushes it to one side. Another few seconds pass by before I'm aware of his arms encircling me. The necklace flashes in front of my eyes and then it's laid on my skin.

'But ...'

He fastens the clasp.

'You're a silver woman. I noticed that on our first date. Yorkshire jet and silver.'

I smile silently, reaching up to touch the pendant, making sure it's really there.

'Now,' he turns me back to face him. 'Never take this off.'

'Never?'

'Ever.'

I touch the pendant again and the imp in me wants to make a point. 'Oh, I get it. You're in charge and this shows that I belong to you.'

'Something like that.'

'So, what are you going to wear to show that you belong to me?'

'Well, I don't do necklaces.' He cocks me a grin and seems a little embarrassed. 'I'll think of something. Maybe a ring at some point.'

I stare at him in disbelief. Have I just misinterpreted that? Or, after only two weeks of knowing me, has he just made some sort of reference to marriage? I shake my head. No, that definitely didn't just happen. I get no chance to think about it any further because in an instant, he closes in on me, wrapping his arms around my body. With one hand, he presses my bottom in towards his crotch, while he moves the other hand across my shoulders, holding me in position. And then his lips are on mine, kissing me with a passion. A wave of desire sweeps right through me, clearing out any last vestige of doubt. I want this man in my life. I know that now. And in spite of all the questions, I need him too. Just as much as he needs me. I have no idea how long it goes on for. Here and there, I hear the pap of a car horn or the tinkle of a rickshaw bell, and I'm pretty sure it's all on account of our show.

'Get a room!' someone calls out.

He doesn't pay any attention. Instead, here at the centre of Seven Dials, he carries on kissing me. I can barely breathe when he finally pulls away.

'Can we go home now?' I gasp.

'Not quite yet.' He catches his breath. 'I need you to meet someone first.'

Keeping his arm firmly in place around my shoulders, he raises a hand and flags down a passing cab. I'm ushered in first. He leaps in quickly behind me and slams the door shut, leaning forwards and giving his instructions to the taxi driver. I try my best to listen in, but I hear nothing. I'm in a daze as he seats himself next to me, motioning for me to shuffle into his arms.

'Maya?' I turn my face to his. 'You need to let me know who told you about that woman. Just trust me on this one. There won't be any comeback for them, but I need to clear this up for once and for all.'

I take a moment to examine his features, finding nothing but pure determination. 'Little Steve,' I admit, knowing full well I have no choice in the matter.

He nods.

'Have you got your mobile with you?'

'Yes.'

I lean down and grab my mobile out of my handbag, offering it to him. He shakes his head.

'Do you have Little Steve's number?'

'Yes.'

'Call him. Ask for the name of the woman who's been spreading rumours about me. I think I know who it is, but if you're going to believe me, then you need to hear it from a third party. Her full name. Just do it.'

I stare at Dan's face before I stare down at the phone. Finally, I flick my way through my phone contacts and call Little Steve.

'Maya, darling,' he breathes as soon as he answers. 'Is everything alright? Lucy ran out of here like a bat out of hell tonight.'

'Everything's fine,' I reassure him.

'She says you've got a painting for us.'

Oh bloody hell, I'd forgotten about that, and I don't have the time or the inclination to talk about it right now because Dan's blue eyes are fixed on me, expectantly.

'I have, but can we talk about that some other time? I need something. It's important, Steve. The woman who told you about Dan, about the ... incident.'

'Oh, yes?'

'I need her name.'

'Why?'

'I just need it, Steve. Please.'

'Okay.' I can hear him wheezing heavily at the other end of the line. I can only imagine what's going through his head right now. 'It's Claudine. Claudine Thomas.'

'Thank you.'

Passing my finger over the end call icon, I lean forwards and toss my phone back into the handbag. When I straighten up again, a strong hand pulls me back towards Dan's chest. He really doesn't want to let me go tonight.

'He gave you a name?' he asks.

'He did.'

'Good. So now you know who we're on our way to see.'

He kisses the top of my head. His arms tighten once more. Biting back the urge to ask any more questions, I spend the entire journey curled up in his embrace while he gently strokes my hair. Somehow, I know this is going to be difficult enough for both of us. I don't need to make it any worse by interrogating him. And besides, I get the feeling that all my questions are about to be answered. At last, the taxi draws to a halt.

'Where are we?'

'Belgravia.' He leans forwards and thrusts a note at the taxi driver. 'Wait for us, no matter how long this takes. I'll make it worth your while. The lady's going to leave her handbag here.'

Helping me out of the car, he leads me up the steps of an imposing Georgian townhouse, set back from the road behind iron railings. Wherever this is, judging by the immaculate state of the place and the Bentley parked right outside, we're somewhere very upmarket indeed. He comes to a halt on the top step, his grip tightening around my hand.

'Whatever you see in here, don't judge me by it. Remember it's all in the past. And Maya.' He places a finger under my chin, tipping my head up towards him. His eyes spark fiercely. 'Trust me.'

He straightens up, allowing a mask to fall into place: suddenly, his expression is unreadable, his eyes empty of all emotion. Reaching out, he presses the bell and seems to hold his breath. It takes several seconds for the door to open, revealing a large man, dressed in pin-striped trousers and a blue shirt. I gaze up at the stranger, entranced by the fact that everything about his face seems to droop: the handlebar moustache, the lips, the chubby cheeks, even the eyebrows. At first sight, he seems to be half-asleep, but he's clearly not. His grey eyes dart about, sharp and observant. The moment they fix on Dan, the rest of the face struggles to raise itself into an insincere smile.

'Dan!' A deep voice resonates through the evening air.

'Isaac.'

I watch as Dan lets go of me. Shooting back an insincere smile of his own, he slips his hand into a set of chubby fingers.

'Well, goodness me! You're back.'

'I am.'

The grey eyes shift to my face. A shiver skitters its way up my spine. There's something about this man that I just don't like.

'And you've brought a friend,' he grins. 'Come in! Come in!'

Taking a step back, Isaac waves us into a large, bright hallway. Immediately, I can see that there's money in this place, what with the marble floor, the antique tables that sit at intervals along the walls and the heavy, gold-framed mirrors hanging above them. He motions towards an open door. Dan places his hand at the small of my back and even here in this strange place, a familiar shimmer of excitement passes through me. I'm shown into a dimly lit room that looks to all intents and purposes like a gentleman's study.

It takes me a moment or two to adjust my eyes to the gloom before I begin to register the contents. In front of an ornate fireplace, two Chesterfield chairs face each other across an antique mahogany table. On the table top, a crystal decanter, half-filled with amber liquid, stands next to a bottle of water and two glasses. The floor is covered with a rug that's worn and thin now, but clearly expensive, and the walls are decorated with dark oil paintings. I take a step forwards, inspecting the paintings, one by one, discovering that they're all of naked women in various sexual poses. It's then that I realise the pictures are interspersed with various objects hanging from hooks on the walls: manacles, whips, gags, paddles …

Oh Jesus, my brain screams out. He's brought you to some sort of high-end sex den!

'Whisky?' Isaac purrs.

'If you don't mind,' Dan answers crisply.

Isaac sets about pouring the drinks.

'And what would you like, young lady?' he asks, glancing across at me.

'Nothing, thank you.'

It takes all of my self-control not to tell him to stop being so bloody patronising. Somehow, I know this just isn't the time for indignation. Play along with the scene, I tell myself. Just bloody well play along.

'The little lady's a tad nervous.' Isaac's mouth twists into a grin. 'She's never done this type of thing before, I can tell.' He hands a glass to Dan and then sinks down into one of the Chesterfields. 'Would you like a seat?' he asks me, waving at the free chair.

'Thank you.'

I perch myself on the edge of the leather and the big man nods at me, letting his eyes rest on my breasts for a little too long before he turns his attention back to Dan.

'You haven't been around for a while. I heard you'd left the scene.'

'You heard right.'

'So, what's this then?'

'A trip down memory lane. My membership's still current.'

'Of course it is. We don't do refunds here.' The grey eyes flick back in my direction. 'And this lovely young thing is?'

'None of your business.' Dan's words scatter themselves into the air, like bullets. In a split second, the atmosphere between the two men has frozen solid.

'Don't you worry, Daniel,' Isaac counters. 'I know my place.' From the way that he's staring at me now, I'm pretty sure he doesn't. His eyes skirt up and down my legs and I readjust myself on the chair, wishing to God that we can just get this over with quickly. 'You've moved on then?' he asks, motioning his glass towards me. 'Initiating fresh blood?'

Finishing off the whisky, Dan leans forwards, depositing the empty glass on the table.

'Whatever I've moved on to, it doesn't concern you. I'm here for a purpose. Is Claudine around?'

Isaac raises an eyebrow.

'Yes, she is. Upstairs.'

'Good. I'd like a private room for the night. And I'd like to invite Claudine to join us.'

You what? My mouth flies open at that. My muscles tense. I'm about to spring up from the chair and flee for my life when I catch sight of Dan's face.

'Trust,' he mouths silently, shaking his head.

'Ooh,' Isaac giggles. Ripples of flab wobble around his neck. 'A ménage à trois, young lady. You're going in at the deep end.'

'Enough of that, Isaac. Have you got a room?'

'Yes.' He stops laughing and narrows his eyes at Dan. 'I have a room available for you, Daniel. I'll get a message to Claudine. I'm sure she'll join you. You were always a favourite of hers.' He sighs, leaning to one side, and sets his glass down on the table. When he looks back up at Dan, his expression is fixed, perfectly serious, half-menacing.

'You'll be careful with my little chick, won't you?' he growls.

'Of course.'

'I've nurtured that one. I'd like to have her returned to me in a decent state.'

'She'll be absolutely fine.'

'Good. You can take your usual room. Any extras?'

'Yes.' Dan glances down at me. His lips twitch slightly before he mutters the next word. 'Whips.'

***

With my hand firmly clutched in his, Dan guides me up a set of stairs and down a corridor. Up here, the décor is just as expensive and sumptuous as on the ground floor, only now the marble flooring has been replaced by a deep red carpet and the lighting is dimmer. Every single door we pass is closed, apart from one. As I'm led past it, I hear a moan. It's a woman's voice. I pull myself to a halt. Dan turns quickly.

'Maya?'

I nod towards the door.

'No,' he warns me.

'I want to know what you did.'

'And how would that help matters?'

'I have a right to know.'

A second long, low moan comes from behind the door.

'Let go of me.' I tug at his grip.

'For fuck's sake, no.'

I glare at him, determined to go through with this. I want to get inside this man's head, and if I'm going to do that, then I need to understand his past. At last, he releases his grip and I move towards the door, pushing it open just far enough to take a peek. At first, it's difficult to see what's going on in the gloom, but slowly it comes into focus. Apart from a bed, there's no ordinary furniture in here: just a leather bench in one corner and what looks like a swing chair in another. But it's what I find at the centre of the room that causes my breath to falter: a woman, suspended from the ceiling in a leather harness. She's face down with her legs parted, bent upward and behind her at the knee. Various straps hold her in place, around her legs, her body and her arms. And she's being fucked ... fucked viciously by one naked, faceless man, while another stands at her head, with a handful of her hair clutched in his fist, forcing his cock deep into her mouth.

'You did this?' I whisper.

I feel him by my side.

'It's consensual. Come away.'

'But this?'

'I told you not to look.'

He takes me by the hand again and urges me further down the hallway.

'But why does she want to be treated like that?' There's no way I'm letting this one go. 'Does she know those men?'

'They're probably acquaintances. And as for why she wants that done to her, I have no idea. That's her business.'

He stops at the end of the hallway, outside the final door, and a shiver scurries its way up my spine. I have no idea what I'm about to be presented with. My brain has only just begun to toss and turn over the possibilities when he opens the door, revealing nothing more than what looks like a plush, luxurious hotel bedroom. He motions for me to enter and I step inside, trying to take it all in, noting a huge four-poster bed, a leather sofa set in the corner, an occasional table. I perch myself on the edge of the bed while he pours a glass of water from a decanter and hands it to me.

'Your hands are shaking. I told you to trust me. There's no need to be afraid.'

'You've brought me to a sex club full of kinky weirdos.'

'That makes me a kinky weirdo. I am a member, after all.'

'I can't believe what I've just seen,' I breathe. 'How did you get into this?'

'I was encouraged. A long time ago. And now, I'm out of it.'

'And you wouldn't come back to it?'

Keeping his eyes fixed on me, he shakes his head, slowly.

'I've found a much better club. Very exclusive. Just two members.' He folds his arms. 'I wish you hadn't seen that. Please don't judge me by it.'

'Degrading women, it's just ...'

'Women told me what they wanted,' he interrupts, 'and I gave it to them. Like I said, don't judge me by what you see in here. This isn't me.'

'Then what is, Dan? Please tell me because I haven't got a fucking clue.'

He drops his head, runs his fingers through his hair and when he looks up again, the expression of pure anguish on his face makes me want to leap up and throw my arms around him.

'I'm doing my best,' he pleads. 'I told you, you just need to give me time. This was a mistake, bringing you here.'

'Then why did you?'

'Because there's no other way to prove what I'm about to prove.'

There's a knock on the door. We both start and turn to look at it.

'Claudine?' I whisper.

He nods and the anguish disappears. Pulling the mask back into place, he seats himself on the sofa, draping his arms across the leather back and crossing his legs. He's completely and utterly composed. It's a masterful performance.

'Come in,' he calls.

The door opens to reveal a tall, red-haired woman, dressed in nothing but a silk robe. She moves into the room, glancing briefly at me before she locks her attention on Dan. In her right hand, she's carrying a whip.

'You're back,' she breathes.

A smile plays at the corner of his mouth.

'I am.'

'I knew you'd come back in the end.'

'I had to come, Claudine. You made it impossible for me to stay away. I hope you've brought my favourite.'

'Of course.' She waves the whip around in front of her face before tossing it onto the bed. 'So, we're here for a threesome then?' Casting a dismissive glance in my direction, she begins to sidle her way across the room, making straight for Dan. He raises a hand and halts her in her tracks. There's something new about him now, something cold and hard in his demeanour, something strange I've never seen before.

'We are,' he says. 'But we're going to take our time.' Raising himself up from the sofa, he nods towards me. 'She's new to this and we wouldn't want to put her off, would we?'

'No we wouldn't.'

'On your knees.'

Without hesitation, Claudine Thomas drops to the floor, her head lowered, and I understand: Dan's playing the dominant now. And he must have played it plenty of times before because, bloody hell, he's good at it.

'What are you in the mood for, Claudine?'

'Anything you want to give me.'

'I'd like to give you this.' Picking up the whip, he runs it across the back of her neck. I can practically see her shiver. 'Head up,' he orders, and she complies. He smoothes the whip across her cheek. 'Do you want me to whip you?'

'Yes. Yes, I do.'

'And why is that?'

'Why?'

'Answer me, Claudine.'

'Because I like it.'

'Not good enough.' He taps the whip against her shoulder.

'Because I love it, especially with you.'

'And are you sure about that?'

'Of course I'm sure.' She seems to notice something in his eyes, a trace of disgust perhaps. 'Why wouldn't I be sure?'

The next few seconds seem to drag their heels. While Claudine Thomas searches his face for clues, Dan continues to stare back down at her.

'Because I whipped you once until you bled,' he presses on, his tone even, perfectly measured. 'Because I lost control and ignored your safeword. Because I had to be pulled away from you.' He pauses. His eyelids flicker momentarily. 'Because I'm a sadist.'

'I don't ...' Confusion takes hold of her face.

'Well, that's the story, Claudine. The story you've been spreading around town.' I watch as she shakes her head. 'You just can't help yourself, can you? You've been spreading your malicious lies because you can't stand the fact that I don't want you.' He stares down at her, his top lip lifting into the beginnings of a sneer. 'So let's just get this straight, shall we?' With a dismissive flick of the wrist, he tosses the whip back onto the bed. 'If I'm guilty of all of those things, then why the hell are you so eager to let me back at you now?'

'I never said anything like that,' she insists.

And that's enough to set me off. 'Oh yes you fucking well did,' I spit.

'Oh, it speaks, does it?' Springing to her feet, she glares at me.

'Yes, it does fucking speak,' I hiss. 'And you did spread that story around. And it's a pile of shit, just like you.'

Claudine Thomas stares at me in amazement. At last, her mouth opens. She turns back to Dan. 'And what's sewage mouth here got to do with it?' she demands.

I'd leap up and chin the madam right now, but I'm distracted by the fact that Dan is holding out a hand to me. And more than that, he's let a smile off the leash. I smile back at him, relieved that the cold, harsh dominant has disappeared for now. My very own Daniel Foster is back in the room.

'Everything,' he announces proudly, curling his fingers inwards. 'Now come along, sewage mouth. I think we're done here.'

Ignoring the gawping red head, I place my hand in his, allowing him to pull me up from the bed and into his arms.

'Satisfied?' he breathes into my ear.

'Satisfied,' I confirm.

'Well thank fuck for that. Now, let's get back to your place. I want you to feel comfortable tonight.' He squeezes my hand. 'You need to be on home ground.'

Chapter Twenty-Six

Shrugging off his jacket, he throws it onto my bed and falters for a moment, catching sight of the edge of the canvas. He pulls it out from where I've stored it safely, down beside the wardrobe, and sets it on the floor, leaning it up against the wall. Taking a step back, he stares at the picture in silence, lost in thought.

'It's finished.' I touch him on the arm.

He gives a start.

'It's wonderful. You're a talented woman, Maya Scotton.'

Arching my eyebrows at him, I decide to change the course of the conversation. I've never been too comfortable with praise.

'Lucy's not back yet. You don't think she's hit it off with Clive, do you?'

'Who knows and who cares? It's time I fucked you senseless.'

With that, he turns quickly, grabbing me by the waist and drawing me close. And although I'm quaking down below at the very thought of a damn good seeing to, the sensible half of my brain has finally come into play, energising me with a new resolve. Gritting my teeth against the myriad of sensations that are kicking off between my legs, I decide it's time to simply get on with the interrogation. My decision was made on the way back from Belgravia: this man is getting nowhere near my special bits until he's explained himself.

'No,' I inform him.

His expression darkens, transforming itself from bright sunlight into shadow.

'I make the rules around here,' he reminds me.

'Not all the time, you don't, Mr Foster. So if you know what's good for you, just sit down on the bed.' I pause for effect, giving him an I-really-mean-this face. 'My rules now.'

'Your rules?' He grinds his crotch against mine, sending a delicious quiver of lust through my core.

'My rules.' I swallow hard, doing my best to press on with the plan.

'Which are?'

'You do exactly as I say.' I wait for a moment, watching as he sucks at his bottom lip. 'No talking unless I ask you a question.' I wait again. His lips begin to twitch. 'And you answer every single one of my questions.' He narrows his eyes. 'Is that understood?' He opens his mouth to speak, but he's far too slow. I get in there first. 'I said is that understood?' With a reluctant nod, he loosens his grip on me and sits on the bed. I let out a sigh, and continue. 'If you want me to trust you, then I need to know more about you, Dan. And if you want this to go any further, then you need to open up to me. You can start with Claudine Thomas.'

At the mention of her name, he winces and I wonder if I should really go on with this. After all, there's been enough trouble today. But then again, I remind myself, after what he's done today, he owes me a few explanations.

'Come on, Dan. Tell me about her.'

'There's nothing to know,' he begins quietly. 'She's just someone I met at the club.'

'I think there's plenty more to it than that.'

'It was sex. That's all. I met her there and I fucked her.'

'How many times?

'I don't know.' He clasps his hands together. 'It went on for a year or so. It wasn't exclusive. I never saw her outside of the club. We had a few shallow conversations here and there. Nothing much. I was never interested in her, not in the way I'm interested in you.'

'But you enjoyed whipping her.'

'Enjoyed isn't the right word.'

'Then what?'

'I don't know.'

I wait for more but nothing comes. Realising that I'll just have to bide my time on that one, I move on.

'So, how far did you go? Did you ever make her bleed?'

'Yes.' He stares at me, his eyes pleading for understanding. 'It was last year. One night, she asked me to whip her hard.' He lowers his head. 'She didn't opt out and nobody had to pull me off. She was begging for more. In fact, she was screaming for it.' He looks up at me again. 'I went too far. I know that, but I stopped myself. It was a wake-up call. I walked out of there and I've never been back, not until tonight.'

'Why did you go too far? That's the question.'

He bites his lip, glancing past me at the picture, as if he's searching for inspiration in the woods of Limmingham. When he begins to speak again, his voice falters.

'I wasn't in a good place. I wasn't thinking straight. I'd had a visit from someone.'

'Who?'

'It doesn't matter. Just someone from my past, someone I never wanted to see again. They turned up at my office out of the blue and it threw me.' Closing his eyes, he runs a hand through his mop of hair. 'Leave it, Maya. Please.'

'I can't leave it. You need to answer all of my questions. My rules.'

'And I will. I promise. Another time.' He holds me with his gaze, silently begging me to let it go, and I do. 'I can't change what I've done in the past.' Reaching out, he takes hold of my hand. 'Don't push me away because of this.'

'I won't,' I reassure him.

'I'll never hurt you. That's all I know.'

'I know that too.'

With a sigh and a nod, he closes his eyes for a moment before getting to his feet and snaking an arm around me. A hand cups the back of my head.

'So, I'm off the hook then?' he asks.

'Not entirely. You've got a little more explaining to do. You can't go sending me flowers and then mess about with another woman.'

'I am not messing about with another woman.'

'Lily's got the hots for you.'

'Trust me, she's not.'

'She wants to get inside your trousers. Is she a madam?'

'What?'

He loosens his grip for no more than a split second but it's enough. I take the opportunity to free myself. Taking a step backwards, I watch as his face travels from shock, through disbelief, and finally lands on amusement. He begins to laugh.

'Don't laugh at me, Foster! She's a madam, isn't she? Or some sort of high class prostitute? You keep her on because you just can't drop your old ways.'

He's laughing so much now there are tears in his eyes. Wiping them away, he draws in a few deep breaths.

'Lily's a family friend,' he explains, smiling broadly. 'I've known her since I was twelve. She's like a sister to me. She's also bisexual, if you must know, and her preference at the moment is female. She's in a relationship and having a spot of bother.'

'What?'

'She came to me for help and ...' He silences himself in mid-flow and stares at me. 'What sort of flowers?'

'Pardon?'

'You said I sent you flowers.'

'This morning. The roses.'

He shakes his head.

'I didn't send you any roses.'

'But the card ...'

My eyes seem to lose their ability to focus. Suddenly, the room is a blur.

'What did it say?' he asks.

'I'm glad I found you.'

The next few moments pass by in silence while I'm dragged under, into the depths, watching the surface as it recedes out of reach. I'm drowning in my own personal nightmare now. If it wasn't Dan, then there's only one other suspect, and my blood runs cold at the very thought of him: the man I left behind in Edinburgh, the man I ran away from ... and for good reason too. I shake my head, trying to jolt reason and logic back into place. I'm just over-reacting. Because it couldn't be him. He gave up on finding me a long time ago. When I finally surface again, I find Dan frowning at me.

'Is there something I should know about?' he asks.

'No. Of course not.'

He watches me closely for a few seconds before taking hold of my arm.

'Then don't worry about it.' He squeezes me gently. 'It's not surprising you've got other admirers. But I can tell you one thing.'

'What's that?'

'None of those fuckers are getting anywhere near you. Now, come here.' He draws me in again, holding me so tight I can barely breathe. He brings his mouth to my ear, nipping at my earlobe and sending a tingle down my neck. 'My rules now, Miss Scotton,' he whispers. 'Your reign of terror is over.' With a smile, he lets go of me and lowers himself back down onto the bed. With his eyes fixed on mine, he unfastens his tie and throws it on the floor. 'Strip for me,' he murmurs, his eyes glinting in the light.

'What?'

'I said strip.'

'I don't ...'

'My rules.' He smiles languidly, unfastening the top three buttons on his shirt and leaning back. 'Now do as you're told.'

I gawp at him for a few seconds before I finally realise that he means it. He actually wants me to strip for him. He's staring at me now, all mean and hot and moody, and I feel myself blush. Okay, so I've already peeled my knickers off for him today, but a full-blown striptease, well that's another thing entirely. But in spite of any reservations, I unzip my skirt, edging it down until it's low enough to drop to the floor. Stepping out of it, I glance down at my bare crotch.

'Still in the stockings.' He grins mischievously while his eyes seem to dance their approval. 'You can keep those on.' He wafts a hand through the air. 'Please continue.'

Keeping my eyes fixed on his, I begin to unbutton my new blouse, parting the material here and there to give him a flash of skin. His smile deepens as I shrug the blouse away from my shoulders. And now for the finale. I reach behind my back, unclasp my bra and gradually release my breasts from the cups. Dropping the bra, I stand in front of him, completely naked except for the suspender belt and the stockings. Silently, he beckons me forwards with his right index finger.

'Now turn around.'

I do as I'm told and feel his hands on my buttocks. The warmth of his touch has me rolling my head backwards in pleasure.

'They're red,' he breathes. 'Have you got anything I can put on them? Something to soothe them?'

'No.'

'Well it won't happen again.' He turns me back to face him, wrapping his hands around my hips. 'Which is a shame.'

He smiles knowingly and I just can't help probing further.

'Why is it a shame?'

'Because you'd enjoy a proper spanking.'

I laugh.

'I can't see that happening. It was bloody painful.'

'Well, that's because I gave you a short, sharp dose. If I'd had time to carry on, believe me, it wouldn't have hurt so much.'

I hear myself snort.

'It's true. Your body releases endorphins.' He talks quietly, dreamily, running a finger across my stomach, urging my legs open and softly exploring my labia. 'And adrenalin too. Your pain threshold rises. Your blood flow increases, especially around here.'

He caresses my crotch in his palm. 'In the right hands, you learn to truly enjoy the pain.' He massages me slowly. 'Give me an hour or so and I could spank you into a stupor.'

'You'd spank me for an hour?'

'Not solidly. It's an art form, believe me, a balance of pleasure and pain. Your body releases its chemicals, I watch for the signs, soothing you when I need to, stimulating you when it's necessary, spanking again when it's just the right time. I could make you come without even getting inside you.'

'That's quite some claim.'

'It's just a fact.'

I can hear my own breath now, and it's beginning to unravel. Jesus, I'm turned on. And fuck, I'm tempted. And before I know what's going on, I can hear my voice making a distinctly strange suggestion.

'Well, maybe we should try it.'

'Maybe we should. But I'd need to restrain you somewhere comfortable, and I'd need to take my time. You'd need to be in the right frame of mind.'

'Not tonight,' I plead.

'No, not tonight.'

He gazes up at me. Sliding his left hand around my buttocks, he continues to massage me at the front, stroking a finger slowly around my clit, working up a ball of warmth between my legs. Removing the finger, he pulls me closer. Immediately, his tongue laps at me, working its way between the folds of my clitoris, over the tip, again finding my spot and swirling over it, lazily. His right hand moves between my thighs, parting them. His fingers push their way inside me, probing deep. Clasping a hand on either side of his head and clutching at his hair, I close my eyes and drink in the pleasure. His left hand tightens against my buttocks, reminding me of the soreness, and the rhythm picks up, his tongue working at the front while his fingers gently thrum inside. I moan again, and again, as the pressure begins to build inside, pulsing its way from my centre outwards. Before long, a deep, exquisite ache takes hold of me. I teeter on the edge for a minute or so, groaning unashamedly. It doesn't take much longer. In an instant, my muscles clench in on themselves, pulsating, rippling, causing me to cry out.

'Oh fuck, that's fucking good!'

With a satisfied laugh, he pulls me down onto the bed, kissing me deeply for an age, pinning me into place with one hand while the other runs up and down my thighs, evidently enjoying the feel of the suspenders.

'Make yourself comfortable, sewage mouth,' he whispers at last, stroking my cheek. 'It's time I changed into my birthday suit.'

Still flushed through with my orgasm, I rearrange myself on the bed as quickly as I can. Daniel Foster stripping off. Now, that's one show I just don't want to miss. Propping myself up on my elbows, I watch as the sex God removes his shirt, revealing his muscles and that ridiculously perfect torso. It's not until his trousers hit the floor that he realises I've got him in my sights. He slows down immediately. Slipping his fingers into his pants, he draws them downwards, edging the material over the end of his cock, stopping for a moment to allow me ogle at its size, before he finally steps out of his underwear.

'Hands up.'

I do as I'm told, watching as he prowls around the room, looking for God knows what. He opens my wardrobe door and lets out a sigh.

'You are one fucking disorganised woman,' he groans, rummaging around on a shelf. 'This'll do.'

He takes out a scarf, a thin, silk number I've had for ages and hardly ever worn. On his way back to the bed, he makes a detour, picking a paint brush out of the crate. Oh shit! My mind explodes. What's he going to do with that? He must have noticed the look of shock on my face because now he's grinning at me.

'Relax, woman. This isn't going inside you.'

'Thank God for that.'

Climbing back onto the bed, he places the paint brush next to me, motions for me to raise my head and blindfolds me with the scarf. It's beautifully soft next to my skin, comforting.

'Now,' I hear him whisper. 'Relax this body.'

I do what I can, but I'm on high alert because I have no idea what he's about to do with that bloody paint brush. The bed dips and he's beside me, his skin warm against mine. He takes off my stockings, patiently unclipping them and peeling them away from my feet. After that, he unfastens the suspender belt and carefully pulls it away from my waist. A few seconds later, my left nipple is tickled by a set of bristles.

'Oh God,' I gasp, my entire body lighting up at the touch. Evidently, he's chosen a brush I haven't used yet, one that's fresh, still soft, unbothered by oil paints and cleaning fluid. 'Oh shit.' I just can't help myself. I begin to writhe under him as the brush is swirled around, lightly, gently, across my breast, round and round in slow, masterful movements.

'How do you like that?'

'Mmm,' I moan. 'A lot.'

'And how about this?'

He moves the brush across my chest, the bristles spiralling against my skin, setting me on fire with sensations. The brush travels downwards, slowly, barely glancing against my skin in some places. It dances its way across my stomach, moving further downwards. He pauses for a moment, urging my legs further apart and slightly upwards so that he can gain full access to my groin. And now, the real pleasure begins. The brush is removed and lands again with delicate touches across the inside of one thigh and then the other. It sends my pulse into a rage, leaving my skin hyper-sensitive, washing my brain through with pleasure. I moan again, and hear him laugh quietly.

'You're beautiful,' he whispers. 'I love watching you like this.'

The bristles travels inwards, tickling their way across my clitoris, down towards my backside and back up along my perineum. He repeats the movement, again and again, until I'm nothing more than a wreck of desire.

'What do you want, Maya?'

'I want you to fuck me.'

'Magic word, woman.'

'Please,' I groan.

I sense a movement on the bed and I know that he's positioned himself above me now. His legs are between my thighs, nudging them further apart. His mouth covers mine, devouring me while his tongue gently probes my mouth. At last, he pulls away. I can still feel his breath against my face as his cock presses at my opening, pushing its way into me, slowly, filling me right up.

'It feels so good to be inside you,' he breathes. The blindfold is taken off and I find his glorious face right next to mine. 'I want to see you. Look at me while I fuck you.'

He withdraws slowly, right to the tip and then slides his way back up to the limit.

'I can't get enough of you, Maya. I've never felt like this before.'

'Like what?'

'I'm the one who asks the questions now.'

He withdraws again and thrusts straight back in. As he pounds the back of my vagina, I cry out in surprise.

'Get your legs over my shoulders.'

What? How am I supposed to do that? I'm not a bloody gymnast! He notices my confusion. Pulling himself out of me, he kneels up on his haunches, takes an ankle in each hand and hooks my legs over his shoulders, raising my backside away from the bed.

'Keep them there.'

I nod mutely. I can't talk right now. Bracing my arms against the bed, I'm having to concentrate for all I'm worth on keeping myself in position. He grabs hold of my calves, holding me in place and enters me again. Jesus, this new angle takes him deeper, fills me more. Immediately, I'm about to explode. I groan deliriously while he stares down at me, his eyes hooded, shot through with lust. He withdraws himself to the very tip of his penis and slowly penetrates me again, repeating the process over and over again, sending shimmers right through me.

'Are you nearly there?'

'Yes.'

'Then let's take you over the edge.' He ratchets up the speed again, pounding into me relentlessly. 'Come for me.'

Pulling back for a moment, he slams into me one last time. I let go on his order. My entire being seems to splinter in an instant.

'Fuck.' His body judders as he spends himself inside me. 'Fucking hell, Maya.' With shaking hands, he lowers my legs and withdraws before collapsing on top of me, wrapping me in his embrace and digging his head into my neck. 'You are one fucking addictive drug.'

I run my fingers through his hair, gazing contentedly at the side of his face. Eyes closed, he smiles against my skin and my heart skips several beats. This man is a million miles away from the arrogant bastard I met a few days ago, an ocean away from the cold dominant who surfaced briefly at the club.

'Dan?' I ask at last.

'Uh huh?'

'The way you were with Claudine Thomas. Why are you never like that with me?'

His eyes flick open.

'How do you mean?'

'With her, you were cold ... scary.'

He props himself on his elbows and gazes into my eyes.

'Sometimes people just put on a front, remember?' He brushes my hair out of my face. 'The first time I ever met you, you saw the real me.' He touches his lips against mine. 'So what's the point of hiding?'

Chapter Twenty-Seven

When I wake up the next morning, he's gone.

Bowling out of bed, I pull on a T-shirt and a pair of knickers, and race into the kitchen to find Lucy sitting at the table, downing a mug of tea on her own. All at once, the contents of my stomach decide to hurl themselves about like electrons inside an atom.

'God I'm thirsty,' Lucy complains. 'I got wazzocked last night.'

I wave a hand in the air. I really don't care how hung over Lucy Godfrey is. I've got more pressing matters to deal with.

'Where's Dan?' I demand.

'Gone home. You've just missed him.'

'Oh for fuck's sake.' I look for something to kick. 'I'm sick of this. He's backing out again.'

'Chill your beans, woman,' Lucy sighs. 'Clive gave him a lift home. Dan said he didn't want to wake you up and he'd be back in an hour. He had to pick something up. Oh, and he said you're spending the weekend with him.' Her eyeballs seem to expand and contract, a sure sign that her brain is trying to remember something important. 'Oh, yes. He said wear jeans and a T-shirt. That's an order.'

'What?'

'Them's his words.'

I slump down at the table.

'But what's he gone to get?'

'Beats me.'

'And hang on a minute ...'

'What?'

'How come Clive's taken him home? What was Clive doing here?'

An uncomfortable silence lurks in the air between us while my dishevelled flatmate opens her mouth and closes it again, at least five times.

'You didn't?'

'I might have,' she mumbles into her tea. 'You're not the only one who deserves a bit of how's your father.' She rolls her shoulders, doing her level best to seem affronted. Before I get the chance to ask for further information, she's already decided to oblige. 'We had a few more drinks last night and I invited him back for coffee. We sat on the sofa and talked for a bit and then it was, you know, ooh, he's looking at my lips and ooh, I'm looking at his lips and ooh, I say, he's leaning in for a kiss, and bloody hell he's fit.'

'He's an accountant with a ridiculous name.'

'He's a fucking fit accountant and I can put up with the name.'

'But Clive?'

'Clive.' She stares at me, utterly determined to see this one through. 'Clive,' she says again, without cracking a smile.

'I'm going to get dressed,' I mutter, getting to my feet.

'Jeans and a T-shirt,' Lucy calls out as I skitter off back to the bedroom. 'That's an order!'

***

Staring at my wardrobe, I decide it's got nothing to offer me today. Yes, I've got plenty of jeans and T-shirts but if Daniel Foster thinks he's going to control me outside of the bedroom, then he can go and get stuffed. I need to make a point, and I need to make it good and proper. In fact, I need a dress. With no other option, I take myself off to Lucy's bedroom. As soon as I open the door, I let out a gasp: it looks like several bombs have gone off in here. For a start, Lucy's clothes from last night are strewn all over the floor, and if I'm not very much mistaken that's a pair of her knickers dangling from the bedside lamp. Doing my best to ignore the carnage, I open the wardrobe and pull out the most flowery, girly, short dress I can find, a cream and pink number, all pretty and feminine and dainty. Taking it back to my room, I slip it on and locate my mobile, fully intending to fire off a quick text to the big kahuna, reminding him in no uncertain terms that when it comes to clothing, he's not the boss of me. As soon as the screen lights up, I let out a groan. I'm faced with a message from Sara:

I really need to see you. Can I come down to stay?

Come down to stay? Jesus! Not likely! That's the last thing I need. And I don't care how badly the gruesome husband is pissing her off, I just haven't got the time or the inclination to help her out at the minute. And anyway, it's not as if I owe her even a speck of sisterly love. What goes around, comes around. She'll just have to cope by herself. Ignoring my sister's plea, I get on with the far more

important task of putting Mr Foster firmly in his place. I tap out a text:
Thank you for your orders. I'll wear what I like, if you don't mind.
The answer is quick in coming.
Of course I don't mind, as long as it's jeans and a T-shirt. X
I stare at the kiss, stunned by its sudden appearance. Now where did that come from? And what the hell does it mean? Before I really know what I'm doing, I'm firing off a reply.
What's with the X?
I spend a good couple of minutes waiting for a response. When nothing comes, I perch on the edge of my bed and begin to wonder if I've pissed him off. Have I just pressed him for a declaration he's simply not ready to give? Shit. I think I have. So now, when he finally turns up on my doorstep, bringing with him whatever he's gone to fetch, he'll be in a grump and I'll be feeling distinctly embarrassed. Oh yes, I'm an idiot. I've definitely gone and done the wrong thing there …

***

I'm standing in the hallway, rearranging my hair for the umpteenth time and still worrying myself stupid over that stupid bloody text when I hear a roar from the street outside. Opening the door, I find a black motorbike parked at the kerb and sitting astride it, kitted out in a set of black leathers, is Dan. While he removes his helmet, ruffling his hair in the process, I shuffle out onto the step and gawp at him. His shoulders slump and he stares at me in despair.

'I told you to wear jeans and a T-shirt,' he sighs.

A sudden realisation dawns on me. I'm being taken out on a huge beast of a motorbike and a skimpy dress is no protection.

'I'll go and change.'

He shakes his head. In one swift movement, he swings his leg over the bike and marches up to the doorway. A gloved hand reaches out and grabs hold of my wrist.

'No, you won't. You've decided to play silly buggers again and you can pay for it.'

'Dan, I can change.'

'And I say you'll stay in this dress.' He tilts his head to one side, looking all rugged and shit hot in his leathers. I just want to yank him inside and strip him naked right now. 'Besides, I like it,' he adds, his eyes twinkling. 'Oh, and in answer to your question about my text.'

A second gloved hand reaches out and grabs the back of my head. I've hardly had time to draw breath when his lips are on mine, kissing me fiercely, deeply.

'Is that clear enough?' he breathes, finally releasing me.

'Yes,' I squeak.

'Good. Then let's get going.'

I stare at the motorbike.

'We're going out on that thing?'

'Yes, we are. It's my preferred mode of transport.'

'But it's only got two wheels. It might fall over. It's dangerous.'

'Don't be ridiculous,' he laughs. 'Besides, I've got a little something for you.'

He motions towards a car that's parked a few feet away. The rear passenger door is open, and standing right next to it, holding a second set of leathers, a pair of boots and a helmet, is Clive. With a grin, he moves forwards and thrusts the whole lot at Dan.

'Cheers, Clive.' Laying the helmet on the seat of the motorbike and placing the boots at my feet, Dan sets about shaking out the leathers. 'So, what are you up to today?'

'Lucy's got the day off,' Clive smiles. 'I said I'd take her out.' He touches me on the arm. 'Enjoy yourself, Maya. I've got to go.'

While Clive disappears inside the flat, Dan begins to go through the rigmarole of squeezing me into a full set of leathers. I'm ordered to take off my sandals, which are tossed into the hallway shortly before my feet are squeezed into the boots.

'Dan, I'm scared.'

He looks up at me, genuinely excited, like a little boy. 'Don't be. You're with me.' He stands up straight. 'You wanted me to open up. Well, I'm going to. I'm going to show you my world.'

'Not more sex clubs?'

He tuts. 'There's more to me than that. Now, get this on.'

He pulls the helmet over my head. I stand there while he fixes the strap under my chin, concentrating on getting it just right before he opens the visor.

'Is that too tight?'

'No, it's fine.'

He wiggles the helmet about.

'Perfect. Let's get going.'

I follow him to the motorbike and watch as he swings himself back onto it.

'You sit here.' He pats the seat behind him. 'Feet on those pegs. Arms around my waist. Hold tight at all times. Whichever way I lean, you go with me. Understand?'

I nod.

'I mean it, Maya. Don't try to go in the opposite direction. You've just got to trust me. In everything.'

I nod again and hoist my right leg over the bike, manoeuvring myself into position.

'Comfortable?'

'Yes,' I shout.

He puts his helmet back on and with a flick of a key, the motorbike erupts into life. Clamping my arms around his waist, I hold on for dear life while he kicks up the stand, revs the engine a few times and pulls out into the road. My heart begins to pound as we turn onto Camden High Street, and then it begins to thud as he picks up the speed. Before long, we've made it through the streets of North London and I'm pretty sure we're on the M25. I have no idea where we're going. All I know is we're in the outside lane more often than I care to think about. But whichever way he leans, he takes me with him, and the further we go, the more I learn to trust him. By the time we finally leave the motorway and begin to hurtle our way along picture perfect country roads, I'm almost certain I'm enjoying the whole experience. At last, the motorbike slows. Taking a right turn through a gateway, we roll forwards beneath a canopy of trees until we emerge into the sunlight, out onto a gravelled driveway that curls to a halt in front of an impressive, Georgian country house. While Dan slows the bike to a crawl, picking his way carefully over the gravel, I take the opportunity to peek over his broad shoulders at what I already know is the family home. After all, I've seen it before … in the photograph on Norman's shelf.

With five huge sash windows on each of its two main storeys, the house is perfectly symmetrical. A third storey sits in the roof where three smaller, dormer windows gaze out over the perfectly tended lawn. On the ground floor, a panelled door is centre stage, perched at the top of a small flight of steps. The whole thing is painted a pale cream colour, a contrast to the vibrant flower beds that line the front lawn. I don't think I've ever seen anywhere quite so beautiful, quite so peaceful and calm. We draw to a halt at the bottom of the steps and when the bike has hummed into silence, Dan takes off his helmet, turns and gives me a heart-stopping grin.

'Home, sweet home,' he smiles. 'You get off first.'

I swing my leg over the back of the bike and lower myself to the ground, immediately fiddling with the strap under my chin. Pulling it loose, I tug the helmet off my head and shake out my hair, hoping against all hope that I don't look a complete mess. God, I'm sticky and my dress has ridden up a few inches into places it really shouldn't go.

I watch in awe as Dan gets off the bike and sets about shrugging off his leather gear. Underneath it all, he's wearing my favourite outfit, the one he wore when he tracked me down to Slaters: tight, black jeans and a plain black T-shirt. Slipping his boots back on, he arranges the leathers across the back of the bike and turns to face me. My heartbeat trips at the sight of him.

'Now, let's see how that dress is doing.'

He unzips the top of my leathers and peels them away from my shoulders, before crouching down in front of me, removing the boots and pulling the leathers off completely. As I step out of them, I realise that the dress is already a mess of crinkles.

'Oh dear.' He smiles up at me. 'You know you really should just do as I say.'

'Never,' I grimace. 'So, I'm guessing this is your parents' house.'

He stands up.

'It was. It's mine now. I've had some very happy years here.'

'In the lap of luxury. I bet you were a spoilt brat.'

Oh bugger, I've done it again. My rotten, stupid mouth has fired off before it's been fully briefed by my brain.

'I wasn't spoilt when I was child, Maya, and I wasn't overindulged. I didn't get every last thing I wanted. In fact ...' He trails off into silence, turning to look up at the house and then back to me. Suddenly, there's a hint of sadness in his eyes. It must have been hard, losing his mum and dad in one fell swoop. 'Come on.' He reaches out a hand. 'I'll show you round.' He glances down at my bare feet. 'We should have brought those sandals. You can't put those boots back on. They don't go with the dress. And I can't have you hurting yourself on this gravel. Here.'

Before I can say a word, he grabs hold of me and swings me over his shoulder, knocking the air clean out of my lungs. Ignoring my complaints, he carries me round to the back of the house and sets me down on the grass. When I finally get my breath back, I take a look around, awestruck by the idyllic scene in front of me: beyond yet more lawn, I can see an orchard and behind that, an ancient-looking wall.

'Good tree climbing.' He points at the trees. 'And there's a kitchen garden on the other side of that wall. I'll take you to see it later, but first we must meet the boss.'

'I thought you were the boss.'

'Not here,' he winks.

He leads me inside, into the cool, through a flag-stoned corridor that makes me think of Jane Austen, and further into a huge kitchen that's kitted out with a fireplace and an Aga, alongside all manner of more modern appliances. An oak table and chairs sit at the centre of it all, and over at the far end a woman, dressed in a plain, grey dress, is busying herself with washing pots at a Belfast sink. She can only be about five feet tall but what she lacks in height, she more than makes up for in width. She seems to sense our presence. Raising her head and swinging round on the spot, she holds out her arms.

'Well, here he is,' she beams. 'Come and give us a hug.'

At her command, Dan sweeps forwards, throwing his arms around the woman and squeezing the life out of her. Finally, he straightens up and turns to me.

'Maya, this is Betty. Betty, this is Maya.'

While Betty shuffles toward me, I take in her face, noting the wrinkles, the lack of make-up, the kindly grey eyes.

'Oh my Lord, she's beautiful.'

'Told you, Betty.'

'Lord above. I never thought I'd see the day.' She takes my hands in hers and stares at me, transfixed, and I wonder what the hell he's told her about me because she seems to be looking at me as if I'm some sort of a goddess. 'I hope you like chops,' she wheezes at last. 'We've got chops for dinner. You're not a vegetarian, are you?' I shake my head. 'Oh, thank goodness for that. I asked Dan but he didn't have a clue.'

I feel an arm around my waist and I'm dragged backwards, out of Betty's grasp.

'I'm going to show Maya around the house, Betty. You can chat with her more over dinner.'

'Six o'clock.' Betty raises a finger and narrows her eyes at Dan. 'And don't you be late, young man.'

Before I can even open my mouth to say goodbye, my hand is clasped firmly in his. I'm guided out of the kitchen and back into the flag-stoned corridor. He takes me further into his home, pushing open a door into what I can only suppose is the main entrance to the house. I catch my breath at the sudden change. We've just stepped out of the gloomy servants' quarters into another world, a world of light and space and air. I'm barely given time to take it all in. Instead, I'm ushered across the black and white marbled floor, past a sweeping staircase and straight into a sitting room. It's only now that my hand is freed and I'm allowed to take a good look around. Turning slowly, I try to register everything. It's a huge room, probably the size of my entire flat in Camden. Tall sash windows dominate two of the sky blue walls, spilling sunlight across the pair of sofas, a coffee table, a fireplace. I catch sight of a television, a bookcase or two, a smattering of antique furniture. And then my attention is drawn back to the walls: they're decorated with watercolours.

'My mother painted most of these.' I turn to find him examining me closely, watching for my reaction to every last thing. 'There's another sitting room on the ground floor, a dining room and a study. But this is my favourite room, the room I tend to use. If you want to know who I am, it's all here.' He shrugs, almost embarrassed and I turn away, overcome by the urge to poke my nose into every last corner of the room. Edging my way towards one of the book cases, I realise that it's crammed with everything from the classics to more recent novels.

'Betty's a big reader,' I breathe.

'Betty reads Mills and Boon.' His arms encircle my waist. A chin comes to rest on my shoulder.

'So, who reads these?'

'Me.' I turn to find him gazing at me in amusement. 'Not so much any more. I hardly have the time. I read English at university.'

'You really are a dark horse.'

He smiles and swings me round. My eyes land on a selection of silver framed photographs set out on a mahogany table. Sliding out of his hands, I move forwards, tentatively. There's the same photograph that Norman has in his office.

'Norman,' I murmur. 'Does he still come here?'

'Yes, he does. Every evening and every weekend. He's married to Betty.'

I turn quickly.

'You're kidding me.'

'Not in the slightest. They've been married for fifty years. Betty's my housekeeper, for want of a better word. I had the old stables converted for them. They live out there, but we all eat together here at the weekends.'

'Bloody hell.' My eyes rove further along the frames, catching sight of a young boy, a younger Daniel with his parents.

'How old are you in this photograph?' I motion towards it.

'Thirteen or fourteen.'

'And this one?' I point to another.

'Eighteen. That was the day I heard I'd got into Cambridge.'

I shake my head in disbelief. Cambridge. My sexy, arrogant, womanising arse of a boss isn't just a dark horse, he's an intelligent dark horse. While my eyes take another sweep of the table, my brain realises there's something missing here.

'Why aren't there any baby photos? And there's none of you as a toddler.'

'I put them away.' He shrugs dismissively. 'I was an ugly kid.'

'Dan,' I laugh. 'No way have you ever been ugly in your entire life.'

'Yes, I have.'

I feel a prickle against the back of my neck. His tone was far too serious then, laced with a warning, and from the way he's staring at me now, his eyes threatening to pull down the shutters, I know I'd better not probe any further. Not yet. Thankfully, I'm saved from the awkwardness of changing the subject when a spaniel skitters into the room. Sliding across the wooden floor, it gathers itself together and comes to rest at Dan's feet. He crouches down and fusses it.

'And this is Molly,' he beams back up at me. 'She's mine. Just like you. I keep her here. No point in locking her away in a penthouse in London. She's got the grounds here, and she's got Betty and Norman.'

'Molly?' I laugh. 'You've got a dog called Molly?'

'Why not?' Straightening up, he takes a step forwards and draws me into his arms, holding me tight. 'So, what do you think so far?' he demands.

'It's lovely. In fact, it's beautiful. I never imagined you were the lord of the manor.'

'I'm not,' he whispers, landing a quick kiss on my lips. 'I'm just the lucky fucker who gets to live here. Now come on. I need to get you into bed.'

My breath catches and the muscles spasm between my legs. Grabbing hold of my hand, he leads me out of the sitting room, back into the hallway and up the grand staircase. On the first floor, he takes the first door on the right. Letting go of my hand, he propels me forwards. I come to a halt, finding myself in a master bedroom, complete with more antique furniture and a king-size bed. The sash window is open in here, and the curtains flutter in a slight breeze.

'Whose is this room?'

'Mine, of course.' He closes the door. 'When I'm here.'

Leaning back against the door, he watches intently as I meander round, running a finger across a chest of drawers, taking in the soft lemon yellow tones of the walls, the delicate lacework of the curtains. At last, I look down at the bed.

'How many women have you had on that thing?'

'I've never brought a woman back here before. Just like I'd never taken a woman back to my apartment before you came along.'

Suddenly, my brain is whirring. Why have I never realised this before? It's a new type of deal for him.

'I really am the first?'

He nods slightly. He's not exactly comfortable admitting this.

'There's never been anyone special?'

'No.'

'I don't understand. You can have your pick of women. Women must throw themselves at you.'

'They do.'

He kicks off his boots.

'You've never had a serious relationship?'

'No serious relationships. No non-serious relationships. I've never been married. Never had any children. No skeletons in that particular closet. I've screwed my way through the past few years without a care in the world, and I'm not exactly proud of myself ... just for the record.'

I stop and stare at him, knowing that I need to get this straight, perfectly straight.

'But Claudine?'

'That kind of thing was purely an arrangement. I've already told you that.'

'Was she the only one?'

'No. There were a few. But it was never anything more than sex, and it never went beyond the club.'

'And what about you and Clive?' He narrows his eyes. 'He told me you used to play the scene together.'

He shakes his head.

'We picked up women in bars and nightclubs. I used to take them back to a hotel room, and that was that. I never saw them again. Is this a job interview?'

'It could be.'

'And are you finished yet?'

'I think so.'

'Good, because I'd like to move on to a practical exercise.'

Pushing himself away from the door, he moves forwards, circling me slowly, running a hand across my back, around my neck, down between my breasts ... further down. I stand perfectly still, closing my eyes, drinking in the sheer pleasure of it all. My nerves are on fire now, my breath torn to pieces.

'Look at me, Maya.'

I open my eyes again, to find him in directly in front of me. Locking me into his gaze, he leans down and takes the hem of my dress, pulling it up over my head and dropping it to the floor. While one hand locks into place behind my back, he massages each nipple in turn through the material of my bra, gently pressing and pinching until they're both erect, alive with sensation. Flustered with desire, I reach out and grab his T-shirt. Pushing it over his head and throwing it to one side, I take a moment to skim my hands over his arms, savouring the hard biceps beneath the soft skin, before I stroke my palm across his chest, sensing that his heart is beating just as wildly as mine.

'Does it meet with your approval, madam?' he asks.

'It's not bad.'

'Well, it gets better from the waist down. Get these jeans off me.'

He nods downwards and I'm amazed to find myself falling to my knees. Working at the buttons in a frenzy, I pull his jeans from his hips, revealing a pair of black pants and a massive bulge.

'Oh, what you do to me, woman,' he breathes, running a hand through my hair. Lifting one leg at a time, he allows me to take off his jeans. And then I move on to his pants, easing them slowly downwards. His penis springs out at me, fully erect, and I stare at it, mesmerised.

'Why don't you have a taste?' he asks. 'An *amuse bouche?*'

I've had just enough time to let out a filthy giggle when a big hand comes to the back of my head, thrusting me in towards his crotch. I have no choice. I open my mouth and accept him completely. His cock slides into my throat, thick and warm and wet with pre-cum. Clamping my lips around it, I begin to suck and pull, tickling at his shaft with my tongue, taking hold of his balls and massaging them firmly, putting into practice every last thing I've been taught by a variety of men over the years. Dan's pleased me enough times recently. And now I just want to please him back. Keeping his hand firmly in place, he begins to thrust his cock into my mouth, slowly at first, rhythmically, but gradually picking up in pace. He's on the verge of coming when he falters, placing a palm on either side of my head.

'I want to come inside you,' he growls. 'On the bed, on all fours.'

I scramble onto the bed and do exactly as I'm told.

'On your elbows. Legs further apart.'

Again, I follow his orders to the letter. Lowering myself down, I feel his warm touch immediately. While one hand steadies me on the small of my back, a single finger probes inside me, slowly massaging up a ball of excitement.

'It's about time I had all of you,' he says at last.

The finger slips away from my clitoris and upwards, tracing its way between my buttocks, and finally coming to rest against the opening of my anus. My heartbeat stalls. God! That? I'm exploding with panic. I've never done that kind of thing before. Even in my darkest days when I'd go with anyone, drunk out of my mind, I never went there.

'It's okay,' he whispers. 'We'll take it slowly. I've got lubricant.'

'But here?'

I turn and find him smiling.

'Yes here.'

'But Betty –'

'Won't have a clue what we're up to as long as you behave yourself and do as you're told. I'm all prepared for you. Stay where you are.'

Through a daze of panic and confusion, I watch as he gets up, pads over to a chest and opens a drawer. He takes out a bottle and a handful of ties. Returning to the bed, he smoothes his hand across my backside.

'Calm down. It was going to happen sooner or later. You need to trust me. Remember? You'll enjoy it.'

I bite my lip as he runs a hand down my spine. I'd like to tell him I'm not so sure about the whole 'enjoying it' thing. As far as I'm aware things are only supposed to come out of that hole. Nothing's supposed to go in.

'Hands behind your back.'

'What?'

'Just do as I say. I want you restrained.'

He leans around me, moving two pillows into place and motioning for me to rest my head against them. Throwing caution to the wind, I sink the side of my head against the pillow, and with my backside still thrust into the air, raise my hands behind my back. They're taken immediately and bound firmly together at the wrists with a smooth length of fabric.

'Does that feel comfortable?'

'Yes,' I splutter.

I close my eyes, hear the click of a lid, feel the cold sensation of the gel. He works it around the edges of my opening, nudges his way in, slowly, calmly, easing me open with first one finger, then two. Immediately, a strange pressure builds up, a completely unknown mixture of pleasure and pain. He pulls back, nudges forwards again, searching his way gradually into unknown territory. On a third withdrawal and a third plunge, I cry out. I've never experienced anything like this before.

'Shush!'

'But I can't!'

'I really fucking want to gag you right now, Maya. Another sound and I'll do it.'

'But I've never -'

'What did I say?'

The finger is removed and I freeze. So he is going to gag me? It's not just a lame threat? He really is going to do that? And I'm actually going to let him? A hand reaches under my throat and urges me upwards. For a few seconds, I'm upright, kneeling on the bed.

'Open your mouth.'

Again, I comply. With lightning speed, a length of fabric is wound between my lips and knotted tightly at the back of my head. I can feel him testing the binds. Obviously satisfied with his efforts, a hand is placed at the back of my head and I'm manoeuvred back down onto the pillow.

'So, now you can't speak.' The words filter through my ears. 'And your safeword is obsolete.'

I groan into the gag.

'But we still need something. These hands.' I feel a touch against my fingers, feathery light, brushing its way across my skin. 'They might come in useful. If you want me to stop, just point. I'm watching. Do you understand?'

I nod. I can barely take it all in.

'Trust me.' A hand is against my forehead now, moving my hair away from my face, gently tucking it behind my ears. 'It won't hurt for long.'

A finger presses into my backside and I gasp. Slowly, it works its way round, stretching me. And all the time, his free hand is clamped against my back, holding me in place.

'I think you're ready.'

My legs are spread further and I'm aware of movement behind me. The end of his cock is positioned.

'Slowly,' he whispers. 'I'm watching.'

His hands move into place, one on each hip, holding me tight. I close my eyes, waiting for the onslaught, and it's not long in coming. His penis broaches me, inching its way inside. Sensing an edge of discomfort, I cry out against the gag but I'm determined not to point. He penetrates further, pushing his way into a place that's never been explored and I hold my breath, waiting to find out whether I'm going to meet pleasure or pain. Reaching round with one hand, he begins to circle a finger against my clitoris, firmly, steadily, creating a knot of pleasure deep inside. And simultaneously, he withdraws his cock, taking it right to the tip before he plunges himself back inside me. He repeats the action, over and over again, while his arm tightens around my waist and the momentum increases. Before long, I'm spinning, clenching, catching my breath as electric shocks shoot their way through my stomach, right into the deepest folds of my muscles. I cry out incoherently, knowing that I'm completely at his mercy, completely given over to pleasure. And it's all I can do as he smashes into me relentlessly.

At last, his breath begins to come apart.

'Now,' he growls.

Without warning, he pinches my right nipple, sending a streak of pain through my breast. I come to pieces immediately. Flushed through with waves of ecstasy, every last nerve and fibre seem to fizz and shake and jitter. He holds me in position for a minute or so, slowly pumping his way down from his orgasm, twitching inside me as the last drops of cum fill up my back passage. At last, he withdraws.

'Stay where you are.'

I bury my face into the pillow, trying desperately to work my way through a mess of emotions. He's just trussed me up and gagged me and taken my arse ... and I loved every minute of it. And more than that, pain sent me over the edge. What kind of person am I? Jeez, I must be a deviant to enjoy all of that. A kinky weirdo. The bed moves again and I feel a warmth on my backside. He's cleaning me up, slowly and tenderly, wiping his cum from my crotch and my legs. At last, I'm nudged onto my side. He releases my hands, unties the gag, and I curl up into his arms.

'Did you like that?' He twists a finger through my hair.

'I bloody did,' I smile. 'I hope you've washed your hands.'

'Of course I have. I've washed my dick too. I'm not finished with you yet. Sorry about the gagging business. I couldn't have Betty hearing you scream.'

'I liked it.'

'Then we'll do it again.' He readjusts his head against the pillow. His eyes glimmer mischievously. 'You're as kinky as me, Miss Scotton. I think I might have met my match.'

Chapter Twenty-Eight

'Where have you been?' Betty scolds him.

'Asleep,' Dan answers quickly, making no eye contact whatsoever.

I grin to myself. In actual fact, he's spent the last four hours either pleasuring me to within an inch of my life or fucking me senseless. I'm surprised the man can still function at all when I feel like I've just run a marathon and swum the Channel.

'Anything I can do?' he asks.

'Yes. Go and fetch Norman.'

He nods at Betty and motions for me to take a seat at the kitchen table. 'You sit down, Maya. I won't be long.'

I watch as he saunters out of the door, leaning down to greet an over-excited Molly along the way. Bloody hell, he really has got a sexy walk. Will I ever tire of gawping at it?

'So, you're Dan's girlfriend?'

I give a start and turn to find Betty's grey eyes probing me.

'I don't really know.'

'Of course you are,' she smiles, placing a glass of water in front of me. 'And judging by what you've got around your neck, I'd say it's pretty serious.'

I reach up and touch the pendant, feeling suddenly ridiculous. Betty must know that it belonged to Dan's mother, and God knows what she must think of me for wearing it.

'It's alright,' she reassures me. 'He told me he was going to give it to you.'

'I just feel ...' I pick up the glass and take a drink.

'Well don't,' she soothes me. 'It's a good thing to see. It's about time he had someone special in his life. I'd like to see him settle down and have a family.' I almost choke on the water. 'He'd make a good dad.' She bends down, rummaging through a cupboard. 'And you two would make beautiful babies.' It's a good job her head is still in the cupboard. I'm sure I'm beginning to blush. 'But he'd have to cut back on the work. It's all he ever seems to do.' She straightens up and swings a colander through the air. 'There's more to life, Dan, I've told him that a thousand times but he never listens to me.'

She shuffles over to the sink, drains off the potatoes in the colander and makes her way over to the table.

'Does he come here a lot?' I ask.

'Most weekends. But then he's at it all the time. Up until all hours.' She transfers the potatoes into a serving dish. 'I've told him he'll wear himself out, but he feels the pressure. Old Mr and Mrs Foster left him the business and it's almost like a duty for him to keep it going. He doesn't want to let people down. I've found him at two in the morning before now, head in hands, agonising over this, that and the other. And it gets to him, the stress. He can get a bit snappy, even I know that. But can't we all?' She shuffles back over to the Aga, opens the door and retrieves a tray of chops. 'There was a time last year when I was really worried about him. He was miserable, just miserable, but he pulled himself out of it eventually.' Sliding the tray onto a board, she sets about transferring the chops to plates. 'At the end of the day, he's done a brilliant job. He keeps that company running and Mr and Mrs Foster would have been proud of that, but they'd also want him to have a life.' She turns to face me. 'Maybe he'll change now he's got you. Maybe he'll calm down a bit, take a bit of time off. Maybe he'll realise there's more to life than work. He deserves a bit of happiness after all he's been through.'

What a strange thing to say. After all he's been through? As far as I'm aware, he's led a blessed existence, born into money and raised in a picture perfect country house. She must be talking about losing his parents. I'd ask for a little clarification here, but from the expression on Betty's face, I'd guess she's not too keen on saying anything else.

'So, what was he like when he was younger?'

'Oh, he was a good lad.'

'How about when he was a toddler?'

'Oh, just like any other child.' She waves a hand, as if she's wafting away my question, and then she turns to examine me. 'He's not told you anything then?'

'About what?'

Betty has no time to answer. Before she can open her mouth, Dan returns to the kitchen, tossing a red rose onto the counter top.

'For you, Betty.'

'You're still late,' she snaps. 'And where's my idiot of a husband?'

'On his way in. I just caught him talking to his courgettes.'

She laughs loudly.

'He's going mad. I swear it. He talks to his vegetable patch, Maya. If you can believe it. I swear I'd go mad if I had him here every day. Thank God Dan keeps him busy up in London.'

Pretending he hasn't heard any of that, Dan gets on with the job of searching through a drawer, helping himself to a handful of knives and forks. Circling the table, he lays out the cutlery before dropping onto the seat by my side, cupping his chin in his hands and smiling at me like an idiot.

'Don't listen to Betty,' he whispers. 'She talks bollocks.'

Molly's barks herald Norman's arrival.

'Maya!' he announces. I look up to find him covered in dirt and taking up almost all of the doorway. As soon as we lock eyes, he breaks into a broad grin. 'It's lovely to see you here, my darling.'

'You too, Norman.'

His eyes dance from my face, to Dan.

'Elbows off the table, Dan. Remember your manners.'

Immediately, Dan complies.

'And, Maya?' Norman rolls up his sleeves. 'Remember that thing I told you about? That thing I was worried about? Back in the office.'

'Yes,' I murmur. If I'm not too much mistaken, he's referring to Dan.

'Well, I'm not worried about it any more.' He raises an eyebrow. 'I just wanted you to know.'

'Okay.' Almost certain that this is Norman's way of giving me his blessing, I shoot him a sweet smile. While he wobbles over to the sink and washes his hands, and while Betty busies herself over the gravy, I turn to find Mr Mean and Hot and Moody staring at me, his eyes glinting with intrigue.

'What's going on?' he whispers.

Time for deflection.

'Nothing. And anyway, why don't you tell me what's going on?'

'What do you mean?'

'Norman's just ordered you around.'

He shrugs his shoulders.

'I boss him about at work. He bosses me about here. We both know the deal.'

He takes a swig of water and watches appreciatively as a plate is deposited under his nose.

'Tuck in,' Betty announces proudly.

We take our time over dinner. After Norman tells us what he's been up to in the garden, reminding us that the vegetables on our plates have been produced by his own fair hands, Betty informs us of all the latest gossip from the local Women's Institute. Eventually, I'm asked about my family, grilled on my background and probed about my painting. And while I give my answers, Dan listens intently to it all, quietly clearing his plate of every last remnant of food. At last, when everyone's finished, he offers to help with the washing up, but he's quickly brushed away. Instead, while Norman and Betty fuss and flap over clearing up, he makes tea for everyone in the most exquisite china cups I've ever seen. Handing a cup to me, he takes one of his own and motions for me to follow him.

Stepping out of the back door, I'm aware that I'm still barefoot. But that's no issue. Dan isn't wearing shoes either. The gravel path is narrow here and with a couple of steps, we're safely onto the grass, walking out across a perfectly mown lawn, through the orchard and towards a gate that I already know leads into the kitchen garden. He pauses by the gate. Holding his saucer in one hand, he raises his cup and takes a sip.

'This keeps Norman busy in the evenings and at weekends,' he explains. 'And I keep him occupied during the week.'

'You keep him working at the company so he doesn't drive his wife mad?'

'That's part of it,' he smiles. 'I also keep him working at the company because he loves the company. He helped my father build it up and when I took over, he was good to me. It was a steep learning curve and Norman helped me out a lot. He doesn't do that much anymore, but he's not an idiot. That's why I put him in charge of Tyneside. I knew he'd do a decent job. He'll retire when he's good and ready. I'm not about to take that away from him.'

'Well, that explains a lot,' I murmur.

'It does,' he murmurs back. 'And now I'd like to explain some more. Come on.'

I follow him through the narrow gateway, and suddenly I'm transported into another world, transfixed by an onslaught of colours and scents. I halt for a moment, surveying the scene, taking in the mass of raised beds in front of me that are bursting with of every kind of vegetable known to man, the grassed walkways that criss-cross the vegetable patches, the shower of red roses that dominates one of the four walls, and the pink clematis that seems to have run riot down another. I'm touched lightly on the arm, encouraged to follow Dan through the centre of it all to an arbour at the far end, where we settle ourselves down onto a bench.

'This is amazing,' I gasp.

'All Norman's work.'

Dan leans forwards and places his tea cup on the ground. I do the same. As soon as I straighten up, he takes my hand and falls into a contented silence. I'd like to join him there, but I'm not ready yet. My head is still buzzing with questions.

'So, I get why Norman's in that office,' I begin. 'But what's Jodie doing there?'

He groans and runs his fingers through his hair.

'Come on, you might as well just own up.'

'She's Norman's granddaughter.'

'You're kidding me.'

He shakes his head.

'She was a bit of a tearaway at school. Left with no qualifications whatsoever. Last year, she got in with the wrong crowd, got arrested for shoplifting a few times and managed to land herself with a criminal record. I gave her the job with Norman so he could keep an eye on her. I know she does fuck all and I pay her peanuts, believe me. That's why we need the second secretary in there, just in case Norman actually ever has anything to do. It's a stop-gap. She's thinking about a beauty course.'

'Which you'll fund?'

'Naturally.'

'Daniel Foster, you've got a soft centre.'

'I have not got a soft fucking centre.'

'You're rumbled, Mr Foster.'

'Drop it.'

He turns and gazes at me, obviously trying his best to look pissed off, but he's not doing very well at all. He's definitely smiling.

'Well, you're certainly peeling back a few layers for me today.'

'Would you like another one, Miss Scotton?'

'Yes please.'

'This is my favourite place in the world.'

Feeling his hand slip away from mine, I glance around at the display of flowers. They cover just about every single inch of the wall.

'Sweet peas.' I turn back to Dan, only to find him picking a handful.

'My parents used to sit here every night in the summer, for an age. Sometimes they'd talk. Sometimes they'd just sit in silence. Mum loved the smell of these.'

He offers me the flowers. I take them, gaze down at their delicate petals, and suddenly I understand.

'You,' I breathe. 'Those sweet peas on my desk. That was you.'

He nods.

'I could have picked up the phone and ordered an expensive bouquet from a flower shop.' He gives me a flash of his eyes. 'I thought about it, but this is a piece of me. This means more.'

'So, you got Norman to bring them in for you?'

'No. I drove down here and picked them myself. How goofy is that?'

'It's not goofy. It's wonderful and I love it.' I lower my head. I can't focus on it from here, but I'm wondering about the little, white flower around my neck.

'It's a sweet pea,' he smiles. 'Stylised, but a sweet pea, nevertheless. My dad bought it for my mum because it linked them both to this place.'

'And now you've given it to me.'

He reaches up and touches the pendant.

'I'd like us to stay here tonight,' he says quietly. 'Norman and Betty won't be in the house. They'll go back to the cottage in a while. Would you do that for me, Maya? Can we stay?'

I turn the sweet peas in my hand. I'm not going to deny him this. Why wouldn't I want to stay the night in this beautiful house, with this beautiful man?

'Yes, we can.'

'Thank you.'

I hear him take in a deep breath.

'Dan,' I whisper.

'Mmm?'

'I really could do with knowing what's going on here.'

'What do you mean?'

'Is this a relationship?'

I look up to find him staring at me, a quizzical frown etched across his forehead.

'Define relationship for me.'

'Two people spending time together, enjoying each other's company, having sex and all that.'

'Sounds pretty close.'

'And committing themselves to each other,' I add.

'Then this is a relationship.' His hand returns to mine and squeezes tight. 'I fucking own you and you fucking own me, remember?'

'So, we're girlfriend and boyfriend?'

'If you like. Although I'm probably a little too old to be classed as a boyfriend. Can't I just be your man?'

'I suppose so.' I chew on my lip. 'And I'm your woman.'

'Well,' he grins, 'you're definitely not a girl.'

We sit in silence for a while. He keeps a hold of my hand, slowly entwining his fingers through mine while I watch the shadows climb their way up the walls. And before I know it, I'm lost in a day-dream: I'm married to him now, sitting out here every evening in the summer, watching the children as they run wild around the vegetable patches, squealing with delight ...

Snap out of it, woman, my brain screeches at full volume. Jesus! Where the hell did that just come from? I shake my head, reeling from the shock. In actual fact, I have no idea where that stupid notion just came from, but as quickly as it appeared, I bat it straight out of my head. I may well have fallen for the man, hook, line and sinker, and he may well have fallen for me too, but that's definitely a step too far. After all, he's a recently reformed womaniser, for God's sake, a self-confessed kinky weirdo and a dominating, work-obsessed control freak to boot: not exactly the best choice for a husband and a father. And anyway, in spite of everything he said at Seven Dials, I'm not entirely sure that's he's interested in popping a ring on my finger and then popping out a clan. And more than that, why the hell am I even thinking about this in the first place?

'Penny for them?' he whispers.

'They're not worth that much.'

'I'm sure they are.' Letting go of my hand, he leans down and picks up the tea cups. 'It's getting chilly out here. Time for bed.'

***

Back in the bedroom, I watch as he takes off his T-shirt and slowly removes his jeans. Tugging down his pants, he steps out of them and straightens up, his eyes latching onto mine. My breath falters at the sight of the sharply defined body in front of me. Completely naked, completely unashamed, he begins to move towards me in that self-assured, utterly sexy way of his, and I'm a bundle of nerves, a chaotic wreck of anticipation.

He comes to a halt in front of me, so close I can feel the warmth of his skin even though he hasn't touched me yet. He strokes a finger against my cheek, under my chin, across my neck, and then he reaches down. Taking hold of my dress, he lifts it gently over my head, dropping it to the floor. His eyes rove slowly from my breasts down to my stomach, and then back up to my face. Tilting his head to one side, he smiles in appreciation before he reaches round to unfasten my bra, pulling it away slowly, tenderly, watching as the straps glide over my skin.

And then he sinks to his knees.

He slots a finger into the top of my knickers, drawing them down my legs and away from my feet. Still kneeling, he runs his hands around my calves, moving upwards, around my thighs. Coming to the front, he probes my clit with both thumbs, gently kneading at the folds. I close my eyes, sucking in a jittery breath, and I begin to sway. He almost has me on the edge when he finally removes his thumbs and gets back up to his feet.

'So, what are you going to do to me tonight?' I ask, breaking the silence.

He takes a lock of my hair in his fingers and twiddles it.

'I'm going to worship you.' He captures me with his gaze, holding me there for a few delicious seconds before he adds the rider. 'And neither of us is going to make a sound.'

As soon as I open my mouth to complain, he lays an index finger across my lips. 'No words. No noise at all.'

Wondering what on Earth he's playing at now, I nod but remain silent.

He lets go of my hair, slides one arm around my back and leans down, snaking the other behind my legs. I tingle at the touch of his warm skin as he lifts me and carries me over to the bed where he lays me on the rumpled sheets, positioning himself by my side and propping himself up on one elbow. He begins to trail his fingers lazily across my breasts, watching their steady progress as they travel along my collar bone, down my sternum, further down to my stomach. His fingertips explore every inch of my flesh, again and again, for minutes on end, along my thighs, across my pubic hair, tickling their way around my clitoris. And all I want to do is moan, but I bite back the temptation. All I can hear now is the sound of my own breathing, uneven, catching on itself, quivering at each new sensation.

And then I realise. If there are no words, there are no commands. And if there are no commands, then he's relinquished control. I'm free to worship him right back. Reaching out, I touch his chest, amazed that he doesn't catch hold of my hand or shake his head. Instead, he simply watches as my fingers explore his body. Taking in his contours and his power, I run my palm across his chest, down to his stomach, further down to where I curl my fingers around his hard cock, feeling it twitch in my grip.

He manoeuvres me onto my back and begins to kiss my skin, lightly, softly, every square inch of it, sucking at my nipples, running his nose along me here, licking me there, tasting me, taking in my scent until he comes to my groin where he pauses, nuzzling against my hair. His big hands take hold of my thighs, gently parting them, and he licks a slow, languid line from my clitoris to my opening and back again. And then he homes in on my clit, taking his time, lapping his tongue against the bundle of nerves, working me up into a fizzing ball of ecstasy. I shiver under his touch, listening to my breath as it begins to flounder. I feel myself tense as the pressure within me builds. He slows the pace of his tongue, extending the pleasure for me, holding me firmly on the outsides of my thighs. At last, after what seems like an age, my muscles tighten for a moment before they falter, giving way to an intense, pulsating orgasm. I whimper with delight and his lips are on mine in an instant, soaking up the sound in a long, deep kiss that reminds me to remain silent.

Eventually, he pulls away. Easing my legs further apart and positioning himself between my thighs, he guides his cock inside me. As soon as he begins to move, I'm only too aware that I've become hypersensitive. My muscles begin to flutter again, sending warm ripples of pleasure right into my core. Arching his body above mine and resting one elbow on the mattress, he slides his free hand beneath my back, drawing me up to him. And with his eyes fixed on mine, he falls into a slow, steady rhythm, taking his time, working at one angle and then shifting himself slightly so that my insides spasm at each new new sensation.

Minutes pass by in quiet oblivion. I run my fingers through his hair, across his shoulders, his back, his firm buttocks, urging him into me. And the rhythm continues unabated, while the pressure builds inside me one more time. Sensing that I'm close to the edge, he stops for a moment or two, allowing me to calm my muscles. And then he begins again, pumping his cock into me at a steady, lazy pace. I will myself not to come, not until I sense that moment in him. Gazing up at his face, I wait for the signs. And at last, after what seems like an eternity, they come. His pupils dilate, his breath begins to unravel, his hands tighten against my skin, and his thrusts become urgent. I know it's time. Releasing myself, I trip over the edge into ecstasy, falling into a deep, all-consuming orgasm that undulates inside me and clutches at his cock. Over and over again, as he empties himself, gasping for breath and fighting back the need to cry out, the aftershocks keep coming. And we hold each other tight, touching foreheads, steadying each other through the intensity of it all. And I get the strangest feeling. It's as if I'm falling into a delicious abyss from which I can never escape. It's as if we're sharing our souls.

Chapter Twenty-Nine

'Pick me up in the car later,' I plead. Standing on the pavement outside my flat, swathed in the heat, I'm struggling to unzip the leathers. 'Don't make me put this stuff on again. It's ridiculous.'

He takes off his helmet, swings himself off the bike and begins to help me out.

'This stuff keeps you safe,' he mutters. 'You're mine now, every last bit of you, and I'm not putting you at risk.'

'Then pick me up in the car.'

'Relax.' Fiddling with the zip, he's fully focused on the job in hand. 'Ah, done it.' He unzips the front of the jacket and pulls it over my shoulders, leaving it to hang from my waist while he gives his best shot at straightening out the dress. And then he locks me in with those blue irises. Immediately, I'm a swooning idiot.

'Can't I just come back with you now?'

He shakes his head, drops to his knees and sets about unbuckling my boots.

'Not a good idea.'

He taps my feet, one at a time, and I lift them, allowing him to remove the boots.

'I won't bother you.'

'I've got a shed load of work to do. If you're lazing about on my sofa, I'll just want to fuck you.' He arches an eyebrow and pulls the leather trousers down, slowly, running his tongue across his bottom lip. 'Better you stay here for a bit and get some painting done.'

'I don't see why you have to work on a Sunday.'

Holding on to his broad shoulders, I lift one leg at a time while he peels the trousers over my feet.

'CEO of a building company and all that shit.' He shrugs. 'I'll get it done as quickly as I can and then we'll be clear for the evening. I'll pick you up at five ... in the Merc. I can't get the Jag back until next week.'

I let out a sigh. I'm clearly getting nowhere with my plan to get him to fuck me senseless for the entire afternoon. I'll just have to do as I'm told. And maybe that's not such a bad thing. Maybe I'll start on my next painting. There's already the seed of an idea growing in my mind: a kitchen garden, brimming with sweet peas. A present for Dan.

'And pack a bag.'

'Why?'

'Because you're staying over at mine.' Gathering together the boots and the leathers, he straightens up. And then he leans in, skimming his lips across mine. 'I may be your boyfriend, or your man, or whatever you want to call me, Maya, but I still want you back in those cuffs.'

My heartbeat jumps up a notch or two, and while the sex fairy sets about tweaking just about every nerve and fibre between my legs, something half-expected sparks to life in my chest. It's as if a fire's been set. Radiating outwards from my heart, the heat grows quickly, gaining in intensity at an alarming rate. Suddenly, I know exactly what it is that I'm feeling. And I need to tell him. I can't contain the words any longer. Gazing up into his eyes, I'm on the verge of saying something stupid when the front door is wrenched open.

'You've got to get in here,' Lucy hisses.

I swivel round to find her on the doorstep, distinctly dishevelled in her dressing gown, her hair a matted mess.

'What's wrong?' I demand.

'Bitchface is here,' she growls, her face contorting itself into a look of pure distaste. 'And there's all this wet stuff coming out of her eyes. You've got to rescue us.'

'Us?'

'Me and Clive. We've had her blubbing all over us for the past hour. Get in here now!'

With a wave of an arm, Lucy disappears back inside the flat, leaving the front door wide open.

'Who's Bitchface?' Dan asks.

I turn to find him staring into the hallway, a broad smile spread across his face.

'My sister.'

In an instant, the smile disintegrates. His lips part. He glances back at the motorbike.

'You finally get to meet the root cause of all my problems.'

He shakes his head. Clearly, he wants to make an escape, but I'm not having any of it. While half of me is disappointed that Sara's chucked a massive spanner into the works, the other half's quietly excited to show off Dan to my sister, to rub her face in my happiness while she's at her lowest ebb. I know it's juvenile and I know it's wrong, but I just can't help myself ... even after all these years.

'Come on,' I urge him.

I don't care what's eating him right now. He's got to learn that he can't get his own way all the time. Making sure that he's following me, I watch as he veers away into my bedroom to offload the leathers, and then I press on into the living room where I'm greeted by Clive. Standing by the window with his hands in his pockets, he tosses me a curt smile before he nods towards the sofa where Lucy's busy comforting a crumpled body.

'Sara?'

At the sound of my voice, she gets to her feet and turns to face me. It's been a good few months since I last saw her, but something seems to have taken its toll along the way. She's thinner now, gaunt even, and she's a complete mess. Dressed in a pair of baggy jeans and a frumpy T-shirt, her blonde hair hangs limply around her face, framing a mass of blotchy skin and a pair of reddened, pig-like eyes.

'I'm sorry, Maya,' she sobs. 'Me and Geoff had the most almighty argument. I just stormed out. I didn't know where else to go. I couldn't go to Mum and Dad's. I didn't want to upset them.'

'It's okay.'

Overcome by a sudden dose of sisterly love and instantly regretting my plan to showboat, I edge my way around the sofa and wrap her in my arms. She may well have been the bitch from hell in her youth, I remind myself, but when all's said and done she's still my flesh and blood.

'It's not okay,' she complains into my shoulder. After keeping her head buried there for a minute or two, she finally straightens up and with the back of her hand, wipes all manner of bodily fluids away from her face. Sucking in a deep breath, she seems to steel herself before firing out the next words. 'It's awful, Maya. It's just fucking awful. We're constantly arguing and he's a total shit these days. I don't even feel like I know him any more. And he doesn't care. I just need some time to myself. Can I stay here for a few days? Please?'

'Of course you can.' I glance at Lucy to find her mouthing the word 'no' as if her life depends on it. 'Where are the kids?'

'They're at home. I left them with the bastard. He can look after them for a change. I needed some space. I'm sorry. I should have phoned but I wasn't thinking straight. And you didn't answer my texts.'

'Well,' Lucy sighs. 'We'll leave you two in peace for a bit, shall we? Come on, Clive.'

I watch as Lucy slopes out of the living room, dragging a disgruntled-looking Clive in her wake. And then I hear a low, muffled conversation in the hallway.

'I'm being a pain in the arse.' My sister fights back a sob.

'No, you're not.' I touch her on the arm. 'You can sleep on the sofa for a day or two. I'll see if I can get tomorrow off work and we can talk this through.'

'It's all such short notice.'

'Don't worry. We'll sort something out.'

'I owe you ...'

Her voice fades as her eyes latch on to something behind me. When I turn to see what's going on, I find Dan in the doorway, holding his helmet in one hand, his leathers unzipped to his waist. I catch my breath at the sight of him, but he hardly notices me. Instead, his attention is fixed on my sister.

'Who's this?' she smiles.

'This is Dan.'

Circling her way around the sofa, she reaches out to greet him, but she gets nothing in return. He doesn't speak. He doesn't smile. He simply stares down at her hand. And I can barely believe the change in the man. He's transformed: from relaxed and playful to solid ice in less than five minutes flat.

'Dan,' I prompt him, sensing an edge of anger in my gut. 'This is Sara, my sister.'

Without a word, while the seconds stretch themselves out to breaking point, he continues to stare at the hand. At last, he lifts his line of vision and begins to take in her face. Smile back, for fuck's sake, I will him silently. At least shake her hand. Show some sodding manners! But he doesn't. Instead, he simply studies her features, as if she's a painting that he can't quite fathom.

'Hi Dan.' She's mesmerised by those eyes now. I can see that quite clearly. But it doesn't last for long. I watch as the smile disappears, as she withdraws her hand and takes a step backwards. 'Have ... we ... met somewhere before?'

While a frown lands on my forehead, my brain flips into overdrive. Delving back through Dan's interrogations, it skims its way over his strange obsession with Sara. If they had met before, then that would certainly go a long way to explaining everything.

'No,' he answers coldly, putting a halt to my train of thought.

'Well ...' She falters and seems to flinch. 'It's nice to meet you now.'

'Is it?' He glares at her for a moment or two. 'I need to go.'

Without another word, and without so much as acknowledging me, he turns on his heels and walks out of the room.

'What the hell was that all about?' my sister breathes.

'I don't know.' Just getting the words out takes every last ounce of self-control. I'm simmering with rage and all I want to do is scream. 'Give me a minute. I need to speak to him.'

Abandoning my sister in the living room, I stride out into the hallway. By the time I catch him just outside the front door, I've gone from a simmer to a full-on boil. Grabbing hold of his arm, I tug him round.

'You can't talk to my sister like that. You were bloody rude just then, Dan. It was out of order.'

'Was it?' He runs his fingers through his hair and stares at the ground, his face a mask.

'Yes it was. What's she ever done to you? What's got into you, Dan?'

Without looking up, he fastens the zip on his leathers.

'Nothing.'

'Something has. Five minutes ago, you were Mr Wonderful and now look at you. You're behaving like a shit.'

And that does it. The mask gives way. Crumbling to pieces in an instant, it leaves nothing in its place but pure rage. He points a trembling finger at me.

'I am not behaving like a shit,' he seethes. 'I've got to go.'

Reeling from the shock of his outburst, I follow him across the pavement, back to his bike, watching as he swings his leg over the beast. I'm not letting him get away that easily.

'She thought you'd met before.'

'Well she was wrong.'

'So what is it then? Why are you so angry with her? Is it because of the way she treated me when we were kids?' He shakes his head, but I ignore his denial. After all, it's the only plausible explanation. 'It's not your battle to fight, Dan. It's mine.'

'I know it is.'

'And what about tonight?'

'What about it?' He shrugs on his gloves. 'You'll be with her.'

I laugh. So that's it then? He's plunged into an almighty grump simply because my sister's put the kibosh on his plans for the evening? Well, I suppose I should have expected it. After all, he is a control freak. But if the idiot thinks he can get away with acting like a two year old, then he's got one hell of a wake-up call on the way.

'We need to talk about this,' I inform him, swallowing back the urge to call him a twat.

'Do we?'

'Yes, we do. Tomorrow night.'

'I can't. I'm busy.'

'You're busy?' I stare at him, fumbling for words, registering a tiny shiver of fear as it passes right through me, permeating every single vein and sinew and nerve. I've seen that look in a man's eyes before. I saw it in Tom's eyes. The day he told me it was over. 'So when will I see you again?' I ask, disgusted at the weakness in my own voice.

He pulls on his helmet and fastens the buckle beneath his chin.

'I don't know. I need some time to myself.' He waits a few seconds before he flings the final insult in my direction. 'This was a bad idea.'

I have no time to ask him what the fuck he means by that. Before I can open my mouth, he flips down his visor, turns the key in the ignition, kicks up the stand and manoeuvres the bike out into the road. With a flick of the wrist, he accelerates away from me, rounding the corner onto Camden High Street and disappearing from view. And I'm left there, standing by the roadside, listening to the roar of the motorbike as it melts away into the din of North London's traffic. And I don't know whether it's shock, or anger, or a combination of the two. But I begin to shake.

***

At last, after a good five minutes spent rooted to the spot, I finally manage to rouse myself. I'm on autopilot now. I've tidied away my emotions, cramming them into some dark cupboard at the back of my mind and slamming the door shut. It's the only way to get through the day. Shuffling back inside the flat, I discover that Sara's migrated to the kitchen where she's perched herself at the rickety table. With a nod in her direction, I open the fridge door and let out a thankful sigh when I find a bottle of wine.

'Want a glass?' I ask, rescuing the bottle.

'But it's only eleven thirty.'

'And?'

'I know you're pissed off right now, Maya, but you don't need to drown your sorrows.'

'Oh come on, Sara. Live a little. The men in our lives are dicks. Let's get pissed.'

I hold up the bottle in front of her face, waving it from side to side.

She frowns. 'Okay then.' She waggles a finger at me. 'But don't make a habit of this.'

I retrieve a couple of glasses from the draining board, set them on the table and fill them to the brim.

'I'm sorry,' Sara groans, picking up a glass. 'I've ruined your day.'

'He's the one who's ruined my day.'

I slump into the chair opposite my sister, pick up my own glass and swig back half of the contents in one go.

'What's wrong with him?' she ventures.

'No idea.'

'Is it because he was expecting to have you all to himself?'

'I don't know ...' And I really don't.

'Well, I don't think he likes me.' She turns the glass around on the table. 'Why is that?'

I shake my head, knock back the rest of the wine and pour myself a second glass.

'You recognised him.' Somewhere in the darkest recesses of my brain, neurons seem to have fired. My brain is back in action. 'You asked him if you'd met before.'

She shrugs. 'I don't know. He just seemed familiar, that's all. I couldn't put my finger on it.' She takes another sip of wine. 'What's his full name?'

'Daniel Foster.'

She shakes her head. 'That doesn't ring a bell. And he's bloody gorgeous. I'm sure I'd remember if I had met him before. Where's he from?'

'Grew up in Surrey. Parents owned a building company. They died. He took over. It's where I'm working at the minute.'

'He's your boss?'

'Yes.'

'Holy shit, and you're ...? He's your boyfriend?'

'Perhaps.'

I take another swig of wine, reminding myself that if a man's truly boyfriend material, then he doesn't storm off when your sister turns up out of the blue.

'What's going on?'

I'm jolted out of my reverie by Lucy's voice. Glancing up at the kitchen doorway, I find her standing in it, backed up by an incredibly serious looking accountant.

'Dan's gone,' I inform them.

'What?' Lucy gawps.

'He took one look at Sara and stormed off.'

Clive manoeuvres himself around Lucy and into the kitchen.

'Clive,' I sigh. 'Can you explain this?'

He leans back against the sink. 'No, I can't.'

'You don't have any idea what would make him do that?'

He shakes his head. 'Whatever it is,' he reaches into his pocket and takes out his mobile, 'he'll calm down eventually and talk to you about it. But you're not going to force it out of him. I know him well enough to know that.'

He slips into silence, squinting down at his mobile, concentrating on tapping out a text. Obviously a message to Dan.

'Well, we're going to go out for the day,' Lucy pipes up at last. 'We'll give you two some space. Come on Clivey.'

On any normal day, I'd shoot my friend a look of sheer disbelief. It didn't escape my attention that she just came up with a pet name for her pet accountant. And it also didn't escape my attention that he smiled in return. But it's not any normal day. In fact, it's a crap day, the sort of day that calls for much more wine than we've got in the flat. If I'm about to listen to my sister's catalogue of woes, then it's something I'm going to endure in a pub. I glance down at my scrunched-up dress.

'I'm going to get changed,' I announce. 'This bloody thing is getting on my nerves.'

While Lucy hauls Clive off into her bomb site of a bedroom, Sara follows me into mine, glass in hand. I watch as she settles herself on the edge of the bed before I set about changing into my customary summer pub outfit: combats and a strappy T-shirt.

'I'm sorry,' Sara whispers.

'You've got nothing to be sorry for.' I rummage around in my wardrobe, pulling out the first things that come to hand. 'Let's just forget about Dan. He's doing my head in. Tell me what's been going on with you and Geoff.'

'He's a selfish prat. He's always out with his mates. If he's not playing football or watching football, he's down the pub talking about football. I'm fed up, Maya. He leaves me alone with the kids all the time.'

'He's done that for years.' I take off the dress and toss it into a corner.

'I know. I've just come to the end of my tether.'

'Then get another tether.' I put on a T-shirt. 'Either that, or get a divorce.'

Her eyebrows seem to shoot up her forehead.

'A divorce?'

'Yes. A divorce.' I step into my combats and zip them up. 'He's not likely to change and you're not happy.'

'A divorce.' She gazes out of the window and takes an enormous gulp of wine. 'Mum and Dad won't like that.'

'They'll like anything that makes you happy. And besides ...' I'm not really sure I should add on the next bit. 'They never really liked him anyway.'

She turns to gape at me, finishes off her wine and seems to think for a moment or two. At last, she smiles. 'Well, that's me sorted then. How about you?'

'What about me?'

'You and Dan? How long has it been going on?'

'A few days.' I shrug. 'But I think it might be over now.'

'Clivey seems to think he'll come back.'

'Clivey's an accountant. What does he know?'

She nods her head, opens her mouth to speak and then closes it again, her attention waylaid by something in the corner of the room.

'Wow!' she breathes, scrambling round to the foot of the bed. 'You're painting again!' She points at the canvas. 'It's brilliant! I love it, Maya. God, I've got a talented sister. Are you going to do more?'

'Yes.'

'I'm so happy for you. What made you start again?'

It's not a case of what, I'd like to tell her. It's a case of who. Daniel Foster made me start again, and if I've got nothing else out of this disaster of a relationship, then at least I've got my mojo back. I reach up and touch the pendant, a reminder that I want so much more than that. He may well be doing my head in right now, but I'm still in love with the man.

'Right,' I breathe, feeling my heartbeat jitter. 'Go and sort yourself out. We're going out for the afternoon. And we're going to get blasted.'

***

By the time we stagger back into the flat, fully laden with two ready meals, three bottles of wine and a selection of chocolate snacks, we've already said it all. Holed up in a local pub, we've put the world to rights, identifying the only possible solutions to our respective problems: Sara needs to leave her husband and I need to carry on painting, irrelevant of the man who may or may not be in my life. After half-heartedly picking our way through two platefuls of something that looks suspiciously like dog sick, we spend the evening watching crappy television, drowning our sorrows in silence, flicking our way through the endless channels of crud until we finally settle on Bruce Willis in a vest.

'*Die Hard,*' Sara slurs. 'Just what I need. I can't be doing with romance or any of that shit.'

'Me neither.' I hiccough. 'Romance is a bunch of shitty crap shit.'

'What's that fucking noise?' Screwing up her nose, Sara shuffles about on the sofa, finally realising that the 'fucking noise' is, in fact, the ringtone of her mobile. 'Oh,' she sighs, pulling the mobile from under her backside. 'Oh, fuck it. It's Mum.'

'Answer it,' I instruct her.

'Oh, for fuck's sake.' Drunkenly, she swipes her forefinger across the accept call icon. 'Hi Mum.' She holds the phone away from herself for a moment before slapping it back against her ear. 'Yes, I've walked out on him. How did you know? What?'

Shooting up from the sofa, she staggers off into the kitchen, leaving me with Bruce Willis and a handful of German renegades. When she finally returns, Bruce has already managed to despatch at least half of the opposition, cutting his feet to shreds in the process, but I've barely paid attention to any of it. I've been thinking about Dan.

'What's up?'

'That bastard,' she sneers, pushing her mobile onto the coffee table and collapsing back onto the sofa. 'He phoned Mum and asked her if I was there.'

'What's bad about that? He's the father of your children.'

'He's a shit. He just wanted to make me look bad in front of her.'

'I'm sure he didn't.'

'I'm sure he did. Anyway, she's happy I've left him, and she doesn't want me to go back to him.'

'There you go.'

'And she wants to meet your new boyfriend.'

'What?' I straighten myself up, sending a bag of Maltesers plummeting to the carpet. 'You didn't tell her?'

'It just kind of came out. He's invited next Saturday to Dad's birthday bash.'

I stare at my own mobile. It's languishing on the coffee table, in between a half-eaten Chocolate Orange and a box of Ferrero Rocher. Not one single text from Dan.

'Look, Sara, I'm not even sure he's my boyfriend any more. Can we just drop this?'

My mobile starts to ring. I huff out a sigh and answer it.

'Mum,' I breathe, without even checking the caller ID.

'Sara tells me you've got a new man in your life. She says he's bloody gorgeous and I want to meet him.'

'Get straight to the point, why don't you?'

'Bring him to your dad's do. No excuses.'

'I'll see what I can do.'

'Get here for one. I'll call Lucy in the week and make sure she knows about it. I'm sure you'll forget. Oh, and tell your sister she's doing the right thing. That husband of hers is a knobhead.'

'Mum!'

'I speak the truth. See you on Saturday. Got to go. Pam's reading circle starts in twenty minutes.'

Sliding the phone back onto the table, I pick up my wine glass and take a huge glug.

'So,' Sara mutters, picking up her own glass. 'I've been thinking about Dan. I've been thinking about why he took an instant dislike to me. Did you tell him about the things I did?'

'What do you mean?'

'Did you tell him I was the world's worst big sister?'

A few seconds of silence pass between us. We've never spoken about this before. She's never admitted to what she did, and I've never alluded to it. Up until now, it's all been apparently forgotten, brushed aside, nudged out of sight. But in those few precious seconds, we gaze into each other's eyes and silently acknowledge the past. And somehow, it seems to open the gates.

'I told him about some of the things,' I murmur.

'Such as?'

'The thunder thing and the arm thing.'

'Is that it?'

'Yep.'

'Jeez, you left a lot out.' She stares at the coffee table, eyeing up a packet of chocolate brownies. 'I'm sorry, Maya. I don't know why I was like that.'

'It's all water under the bridge.'

'It's just that ... some of the things I did, some of the things I said - they were unforgivable.'

'Don't beat yourself up about it. We all move on and we all change. You've changed.'

'I know. Life's taught me a few lessons. I just wish I could go back and change the way I was.'

'Well, you can't, and just for the record, you are forgiven.'

Simultaneously, we lean forwards, place our wine glasses on the coffee table and dive in for a short, uncomfortable, drunken hug. And then, simultaneously, we release each other and reach for our mobiles.

'Who are you texting?' I ask, although I already know. While my phone has remained resolutely silent for most of the day, hers has been inundated with messages from the idiot husband.

'Geoff.' She taps out her message and proudly displays it to me. 'Bruce Willis has inspired me.' I struggle to make out the words, but giggle as soon as they come into focus. *Yippee Ki-yay, motherfucker!* 'And who are you texting?' she asks, merrily prodding at the send icon.

'Nobody in particular.'

I'm not about to confess that I just can't leave him alone. He may well be playing silly buggers again, but I'm not prepared to join in this time. Somewhere, in amongst all the wine and chocolate and words, I've decided to send him a text. Just one. And if he doesn't reply, then I'll leave it at that. I type in the message and fire it off into the ether. Two words. Nice and simple. And they say it all. *No running.*

Chapter Thirty

I spend the night lying on top of the bed covers. I can't sleep. It's not helped by the heat or the alcohol swirling about in my veins or the pigeons fighting outside my window, or by the fact that I can still smell his scent on the bed sheets. Every now and then, I pull them close to my face and drink in the fresh smell. Every now and then, I check my mobile, only to find that he hasn't replied to my text. Every now and then, I touch the pendant that's still around my neck, wondering what was going through his mind when he decided to give it to me. Was this commitment? And if so, then what the hell was going through his mind when he stormed off? Eventually, at day break, I stand by the open window, clutching a sheet around me and watching the beginnings of Monday morning. The colour's back in the world. But today, it hasn't reached me. Today, I'm monochrome.

***

The week passes in a blur. Hardly aware of time, I'm lost in a daze, waiting for the tears to arrive. But day after day, just like Dan, they fail to show up. On Monday morning, I call in sick and spend the day with Sara, wandering around Camden market, stopping here and there for a coffee and saying very little. I call in sick again on Tuesday. Only this time, after seeing Sara off on the train, I take the tube down to Monument, picking my way along the north bank of the Thames until I'm directly opposite Fosters Construction. From this angle, with the Shard right behind it, the building seems far less imposing than before. And suddenly I'm pricked by inspiration.

Taking a mound of photographs on my mobile, I return quickly to the flat where I shut myself away in my bedroom and start on a second canvas: a storm brewing over the rooftops of the south bank. Somehow, with no contact from Dan, the sweet peas don't seem relevant any more. And somehow, I already know that this is my own way of dealing with the rejection. Consumed by a need to see my anger in front of me, I work into the early hours, watching as the buildings of Southwark gradually emerge from the canvas. Using the photographs, I sketch them out with precision: the cathedral, the Shard, a mishmash of office buildings and there, right there at the centre of it all, the fifteen storeys of black glass that belong to Daniel Foster. On Wednesday, after finally gathering enough courage to call Mrs Kavanagh with my resignation, I remain in my bedroom and begin to paint. By the end of the day, the basics are in place, but it's the storm clouds that have taken shape before anything else. Pressing down onto the buildings and reflected in the waters of the Thames, they dominate the scene, just like they dominate my mind.

Thursday gives me no time to work. Early in the morning, Lucy reminds me that it's time to prepare for Friday night's exhibition. I'm forced to get dressed, to eat a little breakfast, and then I find myself in the back of a taxi, propping up the painting of the woods while I listen to my flatmate's endless complaints about the day ahead. An hour or so is spent hanging the canvas, followed by a few more hours helping Lucy with last minute arrangements. Shortly after six, deciding that everything's finally ship-shape and hunky-dory as far as the gallery's concerned, Lucy turns her attention to me: I'm dragged over to Oxford Street where I'm ordered to buy a little black dress and a pair of killer heels.

'This is the way to deal with heartbreak,' she informs me, guiding me towards the fitting room. 'Put on your LBD and get jiggy with it!'

'I'm not getting jiggy with anything, Luce,' I sigh. 'That sort of crap always ends in disaster.'

'You should wear this on Saturday too.'

The dress is thrust at me.

'Saturday?'

'Oh for fuck's sake, Maya. You've forgotten, haven't you?'

I shake my head.

'Your dad's birthday, twat features.'

My brain finally sparks into life. Dad's sixtieth party. Up until now, it's been the last thing on my mind. And the last thing I need right now is a party.

'Oh shit.'

'Your mummy called me' Lucy smirks. 'I'm going, and I'm taking Clivey.'

Oh great. A car crash of a party.

'But you hardly know him.'

'Whatever.' Lucy waves her handbag in the air. 'She wants to meet my new fuckbuddy.'

'Well, I won't be taking mine.' I stare at the dress, wondering why I'm even buying it. It's not as if I've got anybody to impress. 'Is Clivey driving?'

'Uh huh.'

'Then I'll catch a lift with you two.'

***

After a few glasses of wine and a restless night, Friday eventually lands on my doorstep. I spend most of it painting, enveloped in my own private world of light and shade, wrestling with colour and shape and balance. I'm only dragged back into reality by a text from Lucy, ordering me to get ready and heave my sorry backside down to Soho. Obediently, I take a bath, blow-dry my hair, apply a smattering of make-up and put on my best black underwear, complete with suspenders and stockings. Squeezing myself into the tiny black dress, I take a look at the end result in the mirror. Immediately, my eyes are drawn to the necklace. I have no idea why I'm still wearing it. It's obvious now that I need to return the delicate white flower to its true owner. And I will. But before I do, I'd like to wear it for one last night.

After riding the tube down to Tottenham Court Road, I wander through London's Friday night streets, fighting my way past the hoards of tourists until I make it to Slaters. Pushing open the glass door, I come to a halt. The usual serene atmosphere has disappeared for the evening. The place is packed. I falter for a moment, sensing a twinge of apprehension in the pit of my stomach, only too aware that this is a new beginning for me. Daniel Foster may well have disappeared, leaving me with a huge vacuum in my heart, but somehow, somewhere along the way, he also managed to put me back together again. Taking a deep breath, reminding myself that I'm well and truly back in business, I step inside the gallery.

'Maya!' Lucy calls from the other side of the room. 'Good God, woman! You look stunning! Get over here!'

I pick my way through the crowd, to where Lucy's stranded with a bad-breathed, shih tzu-holding man.

'Have you sold many?' I ask.

'Quite a few. Yours has gone.'

'Already?' I glance around, anxiously. 'It wasn't Dan, was it?'

'Don't know. It was some representative, buying on behalf of a mystery collector.' She scans the gallery. 'Whoever it was, they've paid three grand for it and I'd say that's a good start. And you're getting plenty of interest. Look at that little lot.' She waves over to where my picture's displayed. A group of three or four important-looking types are gathered round it, deep in discussion. 'The bloke in the corduroy jacket's a big collector of stuff like yours and he's well interested. Come and say hello.' She grabs me by the arm and drags me over to the group, introducing me, thrusting me into the middle. I have no say in what happens next. Suddenly, I'm being bombarded with praise and questions. A good ten minutes pass like this before I'm finally rescued.

'Darling!'

I'm swivelled round on the spot by a chubby set of fingers, and find myself gazing down at Little Steve. 'We love your picture, simply love it. You have to do more!'

'I'm working on something right now.'

'Oooh!' Little Steve screws up just about everything that he can screw up: eyes, nose, mouth, shoulders ...

'We have some news for Maya,' Big Steve weighs in from behind.

'Ooh, yes.' Little Steve unscrews himself and pulls on a serious face. 'We're selling up.'

'What?'

'Selling up,' Little Steve repeats himself. 'We've found a buyer.'

'Who?'

Little Steve pretends to zip up his lips.

'Can't say, darling. It's all hush-hush.'

'What he means is,' Big Steve smiles, 'we haven't got a fucking clue yet. It's all going through a third party. But don't you worry. You'll get plenty of exposure, even after we've bowed out. Lucy's bound to see to that.'

'She'll keep her job?'

'Absolutely. All part of the deal. She's getting a pay rise too. Me and Little Steve have done our time. We've got places to visit, things to do. We're buying a camper van, doing a grand tour.'

'God help Europe.'

Little Steve squeals with delight and slaps me on the back.

'I'm so glad you're painting again.' He calms himself. 'Now, go forth and network!'

The next hour flies by in a whirlwind of small talk as I slingshot my way from one group of people to another. Eventually, finding myself next to the staircase and silently cursing the killer heels for wrecking my feet, I decide that what I really need right now is a quiet sit down. Nobody seems to notice as I take the steps down to the basement in search of a friendly chair. It's deserted tonight, the main lights switched off, the darkness broken by nothing more than a thin shaft of light falling from the open office door. I'm halfway across the room when a voice catches me from behind, causing my feet to stall.

'Maya.'

I turn slowly, sensing a floodtide of fear in my veins. I already know who's standing behind me in this dark basement. It's been five long years since I last heard that voice, but I'll never forget it. Deep, laced with an edge of the upper class and just the slightest trace of a Scottish lilt, the very sound of it throws me into automatic mode. Paralysed by shock and disbelief, I watch as the scene unfolds.

At first, I can't see his face. His tall, stocky frame is silhouetted against the light from upstairs. But when he takes a few steps forwards, his features finally snap into focus and I flinch. While his grey eyes flick their way down my body, I stare at him, dumbfounded. At last, his mouth twists into something that's clearly meant to be a smile. But the eyes remain hard, soulless.

'Aren't you going to say hello?' he demands.

My mouth kicks into action.

'What are you doing here, Ian?'

'Long time no see. Don't I get a kiss?'

He raises his wine glass to his lips and takes a swig. He's already drunk. That much is obvious from the way he's swaying from side to side. He stares at me lecherously.

'No, you don't get a fucking kiss. How did you find me?'

'It wasn't too hard.'

He stays exactly where he is, only inches away from me, glaring straight into my eyes, and I register everything: his short, black hair, his sharp, angular features. At first sight, any woman would find this man attractive. Everything about him is perfect, but underneath that flawless exterior, I know for a fact there's no real emotion, just an overwhelming desire to possess.

'Did you like your flowers?' he demands.

'What flowers?'

'Your roses?'

I take in a sharp breath. *I'm glad I've found you.* So, I was right after all. It *was* him.

'Tell me how you found me.'

'Easy.' He grins. 'Some prick turned up at my door a few days ago. He wanted to buy your painting, the one you did of the coast near my house. Remember? The one you exhibited in your graduation year. The one I bought. The one that brought us together.'

'We were never together,' I snarl.

'Oh yes, we were.' He licks his lips. 'I fucked you, Maya. A lot. I think that's classed as a relationship.'

Well, perhaps it is. But it was one that I chose to end when I realised he could be violent. A hand reaches out and grabs me by the arm. Adrenalin fires through my body.

'You ran away from me, Maya. I tried to find you, but you went to ground. I let it all go for a while there. But then fate played into my hands, and I met the wonderful Mr Foster.'

'Dan?'

'I let him have the painting, but I insisted on sending it to him, insisted I needed a few more days with it before I let go. He gave me his address, and Bob's your uncle.' He sniggers now. 'He's a swanky bastard, isn't he? Swanky, big flat on The Thames, swanky cars, swanky suits ...'

'You've stalked him?'

'I've been down here for a couple of days. I had a look. Had to see what the competition's like.'

'There is no competition.'

'I've got just as much money as him, if that's what you're after.'

'It's not what I'm after. And he earns his money. He actually works for a living, not like you.'

'Ooh, harsh. I can't help being a poor little rich kid.'

'No, and you can't help being a bastard either. I don't want anything more to do with you.'

'Come on, now. What we had was incredible.'

'What we had was shit.'

'I want you back.'

'That's not going to happen.'

He drops his glass to the floor. It explodes, smashing on impact, splintering into a thousand tiny pieces. My body jolts. My brain discharges an order to run. I'm about to move when a pair of hands lock themselves onto my shoulders, pushing me back against a wall.

'Get off me!' I scream.

'I want you back and I'll have you back.'

'I was never yours in the first place.'

He lurches forwards, pressing his mouth against mine and I struggle, turning my head to one side. He grabs hold of my hair, forcing my head back into place. I try to lift my leg, to knee him where it hurts, but he has me pinned flat against the wall. I open my mouth but I'm silenced immediately with a hand.

'No screaming, baby.'

One minute he's all over me, and the next he's gone. I straighten up, gasping for breath, watching in amazement as he's slammed against the wall. Even before my eyes have fully focused on the scene, I know who's joined us in the gloom. It's Dan who's just pulled Ian Boyd away from me, Dan who's currently punching and kicking the life out of him.

'No!' I cry out. 'Stop! You'll kill him!'

'That's the fucking plan!'

'No!'

Ignoring my cries, he carries on, ramming his fists into Boyd's stomach, occasionally landing a blow against his jaw. I'm about to launch myself into the fray when I'm pushed to one side.

'Enough, Dan!' Clive shouts. Clamping his arms around Dan's waist, he pulls him away. 'Calm down, for fuck's sake! Lucy's about to call the police.'

'Let her!'

He struggles for a moment or two before he gives up, glancing at me, and then back at the man who's currently slumped against the wall.

'You?' he breathes in disbelief. 'Ian Boyd.'

'The one and only.' Boyd straightens himself up, wipes his bloody nose against the cuff of his suit and stares at Dan. 'So, did Mr Swanky Pants get his painting?'

Narrowing his eyes, Dan turns to me. 'How do you know this piece of shit?'

'He's the reason …' I hear my voice falter. 'He's the reason I left Edinburgh.'

I hardly know what happens next. Out of nowhere, I'm consumed by a perfect storm of emotion: everything I've ever locked away from view, everything I've ever refused to acknowledge, about Boyd, about Dan, everything hits me at once. While the floodgates finally open and I begin to sob, my body seems to crumple under the impact. My head fills with darkness, my legs give way beneath me … and I begin to fall.

***

When I come to, I find myself in the passenger seat of a Mercedes-Benz.

'Boyd,' I mutter. 'Where's Boyd?' Sitting up straight and glancing out of the window, I discover that we're skirting the edge of Trafalgar Square. At least I think we are. My head is a fuzz of confusion.

'Gone. Clive threw him out. Are you okay?'

I turn to face Dan, and even though I should probably hate him right now, I'm surprised to sense that familiar twinge of desire between my thighs.

'I'm fine.'

I shake myself further into consciousness. I can barely believe what's going on here. If I'm not very much mistaken, the car has just swung onto Whitehall and I'm being driven back to his apartment.

'You passed out, Maya.'

'I said I'm fine.'

He glances at me.

'So, what's the deal with Boyd?'

I sense a prickle of annoyance. I've spent the last few years of my life trying to blot the bastard out of my mind. The last thing I need right now is to drag him back out of the shadows.

'I don't want to talk about it.'

'You don't have any choice. I need to know.'

'Why?'

'Because I need to make sure that you're safe.'

I hear myself laugh at that.

'And why would it bother you whether I'm safe or not?'

'Because you're the woman in my life.'

And that does it. Irritation springs into action. If Daniel Foster thinks he can simply turn up out of the blue and sweep me back into his life without some heavy duty explanation, then he's got a nasty surprise in store.

'Come off it, Dan. How can I be the woman in your life? You've just blanked me for the best part of a week.'

'There were reasons for that.'

'And I need to know them.'

'Not right now.'

'Why not?'

'Because right now, you need to tell me about Boyd.'

'I don't need to tell you anything.' Downing Street flashes past us on the right. 'And I don't want to go back to your place.'

'Yes, you do. Now tell me about Boyd.'

Anger flares for a split second.

'Fuck you.'

I turn to the window, watching as Whitehall gives way to the Thames. At the south side of the bridge, we circle the roundabout. Almost immediately, Lambeth House veers up in front of us. He waits in silence as the garage doors open before edging the car forwards into the dark. At last, the Mercedes draws to a halt. He gets out, slamming the door, and within seconds the passenger door is opened. When a hand appears in front of my face, I ignore it.

'We can do this the easy way,' he sighs. 'Or I can drag you out of that seat, kicking and screaming. Your choice.'

Glaring up at him, I decide to go for the easy option. I push myself out of the car, straighten up and begin to move forwards, slowly. I've barely taken three steps when I feel a hand at the bottom of my spine. I fizzle at the contact. Jesus, I've missed it. And shit, there's no way I'm ever going to be able to resist. I know that much. As we ride the lift, the hand stays firmly in place and while I stare resolutely at the floor, I know his eyes are fixed on me. By the time we step inside his apartment, I'm a quivering wreck. If I'm ever going to get an explanation out of this man, then I need to break the contact. Pulling away from him, I make my way over to the window where I stand with my arms folded, staring out over the Thames. Before long, I'm aware that he's standing by my side.

'I thought we were over,' I murmur.

'Whatever you thought, you can just forget it.' He touches a finger against the pendant. 'You're still wearing this.'

'No running,' I whisper. He doesn't say a word, leaving me with no option but to push on. 'Where have you been?'

'I needed some time to think.'

'You could have sent me a text.'

'I'm sorry.'

'You said you'd never hurt me again. You hurt me this week.'

'I said I'm sorry.'

'And that's not good enough. Everything was fine until you met Sara. You need to tell me exactly why you hate her so much. And while you're at it, you can tell me why this was a bad idea.'

'And you can tell me about Boyd.'

'If you're not going to talk, then I'm out of here.'

He's on me in an instant, knocking the wind straight out of my lungs and the sense out of my brain. While one hand moves around my back, pinning both of my arms in place, the other is clutching at my hair, holding me tight while he brings his face up close to mine.

'Don't even think about it, Maya. You don't get to make the rules tonight.'

'Piss off, Mr Foster.'

The grip tightens.

'You're the one who's going to talk.'

'Not fucking likely.'

'Boyd,' he growls.

'Sara,' I growl back.

His lips land on mine, kissing me with a violent passion, his tongue probing its way around my mouth, sliding against mine, thoroughly marking its territory. And I give in immediately. I kiss him right back. I have no idea how long it goes on for. When his mouth eventually releases mine, his hands are removed for a split second before I'm grabbed by the wrist and guided towards the stairs.

'What are you doing now?' I protest.

'Patience.' He practically hauls me up the steps, two at a time. 'You'll find out.'

Chapter Thirty-One

I'm expecting to be dragged straight into the bedroom, but instead he takes me across the landing. Pushing open the first door on the right, he flicks on a light and urges me forwards. I stagger to a halt, confused by what I see. At first, I wonder why he's brought me into his gym, but on closer inspection I realise that this isn't a gym at all. The room is windowless, the floor carpeted. And apart from a set of built-in wardrobes that stretch along the length of one wall, there's nothing else I can call furniture, just some sort of elaborate vaulting horse to the left, and directly in front of me, fixed to the opposite wall, a large wooden cross that's been set at an angle and fitted with manacles.

'It's a St Andrews cross,' he says quietly from behind me. 'Standard fare in the world of kink. And that,' he motions towards the second contraption, 'is a spanking bench.'

'Spanking?'

'You wanted to try it.'

'Yes, but when did you ...'

'I ordered them on Monday. They arrived yesterday.'

'Priceless.'

So, all the time, while I was agonising over whether or not we were finished, he was busy planning the next stage of our so-called relationship.

'We'll be using the bench tonight. Why don't you go and take a look?'

Fighting the urge to run, I manage to take a few jittering steps forwards and reach out, touching the wide, padded rest at the centre of the bench. To either side of it, I notice two further rests, narrower this time, and still padded: the lower one evidently for my knees and the higher one for my arms. Both sets of side rests are fitted with cuffs, clearly for my ankles and wrists. And everything is covered with a rich, red leather. I stare at it, open-mouthed, waiting for my brain to form a sentence.

'You're going to torture me?'

He laughs. 'Absolutely not.'

I swing round to find him standing behind me with his arms crossed, looking as cool, calm and collected as you like. Every last bit of me begins to tremble ... and it's not with fear.

'I don't understand.'

'You will later.'

'And what if I say no?'

'You're not going to.'

'You can't spank me into talking.'

'Oh yes I can.' He unleashes a smile. 'And it won't be the pain that makes you talk.' Boring into me with his blue eyes, he takes a good, long pause before he issues the first order. 'Turn around.'

I swallow hard, clenching my fists, willing my brain to locate the single shred of sense that would put an end to all of this right now. I should really insist on going back downstairs and talking things through. But I don't. Instead, overwhelmed by lust and curiosity and the absolute need to prove him wrong, I simply obey.

'This is a seriously sexy dress.' He peels the material upwards and over my head. 'It gave me a full-on stonker as soon as I saw it.'

'Nice. I'm pretty sure the knight in shining armour isn't supposed to rescue the damsel in distress with a massive erection.'

'He always does it with a massive erection, Maya. You just can't see it underneath all that chain mail.'

I smile to myself as he removes my bra, leaving my knickers and stockings in place. His right hand curls around me, slowly brushing its way across my skin, up to my left breast where his thumb and forefinger close around my nipple and begin to pull.

'Now,' he breathes into my ear. 'Let's get down to business, shall we?'

Snaking his left hand round to my stomach, he wastes no time. Thrusting his fingers into my knickers, he begins to massage my clit, rubbing firmly against the most sensitive spot, causing me to close my eyes and throw back my head at the sudden rush of pleasure. And before I know it, I'm groaning for England. He buries his face into my neck, kissing me, licking me, nipping at my flesh. I'm almost there when his right arm tightens around me and he squeezes my nipple, causing a flash of pain to sear its way through my chest. I cry out in shock as I'm tipped over the edge into an orgasm, twitching and convulsing in his arms.

'Ready to talk?' he demands, taking his hand out of my knickers and clamping his arm around my waist.

'Not likely,' I gasp.

'Then it's time to get you strapped in.'

Still holding me, he begins to move towards the bench.

'Do you need the toilet?'

I shake my head.

'Be sure about that, Maya. I'll be keeping you here for quite a while.'

'I'm fine.'

But I'm not. My heartbeat has gone wild. I'm in a total panic. I can't believe I'm doing this. At last, he releases me from his grip and I know what I have to do next. Climbing up onto the bench and shivering at the touch of leather against my skin, I adjust my breasts, making sure that I'm completely comfortable. By the time I've settled myself into position, he's taken off his shirt, his shoes and his socks. He's wearing nothing else now but a pair of black jeans, and my God, he looks fucking gorgeous. I watch in awe as he turns down the lights, leaving the room bathed in a soft, low glow. Pacing over to the wardrobe, he slides open a door, pulling out something that looks like a cat o' nine tails. Finally, he approaches me, dropping the mysterious item to the floor.

'I'm going to restrain you now. Remember your word.'

'I won't need it,' I smile. 'And you won't be extracting any information from me.'

He raises an eyebrow.

'Pride comes before a fall,' he warns me.

He fits the leg cuffs first, tightening them around my ankles, checking them thoroughly before he turns his attention to my arms, wrapping the cuffs around my wrists. I turn my head to the side, resting my cheek against the leather, and find his face close to mine.

'Comfortable?' he asks. I smile my reply. 'Good.' Tenderly, he moves my hair away from my face. 'Then I'll begin.' He kisses my cheek. 'You'll be singing like a canary before you know it.'

'Do your best.'

A palm is smoothed across my back, slowly taking in every square inch of skin before it comes to rest at the bottom of my spine.

'You're beautiful, Maya. You have a wonderful backside.'

'Thank you.'

A second hand runs its way across the black silk of my knickers.

'I'll start light, and build up from there. This is your warm up. Try to relax into it. Don't let your brain fight against the pain. Soak yourself up in it. Try to experience it as if it's something new. And breathe deeply. Concentrate on your breathing. Try to keep it as controlled as you can. Do you understand?'

'Of course.'

Immediately, he slaps me lightly on the right buttock. I try my best to follow his advice, but my body seems to want to crease itself up into a ball.

'Relax.'

He slaps me again, on the left buttock this time, quickly, lightly. The sound of the slaps echo around my head.

'How does that feel?'

'Fine,' I lie. Already I'm wondering if I'm going to make it through the entire session.

'Trust me,' he says gently. 'I'm going to increase the intensity now. Remember what I said.'

He begins to slap harder, moving from one buttock to the other, quickening the pace. One slap follows the other without a break, and I quickly lose count. I'm too busy fighting the need to cry out, to tense up and tug at the bindings. Closing my eyes, I try my damnedest to accept each new stinging sensation, to keep my breathing under control, but it's next to impossible. I'm about to scream out my safeword when he finally comes to a halt.

'There's some colour to your skin now.' He pulls my knickers down to my thighs. 'The blood's starting to flow.'

'Is that it?'

'No. There's plenty more.'

Without another word, he pulls the knickers back up and rains down another long session, harder this time. At first, I flinch, my fists tightening around the leather rests. My buttocks are truly on fire now and I'm vaguely aware that I'm wet around my crotch. He slows the pace, still moving from buttock to buttock, the hand firmer at the base of my spine, holding me in place. And maybe I'm becoming delirious, but between the waves of pain, I think I'm beginning to understand: my body is weakening under his touch, growing ever more vulnerable with each new stroke, and my brain isn't too far behind.

'That's your warm up done.'

'Warm up?' I choke. Raising my head from the leather, I realise that he's stopped again.

'Warm up,' he confirms. 'Now, we give the endorphins a chance. How do you feel?'

I blink a few times.

'My bum hurts.'

I feel his hand against my cheek.

'You're doing well. No struggling, no yelping. I'm proud of you. Now, let's get these knickers off.'

He tears them off in one go, and then he's in front of me.

'This is a flogger.' He shows me the leather fronds, running them through his fingers. 'I'm going to use it now. This is going to be gentle. We're just keeping things going while your body reacts. Do you want me to stop?'

'No.'

Fuck it. Why did I say that?

'Your choice.'

A different sensation hits me this time. He taps the lengths of leather against my buttocks, over and over, before he trails them slowly up and down my spine. He runs a hand across my skin, over my back, down to my buttocks. And then the flogger begins again. While the same routine is repeated for minutes on end, I sink deep into the leather, relaxing totally, soaking up the endless, dancing tingles. I'm pretty sure I'm half way to being hypnotised when he comes to a halt. I feel his fingers at my clit, patiently arousing me while he delivers the next round of spanks: quick, upward movements this time, interspersed with rests. Desperate to come, I squeeze my thighs against the leather, and my brain tosses and turns on itself. I'm losing my grip on rational thought, losing sight of the line between pleasure and pain. After a brief respite, the slaps return, harder this time, while his fingers continue to work me up into a storm. I'm nearly there when he stops again. I groan my disappointment.

'Your pain threshold is higher now, Maya. Adrenalin is pumping through your body. Your blood flow is increased, especially here.'

He cups a hand around my vagina, pressing hard against my clitoris. The pressure sends ruffles of warmth undulating their way through my groin. I moan loudly and hear him chuckle again. Alongside another round of hard slaps, he returns a finger to my clit, increasing the pace of his movements. I close my eyes, focusing on my impending orgasm, willing it to arrive sooner rather than later. I'm breathing quickly now, gasping. Another handful of slaps rain down on my buttocks and I finally come, consumed in a sudden rush of heat.

'Oh, God,' I groan.
'Ready to spill the beans?'
'No. Not until ...'

Out of nowhere, a single hard slap lands on my left buttock. I cry out, more in surprise than pain. A second slap lands on my right buttock and my body jolts. Finally, he begins to spank my vagina, again and again, with short, upward movements. Each spank sends me wild. I can barely believe it when I begin to convulse in a second, intense orgasm.

'Open your eyes,' he murmurs into my ear.

It takes all my energy to comply. I find him standing by my side, staring down at me from under hooded eyes. He reaches down and unfastens his belt, sliding it out of his jeans, slowly, making a show of it while he continues to stare at me. He pulls it tight between his hands.

'Not that,' I mutter, amazed that I can push out the words. Out of nowhere, I'm woozy. I feel as if I've been drugged.

'I'll use this if I see fit,' he says sternly, and my muscles clench again.

He hangs the belt over the end of the bench, right in front of my eyes. My heart begins to race, a real sprint, as I gaze at the belt. Shit. No. He can't use that.

'Ready to sing?'

A sentence. I need a sentence.

'You're getting nothing, you bastard.'

He stares down at me, his eyes gleaming, and he begins to unbutton his jeans.

'Well, if you're not going to talk, then I might as well just fuck that luscious cunt of yours.' He leans down and kisses me gently on the forehead. 'But all in good time.'

He disappears again and I feel his hands on me, running their way tenderly across my buttocks one more time. One hand comes to a halt, holding me in place while he begins to administer the slaps again, each one stinging as badly as before. But something has changed now. Another flow of chemicals must have been released into my body because now I can barely keep my eyes open, and in spite of the pain, I'm wonderfully relaxed. I can barely think now. My brain seems to have washed itself out.

'Talk,' he breathes, halting his flow.
'No.'

His fingers enter me. They're quickly removed.

'You're ready for me.'

He begins to nudge his cock inside me. He doesn't take his time. Filling me completely, he clamps his hands around my thighs and begins to pump with a steady, unrelenting pace. I hear moans and groans, and realise that they're mine. The pressure builds almost immediately.

'I can't ...' My words fizzle out into nothing. I have no idea what I was about to say.

'This is beautiful, Maya. You're beautiful.'

He picks up the rhythm, pounding into me harder now.

I open my eyes and gaze at my hand, surprised to find that it's limp. A shimmer passes up my spine. Another flings its way through my groin. I'm moaning again, only louder this time. I can feel everything so acutely now, his crotch thrashing against my buttocks, his hands on my flesh, every twitch of his cock inside me.

'Jesus!' he cries out as he empties himself inside me.

With a single slap at the side of my right buttock, my muscles seem to implode. I'm barely aware of what happens next. I know that he withdraws himself. I hear the final slaps and even though I know that they're the hardest yet, my body welcomes every single one of them. My brain has long since stopped complaining about the pain. In fact, I don't think it even knows what pain is any more. All I sense is pleasure.

***

I'm curled up next to him. Somewhere. I don't know where. I can see windows. The blackness of a night sky. The lights of a jet. I'm wrapped in a throw, leaning my head against a warm chest. And I can hear a voice.

It's mine.

'I met him in my final year. He was a rich kid. Spoilt.'

Fuck it. I'm talking. I'm spilling the beans, and there's nothing I can do about it. Whatever he's done to me, my brain has taken a hike. And even though I've not touched a drop of alcohol all day, I feel drunk. I seem to have lost all my inhibitions, my stop button, my filter ... the lot.

'Go on,' his voice encourages me softly. A strong arm is holding me, a hand stroking my hair.

'He had a huge house out by the coast in Fife, fast cars, a flat in Edinburgh. Family wealth. He never worked a day in his life. Have you drugged me?'

'No, Maya. Keep going.'

I take in a deep breath and let it go.

'Lucy had a part time job in a gallery in Edinburgh. She got them to exhibit a painting of mine. He was there that night. He bought it and I was taken in by it all. He was Prince Charming. He asked me out and I said yes. The first few months were great, but then I started to realise there was something about him, something I just didn't like.'

I falter. I'm coming back to reality now. I'm on a couch, a leather couch.

'Go on.'

'It started small, little comments about the way I dressed, telling me what to eat, how to do my hair, how to do my make-up. And then he started getting arsey if I wanted to see my friends.'

'He had no right to do that.'

'He told me that he owned me, just like you tell me that you own me. But he meant it completely. He really did think I was his possession. One night, when we argued ...' I swallow, realising that I'm going too far.

'What happened?'

'He ...' I listen to my own breathing. It's in tatters. 'He hit me.' I swallow again. 'I'm not an idiot. I knew I had to get out. I went home and I finished it by text. I couldn't do it to his face because I just didn't know what he'd do.'

Silence unfolds, spreading itself out across the air between us. At last, the arm tightens.

'You should have told me this before.'

'I couldn't.'

'I never would have spanked you if I'd known this.' I turn to face him, finding an expression of pure anguish. 'You shouldn't have let me do that.'

'It's okay.' I reach up and stroke his cheek. 'It's different with you. I don't know why. It just is. Everything you do brings me pleasure.'

I run my thumb down the side of his face, around his chin.

'We aim to please,' he whispers, taking hold of my hand. 'So, tell me. When you finished with Boyd, how did he take it?'

'Not well. He started hounding me, turning up on my doorstep at all hours, texting me, calling me, threatening me. I went to the police but they weren't interested. How did you do this? How did you make me talk?'

'Trade secrets.'

'I feel like ...'

'You just reach a point where you're suggestible. That's all. I've seen it plenty of times. It's wearing off now, but you might as well carry on. What happened to make you leave Edinburgh?'

I let out a sigh.

'He turned up at my graduation party. Drunk. I was looking for the toilet when he got me.'

'Got you?'

I press my index finger against my forehead and close my eyes. 'He got hold of me and forced me out to the back of the building, and then he tried to ...'

His body grows tense against me. 'Maya?'

'He didn't do anything. He didn't get the chance. Lucy turned up. She'd seen it all.' I open my eyes to find him gazing down at me. 'Me and Lucy, we'd planned on staying in Edinburgh, but after that, I couldn't. So we made the move to London. Lucy got the job at Slaters. I got a job as a waitress. We shared a flat in Peckham to start with. And then I met Tom.' I suck in a shaky breath. 'He was everything I thought I ever wanted. He looked after me. He protected me. I'd stopped painting, but I thought it was fine. I thought I'd get married and raise a family. I thought I'd find some sort of fulfilment in that. I invested everything in that relationship. But then he walked away. And I had nothing. Not even painting.' I hesitate. Should I really tell him the next bit? Yes, I decide. Whyever not? I mean, I've already told him the rest. 'I went mad.'

His eyes narrow. He tips his head forwards.

'It's okay,' he soothes me. 'I don't care what you did. It doesn't change anything.'

'I slept around, I drank too much, and then I kind of folded in on myself. Lucy propped me up through all of this. Her flatmate in Camden moved out a few months ago and I moved in. I'd only just started getting myself back together again when I met you. You were right, when you said I had a crippling lack of self-esteem. You were right. It's still there. You couldn't work out what knocked me back down after art college. Well, it was men. And when I met you, I thought I'd get knocked down all over again.'

'And the way I've behaved hasn't helped that.'

I shake my head. 'You've dropped me twice now, Dan. I can't take much more.'

'It won't happen again.'

'But why has it happened so far?'

I hear him let out a breath.

'The first time, it was because of something Clive said. He thought I'd destroy you and he had a point. The way I used to be, I would have done. But I'm not that man any more.'

'And last week?' I urge him. 'I've told you about Boyd. You've got to tell me.'

'And I will. Soon. I promise.' He touches my cheek. His eyes plead with me and I fold with a silent nod of the head. 'Now, stand up.'

'What?'

'I said stand up. I've got something to show you.'

Obediently, I get to my feet and pull the throw around myself. I stay where I am while Dan gets up and makes his way to the door.

'This was intended to be an office, but I've never used it. When you came into my life, a better idea occurred to me.'

He flicks on a light and immediately I'm frozen to the spot, fixed there in a state of complete surprise. The room is at the end of the block, and while the two internal walls are blank plaster, the two outside walls at the corner are made completely of glass. The view gives out over the Thames. I stagger towards the windows and gaze out to where a thousand lights twinkle against the darkness. I turn around, catching sight of the leather sofa, a huge wooden sideboard and an easel. An array of paints, brushes and palettes are laid out across the sideboard while a range of canvases in a variety of sizes are propped up against a wall.

'A studio,' he explains. 'For you. Everything you've got back in your flat, it's here too ... and more.'

I head for the sideboard, hesitating for a moment before I set about picking up one tube of paint after another.

'The light in here during the day is perfect. And it's quiet up here. You won't be disturbed.'

'You've been busy.'

I turn to face him, caught immediately by the sight of a painting hanging on the wall behind his head. I gaze at it, mesmerised, remembering the few days I spent on a clifftop in Scotland, desperately trying to capture the power of the sea.

'How did you track it down?'

His answer floats through me.

'I'd already spoken to your tutor. He remembered you'd sold a piece at a gallery. I called the gallery and they pointed me in Boyd's direction. When I was up in Edinburgh, I went over to his flat and viewed it. He agreed to sell it to me.' He takes a step forwards and unhooks the painting from the wall. 'I thought it would be a welcome surprise. I thought it would remind you of where you came from. I thought it would help you to get painting again. I didn't know it would bring him back into your life.' He turns the painting round and rests it against the wall. 'I'll get rid of it. I'm sorry.'

I shake my head.

'No. Don't. When I painted it, I was happy. I just need to remember that.'

He circles back round the sofa, settles himself down, snakes an arm across the back and pats the seat next to him. As soon as I take my place, the arm closes around me.

'I want you to be yourself, Maya. And that means you need to paint.'

'I know.'

'You've made a start, but you can't work in that god-awful bedroom. This is perfect for you.' He watches me for a moment, gauging my reaction. 'This isn't me controlling you. This is me encouraging you. And if you don't want to work here, then you can find somewhere else and I'll pay for it.'

'You can't do that.'

'I can.'

I glance back at the seascape. 'Did you buy my painting? Tonight? The one of the woods?'

'I did.'

'Why?'

'Because it's too precious to sell to a stranger. One day you'll understand.' His eyes flicker, as if he's just gone too far. He brings himself back quickly, flipping the subject.

'And Boyd won't hurt you again. I'll make sure of that.'

'You can't stop him, Dan.'

'I can make sure you're protected.'

'How?'

'I'm stinking rich, remember? I can afford body guards. I'll have you protected. And while I'm at it, I'll look into ways of getting the bastard to back off.'

'You don't need to do that.'

'I stirred up the hornet's nest and I'll sort it out. If I can't protect the woman in my life, then what can I do?'

I steel myself. It's time to inform Mr Foster of the truth. No more holding back. He'll just have to deal with it.

'I'm not just the woman in your life,' I whisper. 'I'm the woman who loves you.'

He takes in a deep breath and gazes into my eyes. I could stay here forever, lost in the swirls of blue.

'I love you, Dan. And I know you probably don't feel the same way, but ...'

A finger lands on my lips and I sink into silence. He shakes his head.

'I want you to move in,' he says.

'What?'

'You heard me. I want you to move in. Here. Into this apartment.'

'Dan, this is a bit quick.'

'You're not safe in Camden. This place is more secure. I'm not taking any chances.'

'But ...'

'And it's a permanent move. Just for the record. You get to devote all your time to painting and I get to fuck you whenever I like. As far as I can see, it's a win-win situation.'

'But you've never done this sort of thing before. What if ...'

'Bollocks to what if. Tomorrow, we go and get your stuff.'

'But Lucy.'

'She'll be fine.'

'But I need to talk to her about this. And I need to tell my family.' I come to a halt. 'Oh, shit, no,' I gasp. Suddenly, out of the mess in my head, my brain has decided to remember something. 'It's my dad's sixtieth tomorrow. He's having a party. I've got to go. Shit. Lucy's going. She's taking Clive.'

'I know. Clive told me. It's a little strange, don't you think?'

I smile.

'My mum wants to meet him. She's known Lucy for years. She's almost as interested in her love life as she is in mine.'

'Fair enough.' He shrugs his shoulders. 'Clive can drive the pair of you up there.'

'What? No. You've got to come. Mum wants to meet you as well.'

His face ices over.

'I can't.'

'Why not?'

He shrugs again.

'I've got a few files to read through.'

'Then do it on Sunday. Dan! This is the least you could do for me.'

'I can't.'

'Don't be an arse. If we're about to live together, then I think you should meet my family. They know about you and they want to meet you. They'll think it's odd if you don't turn up. They'll think it's rude.'

He sighs now, deep in thought.

'I'm not happy about this,' I push on. 'If this is a relationship, then we've got to share each other's lives, and we've got to share properly.

You've shown me where you come from. Now I want to show you where I come from. You're just being selfish.'

He bites his bottom lip. 'You're right.'

'Then change your mind. Because if you don't, there's no way I'm moving in.'

He stares at me for a few moments. All manner of emotions flash through his eyes.

'And besides,' I add. 'This is the perfect opportunity for you to make it up to my sister. You were awful to her last Sunday.'

He reaches up and touches his forehead, closes his eyes and seems to swallow. Why the hell is this so difficult for him?

'You've got to come, Dan. And you've got no bloody choice in the matter.'

'Okay,' he mutters at last. 'I'll do it.'

Chapter Thirty-Two

I watch as the cluttered streets of North London give way to the suburbs, as the suburbs slowly unravel, leaving us with nothing more than a patchwork of fields. He drives on in silence, leaving the Satnav switched off, paying no attention to the signs that flash past us. It's as if he's on autopilot ... as if he's memorised the route. And all the time, the sky darkens while clouds rally in the air above us.

'Do you think there's going to be a storm?' I ask, shifting about in my seat.

'Yes.'

I wait for him to elaborate, to reassure me, but nothing comes. Instead, he goes back to staring at the road and I shift about in my seat some more, sensing a knot of anxiety in my stomach. I'm about to introduce my family to the new man in my life, to the man I'm about to live with, and on my dad's sixtieth birthday of all days. The last thing I need right now is a flash of lightning or a thunder clap. But as much as it's niggling at my thoughts, the possibility of a storm is the least of my worries. My biggest concern right now is the silent man who's sitting next to me. I watch him furtively, trying to read the inner workings of his mind, but it's next to impossible. The shutters have come down. Speaking in nothing more than clipped monotones, he's simply blocked me out, and for the life of me, I can't work out why. For the last hour or so, I've done my best to catch hold of a clue, but there's been very little to go on. Nothing apart from a flicker in the eyes or a tremble in the fingers. At last, deciding that enough is enough, I touch him on the leg. He gives a start and turns briefly, faking a smile that leaves me in a mire of confusion.

'Are you okay?' I venture.

'I'm fine.'

'But you've been quiet all morning.'

And not just all morning, I'd like to add, but I'm not going to bring that up now. I won't ask him why he changed last night, why he slipped off into his own little world for the best part of an hour. And I certainly won't ask him why he took me back to his bedroom and made love to me with a new sense of urgency, as if it was our last night together.

'I've got a lot on my mind,' he says at last. 'I'm alright. Don't worry.'

Don't worry? If it wasn't totally inappropriate, I'd laugh at that. How can I not worry? I'm about to throw Mr Mean and Hot and Moody into the midst of my mad family circle. He's about to be bombarded with meaningless small talk and mauled by questions, and he hardly seems in the right frame of mind for it. As we push further into the countryside, I settle back into silence, occasionally glancing across at him while my brain picks its way through the things that might be on his mind. Perhaps he's worrying over Boyd. Perhaps he's nervous about seeing Sara again. Or maybe it's just the idea of meeting my parents. I have no idea what's eating him but whatever it is, it's too late now to sort it out. The scenery is already far too familiar. Quaint villages. Country pubs. Houses decorated with Norfolk pebbles. We're nearly there.

Before long, we begin the descent into Limmingham. Down below us, the rooftops slide into view, and now I can clearly make out the mishmash of Victorian hotels and guest houses, the clutter of seaside shops and private homes, the squat, square tower of the church. And behind it all, shimmering darkly under the coming storm, the sea reaches up towards the horizon, nudging at the clouds. Feeling a shiver in my gut, I peer to the left, to where the newer housing estates spread themselves out along the coast, including the one where I grew up. Any minute now, we'll be immersed in the chaos of my parents' home, and suddenly I'm dreading it more than ever.

An idea flips into my mind.

'I'd like to show you something,' I announce. 'Before we go to Mum and Dad's. Take a left just up ahead.'

Without question, he follows my orders, turning the Mercedes into a narrow road that's flanked by pine trees. Before long, we come to a dead end, pulling up in a deserted car park.

'You'll like this.'

Unclipping my seatbelt, I push open the door and get out, waiting for him to join me. It seems to take an age before he's by my side. Gripping him by the hand, I lead him away from the car park, following a path between the pines until at last, we reach a patch of older woodland. It's peaceful here. We're surrounded by birch and oak, thick trunks and gnarled branches that twist and turn on themselves against the sky. Apart from the occasional birdsong and the dull rush of the sea, there's no sound at all. Taking a seat on a log, I beckon for him to join me. He sits beside me, gazing round for a moment or two before the peace seems to take hold of him and he gathers his senses.

'This is your painting,' he whispers, glancing up through the branches. 'These are your woods'

'You're right.' I smile at him. 'This was my sanctuary.'

He smiles back at me, but it doesn't warm my heart. There's something desperate in those eyes, something distinctly unsettling. He takes an unsteady breath and in spite of his claims, I know he's not fine at all. Perhaps I should distract him with a little local folklore.

'It's supposed to be haunted,' I explain. 'There was this boy who disappeared when I was little and you know what kids are like. They all said he was murdered, that his body was buried here. They all said he haunted these woods.'

He stares up at the sky.

'He became a ghost?'

I laugh at the innocence of his question.

'Of course not.' I shake my head and smile, trying to lighten the atmosphere. 'My dad told me the truth. He didn't get on with his family. He just went to live somewhere else. Nothing quite so dramatic.'

He nods. 'Real life's never that interesting. Just seedy and painful and ...' He drifts off again without finishing his sentence.

I reach out and touch him lightly on the arm. He flinches.

'Dan?' He seems so young, so vulnerable. It's exactly the look I drew at work. 'Are you really okay?'

'Like I said ...' He shrugs his shoulders. 'I'm fine.' He stares ahead, into the shadows. 'I don't want you to think I don't want to meet your family. It's not that at all.'

'Then what is it?'

He breathes in deeply and stands up. Thrusting his hands into his pockets, he kicks at a pile of twigs and then turns slowly, fixing his eyes on me. His lips part and for a few short seconds I'm certain he's about to tell me something. But the moment disappears as quickly as it arrived. He turns away, his next words almost lost beneath the sound of the leaves rustling in a sudden breeze.

'What I feel about you won't change.'

'What do you mean?'

'Exactly what I say. Whatever happens between us, it won't change.'

I stand and take his hand in mine.

'It's the same for me,' I reassure him. 'Now come on. They'll be expecting us.'

***

I direct him back along the roads into Limmingham, through the narrow, winding streets of the town centre and out into the suburbs. It's not long before we pull up outside my parents' home. He cuts the engine and stares out of the window, his attention fixed on the row of nondescript, semi-detached houses at the opposite side of the road. Deciding it's best to make a move, I get out and wait, checking the sky above us, noting that the air is heavy now, brooding with the promise of thunder. The slam of a car door jolts me back into the world and I find him standing on the pavement, still gazing down the road, transfixed. Approaching him slowly, I take his hand one more time, and this time I can really feel it. He is shaking.

'Are you ill?'

'No.' He takes his hand out of mine. 'Please don't fuss.'

'But you're shaking. Why are you shaking?'

'Just nervous.' He forces a smile. 'Nervous about meeting Mr and Mrs Scotton. Nervous about making a good impression.'

'You'll knock them for six.'

I shrug my shoulders and walk up the drive, making for the side door, knowing it's never locked during the day. Glancing back to make sure Dan is with me, I open the door and the smell of food hits me immediately. And so does the sight of my mum. Dressed in her usual neat pair of slacks and floral print blouse, she's standing at the counter. She turns, nods and then goes back to faffing about with a packet of cocktail sausages.

'Oh, Maya! You're here.' She pours the sausages into a bowl.

'I told you I would be.'

'I'm all in a tizz. I haven't even got time to put these on sticks.'

'Do you want any help?'

'No.' She wafts a hand about dramatically before moving on to rearranging a huge plate of mini pizzas. 'Maybe later. We've got more people coming over tonight. Auntie Barbara, Uncle Brian, Sharon and Gary ...' She reels off the names of half a dozen other relatives I haven't seen in years. 'But it's just us for now. Your dad's in the living room with Sara and the kids.' She motions towards the living room door. 'Geoff's not coming. She's chucked him out. And a bloody good job too. That man's a lazy arse.' She tugs at a packet of tomatoes. It explodes, ejecting tiny red balls all over the counter. 'And Lucy's here,' she sighs, gathering the tomatoes back together and scooping them into a dish. 'She's brought a lovely young man with her.'

'There you go,' I reassure Dan, giving him a nudge. 'Your reinforcements have arrived.'

He stares at me for a moment, then nods.

'Oooooh,' Mum purrs. Catching sight of Dan, she spins round on her heels. 'Hello, you.' Wiping her hands on her apron, she shuffles forwards. 'You must be Daniel.'

'Dan.' He coughs uncomfortably. Taking her hand in his, he lands a quick kiss on the back of it. 'It's lovely to meet you, Mrs Scotton.'

Mum cocks her head to one side and examines his face.

'Audrey,' she whispers. 'Call me Audrey. You have lovely blue eyes.'

'Mum!'

'Well, he does, Maya.' She scowls at me. 'Oh, for God's sake, you're going to have to marry this one.' She's pointing at him now, waving a manicured hand around in the air. 'You'll have gorgeous children.'

'Mum!'

The ghost of a smile flickers across his face.

'Well,' Mum sighs. 'You'd better take Daniel through to meet the birthday boy. Go on.' She ushers us towards the door.

Glad to escape the unwanted attention, I lead the way into the living room. With the three piece suite crammed into one end, and the dining table at the other, it's a small room at the best of times. But today, it's overflowing with bodies. Seemingly oblivious to our arrival, my dad is busy arranging plates of food on the dining table while over in the corner, Sara's flumped into an armchair. Spread out on the floor in front of her, her two young sons are playing with a massive collection of toy cars.

'That's Ethan,' I inform Dan. 'He's six. And Damian's four.'

He nods silently.

'You made it!' Lucy smiles from the sofa where she's currently draped all over Clive.

'You okay?' Clive asks, raising an eyebrow at Dan.

'Of course.'

And why has he just asked that? Before I can ponder over it any more, I'm pounced on by my dad.

'Maya.' He slaps his big hands on my cheeks, pulling my head forwards and planting a soggy kiss on my forehead. 'Thank God you're here. Are we going to get pissed?'

'Not today, Dad.'

'Your sister's already on her third glass.'

He nods towards Sara who raises her glass and takes a mouthful of wine, staring over the rim at Dan, a frown on her forehead.

'And this must be Daniel.' He clasps the new arrival's hand, shaking it furiously while he sinks into silence.

'It's good to meet you, Mr Scotton,' Dan smiles.

Letting go of his hand and remaining silent, my dad smiles back. A hint of curiosity flits across his eyes.

'I never forget a face,' he mutters.

And in that instant, I sense it: a barrier of mistrust descends between the two men in my life, leaving confusion on one side and an ice-cold layer of reserve on the other.

'Dad?'

He snaps himself out of his reverie, glancing around the room.

'Can I get you a drink, Dan?'

'Water please,' he says quietly. 'I'm driving.'

'Bloody hell. What's that all about? We could have put you up for the night. We could have had a session.'

He slaps Dan on the back and scuttles away into the kitchen, returning quickly with a tumbler of tap water and a huge glass of wine for me.

'I said no, Dad,' I complain.

'And it's my sixtieth birthday. I say yes. Get it down you.'

He thrusts the glasses at us, and we accept them, standing awkwardly for a moment or two, listening to the sounds of toy cars being smashed together.

'So, what do you do for a living, Dan?' Dad asks. 'Maya's told us nothing.'

'Construction.'

'You're a builder?'

'Not exactly. I run a construction company.'

'Ooh,' Mum calls out from the kitchen. 'We want a new conservatory. Do you do conservatories?'

'Not really, Mrs Scotton.'

'That's a shame. And are you rich?' she asks, stumbling through the doorway, brandishing a plate of sandwiches.

'Mum!'

'It's okay,' Dan interrupts with a shrug. 'I suppose you could say I'm financially stable.'

'Well, that's it then.' Mum slides the plate onto the table, turns and claps her hands together. 'You're definitely going to marry my daughter.'

I let my head fall. This really is too much for anyone to bear.

'Mum, please just stop it. We've only known each other a couple of weeks.'

'Well, sometimes you just know,' she insists. 'When I met your dad, I knew straight away. There he was, selling ice creams down at the beach front, and I took one look at him and I said to my friend, that's the one. That's the love of my life. It was the same for him. He asked me to marry him a month later. Is that how it was for you, Daniel?'

He smiles uncomfortably. There's something endearing about seeing him like this, ripped out of his natural environment where he's in control of everything, marooned in the middle of the normal world, with my parents.

'Say hello to Sara,' I whisper into his ear. 'And apologise.'

With a sigh, he makes his way through the chaos of the toy cars, almost tripping over Clive's legs in the process. I watch as he leans over, speaking earnestly, as my sister gazes up at him and finally nods.

'Come and sit down.' Dad motions for me to join him at the table. Squeezing myself into position, I comply.

'What do you think?' I ask.

'Where's he from?' He picks up a sandwich and waves it in Dan's direction.

'London.'

'Are you sure?'

'Of course. He grew up in Surrey.'

'Only I never forget a face.'

I examine my dad's expression. For the life of me, I just can't work out why he's so interested.

'If you'd met him, Dad, you would have worked it out by now.'

'Sometimes it just takes me a few minutes.' He takes a bite of the sandwich and chews thoughtfully.

'Well, good luck.'

'All done,' Dan mumbles. Seating himself next to me, he places his glass of water on the table, in between a mound of cocktail sausages and a plateful of pork pie slices.

'Dig in,' my dad urges him. 'We've got more for later. Come on you lot!'

At last, after much fussing, all the adults are seated around the table, while my two nephews settle for a picnic on the floor. And while we set about wading through the mountains of party food, Mum grills Dan on his company, his background and his upbringing. Apparently satisfied with his curt answers, she moves on to Clive who's half way through his explanation of what he does at Fosters when I notice that my dad is staring resolutely at Dan.

'Your eyes,' Dad muses. 'I just can't put my finger on it.'

Dropping his food onto his plate, Dan picks up the glass of water and takes a sip. I notice that his hands are trembling again. And then I notice that the conversation has fizzled out. I glance around the table, from Lucy who's far too busy biting into a lump of pork pie to notice anything much, to Sara whose attention is fully fixed on Dan, and finally to Clive. Holding a forkful of salad in one hand, he's simply frowning at my dad, waiting for his next words. They're not long in coming.

'I never forget a face. Audrey, I never forget a face, do I?'

'No, you certainly don't,' Mum smiles.

'I just can't work it out.' He continues to stare at Dan, and I'm about to inform him that he's being rude when he waves a finger in the air. 'I've got it! I know who you remind me of. It's that boy, that boy from down the road.'

Taking a gulp of wine, Mum narrows her eyes and shakes her head.

'Which boy?' she demands.

'You know, the one who went off. You remember, Audrey. The kids round here used to think he'd been murdered.'

Something stirs at the back of my brain, something unseen and unwanted. It begins to shuffle the evidence.

'The ghost?' I ask. 'The ghost in the woods?'

'That's the one,' Dad laughs. 'Only he never got murdered.'

I watch as my mum shakes her head, and then I turn to Dan. He's staring down at his plate now, his face inscrutable.

'The Taylors,' Dad goes on. 'That was the family.' He shoves a mini pizza into his mouth and chews happily. 'They had the two girls, didn't they? And then there was the boy, the one who went away. What was his name?' He gazes down at his plate, his brain obviously working at full pelt. A few seconds later, his head flips up. 'Daniel!' he exclaims. 'He was called Daniel too. Well, there's a coincidence. Daniel Taylor. You remember him, don't you, Audrey?'

'Daniel Taylor,' Mum muses. 'Yes, Daniel Taylor. He had bright blue eyes, just like yours.' She takes an uncertain peek at Dan before she goes on. 'You wouldn't remember him, Maya. You were just a little dot at the time. But Sara was in his class at school, weren't you, Sara?'

'Yes.'

A hiss. The word comes out as a hiss. And then it fades into nothing. Only the children are eating now, happily oblivious to the events unfolding next to them. And while the silence seems to stretch out forever, my eyes focus themselves on Dan, just like every other pair of eyes around the table. His head is dipped.

'You really do look like him,' my dad smiles at last. 'I never forget a face.'

My brain stirs again. And then it begins to lay out the cards, one by one, making connections that I just don't want to make. His anger towards my sister. His reluctance to come to Limmingham. His words about my painting. One day you'll understand.

'Dan?' I touch him on his arm. 'What's going on?'

He says nothing. He does nothing. The silence returns, holding court for a few moments before it's broken by my sister's voice.

'It's you, isn't it?' she demands quietly. 'That's why you can't stand me.'

His lips part. He shakes his head.

'What's going on?' I hear my own voice quivering its way through the air. Again, he doesn't respond.

'It is you,' my sister presses.

'Dan?'

There's a sudden flurry of action at my side. Pushing back his chair, he gets to his feet.

'I should go now,' he announces coldly. 'It was nice to meet you, Mr Scotton. I hope you enjoy the rest of your birthday. Mrs Scotton, thank you for the meal. I'm sorry.'

I watch in disbelief as he leaves the room. Finally gathering my wits about me, I push back my own chair back and follow. Scurrying through the kitchen and out through the open back door, I catch him halfway down the drive.

'Wait!' I shout.

He swings to a halt, but he doesn't turn.

'Aren't you going to tell me what the fuck's going on?'

'He's been lying to you. That's what's been going on.' My sister's voice grabs me from behind. 'And now he's been caught out.' She comes to stand at my side. 'I knew we'd met before. We were at school together. You are Daniel Taylor.'

He turns slowly.

'My name is Daniel Foster.' He clenches his fists. His entire body seems to be coiled up now, ready to explode.

'So what? You changed your name. But you're still the boy from down the road. Go on! Admit it!'

I glance between them, trying desperately to make sense of it all.

'Yes,' he growls. 'It's me. What of it?'

I catch my breath, staring at the man I thought I knew, struggling to keep my balance while thoughts whip themselves up into a whirlwind. Everything he ever told you, a voice cries out, everything you came to trust and love, it was nothing more than smoke and mirrors.

'But how can you be?' I glance down the road, towards the house where the Taylors used to live. I remember them now. I remember the girls, but not the boy.

'You never told her,' my sister grimaces. 'Why didn't you tell her who you were?'

Silence cloaks us while up above the clouds gather, threatening to disgorge themselves at any minute.

'Dan!' I shout. 'Just tell me who you are! How the fuck can you be Daniel Taylor?'

'Why don't you let your sister tell you?' His words scratch at the air. His eyes flash darkly as he stalks his way back towards us. 'Go on, Sara. But make sure you don't leave anything out.'

I turn to find my sister shaking, her mouth open, her eyes wide with fear. For a moment, I'm distracted by the fact that we've been joined by Clive and Lucy, that Clive is edging his way towards Dan, holding out a hand, nervously, as if he's approaching a dangerous animal.

'You can't do it, can you?' Dan seethes, drawing my attention back to his face. 'Because if you tell her about me, then you'll have to own up to what you did.' He points a finger at Sara and for a split second, I wonder if he's actually going to lash out.

'Dan, no!' Clive springs forwards, grabbing Dan by the arm. 'Don't do this here. Go home and calm down. I'll bring Maya back and you can explain later.'

'I don't want him to explain later!' I spit. 'I want to hear this now.'

Dan shakes his head. Breathing hard and fast, he shakes himself out of Clive's grasp and moves closer to me, locking me into his gaze.

'Alright, Maya. If you want to know the truth, I'll give it to you.' He points down the road. 'Number fifteen. I spent the first ten years of my life in that fucking house.'

'Dan.'

He shoots a glance at Clive and shakes his head.

'My real dad walked out before I was born. I never knew him. But I knew my step dad alright. And he was a bastard.'

Clive reaches out again. He's shaken off for a second time.

'And I mean a real bastard, Maya.' He chews at his lip for a moment before he speaks again. 'My sisters were his kids but I wasn't, and he hated me for it. My sisters had everything.' He reaches up and touches his own chest. 'I had nothing.'

His words filter back into my head: *I wasn't spoilt when I was child, Maya, and I wasn't overindulged.*

'Dan, not here.'

Ignoring Clive, he presses on.

'My sisters were well dressed but I wasn't. My clothes were always in tatters, always too small, always wrong ...'

It's not nice, is it? Wearing the wrong clothes?

'Do you like the story so far? Do you want to know the rest? Do you want to know how he poisoned my mum against me? Do you want to know that I was filthy because my clothes were never washed? That I was never allowed in the family bathroom? That I stank?'

He grabs me by the arms and I flinch.

'Or do you want to know that they didn't feed me? That I had to scavenge for food? That I got thrown out of my bedroom and had to sleep on a mattress in the outhouse?'

'Dan!'

'No, you don't want to know any of that, do you, Maya? Because then you'll never be able to look me in the face again.'

I open my mouth to speak, but nothing comes.

'And now we get to the good bit.' He squeezes my arm. 'The bit about school.' He turns to my sister.

'This needs to stop,' she pleads.

'No, it doesn't. Maya needs to know the truth. She needs to know that you bullied me relentlessly. She needs to know that I couldn't go anywhere without your taunts, that you had every single child in that school following suit, that you made my life a fucking nightmare.'

'And I'm sorry for that.'

'Well, it's too late.'

I hear a gasp.

'That night,' Sara murmurs. 'The night you disappeared, there was an ambulance.'

He opens his mouth to speak and falters. His eyes soften, flicker for a moment, and the anger has gone.

'There's only so much you can take,' he whispers at last.

'You tried to ...'

I can't bring myself to finish my question, but he knows what I mean. He nods, swallows and looks to Clive for help. For a few seconds, the two men stare at each other before Dan releases me, turning away, leaving Clive to fill in the gaps.

'He was ten years old,' Clive explains quickly. 'He tried to cut his wrists. One of his sisters found him and called the ambulance. Social Services were called in at the hospital. Dan was taken into care. Two years in a children's home, and then he was adopted.'

'That's why,' I whisper. 'That's why there were no photos.'

Dan turns back to face me.

'And what Betty said. She said you deserved some happiness after everything you'd been through. That's what she meant.'

He nods, but I barely register it. My brain has sparked into life.

'Clive knew all of this.'

'Of course he knew, but it wasn't his place to tell you.'

'And that's why he warned me off. He said you'd latched onto me for a reason. That was the reason.' He reaches out to me. I take a step backwards. 'You knew who I was right from the start. You and me, this was no coincidence.'

His shoulders slump. He runs a hand through his hair and takes a deep breath. 'A quirk of fate.'

'But I don't ...'

'Fate brought you into my building.'

'You knew?'

'I knew exactly who you were when I first called you.'

'But how?'

'I'm a control freak, remember. I skim over the details of all the new staff. When yours landed on my desk, I couldn't believe my luck. Your dad might never forget a face but I never forget a name, especially not that name. Maya Scotton. Sara used to go on about you at school. I knew exactly who you were.'

Suddenly, I feel sick.

'It was too good an opportunity to miss.'

'Dan, there's no need for this.' Clive's voice intervenes. It's ignored.

A hand reaches out to me.

'I need to be honest with you, Maya.'

'Am I getting this right?' I bat the hand away. 'You used me to get to my sister?'

'It crossed my mind.'

'So, what was the plan? Revenge?'

'I don't know. I wasn't thinking straight. All I knew was I wanted to meet you. That was it. I didn't know what else I'd do.'

'You used me?' I blink a few times and stare at the ground. My brain has just laid out another card, a fresh piece of evidence. 'That was you,' I breathe. 'That was you outside my flat on the motorbike. Fucking hell.' I look back up at him. 'I can't believe I missed that one. It was my first day at work and you were stalking me.'

'Researching you.'

'Planning exactly how to use me.'

'It wasn't like that. As soon as I laid eyes on you, things changed.'

'Did they?' I laugh.

'Yes, they fucking did.' He grabs hold of my arm, drawing me into him. 'I'm not proud of it, but I'm not going to lie to you. A few minutes of madness. That's all it was. Are you telling me you never once thought about getting your own back?'

I shake my head, knowing damn well I've thought about it plenty of times.

'Oh come on, Maya.' He shakes me. 'We're all human, for fuck's sake. You're not going to hold this against me.'

I pull my arm away from his grasp.

'And you're not going to tell me how to react.'

He's panicking now. I can see it clearly in his eyes.

'You don't know me,' I breathe. 'That song you played in the car. It was a message.'

He holds out a hand.

'I wanted to tell you who I was. So many times I wanted to tell you, but I couldn't. I got in too deep, too fast and I just couldn't. I never meant to deceive you.'

'But you did deceive me, Dan. You kept telling me to trust you, and I gave you my trust.' I hear myself laugh again. 'I trusted a man who didn't even exist.'

'I *do* exist. I'm Daniel Foster. That's my name. That's who I am.'

'And it's just a name. I don't know you at all. And I certainly can't trust you. And do you know what the worst thing is?' I wait a moment before I let out the answer. 'You don't even know yourself.'

There's a rumble in the distance. The clouds are breaking now. The first spots of rain begin to make landfall as the storm sweeps in from the sea. I need to get inside. I need protection. I need to hide from it all.

'Maya, this isn't the end.'

'Yes it is,' I snarl, determined to see this through. 'Just get in the car, Dan, and leave.' Washed through with fear and dread and determination, I look into his eyes for one last time before I walk away. 'It's over.'

Author's note

Thank you for reading my book! I would love to hear from you. You can contact me on my Facebook page:

www.facebook.com/pages/Mandy-Lee/424286884398779?ref=hl

Or on my website:

http://www.mandy-lee.com

I certainly hope you had as much fun reading my book as I had writing it. If you liked it please tell a friend - or better yet, tell the world by writing a review on Amazon. Even a few short sentences are helpful. As an independently published author, I don't have a marketing department behind me. I have you, the reader. So please spread the word!

Thanks again.

All the best,

Mandy Lee

Printed in Great Britain
by Amazon